Everybody loves Jacqueline Marten!

"Jacqueline Marten's stories are satisfying on every
level and will hold the reader fascinated right
up to the last exciting scene."
—bestselling author Dorothy Garlock

" . . . Nothing short of brilliant."
—bestselling author LaVyrle Spencer on *Nightmare in Red*

"Ms. Marten's writing style is free-flowing, almost
poetic, gently pulling her readers along into the story.
An amazing portrait of nineteenth century life and a
must for history buffs and romance fans alike."
—*Rendezvous* on *Moonshine and Glory*

"Jacqueline Marten is a vibrant, colorful, and
powerful writer of exciting and original romances; an author
who stands head and shoulders above her peers!"
—Harriet Klausner, *Affaire de Coeur*

"An imaginative, enchanting novel."
—*Chicago Sun-Times* on *Dream Walker*

"Slick . . . watch for her!"
—Los Angeles Times on *Visions of the Damned*

Turn the page and see why!

SHE'D ONLY THOUGHT THE COACH WAS EMPTY!

She tore off one slippery mitten with her teeth, pulled open the door, threw her portmanteau inside and scrambled up into the dark interior of the coach. She pulled the door shut, plumped herself down, then nearly screamed and pivoted around. She was sitting on someone's lap!

She was staring into a pair of vivid and very amused blue eyes!

"I never believed in fairy godmothers before," drawled a voice that seemed equally entertained. "But I have to believe they exist when a mere five minutes ago, I expressed a wish that I be given a comfortable armful to keep me warm."

Horrified and blushing as she had never in her entire life blushed before, Gaby stared into the blue eyes.

One arm encircled her waist and the other tilted her backwards. "And a very lovely armful you are, my girl," said the drawling voice. "Extremely charming, definitely warming . . . Now to further test my fairy godmother's gift."

Then he was kissing her . . . Dear God, how he was kissing her! It was surely her duty to deny him, but just as surely not her desire. Nothing in her life before had prepared her for the overcoming, overwhelming, overmastering emotion of this blue-eyed stranger's kiss. He had turned her chilled body into a raging inferno, transfused her arteries to streams flowing with lava, converted her bones to liquid fire.

She managed to disengage her mouth. Thankfully, her head seemed to be slowing down in its dizzying rotation.

"You have very peculiar reactions, sir."

"My dear girl, you have never said anything wronger in your life. My reactions at this moment are exactly those you might have foreseen."

"I might?" Gaby squeaked.

"Yes, Mistress Innocence. Surely you know you are driving me out of my mind?"

"How very strange." Gaby blinked up at the roof of the hackney. "I do not feel anything much happening in my mind. It all seems to be in my body. I think my insides are sliding upside down."

"Mine, too," he said, and fell to kissing her again.

DARCY'S KISS

JACQUELINE MARTEN

PINNACLE BOOKS
KENSINGTON PUBLISHING CORP.

PINNACLE BOOKS are published by

Kensington Publishing Corp.
850 Third Avenue
New York, NY 10022

Copyright © 1996 by Jacqueline Marten

All rights reserved. No part of this book may be reproduced in any form or by any means without the prior written consent of the Publisher, excepting brief quotes used in reviews.

If you purchased this book without a cover, you should be aware that this book is stolen property. It was reported as "unsold and destroyed" to the Publisher and neither the Author nor the Publisher has received any payment for this "stripped book."

Pinnacle and the P logo Reg. U.S. Pat. & TM Off.

First Pinnacle Books Printing: April, 1996

Printed in the United States of America
10 9 8 7 6 5 4 3 2 1

To

"Friends at the dread CIA"

And in memory of

*four of General George Washington's
amateur intelligence agents in New York—*

*Hercules Mulligan, Irish-American tailor
Haym Salomon, Jewish-Polish merchant
Robert Townsend, conscience-ridden Quaker*

*The unknown woman, Spy #355, who died
aboard the British prison ship Jersey
in the New York harbor*

One

The Reverend Mr. Timothy Edgar Foote extended his cup and saucer for a third refill. He did so without troubling to emerge from behind the newspaper he had been rattling vigorously to express his displeasure at its treasonous contents.

On his right hand, Gabrielle Foote serenely continued her reading of a paperbound pamphlet. She appeared better satisfied with the point of view. Without so much as lifting her eyes from Thomas Paine's *Common Sense,* she reached for the teapot and skillfully poured the exact amount her absentminded parent desired.

Since his wife's death three years before, on the first of December, 1773, Gaby had acquired considerable and necessary expertise in anticipating the Reverend Foote's needs and wants, and in preventing spills.

Her father drank far more tea as a widower than he had done as a happily married man, his bereavement having occurred in the very same month that a mob of unruly patriots masquerading as Indians dumped the East India's three hundred and forty-two chests of the precious leaf into Boston Harbor.

The distance between that harbor and his home was two-score miles, but the Reverend Foote had proclaimed both there and abroad, as well as from the pulpit—usually with a loud pounding of one fist on the nearest piece of furniture—that the noble British beverage would always be served under his roof.

Defiantly, he doubled his own intake. Prudently, he chose not to notice that over those years Gabrielle drank plain hot water infused with herbs. None knew better than he that—behind his daughter's air of smiling compliance—was a stubborn streak inherited from her mother.

His tolerance had been sorely strained only the week before at the discovery that, while making a fair copy of his Sunday sermon (to add to the collection he secretly hoped would one day find a publisher) Gaby had scribbled a note in the left-hand margin: *Papa, if tea is such a British brew, why do we need the services of the East India Company to transport it from Far Eastern climes?*

His wife had been his copyist until just before her last brief illness. She had been given to the same kind of frivolity as their daughter, he reminded himself, unaware as he did so that thoughts of his beloved Annabel greatly altered his expression.

Gaby's flickering glance took note that the chiseled perfection of his features had somewhat softened. Really, she decided pensively, in his forty-fourth year, her father was still a handsome man.

She sat still and silent, only pretending now to read. Not for worlds would she have intruded on his private reverie. It was obviously a happy one. He was smiling now; he looked almost boyish.

A serpent invariably creeps into the Garden of Eden, the Reverend Timothy reflected wryly the next minute, his face resuming its habitual look of chilling austerity. This particular specimen came, as it so often did, in the shape of Elsie, a less felicitous portion of Annabel's generous dowry. (Much too generous, many had sniffed jealously at the time, for an impecunious parson with no greater lineage than three generations of honest New England farmers.)

Even when the pewter serving tray she carried was empty, Elsie bore it in both hands; so the family was quite accustomed to the hearty thump of her plump posterior against a door that swung open from the kitchen into the dining parlor. (Annabel used to giggle deliciously that Elsie's bottom must be permanently black and blue.)

"You've probably et enough," Elsie informed her employer. Then, without waiting for affirmation or denial, she started piling dishes onto the tray.

"Papa may want another cup of tea, Elsie dear," Gabrielle mentioned mildly.

Elsie hefted the teapot. "Ain't none," she announced in triumph and placed the pot with the rest of the crockery on the tray.

"I have no time, daughter. I must leave at once for a meeting in town," the Reverend Foote said frostily, more for the benefit of the maid than for the young mistress of the house.

"Humph!" said Elsie. "Then I can get on with my work. There's some of us not able to spend an entire day in idle talk."

"If you expect to be gone for several hours, Papa," Gaby told him hastily, "I think I shall turn out your study. The books need dusting, and I would like to clear your desk and give it a really good polish."

She nudged him out of the dining parlor as she spoke and through the open doorway that led to an entrance hall. There, she stood on tiptoe to kiss his cheek, reserving her laughter till after he had donned his black tricorn and cape and departed the house. She was still laughing when she entered his study.

A minute or two later Elsie came bustling in, bearing cleaning cloths, a jar of beeswax, and a short kitchen ladder that would permit Gaby to reach the topmost bookshelves.

"Thank you, Elsie," said Gaby meekly, knowing full well that to insist she could have carried these items herself would only have produced the same well-worn answer, "I'm the one takes a wage to fetch and carry."

When she was alone again, Gabrielle sat down at her father's desk, her laudable intention of dusting and polishing quite forgotten. She faced a charming miniature of her mother. It had been painted in watercolors the year of her own birth and showed a smiling happy Annabel, more generously endowed than her slim, slightly taller daughter but with the same devilish dare-me spark in her eyes, the same impish smile lifting the corners of her mouth.

Their coloring was quite different, for Annabel had been divinely fair and blue-eyed while Gabrielle owed to a Huguenot great-grandmother hair that was glossy and black, and slanted brows that seemed to swoop over rather than frame a pair of brilliantly alive, all-too-often mocking dark eyes.

"Mama," Gaby said aloud, lifting up the small portrait, "I'm worried about Papa. Not just his politics either, though I think there's just so much longer the patriots are going to give him sympathy over losing you and the license due to a man of the cloth. He just doesn't understand . . ."

She smiled apologetically as she set the miniature on the desk again. "We've talked of this before . . . how sometimes he listens without really hearing. The mood of the people has changed so much since General Washington first took over the army in Boston."

Her mother might have been sitting opposite her, she leaned forward so earnestly to confess, "I might as well tell you the whole truth. He's getting pompous again and—and stuffy . . . Well, you know better than I, how he can be, without you to tease and laugh him out of self-importance. It's only because he misses you so much, Mama. There are so many times when I see the same lost, bewildered look about him that he had when he kissed your hands and then your lips and said good-bye, as though he couldn't believe this terrible thing had happened."

She clasped her hands on top of the desk. "Every widow and elderly maiden from here to Nantucket has made a stab at him. I spend half my time chaperoning him, and he's getting mighty skittish about spinsters. I believe he's been dabbling so much in politics to keep all his hours occupied. I never thought I would say this, nor even consider it—but I think it might be best for Papa to marry again. I would like to find him someone special. Not another *you,* Mama. No man could expect two like you in a single lifetime. Just someone who would love him and laugh with him and understand his ways so as to bring out the best in him the way that you did. Remember that day you explained to me about Papa . . . actually about all men . . ."

She could recall as though it were yesterday the beautiful June morning that she was sure God had sent to order for her fifteenth birthday. At breakfast her parents had overwhelmed her with the gift of a heart-shaped locket on a slim gold chain and a leather bound set of Mr. Richardson's novels.

After she and her mother skimmed through their morning chores, Gaby had picked up the picnic basket prepared by Elsie. They had walked lightheartedly along the wagon road, then headed up the mountain to a lovely jewel of a fishing pond where they liked to picnic.

Most of the way there, they talked nonsense, but after the long climb and a leisurely lunch while they sat on the grass verge, with their bare legs dangling in the water, Annabel suddenly turned serious.

"Gabrielle, you are fifteen today, almost a woman. It isn't a sensible step to take, but many girls marry when they are your age or not much older than you. Your father and I would be much happier if you waited until you reach an age of—not so much of greater wisdom as—well, as of self-knowledge. At twenty, you are more likely to know what manner of man is most likely to make you content."

"Is that because you were twenty when you married Papa?" Gaby asked, grinning.

"No, indeed," her mother answered seriously, shaking her head. "I think this way because, if your Papa had proposed to me when I was fifteen, I would have refused him. I would have laughed at the very idea of becoming a minister's wife. I wanted someone dashing and romantic like the journeymen painters who never stayed in one place more than a few days . . . or a fisherman. Not, you understand, the ordinary lobsterman who was never out of sight of his own piece of land but the ones who went to exciting places like the Orient and were gone for months at a time, leaving wives never certain their husbands would come back from the sea. I was in love—so I thought—with a ship's captain when I had turned sixteen."

"You were in love with someone else besides Papa!" Gaby said incredulously. "What happened to him?"

"What happened? Well, he went on one of his romantic voyages and, since what I felt for him was romantic folly rather than love, by the time he came back, I was seventeen and scarcely remembered him."

"Then Papa came along?"

"Not quite." Annabel grinned back at her now-solemn little daughter. "I think there were two more of my fancies, no, three—I almost forgot the Scottish tea merchant. I had a passion that month for red hair. By the time I was nineteen, your grandmother was moaning that the man had not yet been born who could last in my affections more than a fortnight. It was *then* that your father came along."

"And you fell in love with him all at once?"

"Mmm . . . no, I would say that I fell in love with him rather slowly. Oh, I liked his looks—how could one not? He was and still is extremely good-looking, but my plans for the future did not include a parson, especially when the parson in question—however handsome—seemed so sober and—and—"

"Stuffy?" put in Gaby slyly, and her mother tried to look severe but ended up laughing.

"Yes, you impudent creature. Stuffy. As I said, I was only nineteen."

"What happened next?" Gaby inquired eagerly.

"Well, I encountered your father on a number of social occasions. Gradually, I noticed something about him that I more than just liked. I greatly appreciated his manner of talking to me as though I were a reasonable and intelligent human being."

Gaby looked perplexed. "Why would he not?"

"Ah, but you see, I had noticed that most young men, most middle-aged men and most older men did not. They hardly *conversed* with women; they talked *at* them, and in an indulgent, patronizing way that I found intolerable. After all, we eighteenth-century women of America are different from our sisters in England. For the most part, we Colonial ladies are encouraged to be independent and able to manage for ourselves, even if it means dabbling in what are so often considered strictly 'men's affairs.'"

"And Papa did encourage you?"

"Well, the first thing I admired was his open-mindedness when we had a discussion about religion. We both began with a belief in the same God—but from there we diverged on almost every particular. Your father held by the exact word of the Bible, while I held that most of it was writ many years after the events by mortal men, and that the entire concept of Christianity—indeed, of all religions—was bound up in the Ten Commandments and the Golden Rule."

She smiled ruefully at her daughter. "I would never have dared to speak so to Reverend Shuttleworth. He would have scolded me at length and prayed over me even longer . . . but your papa only said that, if I lived my life by those standards, I could hardly do better. Then he smiled down at me—we were at a church supper; I was sitting and he was standing—he courteously bade me good-night and went off to talk to Dorcas Bigelow, who was quite pretty but so painfully shy, she never knew how to talk to young men and therefore seldom attracted any. He—your papa—stayed at her side for a full half-hour . . ."

She seemed to fall into a happy daydream, which her daughter's firm voice finally penetrated.

"You kept track of the time, Mama?"

"I did indeed, you hussy, and I must confess that, although I liked Dorcas Bigelow and wished her well, I was miffed that the two of them were having such an animated conversation. He stayed with her twice as long as he had with me."

"But you did see him soon again?"

"Oh, on public occasions, I saw him any number of times, and we always managed some private conversation. Every added meeting confirmed my good opinion. In discussions of politics and literature, too, we disagreed but always intelligently and invigoratingly. It became a challenge to pit my wits against his. At the same time, I found it quite deflating that he appeared to be completely uninterested in me as a woman. The only time he came to call was the single necessary visit of ceremony to every family in the parish. I happened to be out of the house at the time, and I had the most lowering feeling that he had deliberately arranged his visit to coincide with my absence."

Gaby looked shocked. "Why would you think so?"

"Oh, things . . ." Annabel returned vaguely. "And my mother said . . ."

"What did Grandmother say? Mama, stop making me drag the whole story out of you piecemeal!"

"She noticed I was not pleased about being out of the house when he called. She told me that, since a penniless parson could not aspire to a girl with my lineage and dowry, she thought that the young man was acting wisely in avoiding temptation. He was sensible to approach only young women in his own sphere as, naturally, a minister must be seeking a wife."

"Oh, Mama, how romantic!"

"It wasn't romantic at all!" her mother retorted tartly. "I was furious at her as well as at him for such snobbery and—being much like you, miss"—she tugged at a strand of Gaby's hair—"I very impetuously said so. I think it would have earned me a box on the ears for such impertinence if it were not that I think she had purposely provoked me into understanding my own heart."

"And did it?"

"Oh, my, yes! I jumped up, crying out most unbecomingly, 'Sphere be hanged! We are cast in the same mold, he and I!' Then I rushed out of the room, out of the house, to be alone to think. All the odd bits of the puzzle that was love seemed to come together for me in one perfect picture. I realized that, first, for a girl, and perhaps for a man, too, there may be silly infatuations based on pleasing features and fairylike fantasy. Sometimes the marriages resulting from such infatuations turn out well, but more often they fail. Next are the marriages of good sense . . . a housewife for him, a provider for her, children for both. It's a matter of chance whether or not the couples in these unions rub along reasonably well together."

Annabel hugged herself, her voice happy and lilting. "But

there I was all alone in a field of buttercups, whirling round and around and around, as I visualized a relationship that made fantasy pale by comparison. A marriage not just of hearts but of minds, every day a challenge, every faculty put to use . . . every passion. But was there passion? It seemed to be rising in me . . . so much so that I felt as though I were being sucked down into the cone at the heart of a tornado. I could only pray out loud—I fairly demanded of God—that the Reverend Mr. Timothy Edgar Foote was caught up in the whirlwind with me!"

Two

Mother and daughter sat for two minutes in complete silence before Annabel explained most unnecessarily, "I do *not* have a great deal of patience, especially in a matter of importance."

Gaby promptly lowered her face to her propped-up knees to smother a laugh while Annabel continued, "Since *he* would not court *me,* I quite simply started a pursuit of him. I managed to pop up unexpectedly in places where he would be. I teased and tormented him. I talked seriously one moment and started flirting the next. After several weeks, the only thing that gave me enough courage to continue was that one day we met—this time truly by chance—in the churchyard. I had just knelt to arrange fresh flowers on my baby brother's grave, and I was talking to Charlot, as I always did, when I became conscious of a shadow over the grave and me. I looked up to find your father standing just behind me and . . . for seconds only . . . I saw everything I had ever wanted to see written on his face."

"Did he propose to you then and there, Mama?" Gaby sighed ecstatically.

"Certainly not. He drew himself up and gave me that cold stiff air he puts on when he is displeased. Before he could speak, I gushed that I had been longing for the opportunity to tell him that I would like to join the church choir. Poor man, he was fearfully embarrassed."

"Why should he be? *I* sing in the choir."

"Yes, my dear daughter. But you have a lovely singing voice, and the whole town knew that I sang like a frog. Everyone had warned him, at all costs to avoid having me in the choir. I acted so reverent at first and then so hurt when he stammered out there was no extra robe that I managed to make him feel quite guilty. Having done so, I was up and away, flinging over my shoulder, 'Are you guilty of the sin of pride, sir, in desiring a pure voice rather than a pure woman for the choir?' He has never, *never* acknowledged it to me . . . but one day I will discover the truth. I think he swore aloud at me."

Gabby giggled. "Oh, I would dearly love to hear Papa swear."

"I," said her mother grandly, "am the only woman in the world your father has ever had the inclination to swear at!"

"The proposal, Mama? His proposal! I am growing impatient, too."

"Well, it took another two weeks. My own papa told me that Joan Simpson had just been confined, and I knew there would be no supper for them that night as her husband Ralph, though an excellent farmer, was helpless in a kitchen. Joan's sister lived in Braintree and would not get the message to come until the next day. As I, with my basket, arrived at my friend's, your father was just leaving.

" 'Do wait for me, sir!' I said to him hastily. 'I would be glad of some company along the road if you are going my way. I shan't visit with Joan today, she will be too weary. I intend just to deliver their meal.'

"I sailed by him without waiting for an answer. I knew courtesy demanded that he wait, since I had not really given him a choice. I dumped the basket into Ralph's welcoming arms. 'My felicitations,' I said, then fairly flew into the bedroom.

"I bent and kissed Joan's forehead. 'I'm so happy for you,' I told her. 'I will come to admire your no-doubt superior son tomorrow, but I must fly now in pursuit of a father for my own future progeny.'

"She shrieked, 'Annabel, come back here and explain,' but I was out of the room and out of the house, too, before she finished calling. Your father was waiting outside, and he looked at me with extreme approval as we walked along the road, at the same time being careful to keep a foot of space between us.

" 'A kind and neighborly act,' he told me.

" 'I have known Joan all my life, Mr. Foote,' I told him, at my most demure. Then I smiled as engagingly as I could. 'You must not be ennobling my character because I do a slight act of kindness for a friend,' I added softly; and at once he was all minister. He said stiffly . . ."

"You mean," Gaby interrupted her mother cheerfully, "at his *very* most pompous?"

Annabel pulled her daughter's hair again. "Rude child! Well, if you insist, yes, at his *very* most pompous . . . He said, 'There is no such thing as a *slight* act of kindness.'

" 'Now,' I retorted, 'you sound just like the Reverend Mr. Foote in his pulpit. Will you make soup, boiled chicken, and rice pudding the subject of your next Sunday sermon? Do you not sometimes long to throw your hat across the road, unbend your back a little, and speak to me as a man to a woman?' "

"Oh, Mama," Gaby breathed, "that was quite forward of you, was it not?"

"Exceedingly forward."

"What did he say?"

"He came closer to me, halted, and gripped my elbow so firmly, I had no choice but to stop, too. I looked at him in an inquiring sort of way, surprised to see a rather strange smile on his face. 'Miss Annabel Forsyth,' he said to me, 'for some weeks now, you have behaved so as to invite either a spanking or a kiss. State your preference. I am entirely at your disposal, quite willing to give you one or the other of the two—even, if you wish, both. It must be your own choice. No, my dear Miss Forsyth, do not try to slap me. I am stronger than you and able to prevent it. Please tell me which—or what—you want. I await your command.'

"We were standing at the side of the road, and he was unprepared for my next move. I shoved him so hard and unexpectedly, he fell over backwards into Ralph Simpson's cornfield. He was just trying to prop himself up on his elbows, looking decidedly wrathful, when I followed him down. I flung myself onto him, petticoats flying up. His elbows gave way and he fell flat on his back again. I looked down at his beautiful face and his angry eyes and sang out, 'I choose to have a kiss, Reverend Foote, or may I now call you Timothy?' Then, not giving him a chance to answer, 'Yes, I think I shall. Timothy, dear, *dear* Timothy, I do so want a kiss and intend to ask for it most biblically. Have you done much studying of the Song of Songs, Which Is Solomon's; or do you think, like Reverend Shuttleworth, that it crept into the Word of the Lord most improperly? It happens to be *my* favorite part of the Book of Books.'

"I lifted myself from his chest a little, Gaby, the better to look at him. I said"—she bit her lip, glanced doubtfully at her daughter for some seconds, then shrugged and resumed her story. "I said, *'Kiss me with the kisses of your mouth, for thy love is better than wine, therefore doth this virgin love thee.'* Then I bent my head and did not so much kiss—what did I know about kissing?—as rub my lips against his."

Gaby stayed still with shock while Annabel smiled dreamily. "My mouth was still on his mouth when he heaved me up and over and onto the flattened patch of the field where he had been lying. It took only seconds for him to be lying on top of me, and it was an altogether different sensation. His body pressed down on mine so heavily, it was impossible for him not to feel every line of my body. God knows I could feel the strength and the changing contours of his; it was exciting, but I was beginning to be just the least bit frightened, too. What's more, he knew it. There was a strange smile on his face. He had the look of a—a conquering male.

" 'The next time you equate me with Reverend Shuttleworth,' he whispered in my ear, 'I shall not give you the choice that I did a few minutes ago. Yes, my adorable, infuriating Annabel, I have studied the Song of Songs, and yes, there will come a time, *my well-beloved, when I shall lie all night betwixt your breasts. Behold thou art fair, my love, yea, pleasant, also our bed is green.'*

Then his mouth came down on mine, and there was not mere rubbing. He kissed me, and he kept right on kissing me while the birds sang and the scent of the corn permeated our clothes and our bodies and the whole world seemed to stand still for us. I thought I would die of happiness. Then just as suddenly as he began, he stopped. He leaped off me and, while I lay blinking up at him, he said quite harshly, 'I will take you home.'

" 'Wh-what's wrong?' I stammered, but he just reached down, took hold of my nearest arm and yanked me to my feet.

" 'Brush yourself off,' he ordered me quite unpleasantly.

"I saw the necessity for it. There were bits of grass, corn silk and dirt on the back of his shirt and breeches, so there must be on my clothing, too. I began to brush, vowing to myself I would not give him the satisfaction of seeing me cry.

"When I felt sufficiently neat, I said not a word to him. I just turned and started for my home again. He had to take a few long quick strides to catch up with me.

" 'I do not need an escort,' I told him coldly.

" 'Annabel,' he said gently, *'though thy love may be better than wine,* did you really wish me to take this virgin, who professes to love me, in a cornfield?'

"This time it was I who stopped in the middle of the road. So did he. We faced each other with slightly less antagonism this time.

" 'Yes,' he answered my unspoken question, 'it is what might have happened if we had continued longer in the same way. I am a man before I am a minister.'

" 'I'm sorry if I misjudged you,' I said contritely. 'You may as well know that I have a rather quick temper.'

" 'I suspected as much,' he answered dryly, and we walked on in silence."

"Every minute I was expecting him to propose, but he said never a word. I was beginning to get angry all over again when we reached the hilltop that gave us a view of my house. There, before I could guess what he intended, he fell back a pace and dealt me a light whack on my bottom."

"I knew full well it was more of a caress than a slap, but my dignity required that I demand an affront, 'Why did you do that?' As I spoke, I tenderly massaged the tingling area of my backside.

" 'Just a loving reminder that you are not going to have it all your own way in this marriage.'

That was an intolerably arrogant assumption!

" 'There isn't going to be any marriage,' I declared haughtily and started to run. He ran right after me. 'Oh, but there is, and it is going to be as soon as possible.' He pulled me back into his arms . . . There is no surer, stronger, safer shelter in all the world, Gaby, than the arms of a beloved man. Between kisses, he made me promise not to keep him waiting long."

"Mama," Gaby said tentatively, "could you tell me about the—you know—the *taking* part. The wedding night business. We girls all discuss it a good deal, and when Joan married, and Susan, too, we tried to get more information, but they primmed up about explaining. Partly, I *do* know but watching the rooster was *no* good at all; women don't lay eggs. When I tried to climb the fence one time to see Mr. Frome's bull servicing the cows, he chased me away and threatened to tell Papa. How does it work—I mean, the exact way—between a man and woman?"

Annabel hesitated a moment, then looked tenderly at her daughter . . . and told her.

Gabrielle's eyes got wider and wider and wider.

She said once, "But Mama, I've seen lots of boy babies. It's small and soft."

She said next, "But Mama, how could anything stretch that much and not hurt awfully?"

She said incredulously, "But Mama, why would a grown man want to do that to a woman? Babies do it for nourishment!"

When Annabel finally finished her explanation, she asked her daughter, "Do you have any other questions, Gaby?"

Blushing a bright red, Gaby turned away from her mother and shook her head decidedly. "Mama, I don't want to hurt your feelings, but the whole thing sounds disagreeable—not to say embarrassing—and as though it might be painful. I just can't picture you and Papa . . . ugh! . . . or me and *any*one, not *any*one, not ever!"

Annabel said softly, "My dear little daughter, there are women who can be equally happy or equally unhappy married to any one of a score of men. There are women for whom, to be happy either in marriage or in life, there can only be one man. A relationship I find beautiful and exciting with your father would be disgusting to me, too, with any other man."

Gently, she turned Gaby's face toward her. "I think you are of the same temperament, Gabrielle. For you, too, there will be one man, one love, one kiss. Wait patiently. However you feel about what I have just described, you cannot have reached your fifteenth year without having experienced physical sensations and unsatisfied yearnings which have everything to do with this discussion. Don't be ashamed of them; they are natural. Don't be fearful of what men may begin to feel for you or you for them, now that you are becoming a woman. It's not important if love happens quickly or slowly, on the instant or over a period of time. When love comes—when you think it has come—involve your head as well as your heart. Your body will speak its own needs, and you will be able to reach out for happiness."

Three

Next morning's breakfast in the Foote household was a reprise of the day before, except that, while her father read his newspaper, Gaby chose to amuse herself with the first volume of the vicissitudes of a lachrymose young lady named Clarissa. The silly sentimentality of the heroine amused her so little, she took a firm resolve to avoid reading any one of the six books that completed the series.

Her father was equally annoyed. "That fellow Pythias again," he fumed, lowering the newspaper a trifle. "He should be thrown out of this colony."

Color slightly heightened, Gaby allowed the word *colony* to slip by. "May I read it? He isn't always serious, you know, Papa."

He handed over the paper, stating in ministerial tones, "Serious or not, he is a troublemaker and a traitor to his country."

"Papa, one must be fair. The patriots believe America, not England is their country."

A minute later, she gave a little gurgle and seconds later, laughed outright. "Oh Papa, it's true this appears to take a political position but actually it is only a bit of satire poking fun at British rule here." She hummed a little to herself. *"I think it could be charming set to music. There is a lilt to it. Listen."*

Without waiting to see if he were willing, she read aloud, in a decidedly lilting manner.

With a heigh nonny non
And a hie nonny no,
Would it not be fun
If the British were to go
Back across the ocean
To their stuffy little isle
Where Parliament could tax 'em
And the King could smile
At the willingness of Britons
To support their German Royals
(Only we Americans
Deny them proper spoils!)

With a heigh nonny non
And a hie nonny no
Plus that other very British phrase,
What ho!
Here in America, you must confess,
The British have created
An unholy mess.
If we could be free of them,
If not one was left . . .
Would we be amenable
Or would we be bereft?
Lack a day!
Oh, I say
Do we want them well away?
Take a guess.
Would we all be happier?
         Yes!
            Yes!
               Yes!

"Really, Papa!" Gaby returned the paper to him with a very Gallic shrug copied long ago from Annabel. "It's just a charming bit of nonsense. There's no use in your getting choleric about it."

" 'Yankee Doodle' was a similar 'charming bit of nonsense,' " her father pointed out acutely, "and it is now being used by the rebels as a rallying call."

Gaby smiled, then shrugged again. "You have me there, Papa, " she admitted, adding thoughtfully, "I am sure this fellow Pythias would be pleased and proud to have his doggerel used in a like manner by his countrymen. Still, in all fairness, even *you* must admit that the British *have* created an unholy mess here, and all on account of their failure even to try to understand how Americans think. To say nothing of the fact that they treat us as an inferior brand of Englishmen and Englishwomen! Recollect, it was they, not us, who first started singing 'Yankee Doodle,' and they did it—you know they did—to mock us. Now they are annoyed because we use the song pridefully instead of hanging our heads in shame."

"There are times when you sound as much a rebel as any one of them," the Reverend Foote said critically, ignoring her arguments.

"I believe as Mama did," Gaby said seriously, "that to draw the right conclusion, one must always try to listen to both sides of the argument."

Without any reply, her father again disappeared behind his newspaper while Gaby sat, staring dreamily into space.

They were equally startled when Elsie erupted into the room. Not only had she left her tray behind and used one hand to thrust open the door, but she was loudly lamenting, "Oh, dear, what's to be done, what's to be done?"

Gaby rose swiftly and went to the maid. "Elsie, dear." She put an arm around the servant's shaking shoulders. "What is it?"

"There was a loud knocking on the kitchen door. When I went to answer it, there was no one there, but I heard rustling in the bushes, so I well knew where the pesky critters were hiding themselves. I thought to myself, it's them Clark boys again, always up to some devilment, I'm going to complain to their pa. Then I saw this." Dramatically she produced *this* from the folds of her apron. "Right out in clear view it was, on the top step."

Gaby paled and the Reverend Mr. Foote's first loss of composure gave way to lips tightened in anger and nostrils flaring in disdain. He plucked the object that had caused so much distress out of Elsie's hand. It was a large ball of cold tar all covered with feathers.

"There, Gabrielle, *there* are your misunderstood patriots, cowards all, unwilling to show their faces when they deliver a message!"

"Papa, are you mad?" Gaby cried impulsively. "You know full well that this is only a warning. Next time—if you allow them a next time—they will not knock and run off. Then you will indeed see their faces, unless the hot pitch running down your face as they tar and feather you gets into your eyes and blinds you, as it has blinded some."

"Rubbish!"

Gaby snatched the ball of tar away from him. "Papa, I know you are not a fool, but to dismiss this as rubbish is foolish beyond words!"

"Gabrielle! I allow you a great deal of license in what you may say to me, but this is going too far."

"On the contrary," his daughter disagreed, "I have not gone far enough."

He turned swiftly to the maid. "Elsie, please leave us. I wish to speak alone with my daughter."

Gaby turned even more swiftly. "No, Elsie, stay!" she ordered defiantly. "We have a decision to make that concerns all three of us. Papa, please don't be angry with me . . . Elsie will only listen at the door if you send her away . . . and she has as much of an interest in this decision as the two of us. If we are to leave the State of Massachusetts—and it appears now that we must—then Elsie must decide if she is to go with us. Ours has been her home much of her life. Mama was only seven when Elsie came to work for my grandmother."

Mr. Foote began to admonish his daughter, her insubordination no longer looming so greatly in his mind as the notion that he would turn tail and run because a pack of cowardly curs delivered an anonymous and traitorous warning.

"It will remain anonymous only for twelve to twenty-four hours!" Gaby cried out passionately. "That is the longest interval that has ever elapsed between the delivery of one of those"—she pointed, shuddering, to the ball of tar—"and the carrying-out of the sentence that is bound to follow if you refuse to take it seriously."

"I am a minister, chosen to do God's work in this town and to spread His Word," her father said not altogether calmly. "It behooves me to set an example, not only by what I *say*, my dear daughter, but by what I *do*. What will my people think if I flee at the contemplation of personal danger?"

"They will say what they are already saying. The rebels will be joyful to see you go and claim that you did well to save your hide. The loyalists—there are far fewer of them than you realize, Papa—will believe that you did well to save your life so as to be able to fight for your beliefs another day."

"My dear, you perturb yourself unnecessarily—"

"Damn it to hell, Papa, I perturb myself not enough!"

"Gabrielle Renée Foote!" thundered her father. "How dare you—"

"I saw him." Gabrielle began to weep noisily. "I saw Jonas Smith the day they tarred and feathered him. Oh God, Papa, it was horrible. The broadsheets and the newspapers do not begin to tell the half of it. They make it seem frolicsome. *Frolicsome!*"

"My dear little girl, why did you never tell me?"

"I didn't want to speak of it. I didn't want to think of it. And I was so ashamed that Americans—my own countrymen—should so—so—"

"You were present at the actual tarring?"

"Oh, dear God, no! I am grateful I missed that. They said his screams of agony as they applied the boiling tar to his naked body could have been heard for a mile. It was when they were riding him out of town on a rail that I came upon them—those loathsome bullies who call themselves patriots. He—Mr. Smith looked like some kind of monstrous oversized chicken . . . and it was obvious the rail between his legs gave him great pain. Years ago, when I was just a little girl, I heard the story of another poor man . . . I think it may have been in Ipswich . . . who went out of his mind from a similar experience.

"Papa, dear Papa." She tried to sound calmer as she went to him and reached up to put both hands on his shoulders. "I know you are reluctant to seem a coward when in reality, you will be acting like a man of sense. You must leave this very day. The only choice offered you is to go in health and on horseback or in pain and shame, possibly scarred for life. Did you know—I inquired into it after I saw Mr. Smith—that for weeks after a tarring, the victim's burned skin comes off in strips?"

He stood, frowning, and Gaby began to cry again. "How can you hesitate if you love me? Mama's parents and your own are all dead . . . much of our family is in England . . . Since we lost Mama, we have only each other and Aunt Emily in New Jersey . . . Papa, it is you who has always preached to *me* that *pride goeth before destruction and an haughty spirit before a fall.*"

"Gaby, my—"

"No, no, look into your own heart, Papa. Are you not concerned more with what others think of you—in short, of not appearing to be a coward? Does your own pride matter more than what will become of *me* if anything happens to you? I have already had to deal with the agony of losing my mother. Must I mourn my father, too? Or, perhaps, if I am more fortunate, only have to spend the next twenty years of my life as your nurse?"

"Gaby, my—"

"Reverend Foote, sir," Elsie interrupted most unexpectedly and more respectfully than she was wont to speak to him, "Gaby is in the right of it. You must leave this very day . . . the sooner, the better. She and I can settle the house by ourselves and come to you afterwards."

"Go myself and leave you both here!" he cried, aghast. "I could never do so. Suppose the crowd—in fury at finding me gone—turned on you?"

"No danger exists for *us,* Papa, only for you. I am believed to have patriot sympathies, and Elsie does not dabble in politics."

Tactfully, she refrained from mentioning that any mob coming to their house would be so elated to have driven the Reverend Mr. Foote out of town, they were more likely to build a bonfire of victory than turn on his women-folk.

"One of my cousins is a Son of Liberty," Elsie announced surprisingly, "and my brother—Well, you can take my word for it, sir, Gaby and I will do very well and be able to follow you soon." She looked at them both. "Where will we go?"

Gaby and her father spoke together.

"Aunt Emily urges us to visit in every letter."

"My sister Emily's would be a refuge until we formed other more permanent plans."

As they all smiled, he added curtly, "At least we may be thankful that General Washington and his rabble have been forced to retreat across the Delaware into Pennsylvania. Good British troops hold most of New Jersey."

Elsie gave a short sharp nod and disappeared into the kitchen, but Gaby and her father showed no inclination to finish their interrupted breakfast.

"Let us go upstairs, so I can help you with your packing, Papa," Gaby offered. "I think you need not take more than you will require for a week. I will bring all the remainder of your wardrobe afterwards. Do not worry. I shall take particular care of your papers and books. Perhaps you should stop at Mr. Knight's on your way out of town to tell him I have the authority to act in your name to rent or sell the house . . . some of the furniture, too. Never fear, I will keep Mama's spinet and spinning wheel and her little desk . . . I will know what you would not wish to have left. When all is done—and you may be sure I will try to be speedy—I shall hire someone, perhaps one of the Trumbull boys, to take our belongings to my aunt's by wagon."

Little more than an hour later, with—stuffed into his saddlebags—the two small portmanteaux containing the precious miniature of his wife, the smallest of his three Bibles, and the manuscript of his sermons wrapped in a week's supply of clean clothing, the Reverend Mr. Foote took leave of his daughter as well as of the house in which he and Annabel had lived the last happy years of their life together. He tied his horse to an oak tree along the path that led to the churchyard.

At Annabel's grave, he knelt for a brief prayer and a longer, heart-wrenching good-bye.

There were rare tears in his eyes as he mounted his horse again. Only one task left.

The lawyer quickly drew up the power of attorney Gaby would need and promised to deliver it to her before nightfall. When it had been signed, with Mr. Knight and his clerk as witnesses, Timothy Edgar Foote, heavy of heart, wretched in spirit, mounted his horse again to ride out of the Colony of Massachusetts, where he had been born and lived his entire life, except for the years in Divinity School at Yale College.

He was a practical man of God, not given to wild speculations nor forebodings of evil, but as he turned his face toward New Jersey, a voice inside him kept whispering that he might never again see his home or his Annabel's grave. As he rode, quietly he wept.

Four

Gaby and Elsie arrived at her Aunt Emily Van Raalte's house in Princeton, New Jersey on the twentieth of December, 1776. It was midafternoon, and the housekeeper, Mrs. Cornwall, alerted by the rumble of wagon wheels along the driveway of the handsome red brick mansion, had rushed to the back parlor to inform her mistress.

Mrs. Van Raalte was waiting at the open door when the wagon stopped and Gaby tried to hop over its side, not without difficulty. Under a thick black hooded cloak that seemed to spread out from her body like inflated wings, she looked like a great balloon puffed up with air.

A red-nosed young man, warmly but not so bulkily dressed, jumped down from the driver's seat and rushed to assist her in extricating Elsie from the wagon. Since the maid was naturally plump and even more cumbersomely clothed than Gabrielle, it was no easy task.

"Come in, come in," Aunt Emily called to the two women. "My dear, you must be half frozen. Young man, you drive around to the back and tell one of my men to see to the care of your horse. Remind him to make sure afterwards that both horse and wagon are well hid. Then return here for food and a dram of hot rum punch. The kitchen entrance will be nearer. My housekeeper will see to you."

Isaac Trumbull grinned his appreciation of this invitation and again climbed onto the wagon seat. As he drove off, Emily Foote

Van Raalte shepherded her niece and Elsie into the house and slammed the door shut tight.

All sighed in pleasure and relief to be out of the cold; Gaby and Elsie willingly allowed their hostess to shoo them ahead of her to the small back parlor.

"I use it in preference to the large front parlor in winter," she explained, "because it is easier to keep warm and toasty."

They had pleasant proof of this in the blazing fire on the hearth of the small room. It spread warmth to every corner, even near to the window. With a cry of pleasure, Gaby tore off three pairs of wool mittens and held her hands close to the blaze.

Her aunt, wishing to embrace her, was prevented by the multiple layers of clothing.

"I declare," said Aunt Emily, assisting both visitors off with their cloaks. "I don't know whether to laugh or to cry." She seemed on the point of doing both. "Your father will be vastly relieved. These last few days he has been constantly on the fret. I only kept him from going after you by convincing him that he would be bound to take a different road and pass you by."

"It happens to be true," said Gaby thankfully, while she unwound a wool shawl tied around her head and ears. "I am glad you had such good sense, Aunt Em. I would have gone out of my mind with worry to arrive here and find Papa gone back home."

She had kicked off her boots, stepped out of three heavy skirts (down to four petticoats) and unbuttoned two wool vests, which even then did not disclose her shift. She had still to unwrap a second shawl from about her chest and middle. Lastly, she removed several pairs of thick knit stockings and wriggled bare toes before the fire in speechless ecstasy.

Elsie had acquiesced in the removal of hooded cloak, shawl, and gloves, but otherwise stood, overdressed and beginning to thaw out, in the center of the room.

Gaby sprang to her feet. "Let me help you off with your things, Elsie. The fire will feel wonderful to you on your bare hands and feet."

Elsie fended her off. "Now Miss Gabrielle, stay right where you are. Bare my limbs in public is something I have never done before and have no hankering to do now."

Gaby stared at her, astonished. *"Miss* Gabrielle. What's got into you? We are all women here."

"I know my place," stated Elsie primly, and *Miss* Gabrielle's eyes rolled heavenward, as though imploring Him for patience.

During this clash of wills, Aunt Emily had calmly picked up a small brass bell and was now ringing it vigorously. The housekeeper responded in less than three minutes.

"Mrs. Cornwall," Aunt Emily said with calm authority, "my niece's nurse is extremely weary. Will you see that Polly lights a fire in the room that was prepared for her and warms the sheets? Oh, yes, until the baggage is sent over, lay out one of my flannel nightdresses. Please inform me when the chamber is comfortably heated." She turned graciously to Elsie. "Will that suit you, ma'am?"

Elsie nodded stiffly. "Thank you, ma'am, it'll suit me fine; but my name is Brown, Elsie Brown, though plain Elsie is more than good enough. I'd as soon go along with Mrs. Cornwall now. After what we went through on this journey, a few minutes in a cold chamber don't seem much to fuss about."

"Very well," Aunt Emily said calmly. "When you serve our tea, Mrs. Cornwall, let Polly bring up a pot to Miss Brown, and later she will have a supper tray in her bed. The tea, by the by, she told Gaby, "is of home-grown ingredients. Not as tasty as China or Ceylon but more patriotic. Your Papa hates it."

When Mrs. Van Raalte and her niece were finally alone, Aunt Emily allowed herself to laugh so hard, she was forced to wipe tears from her eyes. "Annabel always said that your Elsie was a character, but she loved her dearly."

"So do I," said Gaby, giggling. "You do understand that if *I* had ever demanded that she prefix my name with *Miss,* she would have been out of the house at once, never to return. But since we are in a fine New Jersey mansion"—she sketched a mocking half-curtsey to her aunt—"we must show the natives that we are fully aware of the customs appertaining among the gentry."

As she straightened up, her aunt took her by the chin and shook her head wonderingly. "How can you look so very different, my dear Gabrielle, and yet remind me so strongly of your mother? I think it must be because your brave spirit shines through, just as Annabel's did." She hugged Gaby fondly. "I am so happy to have you here but grieved for you that you had to flee your home. Oh, war is a wicked thing . . . and yet, in this case, what other choice do we have?"

"We, Aunt. What *we?"*

"America, of course."

Gaby cocked one eyebrow in surprise. "Why, Aunt Emily, that sounds like Whig talk."

"Naturally, since I happen to be one!" Emily Van Raalte said stoutly.

"Heavens! Does Papa know? And where, by the way, *is* Papa? How is his health? Has he recovered a little from the grief of being forced from our home?"

"I think," the Reverend Foote's sister said slowly, "that to have been forced from his home is a grief that will never quite leave him. The sorrow diminishes in time, but it can remain a bruise on the spirit."

She blew her nose briskly and sat down in a rocker near to the fire, indicating that Gaby should do the same. Instead, Gaby drew up a hassock and sat at her aunt's feet.

"I must admit," she was told, "that the first three days Timothy spent here, I was like to lose my mind, as well as my patience, reassuring him every hour on the hour that he had done the right thing. He was so ashamed and worried to have left you with only Elsie to bear the burden of settling the household."

"Ha! I would rather have had one Elsie to assist me than a regiment of Papas."

"So I thought, myself, but was fortunately too tactful to say it aloud. But how did you happen to come in the wagon with your furnishings and clothes, my dear? I made sure Timothy told me that, after the wagon left town, you and Elsie would travel by stagecoach, arriving ahead of it."

"That *was* our first plan, but when we inquired into stage travel . . . the varying routes, the changes, the stage inns—it began to appear to me that, as well as being quite expensive, there was no great likelihood of its being faster or more comfortable. I could hardly believe it would take three days by coach for each ninety miles—and that, when the roads were better, mind. So Elsie and I talked it over and agreed that it might be just as well to travel along with Isaac on the wagon."

"But the cold in an open wagon! The bumping on the road!"

"We cushioned ourselves well, and you saw how we were dressed. The wagon was not that packed since I rented much of the furniture with our house. But we did take two of the thickest mattresses, several featherbeds, and Mr. Trumbull—Isaac's father—contributed two bear furs, which, poor man, he expects to have returned to him."

"Will they not be?"

Gaby hesitated. "I fear not. You said you were Whig, Aunt Emily, so perhaps you will not be too shocked . . . though I would much prefer that you not tell Papa . . . he has had enough to bear. I could not just rent the wagon and Isaac's services because he does not plan to return home. He is determined to enlist in one of General Washington's Massachusetts Regiments. He had to make his plans secretly because the Trumbulls are as Tory as Papa . . . that's why they helped us so much . . . for Papa's sake. Isaac has two brothers and a cousin in the Loyal New Englanders Regiment."

"You are quite right. It would be wise to keep this family saga from your father. He would begin to blame himself for putting temptation in the boy's path."

Gaby wrinkled her nose. "I don't think he could do that. Isaac told me he had been planning to run away and only delayed a few days because this marvelous opportunity came up. I bought the horse myself from a farmer outside town and Isaac told me the worth of the wagon—exaggerating a little as New Englanders tend to when they make a bargain—and I left a sum with our attorney to give to Mr. Trumbull. I figured that an extra horse might always come in handy, and perhaps you can use the wagon on the farm?"

"Without a doubt, my dear. In New Jersey a horse is considered a woman's most prized possession. It gives her freedom of movement, and the thieving British have helped themselves to all they can lay their hands on, to say nothing of wagons full of produce."

Gaby stretched voluptuously, then yawned. "How has Papa been spending his days, other than in worrying?"

"Unfortunately, he had the additional disappointment of my having to scotch a plan he had conceived of to keep you both in funds without having to dip into your capital. He thought he might be able to obtain a teaching post here at our College of New Jersey."

"Yes, he mentioned the possibility to me while we were packing his portmanteau. He has Latin and Greek as well as Hebrew, and even a thorough grounding in mathematics, which he has vainly tried to impart to me. Is this insufficient knowledge for a post at the college?"

"More than sufficient. My brother's credentials are excellent; his politics, I fear, are quite wrong. The College of New Jersey is presently a hotbed of radicalism, although who knows about next week? Also, a good part of the student body has gone off to war on one side or the other. Most of our population is woefully like our changing climate. Whichever wind prevails, that is the one chosen. My friend Annis Stockton is a case in point. Her husband Richard owns extensive lands, so for a long time, he chose the course of moderation. Then, as sides were being taken and choices forced, he finally went to Philadelphia to take his seat in the Congress. He arrived there only days before Independence was proclaimed, so Annis may well be the only woman in America to have both a husband and a son-in-law—Dr. Benjamin Rush of Philadelphia—as signers of the Declaration."

"But that is a thing to be proud of!" Gaby protested.

"History will no doubt decide whether you are right," her aunt said dryly. "Unfortunately, after Washington's double defeat in New York . . . Long Island and then Manhattan lost . . . the general was forced to retreat toward Pennsylvania, and Richard did what he felt he must do to survive and took the British Oath of Loyalty. Many, many have done the same without notoriety, but the Stocktons were too prominent as well as being great friends of Governor Franklin. But then so am I. Poor William; he served our state well for such a long time, and one cannot fault him for sincere conviction. It has been no small burden for him his entire life," she ended calmly, "to be known as Benjamin Franklin's bastard."

Gaby blinked a little. She was not—Annabel's daughter could never be—a prude, but she had never before heard such a word on a lady's tongue.

Her aunt smiled down at her. "Not missish, are you, Gaby?"

"I do not think I am," Gaby answered honestly, "but I must admit that I have never heard that particular word spoken in a parlor."

"I am so accustomed to my own society or that of—" She hesitated, then continued briskly, "Naturally, I am more careful in your father's company . . . not because I think it wrong, you understand, but I don't wish to shock or sadden him. I am quite attached to Timothy, even though we are as different"—she laughed quite cheerfully—"as chalk from cheese. Oh, goodness!" She struck her forehead a light blow. "Where have my wits gone begging? It is of your Papa's activities we started to speak. With so many men gone off for soldiers and others in hiding or staying out of public view, our primary and secondary schools have suffered, too. My neighbor, Thomas Stuckley, for one, had three sons in need of instruction. He was most happy to set up a schoolroom in his dining parlor and hire your father as tutor. Within days, first one and then another gentlemen were asking him to accept other children in need of lessons, so now one of the smaller Stuckley barns is turned into a schoolhouse, and your father has eleven pupils."

"Papa and I have funds. You do remember, don't you, Aunt, that Mama brought him quite a good dowry?"

"I remember quite well. Timothy and I were thought to be doing quite well for ourselves, a farmer's children marrying so high. In your father's case," she said with studied nonchalance, "it was quite true—but not because of money. Annabel was a pearl beyond price."

"But—but . . ." Gaby did not quite have the courage to ask the question on the tip of her tongue. "All I meant, Aunt Emily, was that Papa and I could rent a house of our own, with enough space for schoolrooms. We need not impose on you too long."

"I would not hear of it!" her aunt said firmly. "There is no question of imposition! You are my family, my only family."

"But did not your husband have relations here in Princeton?"

"My husband's parents are dead," her aunt said in a voice as clipped and final as the shutting of a door. "He has two brothers in Brunswick, one sister and a family of cousins in Elizabeth Town. We do not visit. Ah, good, here is our tea."

There was the bustle of setting out cups and saucers after Mrs. Cornwall left. Then Aunt Emily looked across at her niece with a faint smile. "You are burning to ask some questions, Gaby, and another day I will answer them. For the moment, let it suffice to say that the happiest day of my life was the day I buried my husband. Do you wish cream in your tea?" She paused a minute, listening. "I believe your papa is at the door."

Five

"Papa. Papa dear." Barefoot, wearing only her shift and petticoats, Gaby flew through the hallway and flung herself into her father's arms. His tricorn and cloak fell unheeded onto the carpet.

"Gabrielle. My dear Gabrielle." When he held her off from him to look earnestly into her face, there was such joy on his own as she had not seen since the death of his beloved wife. "I had quite given up my hope of Heaven," he said simply. "I knew if I had allowed harm to come to you, I would never be able to face your mother there."

Although her throat felt too clogged to speak, she managed to smile and then say buoyantly, "Nothing harmful happened to me except for a cold bumpy trip on a wagon that I—*we* bought from the Trumbulls, and my greatest suffering was having to listen to Elsie snore from Massachusetts through New York to New Jersey. We must have been overworking her for years, Papa, because she slept most of the way and is in bed right now."

The Reverend Mr. Foote stooped to pick up his cloak and hat and found himself staring at his daughter's bare toes. As he stood up, he was shocked to notice for the first time that she wore only her shift and petticoats.

"Gaby! You are in a state of undress! Have you just come down from your bedchamber?"

"I know I look indecent," said Gaby just as buoyantly, grinning at his shock. "No, I was not in my chamber, I was sitting in the parlor with Aunt Emily, talking just as I am. Forgive me, Papa, but I have had a surfeit of clothes since leaving home. To stay warm during the day, Elsie and I huddled under featherbeds, wearing three outfits each, and the inns we slept in overnight offered not much more comfort. Aunt Emily will confirm we were so heavy with clothing, we could scarcely move."

"Aunt Emily does indeed confirm it," said that lady from the doorway of the back parlor. "Come have a cup of tea, Timothy. You look tired and cold; it will refresh you."

Gaby danced ahead of her father, and this time, she knelt on the hassock so as to be able to reach the table. She poured out his tea, adding just the amount of cream and the dash of sugar she knew he liked.

"The sight of my daughter," he said above her head to his sister, "was the greatest refreshment there could be. But I will be glad to have the tea as well . . . if," after pausing to take a sip and grimacing, "this substance deserves that honorable name."

"My dear Tim," said his sister, sipping her own beverage as though it was a rare nectar, "I am afraid that as well as having to get used to New Jersey tea, you must learn as well to accustom yourself to New Jersey ways. When I first came to the colony, the informality that reigned, even among the gentry, was one of the pleasanter aspects of my new life. Our nearest neighbors then, the De Pooles, had three unmarried daughters known to all the neighborhood as the nymphs. The first time I went to call—the weather, I recall was oppressively hot and humid—you can imagine my surprise and delight to find Mrs. De Poole and her girls seated in the hallway, where doors at opposite ends of the house created a funnel of cool air. They were all dressed—or perhaps," she added with a touch of mischief—"you, Timothy, might say all in the same state of *un*dress as Gaby is now. They were totally unembarrassed and friendly and came barefoot with me into the parlor."

"Oh, Aunt Emily, what an enchanting picture!" Gaby burst out. "Perhaps come summer, I should do the same. I shall sit in your hallway and sew or spin. It might bring me an acceptable suitor. I think," she added teasingly, "Papa fears sometimes he may have me on his hands for life."

Her aunt spoke up suddenly and harshly, "Never, *never* marry to please your family, child."

"Of course, I will not, Aunt Emily," Gaby reassured her at once. "It is just a jest we have between us. Papa is the most indulgent of fathers, even though my frivolous ways try him sorely at times."

The strained look left her aunt's face, and after another half hour's pleasant chat over the tea cups, she led Gaby up to the cheerful bedroom she had chosen for her. It had flocked wallpaper, flowered curtains and a glowing fire in the fireplace.

All the clothes Gaby had discarded in the back parlor were laid neatly on the sleigh bed. A basin of steaming water and clean towels were set out on the nightstand.

"It is a lovely room, Aunt Emily." Gaby embraced her fervently. "Thank you so much for everything."

A little later, when Gaby came downstairs again, soberly dressed in one of her dark traveling gowns, her aunt told her quietly that Isaac Trumbull had been invited to have supper with them but declined in horror. "He said," Aunt Emily quoted laughingly to her niece, " 'Ain't no way, ma'am, I could set down to table with Parson and lie to his face. He'd have the truth out of me, sure as shootin', so if it's all the same to you, ma'am, I'll just bide in the kitchen for supper, sleep in the barn, and slip away unnoticed-like in the early morning. They tell me the independency troops are just a whoop and a holar acrost the Delaware. I'll take the ferry and stumble on them somehow.' "

"That's Isaac." Gaby giggled. "I will slip out to the barn after supper to say good-bye to him and give him a bit of money for himself."

"I already did," said her aunt, "when he brought over your clothing and the boxes marked 'Open at Aunt Emily's,' which are all stacked in the front parlor. Mrs. Cornwall is readying for the morning a package he may find more useful even than money. Eggs, some cheeses, fresh loaves and—if he wants to take the trouble—he can wring the necks of a couple of chickens to take along."

The Reverend Mr. Foote strolled into the room and asked in high good humor, "What mischief are you hatching with all this whispering?"

Gaby smiled innocently. "Aunt Em was just telling me that our boxes are in the front parlor, Papa. There is one that's full of Massachusetts newspapers for you. I collected them all from the day *you* left until the day *we* left."

Seeing her father's wistful look, she told him firmly, "No, Papa, not everyone is a table reader like you and me. I am sure Aunt Emily prefers a little conversation."

"Considering the state of your temper, my dear brother, every time you read a newspaper article that displeases you," Aunt Emily agreed just as firmly, "I definitely would prefer conversation. You can ruin your digestion as much as you wish *after* we eat and without ruining mine in the process."

When their meal was over, Mrs. Van Raalte and her niece went straight to the small parlor and took their places on rocker and hassock, resuming a spirited discussion on current literature. The reverend joined them shortly afterwards, his arms piled high with newspapers. He seated himself in an upholstered armchair near a table that held a brace of candles. From time to time, his extraordinary grunts and ejaculations caused the two women to exchange mirthful glances.

"I knew it. Nothing keeps the fellow quiet!" he exclaimed at one point.

"Has something displeased you, Papa?" his daughter asked with an air of great solicitude.

"That damned fellow Pythias displeases me!" he exploded.

"Papa!" cried Gaby in shock. "You swore! And Mama told me once that *she* was the only one in the world you were ever tempted to swear at!"

Mr. Foote dropped the paper on his lap, smiling in tender recollection. "When did your Mama say that?" he inquired of his daughter.

"On my fifteenth birthday when she and I went picnicking. Is it true?"

"It is true," he admitted guiltily. "She was the only woman. This fellow Pythias is another story." He rattled his newspaper. "Just listen to this." He cleared his throat loudly. "It is titled *A Small Warning to Great Britain.*"

"Clever," Aunt Emily broke in. "*Small* as a contrast to *Great*."

"Yes, indeed, most clever," Gaby responded solemnly.

"If I may continue—?"

"Certainly, Timothy."

"Of course, Papa. Do read on."

> Beware
> You who dare
> Try so hard to subdue us.
> The way
> We reply
> Will long make you rue us.

"Is that all?" asked Gaby. "I must admit I am rather disappointed, Papa. She is usually a great deal more entertaining and has much more to say."

"It may be short, but it is decidedly to the point," Aunt Emily disagreed. "Most poets, Gabrielle, say all too much about all too little."

"But Pythias is more of a political observer than a poet."

"I think he is a little of both."

"Truly?" Gaby looked so enormously gratified that Aunt Emily—while she reflected seriously about the giveaway pronoun *she*—pushed her spectacles farther up her nose to inspect her niece.

Gaby jumped up from her hassock. "I think I will go up to bed. It has been"—she pretended to yawn—"a very long day."

Once in the hallway, she hurried to the closet and helped herself to a cloak and a pair of heavy boots. She left the house quietly and walked quickly to the barn to bid Isaac good-bye. It was half an hour before she returned to the house, this time using the kitchen entrance.

Aunt Emily and Mrs. Cornwall stood together in the pantry adjoining the kitchen. They were engaged in an earnest and somewhat furtive conversation. Gaby hesitated, not wanting to disturb them. Then she couldn't help overhearing words that kept her absolutely still, listening deliberately.

"Now that he is assured of my niece's safety, my brother has agreed to accompany Mr. Stuckley to New York—on Tory business, I suspect—so he will be safely away. Since a school holiday has been declared, they may well stay a week. Since they leave on the morning of the twenty-fourth, I will announce that our meeting is at dusk on that day. We can send Abe around with the notes tomorrow."

"What about your niece?" Mrs. Cornwall asked to that young woman's great surprise. "Should I slip a few drops of laudanum in her afternoon tea, just enough to make her sleepy without any harm done?"

"I believe," Aunt Emily said thoughtfully, to the eavesdropper's equal astonishment, "that it will not be necessary. I think I may be able to confide in Gabrielle."

"If you are sure of her," Mrs. Cornwall said dubiously.

"I am . . . or will be. You may tell Abe the notes will be ready in the morning. Both women turned toward the kitchen, and Gaby flattened herself against the wall so as not to be seen; but they were only reaching for their candlesticks on a shelf.

She remained quietly in the darkness for what seemed a long five minutes, then crept quietly upstairs.

Once safely undetected and in her room, she took from under her pillow a schoolroom exercise book she had once used for grammar lessons. Both sides of the precious empty pages at the back were used for her uncorrected scribblings before being transferred to the even more precious writing paper that she sent to the newspapers. There were three crossed-out, corrected, at times almost indecipherable versions of her latest poem, "Tempest in a Boston Teapot." Was it ready to post?

She sat down on the side of her bed and muttered the words aloud.

'Twas mid-December
Of '73
(A night that will live
In history)
When two-hundred
Sons of Liberty
A Boston Tea Party
Did attend,
Their object?
To brew a special blend,
So special it would
Forever end
The drinking of taxed tea.

Much against British wishes
The tea was tossed to the fishes
And across the ocean, reprisals
Were ordered for our land.
   The British—they acted like British
   Unable to understand
   America sprang up from British seed
   But American soil grows a different breed . . .

Then and there in '73
We knew that this conflict had to be
It was never simply the price of tea
But a question of personal liberty!
No more were we willing to bend our knees
To British directives and British decrees
   We're Americans—damn it!
   We're different . . .
   We're we!
      We want—
         We need—
            We shall be free!

Perhaps, she thought humorously, I should ask Aunt Emily's opinion when I speak with her. Impulsively, she ripped the final version out of the exercise book and walked over to the door.

"Come in," Aunt Emily called in answer to Gaby's soft knock.

She was sitting up in bed, in nightcap and nightdress. There was a hand-carved pine lap desk on her knees, and she was writing.

"I thought you were Mrs. Cornwall," she said smilingly. "Is there anything you need, Gaby?"

"Just your confidence, Aunt Emily. I am so pleased you feel you may give it to me as I would much rather *not* have laudanum in my tea, although I think it may be necessary for Elsie. She is so conventional, poor dear."

"Dear me," said her aunt, unperturbed. "That was careless of us. We must conspire together more privately in the future."

"Suppose those notes for Abe—whoever he is—fell into the wrong hands?"

"No harm would be done," said Mrs. Van Raalte at her most tranquil. "I call the meetings a sewing circle, and I do not address anyone by name or use a signature."

"Would it help if I told you I am entirely in sympathy with your rebel politicking? If you would like the proof—here." She held out the poem.

"Yes," said her aunt, hardly glancing at it. "I began to suspect tonight that you were Pythias and confirmed it while you were probably in the barn with Isaac. I hope you will forgive my having gone through your private papers, but I fear," she added twinklingly, "that politicking—as you call it—affects both manners and morality adversely. I think, by the way, "Tempest in a Boston Teapot" is one of your best. No wonder your poor father is in a constant rage at Pythias. Paternal instinct, do you suppose?"

Without being invited, Gaby sank down on the featherbed at the foot of her aunt's four-poster. "Honestly, Aunt Emily!" she sputtered.

"And now, I am afraid," Mrs. Van Raalte continued regretfully, "I have an even bigger shock, perhaps even a great disappointment for you. Although we Regulars are all attached to the cause of American liberty, our meetings are more often called—as is this one on the twenty-fourth—for the very personal purpose of frightening a local wife-beater into better behavior."

"You . . . you *what?* No," as Aunt Emily started to speak, "I heard the words . . . it's their meaning. How can you do what you say? And how do you find out who deserves such treatment? And why—oh dear God, Aunt Emily! *That* is what you meant when you said the happiest day of your life was the one when you buried your husband?"

"Quite true," said Aunt Emily calmly. "Everyone, including my parents, thought I was the luckiest girl in the world when Johann Van Raalte asked for my hand. He was young, rich and handsome while I was dowerless and only passably pretty; I was easily persuaded to believe as they did. Johann was not an older son, but he did own Hillpoint Farms, a very handsome property—now my own—which came to him through an uncle.

"The courtship"—her lips twisted wryly—"was all a woman could ask for. Johann acted the *parfit gentil knight.* Going from Massachusetts home to New Jersey was our wedding trip. My first beating was on the wedding night in a country inn when I did not respond quickly enough to his command to 'take off that damned sack' I was wearing and give him a view of what he was paying for. I lived three years of such hell with him that even these twenty-plus years later, I am not sure how I managed to survive. He was a man who delighted in cruelty . . . to his servants, to dumb animals, but most of all—to that primary source, a bought-and-paid-for wife."

"Would not anyone help you?"

"I ran away half a dozen times, trying to seek refuge with my parents, with friends, even among strangers. He always came after me and used the law to force me back with him. Timothy was still away at Yale College and could not have helped me. In any event, I was Johann's personal property, you must understand. *That* is the law. He had the right to chastise me for my faults. *That* is also the law. I appealed to members of his own family, and they shunned and turned their backs on me, proclaiming me a liar. Then one happy harvest night, as he rode drunkenly home to me, Johann beat his horse one time too many, and the poor beast threw him. He landed heavily on a graveled road that split his head wide open."

Gabrielle moved to the middle of the bed and put her hands comfortingly on her aunt's, whose voice remained amazingly serene.

"When they told me he was dead, I went by myself into the little back parlor—it was kept cold and mostly unfurnished then because Johann thought it a mean little room. All I could say over and over was, 'Thank you, God, thank you with all my heart.' "

She sighed. "Twenty-two years I have been a widow, Gaby, and for me, it is a woman's happiest state. I have even learned"—she gave a wicked little wink of one eye—"from two men I have known rather well during my widowhood that relations between a man and woman may be altogether pleasant rather than hurtful and frightening."

"You w-went to—to—?"

"To bed with them?" her aunt filled in obligingly. "Yes, Gaby, I have had two lovers, one for four years, one for seven. They were both widowers, so no one was hurt by our arrangement, though I would prefer you never mention it to your father. It would grieve him to no purpose."

"Heaven forbid. Did—did they want to marry you, Aunt Emily?"

Her aunt shrugged. "Yes, but without much hope that I would agree. I was both wealthy and independent. Trade that for the shackles of married life, not likely! Risk another man's owning both me and my property. Never!"

She held up her left hand for Gaby to see. "I threw my wedding ring into Johann's coffin before it was closed, and I took a vow at his grave, as a thank-you offering to God for my own salvation, to help any women I could who were in similar circumstances. That vow brought the Regulars into being. And I have also provided sanctuary here at Hillpoint House for runaway wives or serving women. Mrs. Cornwall was the first . . . Cornwall is not her real name. She managed to get here from Virginia; she has been with me for fifteen years. Polly is another, here only since last month. We are sending her on to a more permanent position in Connecticut; she will be farther away and safer there."

"Well, Gaby?" She looked laughingly across at her niece. "Are you disappointed to find my secret doings less exciting than you had believed?"

"Aunt Emily, you command my admiration even more." Gaby leaned forward to kiss her aunt soundly in the middle of her forehead. "You are wonderful."

"And will you attend our meeting at dusk on the twenty-fourth . . . or opt for laudanum in your tea? I should warn you that we wear men's garb."

"Nothing short of catastrophe could keep me from participating."

Six

On the afternoon of the twenty-fourth, Gaby was impressed anew with the neatness and dispatch of the arrangements. Mrs. Cornwall, Aunt Emily and she already wore the homespun men's wear of simple farmers. Only Polly had retained her skirts. Elsie, slightly dosed with laudanum tea was snoring in her bed.

The large front parlor and front hallway were aglow with cheerful candlelight that could be seen through the windows. A buffet table was laid out with cups, saucers and cake plates on either side of the massive silver Van Raalte Queen Anne tea service. Little scattered tables held embroidery hoops, incomplete chair seats worked in needlepoint, altar cloths, and half-seamed cotton work shirts.

A huge copper kettle was placed on the hob, and a last finishing touch was the opening of the spinet, with sheet music placed on the rack above.

Even before dusk, one wagon and one carriage drew up in the driveway just outside the door, and a small horse-drawn sleigh came across the fields. Beshawled and bonneted women of assorted ages and sizes spilled out of these conveyances, left off by their various menfolk. As they ascended the steps of Hillpoint House, the brisk air echoed with shrill cries of "Good-bye" or "Pick me up on time, mind!"

As each woman entered the house, she ran upstairs to Aunt Emily's bedchamber, where a brisk fire had been burning for hours. A trunk full of men's breeches, waistcoats, shirts, coats and tricorns was dipped into. Tallow wax and powder were used to turn women's hair arrangement into men's, and half their number merely slipped on men's powdered wigs.

When they all gathered downstairs, Polly and another woman about Mrs. Van Raalte's age, sat, ladylike, in the front parlor. The woman was sneezing and sniffling into a handkerchief.

"Tarnation, Em!" she said pettishly. "I wanted to be there tonight. I have a special distaste for Luther Burley. The pious, hypocritical, Bible-thumping ones rile me most of all."

"You should not have come out at all tonight with that shocking cold, Maribelle," Mrs. Van Raalte tried to soothe her. "I promise to give him an extra hard lick or two for you. Now that I think of it . . . Polly, would you fetch the brandy bottle from the cupboard, my dear. I think Mrs. Calvert would enjoy a tot before her tea, perhaps with a little honey. You'll have to play the spinet, Maribelle; it's a mercy you know how . . . and remember, Polly," the young maid came running back, bottle in hand, "move about quite a bit, and talk and laugh loudly, so if anyone is passing by, you two will sound like a dozen."

"Who is the new gel?" coughed Maribelle.

"A brave new recruit, my niece Gabrielle Foote. Gaby, this is my dear friend, Mrs. Calvert who—I believe I hear sleigh bells. It must be Abe."

"Let's go, Regulars," said someone else in a deep mannish voice.

They laughed as they bundled themselves out of doors. A huge sleigh with two horses was drawn up in front of the house. All the women dressed as men climbed speedily over the side, laughing and jesting, burrowing down in the hay.

The rather grizzled elderly driver, Gaby took time to note, really was a man. "Does he know what we are about?" she whispered to her aunt.

"Better than you, my dear," Aunt Emily answered. "He had a daughter crippled by a husband who kicked her down a flight of stairs. Old Abe always drives us when we schedule a little rendezvous, and he has driven many a runaway to her place of refuge. I should warn you, Gabrielle, that no matter how much of a frolic it has seemed so far, we are not playing games. Our intent is serious, and our methods may seem crude and even cruel to anyone who has never been a victim herself or endured the grief of seeing a loved one victimized by a brutal man. If you would rather stand watch outside with Abe . . ."

"No, Aunt Em," said Gaby firmly, "I wish to be there with you."

As they turned down a modest lane, there was not a whisper of sound among them. Abe went past a large farm house, then backed the sleigh so it was headed in their return direction. He took out a rifle and laid it across his lap, then handed two pistols to Aunt Emily. She kept one herself and gave the other to the tallest of the young "men." "Your turn, Sal. Stand guard right outside the house."

Sal nodded and ran softly ahead, stationing herself just below the three small steps leading up to the farm house.

"Time for masks?" someone asked.

"Yes," said Aunt Emily.

They all, Gaby, too, took little black cloth masks from a basket and tied them across their faces.

"Now?" asked the same quavery voice.

"Now!" they all roared, and in a sudden rush, with a unified raucous shout, they took the three steps at a run, broke through the front door and crossed the threshold into a parlor, where the family appeared to be assembled.

A woman in her thirties left her spinning wheel to put her arms protectively about two little girls. A young man of about twenty jumped up from his chair.

"Children, upstairs to your room!" cried one of the Regulars. "For their own safety, ma'am." He made a courteous bow to the woman.

She whispered to the girls, and they both scuttled out of the room and up the stairs.

An irascible-looking man, about fifty, was hindered from getting to his feet by a touch of rheumatics. "Get out of my house, you scum!" he roared.

"You do not give the orders here tonight, Luther Burley!" one of the Regulars told him in a voice that sounded at once contemptuous and masculine. She turned to the young man. "Is your maidservant in the house?"

"Who wants to know?" he asked insolently.

"I," said Mrs. Van Raalte and raised her pistol.

"Henry!" his father commanded. "Tell them."

Henry answered sulkily, "She is asleep in the attic."

"Both of you are wise." The pistol pointed to the sofa. "Do sit down, Henry."

Gaby stared. If she had not known for sure, she would never have believed the speaker was Aunt Emily.

One of the Regulars went to each side of Henry and took hold of an arm, twisting it back slightly to keep him from rising. A third stood behind him with an arm-lock around his neck. In a pretense of keeping Mrs. Burley from interfering, she was told to seat herself next to Henry.

While Gaby looked on uncertainly, the four remaining Regulars took hold of Luther Burley, hauling him onto his feet. Mrs. Van Raalte gestured with her pistol, and the four wheeled him about, then positioned him over an arm of his chair, with his head bent uncomfortably low.

Speedily and silently, save for bellows of outrage from their host, his breeches were torn open. As buttons flew all over the floor, both his breeches and smalls, as well as his wool stockings, were pulled down to his ankles, revealing to all, part of a mottled back, fleshy legs, and a fat, pale posterior.

As a Regular stepped forward, holding out a sturdy strip of leather, "As you do to others, so shall you be done by," said Aunt Emily in that strange hoarse voice. She nodded, and the chastisement began.

Each woman took a turn with the switch, delivering lusty blows, while their victim swore so robustly and vowed such signal vengeance that Gaby had no hesitation, when the time came, about taking her turn.

When Aunt Emily exchanged her pistol for the whip, she administered five strokes with a right good will. ("Two for you, Maribelle," she would say later, "and three for me.") She took back her pistol when she was done.

"Those who beat the women of their household cannot hide themselves from us. They who beat shall in turn be beaten. If you require us to come again, tonight's visit will seem gentle. You may tend your husband now, Mrs. Burley. Henry." His guards let go of their hold. "You, as well as your father, take warning for the future from this night's work."

In another moment they were out of the room, then out of the house and all bundled back in the sleigh, which old Abe at once set in motion. Sal and Mrs. Van Raalte held their pistols ready until the farm house was out of sight. A number of the women took wadded pads of cotton from inside their mouths, accounting to Gaby for their changed voices.

They were back at Hillpoint House in another thirty minutes. Polly, watching from a window, saw the approach of the sleigh and flew to the door to admit them.

"Our mission was a complete success, Polly," one of the women said to her; and Polly, who had hitherto seemed to Gaby a quiet, unassuming, meek sort of girl, startled her by exclaiming with loud joyful profanity, "Thanks be to God. One more bleedin' bastard whose had his double jug set on fire for him by us women!"

Mrs. Calvert sat on the sofa, sneezing, sniffling and coughing even more than before they left.

"Take some more brandy, Maribelle," said Aunt Emily solicitously.

"Can't," said Mrs. Calvert succinctly. "There's none left."

"None!"

"If you look around, you may well see why. We had a friendly visit"—she spoke with bitter irony—"from a scavenging British patrol."

"Heavens!" Aunt Emily looked around her parlor for the first time, noting slits in upholstery, draperies partly pulled down and slashes in the wallpaper, wanton, useless destruction all, but not nearly so important as—

"They did not hurt you?" She included Polly as well as her friend in an anxious glance, while the other Regulars fell silent.

"We received very little warning. There was just enough time for me to bid Polly to hide behind the sofa, and I tossed three cakes and two of the loaves on top of her, knowing you would all return, famished. There were half a dozen of the red-coated rascals, and they were already half tipsy but promptly helped themselves to the bottle of brandy and polished it off. Then they started smashing tea cups and created general mayhem, demanding my jewels and money. I said I was a Quaker and had none; those of my faith stored up treasures in heaven, not on earth. So they took my wedding ring. Then they wanted to know why the house was so empty, and I said I was expecting a party of missionaries who sewed for the poor underdressed heathen in faraway countries."

"Oh, she was marvelous!" Polly broke in with enthusiasm. "I nearly gave myself away, laughing, it was so amusing. Mrs. Calvert, she said to them in the most die-away voice, 'Young men, thou art in a sad state of inebriation. Thy mothers would sorrow to see thee.' Then she coughed and coughed and sneezed right on them, moaning out, 'O Lord, I do not dispute Thy will, but why hast Thou afflicted me? My poor daughter and my dear husband taken from me by the pox only a week ago. And now these men wanting what I do not possess.' Then she coughed and sneezed at them again, sighing out, 'I feel so hot and fevered; I cannot breathe.' "

Polly paused to catch her breath while they all broke into laughter.

"What happened next, Maribelle?" everyone exclaimed eagerly.

"As soon as they heard the word pox, they all drew back. When I mentioned being fevered . . ." She shrugged. "They couldn't get away fast enough, although, I am sorry to say, Emily, they paused on their rush out the door long enough to take your Queen

Anne service—all except the tray, which was too heavy. They threw it on the floor; it is badly dented. They also helped themselves to all the silver teaspoons and silver thimbles and made a clean sweep of your pantry."

"And they hurled the breakfast set at the wall for sport, Mrs. Van Raalte," Polly added. "I swept it up, and I'm not sure, Miss Gaby, but I think when they went outside to the back to see what else there was, they may have taken your horse."

"Her horse!" More sympathetic groans rang out than for the tea service or the breakfast set. Gaby decided, amused in spite of her loss, that Aunt Emily had been right. A New Jersey woman appeared to value nothing so highly as her horse!

"Well," said Mrs. Van Raalte practically, as she seated herself, "it could have been a great deal worse if we had all been here." She looked about her at Gaby and her Regulars, many of them not much older than her niece. The British soldiers' disdain for extending courtesies to American women was only too well known; they usually considered them ripe plums for the common redcoats' taking.

"Let us have our tea . . . and whatever food is left. There is a bottle of blackberry cordial and another of rum hidden at the back of the hall closet."

"I'll get it, Aunt Emily," Gaby offered, rising, while Polly crawled in back of the sofa to bring out the cakes and bread. These turned out to be somewhat caved-in and sad-looking, but they provided a feast for the hungry, happy women. Not a crumb was left, and countless cups of tea were downed as well as the entire bottle of blackberry cordial.

When Sal reached for the rum, Aunt Emily removed the bottle from her hand and shook her head regretfully. "Save it for the men when they come to collect you. Between rum and their righteous anger when they learn that only by hiding yourselves in the fields were we all saved from ravishment by the British, no one will dream of connecting us with the little—er—contretemps at the Burley house tonight."

"If it should ever be learned of, which seems unlikely," said one of the Regulars.

"Not one of our previous targets has ever let his punishment be made public," a second pointed out.

"Bullies do not want their own discomfiture to be known," said a third scornfully.

Presently they heard the scrape of boots and then the thud of the door knocker. As man after man was admitted, nothing could have exceeded the innocent look of the gathering. Colonial women plying their needles on behalf of their households or churches.

If their faces were overflushed and they seemed highly excited, it was not to be wondered at, the rum-filled men said later. What a frightening experience it must have been for them, poor little dears. God damn the British!

Seven

"Gaby. Gaby, my dear."

Gabrielle awoke reluctantly from an oddly interesting dream. Aunt Emily and Mrs. Calvert had been sitting together on the sofa, sipping blackberry cordial and gossiping while Henry Burley and an unknown redcoat fought a duel right in front of them. In the middle of the dream duel, the men's fencing foils turned to leather switches. Seeing this, Polly and she, each armed with a basket of pastry, threw their cakes at the combatants, who, at once, fell unconscious to the ground. Gaby began to dance in delight and Polly to sing. She was still dancing when Aunt Emily shook her awake.

Gaby sat up, rubbing her eyes. When she realized it was still night, she asked in alarm, "Is something wrong, Aunt?"

"I have glorious news, Gaby. There has been a second battle fought at Trenton, this time against the British, too, not only Hessians. Washington's troops have prevailed again, and it is certain now that he will continue his advance to the British positions here at Princeton."

"But it is, as you said, Aunt Emily, glorious news, so why do you look so concerned?"

"If there is the American victory we must all pray for, your father cannot return to New Jersey, Gabrielle. I thank God, as it is, he encountered his old college friend and delayed a few days longer. He will be safe in Manhattan, but here in New Jersey, as in Massachusetts, he has been too openly and avowedly a loyalist. Even I could not prevent his arrest."

Gaby stared at her. *"Even you?"*

Emily Van Raalte flushed a little. "Although we have not spoken of it directly—you have been most tactful—I think you realize that I am in communication—that is, I have contact with the army."

"Yes, Aunt," returned Gaby quite politely. "I have been aware that you supply information to the American Army, wherever it is, about the British Army presence here in Princeton."

"Quite true."

Gabrielle shook her head in wonder. "How shall I ever be able to live up to having someone like you in the family?" she marveled. "You manage an estate and farms, assist runaway women, head the organization that deals out justice to males who transgress against wives and tyrannize over female servants. Then, just as a little sideline—to keep life from getting dull, no doubt—you gather secret intelligence for your country."

Having had her laugh and actually caused her aunt to blush, Gaby slipped out of bed and wrapped herself in a flannel robe. "I will write a letter to Papa at once, warning him not to return yet."

"You cannot, Gabrielle, nor can I."

"Why ever not?"

"We would have to give him a reason he would find acceptable, and we cannot give the true one."

"But, Aunt—"

"If either of us did so, Gaby, *she* would be supplying information to the enemy in New York in the event the letter fell into the wrong hands."

She saw the swift comprehension on Gaby's face and nodded in sympathy. But she was not surprised a minute or two later to hear her niece say, "All the same, Aunt Emily, however much I disagree with Papa's politics, I cannot stand by and let him come back, only to be arrested."

"I never thought you could, Gaby," Emily Van Raalte said with great and loving tenderness. "There is a young man downstairs who is on his way back to Trenton. He is willing to deliver you safely to a ferry crossing on the way. Once in New York, you may proceed to Fraunces Tavern and tell your father only this: that you came because you learned—perhaps you could say from Mr. Stuckley—that there is a warrant out for his arrest."

She put a hand on her niece's shoulder. *"Say nothing else.* Now this is important, Gabrielle. Do not speak at all of troop positions, of advances or retreats. If the victory is already won or lost, it will soon be known. If not, silence is all the more imperative. You must not give the slightest clue that you had or have prior information. At present, your father's safety is at stake in New Jersey. If you are indiscreet in New York, I will be endangered."

"I promise you, Aunt Emily, you may trust me. I can, when I wish to, be both silent and discreet. Remember, you said that I was tactful?"

"I know, child, I have the utmost trust in you. Now dress quickly and warmly. I fear you can only take one change of clothes with you. You will be riding his horse double since the British stole your own."

"Once again, damn the British for that if nothing else!" Gaby laughed as she opened drawers and made a swift selection. "You see how very New Jersey I am becoming, Aunt. I now value a horse far above rubies."

"A pleasing metamorphosis," her aunt agreed. "I will go down and fix a breakfast for you both. There is nothing so heartening for a cold journey as a hot meal. Take a plaid blanket from under the tricorns in the dower chest. You can keep it about your legs as you ride and on the ferry, crossing the Hudson. It will be bitterly cold."

Gaby dressed quickly, shivering, more from the chill of the room than from fear. By tomorrow—no, actually this afternoon, since it was well past midnight—she would be with her father . . . surely in time to prevent his return.

Poor Papa. First driven out of his beloved home and church in Massachusetts, now out of his sister's home in New Jersey. How long, she thought in some dismay, would he be safe in New York? As a patriot, it was her fervent wish for General Washington to regain that city. But as a daughter . . .

Her aunt was standing at the foot of the stairs when Gaby descended, carrying a small portmanteau. "Come into the back parlor," she said. "I have your breakfast there."

Gaby dropped the portmanteau and followed obediently. There was a tray on the hot tiles in front of the fireplace. Emily Van Raalte swooped down and lifted it. "Sit!" she said, and Gaby, with a slight smile, took her favorite hassock and had the tray laid across her lap.

"Where, by the way, is your young man?"

"In the kitchen with his horse."

"With his horse? His horse is in the kitchen!" repeated New England Gabrielle in shock. Then she added meekly, "Forgive me, Aunt. Perhaps, after all, I am not become so New Jersey as I thought. I should have realized at once that in such perilous times as these, a horse is a most precious possession and must be guarded. Speaking of precious—you are going to have to deal with a very cross and angry Elsie when she awakes and finds me gone. Tell her, please, whatever story you think will serve you best."

Aunt Emily said placidly, "I will come up with a suitable lie."

"I am sure you will." Gaby grinned. "Now about this young man—"

"He is there and you are here because I wanted to have a private word with you before you left."

Gaby paused in the eating of her oatmeal. "Is there something else I must tell Papa?"

"No, my dear, something else I want you to consider. And, believe me, you are as New Jersey a niece as I could ever desire. If my baby daughter had lived, I would wish her to be just like you. Gabrielle, have you given any serious thought to your own future?"

"I mean to," said Gaby quite seriously, "as soon as I can get Papa married."

"Is he betrothed?" asked Aunt Emily, all amazed. "Why has neither of you said a word of it to me?"

"Because he is not betrothed, not yet, but I have decided, Aunt

Em, that—provided I can find the right sort of woman—it might be the best thing in the world for him to marry again. He needs someone both intelligent and gay, someone who could keep him from getting too set in his ways and becoming . . . you know . . . a wee bit pompous."

"I know only too well, and I think you may be right, but it gives you two hard tasks, Gabrielle, not only one. First you must find the exemplary lady who suits your fastidious taste and his own. Then, even if you get Timothy to the well, you may not be able to force him to drink."

"One step at a time, Aunt," Gaby laughed. "One step at a time."

"Now back to you, my dear."

"Yes, Aunt?"

"My brother and you, his daughter, are the nearest relations I have in the world. I am possessed by a healthy confidence that I shall live to a ripe, cantankerous old age. When I am gone, however, it would please me to know that you will preside over Hillpoint in my place. Household management you already know. I would want you to learn farm management as well. A wise mistress always knows as much as the people in her employ—if she is not to be fooled or cheated. Your consent would give me great joy, Gabrielle, but you would also be providing for your own future."

There was a slight pause.

"Nothing to say, Gaby? How unusual for you."

"It is hard to find the right words, Aunt Emily. You have taken my breath away. "Are there not . . . relations of your husband's?"

"Any number . . . but they will never set foot on Hillpoint Farms, let alone rule here. My husband was so sure of heirs that, until they arrived in the world, all was left to me. Doubtless, if I had not bred more successfully, he would have changed his will by and by. Fortunately, he did not live long enough and all became mine. Hillpoint has never had a master who loved it more than I or served it better. I think, Gaby, you could be a more than worthy successor."

"And after me?"

"Hopefully, your children."

"Then you do not stipulate that I may not marry to receive this inheritance?"

"God forbid. Gabrielle, understand me, I am not trying to order your life . . . well, perhaps in a way I am. If I thought you were proposing to marry some wastrel—a handsome idiot—a gambler . . . I would have to ensure that Hillpoint could never fall into his hands. I love this place, Gaby. To me, it is husband, children, family, not just my home. I pray that you may have all of these and Hillpoint, too, but all in life is chance."

She shrugged. "Should you not wish to marry, or be unable to, at least you will never have to be a servant, governess or poor relation in someone else's household. You will be the respected owner of a fine estate. You must not give me your answer this very minute. Just consider it carefully while you are in New York."

She glanced at her niece's tray. "You are done. Good. I think you should be on your way. The sun is already rising."

Gaby stood up, tray in hand, and followed her aunt to the kitchen.

The young man had finished his breakfast, too, and stood with his hand on the horse's mane. There was no sign on the newspapers protecting the floor that the animal had committed any serious breach of etiquette.

Gaby and her escort smiled cautiously at one another, but no introductions were made.

Mrs. Van Raalte embraced her niece fondly. "Good-bye, my dear. I pray with all my heart that you will be able to get Timothy settled and come back to me quickly."

"Aunt Emily, I will consider your proposal carefully, as you requested, and give you my answer when I return. If I gave it this very minute, you know, do you not, that it could only be yes, dear aunt, one hundred—no, one thousand times, yes."

Eight

The journey to the ferry crossing was as uneventful as it was cold, and neither traveler felt inclined for conversation.

Icy winds whistled about them, and Gabrielle, seated on the horse in back of her escort, was happy to shield herself behind his bulk. Her mittened hands clutched him around the middle, both for balance and the added warmth of his body. She kept one cheek against his back and thoughtfully tried to ensure that he receive a share of Aunt Emily's wool plaid blanket.

At the deserted ferry crossing, he ignored the bell, with the brief utterance, "No use making a noise about being here."

There was a ramshackle hut a few yards away. He picked his way along the icy path and, to Gaby's keen regret, dismounted. She was battered now by blasts of wind from both front and back.

The young man pounded on the hut door.

"What the hell you be wanting?" called a surly voice from within.

"Ferry passenger. Hurry."

"Hold onto your danged horses. You be early."

The young man winked cheerfully up at Gaby, though tears of cold were running down his cheeks. "Double fare if you can speed it up."

The voice became positively genial. "Gimme two minutes to piss and put on my britches."

Seeing the young man flush slightly in embarrassment that she could hear, too, Gaby restrained a gurgle of laughter. A purveyor of secret intelligence . . . and he blushed! How strange men were, thought Aunt Emily's niece, who was feeling a great deal more worldly wise from her short stay in New Jersey than she ever had as the Reverend Mr. Foote's daughter in Massachusetts.

The ferryman came out in almost the stipulated time, bundled in a worn caped coat, with a red wool muffler tied around his ears. As he strode to the boat crossing, Gaby's escort followed, leading the horse.

"Just the lady is going."

The ferryman indicated a rowboat. "Better and faster fer just the two of us. I'll take my money now."

Before Gaby could even extract the fat purse her aunt had slipped into her pocket at parting, her escort was spilling coins into the outstretched hamlike hand, signaling with his eyes that she be silent.

"Your aunt gave it to me. Best not to let him know that you have coin, too," he whispered as he helped her dismount and took her small portmanteau out of his saddlebag.

"Thank you so much for everything," Gaby whispered back fervently.

"You're more'n welcome, ma'am." He ducked his head almost shyly. Then, as he helped her into the boat, he winked at Gaby again and spoke aloud.

"Now remember, Carrie," he said in the affectionately scolding tone a man uses to his women-folk, "I'll be waiting here at six sharp. Don't you keep me waitin' less'n you want me to leave you to walk the five miles home in the cold and dark."

"I promise I'll be on time, Cousin Tobias," Gaby called, then under her breath, "God keep you."

Crossing the Hudson, she blessed Aunt Emily again and again. Without her plaid blanket, she was sure she would have arrived as a large frozen icicle at the isle of Manhattan. As it was, she sat hunched all the way over in the rowboat to protect her face from winds that cut, razor-sharp, at the naked skin. She laid the blanket over her lap and tucked it in behind to cover the backs of her legs.

In spite of all these measures, when she landed in New York, she felt like an ice statue. It was an effort to walk away from the wharf, avoiding several disreputable-looking fellows. She approached the first respectable-appearing man who came by.

"Can you tell me, sir, how to get to Fraunces Tavern? Is it walking distance?"

"Could be walked in fine weather if you had a man in tow, young lady. My advice is to take a hackney now."

"Thank you sir. Where may I find one?" Gaby asked meekly.

"Keep going the way you are, then when you come to a turn, go right and walk on till you reach Broad Way. No problem picking up a hackney carriage there."

"Thank you." She sketched a brief curtsey and walked on, faster and faster, wanting only to escape the cold. To her joy, even before she reached Broad Way, she saw what was obviously a carriage for hire coming toward her. She hailed the driver, waving both hands and the portmanteau.

She was sure he had seen her, but when he seemed to be making no push to stop, with complete disregard for her safety, she ran out to the center of the road. All she could think of was release from the bone-chilling winds.

There was a loud scraping of the horse's hooves on the roadway and even louder oaths as the carriage came to a creaking, screeching halt.

Gaby laid her hands on the horse's bridle to prevent any risk that the precious conveyance would take off.

"I wish to go to Fraunces Tavern," she instructed the driver.

"It can't be done, miss. I'm bound in another direction."

She had learned a useful lesson only this morning. "Double fare, my good man, if you are speedy," she told him loftily.

It must be more effective when a man said the words, she decided ruefully, because the driver only looked more harassed and somewhat regretful. "I tell you, miss, it isn't possible," he expostulated. "I already—"

Gaby was desperate. She let go of the bridle and took hold of the carriage door, saying, "If you have to go somewhere else first, I shall not object to some delay."

She tore off one slippery mitten with her teeth, pulled open the door, with a shrill shriek at the coldness of the latch, threw the portmanteau inside and scrambled up into the dark interior of the carriage on her hands and knees, moaning joyfully to be out of the cold. She pulled the door shut, plumped herself down, then screamed even louder, and pivoted around. She was sitting on someone's lap!

She was staring into a pair of vivid and very amused blue eyes!

"I never believed in fairy godmothers before," drawled a voice that seemed equally entertained. "But I have to believe they exist—when a mere five minutes ago, I expressed aloud the wish that I be given a comfortable armful to keep me warm."

Horrified and blushing as she had never in her entire life blushed before, Gaby stared into the blue eyes. He also had a nose so long and straight, it was the kind one expected to have an extremely snobbish air, only no one could look snobbish who was grinning quite so widely, quite so fiendishly.

An arm encircled her waist and another tilted her backwards. "And a very lovely armful you are, my girl," said the drawling voice. "Extremely charming, definitely warming . . . Now to further test my fairy godmother's gift."

As he lowered his face to her face and set his lips on her lips, it occurred to Gabrielle that this degenerate specimen of manhood should undoubtedly be repulsed. The only problem about her virtuous conclusion was the extreme reluctance she felt to do so.

He was kissing her . . . dear God, how he was kissing her! It was surely her duty to deny him, but it was just as surely not her desire.

Rick Franklin had kissed her once, just before he proposed marriage and Jon Elliot before he got his face slapped for proposing a tumble in the hay. Seth Jacobs had kissed her when she lied to save him from his father's licking and Ethan Aaron when she sewed up his coat after a fist fight. She had been kissed by a couple of boys on her last visit to Boston, Stuart and—what was the other one's name . . . oh yes, Myles. Then there was that Nantucket sailor Jeremy and her friend Alice's cousin Edward from Martha's Vineyard.

Those island boys were mighty powerful kissers . . .

At least she had thought so until two minutes ago. Nothing in her life before had prepared her for the overcoming, overwhelming, overmastering emotion of this blue-eyed stranger's kiss. He had turned her chilled body into a blazing inferno, transfused her arteries to streams flowing with lava, converted her bones to liquid fire.

And now—oh, God!—he was pulling her off his lap and laying her flat-out on the seat. Dear Lord, he was half-lying over her! He was—she couldn't believe the message winging through so many different parts of her anatomy by the delicious pressure of his body on top of hers.

She managed to disengage her mouth.

"Wh-what are you doing in my hackney?" she asked feebly.

"The shoe is on the other foot, my dear. Not that I am complaining, you understand, about the most unexpected and delightful thing that has happened to me in this remarkable land, but it happens to be *my* carriage. I hired and occupied it first, which is what our worthy driver was trying to convey to you—rather regretfully convey, I fear, after your generous offer of double fare."

Gaby said vaguely, "Then *I* intruded on *you*. I suppose—I must beg—your pardon."

Even as she uttered these platitudes, she was admonishing the Gabrielle who lay, dazed and acquiescent, to take firm hold of her head with her own two hands and put it firmly in its place on top of her head. It was spinning around and around and around . . . just like the carved wooden top Papa had once given her.

The only trouble was that she could not get at her hands. They were down at her sides and, like most of the rest of her, quite firmly pinned underneath him.

You are not behaving at all like a minister's daughter, she lectured herself, then said aloud with more suitable prissiness, "I do apologize, sir."

Her companion tried in vain to smother a laugh. "Whatever for? You have my solemn word, I do not feel the slightest need for your apology."

"Th-thank you," Gaby gasped.

"It is *I* who should thank *you*," the gentleman with the blue eyes responded promptly.

"You are very welcome," said Gaby and wondered why, once again, his shoulders shook with such ill-contained mirth. In polite circles *you are welcome* followed *thank you* as surely as the night follows day.

"You have—you laugh so much." Gaby tried her best to become once more her normal sensible self. Thankfully, her head seemed to be slowing down in its dizzying rotation. "You have very peculiar reactions, sir."

"My dear girl, you have never said anything wronger in your life! My reactions at this moment are exactly those you might have forseen."

"I might?" Gaby squeaked.

"Yes, Mistress Innocence. Surely you know you are driving me out of my mind?"

"How very strange." Gaby blinked up at the roof of the hackney. "I do not feel anything much happening in my mind. It all seems to be in my body. I think my insides are sliding upside down."

"Mine, too," he said and fell to kissing her again, this time not just on her mouth. Remarkably, that long nose of his seemed to be adept at pushing garments aside—the tie of a cloak here, the lowering of a bodice there. He was kissing her . . . Good Heavens, he was kissing her behind the ears, taking little gentle nibbling bites of the lobes. His mouth was traveling the length of her neck. It must be her fevered imagination, maybe the dizziness . . . No, it couldn't be happening . . . she had never heard of a gentleman's kissing a lady with his tongue.

Suddenly, underneath him, her body bucked upwards. Heavens above, it really was his tongue, which meant his mouth had to be open . . . and it wasn't on her lips now or behind her ears, not even caressing her neck.

He was kissing her in the most peculiar way, tugging at a very private part of her, alternating his attentions. First, a short exquisite session with the right one; then a period of consummate pleasure and discovery with the left. She should have been shocked and shamed and scared and mad instead of wanting to weep in sympathy for the breast he was *not* lavishing his attentions on, it felt so sad and lonely.

"I have never," said a voice that no longer drawled, no longer seemed amused, no longer sounded indulgent, "not ever taken a girl, not even a whore, on the worn seat of a hackney, and I do not propose—so help me—to start now."

Gaby shook her head again. She felt sure she had just heard something rather odd and was trying to figure out what it could be when a loud fierce groan was uttered directly into her still-tingling ears. Seconds later, one hundred and eighty pounds of raw male weight collapsed on her like a punctured soufflé, driving the breath right out of her body.

As she struggled to get free, her ears were further assaulted by the most picturesque oaths—quite a long string of them—that she had ever heard.

"Please." She whimpered slightly. "Please, you're crushing me."

With apparent effort and one more oath, he managed to get himself up and off her; then he tugged her up, too. They were now seated side by side.

"You need not worry," he said with a touch of self-mockery. "I would flatter myself unduly if I tried to pretend that you are not completely safe with me for the ten minutes or so until we arrive."

He pounded on the roof of the hackney and shouted, "Go to Fraunces Tavern first."

The driver called back, "We are closer to your place."

"Go back to Fraunces all the same."

"Very good, Major."

Major? Major!

That single word was as effective a reviver of sanity as cold water dashed into her face.

Gaby had spent the last two minutes trying to arrange her disordered clothing and get a grip on her disordered senses. She wheeled to stare at her companion.

Even in the dim interior of the hackney, she could now see that his military coat had spotless white facing. She could undoubtedly have viewed her own horrified eyes in the polished black boots worn over his buckskin breeches. His powdered wig shrieked simple elegance, and—tumbled on the floor at their feet—was the all-too familiar helmet of a British officer.

In a futile gesture of repudiation, Gaby pulled the hood of her cloak over her head, at the same time moving away from him.

Flashes of memory from the last quarter of an hour tiptoed in and out of her brain and seesawed in front of her eyes.

"Oh, God." She didn't even realize she was moaning out loud. "What have I done?"

"Nothing," he said briefly and bitterly. "Neither did I."

She was startled into looking at him again. "Are you"—she swallowed. "Are you angry at me about something?"

"At you!" He looked straight ahead now. "No, dear girl, I am angry at myself."

"Why?"

"Why?" he repeated. Then suddenly he laughed. "A moot question, and a good one. I wish I could say I feel hellish because I disappointed you, but in truth, it is my own tarnished image that troubles me. My manhood has never failed me before this morning."

Gaby tugged the hooded cape so as to cover even more of her face. "You need not feel hellish on my account," she mumbled. "I did not—the experience—I confess you caused me to feel some extremely pleasurable sensations."

For almost a full minute, he gaped, open-mouthed, at the tip of a reddened nose and a bit of chin, which was all he could see of her. Then his elbows came down on his knees, he dropped his face down onto his two splayed hands and laughed as he had never laughed before.

They had traveled nearly half a mile before he managed to control himself. When his guffaws were over, Gaby remarked, "I seem to entertain you a great deal."

It was more of a question than a statement.

"Entertain! My dear," he declared extravagantly, "I would not have missed this encounter for a fortune."

He seized one of the mittened hands lying in her lap and pressed a kiss on the top of each finger. Then he turned the hand over, removed the mitten and pressed a second kiss into her rapidly warming palm.

Gaby snatched her hand back and encased it again in the mitten. *He's British! He's British! He's British!* she reminded herself.

She tried to take charge of the conversation, asking with casual civility, "Why—why did you think your manhood failed you?"

"Now you are being too kind," he answered lightly. "Surely you know it is the duty of a gentleman—before he pleasures himself—to pleasure his lady, even if—"

He checked himself suddenly, but Gaby's perceptions in regard to him by now were so finely tuned, she felt she could see into his mind.

"Even if she is *not* a lady? I believe that is how you intended to finish your sentence. You need not fear to offend me, Major," she added airily. "Class distinctions are upheld even here in the colonies."

"Will you have supper with me tonight?"

"I would like to, but I am only in town for a short visit and tonight is already promised."

"Tomorrow night then?"

Gaby shook her head. "Engaged again, I fear."

"The next?"

Their hackney had come to a halt. "Fraunces Tavern," the

driver called down gruffly, and Gaby put a hand on the door latch.

With a firm hold on her shoulders, he prevented her from leaving. "Dinner is the price if you expect me to relinquish my fairy godmother's gift."

"Tuesday night, then," Gaby said softly. "On Tuesday night I am free."

This time he kissed both mittened hands. "I will call for you at eight. Here at Fraunces?"

Gaby nodded.

By Tuesday night, no matter what story she had to weave for Papa, the one place in New York she would *not* be found was Fraunces Tavern!

She tried to leave the hackney again, but he still kept tight hold of her hands.

"You are forgetting one essential," he reminded her. "What name shall I inquire for on Tuesday?"

She opened her mouth to tell him, then closed it quickly. She could hardly give him her real name; he might track her down. She gulped out the first name that occurred to her. "Emily."

"Emily," he repeated teasingly. "Just Emily. No surname?"

With a sudden unaccountable spurt of temper, she retorted, "Yes, I do indeed have a surname, although I am not sure that a soldier who wears your uniform will be particularly pleased with it. I am Emily Washington."

He grinned. "Piquant—like everything else about you. To have a cozy dinner with a Washington may well seem strange. I trust you are not related to the rebel rascal?"

"No," quite spitefully. "I have not that honor."

His eyes danced. "Squelched again."

"Good-bye, Major."

"I prefer *au revoir*, Miss Emily Washington. By the by, in case it is of passing interest to you, my own name is Rhoads, Darcy Rhoads. I wish I could escort you into the tavern, but I am already overdue at headquarters."

Her hands were free at last. Gaby seized her portmanteau and aimed a vicious kick at his helmet as she opened the hackney door. She jumped onto the pavement without waiting for the driver to come and put down the steps.

Without once looking back, she marched into Fraunces Tavern. *Of course, he cannot escort me at the risk of being late for headquarters duty. One does not accord such courtesies to a woman who is not a lady.*

She whispered under her breath words that her Papa would have censured most severely, "That British bastard thinks I am a whore."

Then, sniffling into a mitten, "I hope the driver makes him pay triple fare."

Nine

"Papa," said Gaby, as they breakfasted in the coffee room of Fraunces Tavern the day after her arrival, "we will most probably make an extended stay in New York, so do you not think we ought to secure more permanent lodgings? The prices here are shockingly high, not only for our rooms but for every morsel we put into our mouths."

Her father set aside his *Gazette*. "I feel much the same," he confessed. "It offends my thrifty New England blood to see such waste on every side. The charge for a single cup of tea . . ." He shuddered. "The local people are taking advantage, not only of the army presence here and the scarcity of some products but also of the notion prevailing among some upper-class English that it is ungenteel even to inquire into cost when making a purchase."

"I realize," said Gaby, delighted at such ready agreement, "that you will be extremely busy seeking employment, so why not leave it all in my hands? I have done our budgeting these last years, and you cannot doubt my bargaining ability."

"Of course," she added, after a few seconds of consideration, "our choice may be somewhat limited. We would both prefer a small house of our own, but so many were burned down in the great fire in September, I have heard, and those left standing are so often occupied by the soldiery . . ."

Seeing his frown of worry, she changed her tactics. "In spite of all this," she finished confidently, "I do not despair. And, Papa, pray do not hesitate to spread the word among your new acquaintance that we are in dire need of housing. We must not be too nice to use the services of friends. Remember that as soon as we procure a house or rooms, I will be able to send for Elsie. Then you need not hesitate to allow me to go about alone. Though why, you are suddenly insistent that I have a chaperone in tow confounds me."

"In this instance, you must abide by my judgement," the Reverend Foote insisted quite firmly. "I will happily leave the procuring of our lodgings to you, but—and this is not a request, Gabrielle, it is a paternal command—you must take a hackney everywhere you go. An occupied city is not only filled with officers and gentlemen; it is also overflowing with the masses of common soldiers. Although it grieves me to say so, many of them are the dregs of English slums and prisons."

"Very well, Papa," Gaby agreed with unwonted meekness.

"In fact," he told her after some thought, "I shall hire a hackney for the entire day when you look at housing, so the driver knows he is to wait with you at all times and see to your protection. I do not want you subject to rough handling or even to verbal insult."

For perhaps the fiftieth time in a mere twenty-four hours, Gaby's thoughts flew like homing pigeons to yesterday's ride in a hackney. *A man's hard and definitely aroused body lying on top of hers . . . Strong hands that could hold her effortlessly . . . kisses that singed her mouth . . . a long straight nose capable of dealing with clothing that hindered his movements . . . lips that nibbled at her earlobes . . . a mouth that caressed her neck . . .*

Even as she quivered in guilty, shamed, *delighted* recollection, Gaby's reprehensible sense of humor all but threatened to overcome her. "Yes, Papa," she said, with just the slightest tremor in her voice. "To have my own hackney and driver will undoubtedly be a safeguard."

Dear, innocent Papa. In his eyes, a British officer was always a gentleman and behaved like one!

Forcing her wayward mind back to more earthbound matters, she held out her hand. "May I have the section of your newspaper which lists lodgings for sale or rent? I shall start looking this very morning."

Her father turned the pages and handed her the one she needed. Then he gladly returned to the perusal of his *Gazette,* while his daughter checked over the listings.

They were both finished with their reading matter at about the same time, and Gaby drained the last drop of chocolate from her cup before she said briskly, "There are any number of possibilities. Papa, can you arrange for my hackney while I get my cape and bonnet?"

She was amused to discover, when she came downstairs again, that the driver her father had hired, although close to middle age and only of medium height, was of exceptionally husky build. She also realized—when, instead of assisting her into the carriage, he lifted her up and placed her inside as though she was a featherweight—that he also had enormous shoulders and powerful arms.

Yes, he disclosed in answer to her amused question, in his youth he had been a boxer, and a good one, too, if he said it as shouldn't. But that was many years ago, and now he was a solidly married man with a young son of his own and three older daughters.

"Flighty creatures they are, too, the lot of them, like all females"—he frowned fiercely at Gaby as he gave this dictum—"having to be saved from much foolishness by wiser heads."

Snorting skeptically at her wide-eyed innocent stare as he tucked a lap blanket about her, he delivered a final admonition.

"So don't you be trying to slip loose of me, Miss Foote. I promised your good father to keep an eye on you, and Jacob Hardesty is a hard man to fool."

Gaby gave him her list torn from the *Gazette.* "These are some of the places where I mean to go. You know the city and can decide better than I in which order they should be visited." Remembering suddenly that he might not be able to read, she added hastily, "Shall I spell them out to you?"

Mr. Hardesty smiled kindly at her. "Not to worry, Missy. I

learned my letters when I was five and went to school till ten."
It was evidently a proud boast. "Now these two"—he jabbed a finger at two locations—"I would forget about. They are not fit for gentlefolk like you and the Reverend. Why not go first to the printer's? Full half your listings say to enquire of him."

When Gaby agreed, he shut her inside and climbed up on the driver's seat.

As she rode in solitary splendor through the streets of New York, the ghost of the man who had shared her last hackney ride rode with her. A rather solid sort of ghost with vivid blue eyes and unbelievably active hands. A ghost who could kiss her out of her senses and make her tremble with what she had forced herself to admit last night, as she lay in bed, was pure unadulterated desire! A ghost who had turned out to be a British soldier speaking of his longing for her one moment and in almost the next designating her a whore. An officer and gentleman of the despised British Army with typical disregard and careless contempt for those born in America.

"In short," said Gaby aloud, willing herself to forget him, "a proper made-in-Britain bastard."

After a brief stop at the printer's shop, Gaby spent the next several hours going from house to house. She realized, with increasing depression, that most of the homes and lodgings she saw were available only because they were so poor and mean that the British did not want them.

Her time was so short, she was beginning to feel rather desperate. It was already Friday afternoon. If she did not find suitable accommodations today, they would not be able to move tomorrow or on Sunday, when Papa would expect them both to observe the Sabbath New England style.

They simply had to be out of Fraunces Tavern no later than Monday. Even Tuesday afternoon would be recklessly late. Suppose *he* sent a message or even—heaven forbid!—tried to see her before their supper at eight!

"Mr. Hardesty, this is downright discouraging!" she sighed to him, limping back from half a house. The other half had been destroyed in the great fire and the smell of smoke and an air of desolation still hung about it. She had slightly twisted her ankle near the crumbling entrance.

"Missy," he asked, "would you be interested in a place on Water Street I only heard of yesterday from another driver? It's near where all the New York sea captains built their houses."

"Is it an agreeable area?"

"To my way of thinking, mighty agreeable."

"Of course, I would be interested. Why did you not tell me of it before?"

"Well now, I said to myself when we started out, 'Jacob Hardesty,' I says, 'better if you let the little lady see for herself how things are in New York before I mention this place, seeing as how we drivers make a bit on the side, if she likes it.' You might have thought, otherwise, I was only concerned with my commission."

"Your commission?"

"If you find yourself a place through me, you're expected to give me a bit of a thank-you offering, hard money, you understand; and I share it with the other bloke who tipped me the wink, the same as he'd share with me, was it the other way around."

Gaby said in exasperation, "Jacob Hardesty, *I* am as hard a woman to fool as you are a man! If you think I would not know whether or not you were only concerned with your bit of side money, then you don't know New Englanders at all. Now, if you please, get me to Water Street as fast as you can before someone else has snapped up that 'mighty agreeable' place!"

She was almost bounced off her feet at the speed with which he followed this direction.

The former pristine whiteness of the house on Water Street was smoke-stained; otherwise, it would have appeared charming. A row of hedges enclosed two patches of lawn, now frozen over, but in summer they were no doubt gay with flowers. A red brick walk led to the front door, where Gaby lifted a knocker shaped like a lion's head to announce her presence.

On the third knock, the door opened a few inches and a pale face poked around it. Gaby giggled, and the door swung wide.

"I'm sorry," Gaby apologized, "but it looked so peculiar to see a face apparently unattached to any body."

The young woman smiled, too. Well not so young as all that, Gaby conceded to herself, five and thirty years at the very least. Aloud she said, "I understand that you have rooms to let."

From somewhere inside, a fretful voice called out, "Lydia, Lydia, the door knocker sounded. Who is there?"

Lydia ignored the voice and answered Gaby, "Yes, indeed we do. Please come in."

Gaby, with a backwards wave to Jacob, entered the house and introduced herself.

"The rooms are all on the second floor," Lydia explained. "If you will just excuse me a minute to attend to Mama, I will be able to show them, undisturbed."

"Of course," said Gaby calmly, ignoring Mama's querelous voice which had not stopped demanding Lydia's immediate presence.

In five minutes her hostess returned, but even as they mounted the stairs, Mama's voice followed relentlessly. ". . . get references . . . not let . . . any riff-raff . . . my house . . . lowering of price . . ."

"My mother has been ill, and it makes her a little cross," the woman called Lydia told Gaby with admirable and understated aplomb.

"There are four bedrooms," she explained to Gaby when they reached the second floor. "When the British were here—we had two officers housed with us—each turned one bedchamber into a sitting room, so that they were converted to two sets of apartments."

"How lovely!" said Gaby eagerly, stepping into the first bedroom, which was bright and cheery, well-furnished with solid oak pieces. I think—if we can come to terms—it would be an admirable arrangement for my father and me. We would need a third bedroom for Elsie, who was my nurse as well as housekeeper. But the largest room, we too could use for both a sitting room and a study for my father. My father, by the way, is the Reverend Mr. Foote. We are—I suppose you could call us refugees from Massachusetts since Papa supports the King."

"My own father died a year ago. To my mother's distress, he supported the rebellion."

They suddenly smiled at each other. "Not to *your* distress?" said Gaby.

"No," said Lydia, "I am, as my mother is only too fond of telling me, too much like my father's family, a Cathcart in my ways as well as my looks."

Gaby laughed. "Dear Papa knows in his heart that I am a patriot, but for the most part, he thinks if he ignores the fact, the condition will go away."

After they had inspected all four rooms, Gaby professed herself delighted, especially with those overlooking the river.

"What puzzles me, Miss Cathcart," she said to Lydia, "is why the British would give up two such desirable apartments when they are so distressed for proper housing."

It was Lydia's turn to giggle. "It was all owing to dear, deluded Dr. Parsley, whose diagnosis of any illness is most exaggerated. The worse the ailment, the more credit for the cure, you realize? With him a simple cold is a serious congestion of the lungs; cough once or twice and you are in a tuberculous condition. Mama is prone to colds, but when her temperature began to rise slightly, he at once began to speak to me of the scarlet fever. By the greatest good fortune, he did so in the presence of our unwelcome guests, with the result that, in a matter of hours, they were packed and gone. I have been on the fidget, since they left, to install lodgers of my own choosing before British Headquarters recollects that we have empty rooms."

She looked hopefully at Gaby. "If we could say that you and your father are relations evicted from your homes for loyalty to the Crown, I think we might be safe from further intrusion."

Gaby, at once, agreed to this deceit. "Providing," she added—

as a New Englander, "we can come to proper terms. Now as to rental cost . . ."

This matter having been concluded to their mutual satisfaction, the new lodger inquired whether she ought to meet their new landlady and satisfy her that she and her father were of respectable character and could furnish references to that effect.

Lydia Cathcart lifted her chin. "No, indeed," she said. "If you can obtain written references, which I will show her later, well and good; but the decision, like the house, is mine to make. My uncle left it to my father with the proviso that on his death, ownership reverts to me.

About to say that Mrs. Cathcart appeared not to understand the niceties of inheritance, Gaby managed to control her wayward tongue.

Having agreed that father and daughter might move to Water Street from Fraunces Tavern after breakfast the next morning, so as to be settled in by the Sabbath, Gaby paid a month's rental in advance and collected her note of receipt.

She and Lydia Cathcart shook hands very cordially at the door; and even before it closed, she could hear Mama's shrill, complaining cries of "Lydia, I need you."

Shaking her head at the daughter's patience—which she well knew she would never have been able to match—Gaby ran out to the road to tell Jacob Hardesty the good news.

She realized as she rode back to Fraunces Tavern that it was the last time she need take this particular trip. She and Papa would be settled in their new home the next day, and she would be entirely safe from pursuit by Major Darcy Rhoads, since no one was likely to connect the minister's sedate-seeming daughter to the Miss Emily Washington sought by a British officer.

She would never again gaze at such proximity into those vivid blue eyes or feel those strong hands of his on her body. She would never be subjected to the encroaching intimacy of his kisses.

She would not go in dread of encountering him at Fraunces Tavern. In fact, to ensure her safety, she would never again set foot anywhere *near* Fraunces Tavern!

DARCY'S KISS 83

How fortunate she was to have found a pleasant dwelling place for Papa and herself . . . and to have escaped all danger of the attentions of Major Darcy Rhoads.

Tears filled her eyes and she blinked them away.

They were, of course, tears of joy at her great good fortune!

Ten

The first Sunday at their Water Street lodgings, when Gaby and her father came downstairs, soberly dressed, New England style, for church, they encountered Lydia Cathcart in the hallway.

She looked very far from sober in a lively-hued blue cloak and she was winding a blue and gold scarf around the thick braid hanging unfashionably down her back.

She greeted them with a cheery, "Good morning."

Gaby returned, "Good morning," at the same time her father made a courteous offer.

"If you are on your way to church, Miss Cathcart, I will be most happy to escort you."

"My mother's friend, Mrs. Erskine, has come to spend the entire day with her. I love Mama dearly, but she has been most demanding since her illness. I feel I have earned—and I am gifting myself with—a holiday," Lydia answered gayly. "I am afraid, Reverend Foote," she added, with a rueful look at Gaby, "that church was not the treat I had in mind."

Although he looked considerably taken aback, Mr. Foote responded with polite restraint, "What appropriate treat had you in mind?"

"Oh, a concert or play, to be sure, but, of course, there is none today. I may go down to the pier to watch the ships; it is something I never tire of. Or possibly I could try Bowling Green. The British often have competitive races near there . . . horses, you know, or boxing."

"On the Sabbath!"

"Oh, forgive me," apologized Lydia, coloring a little. "I truly did not intend to shock you, Reverend Foote, but I am grown accustomed to an atmosphere that encourages more openness. A bustling city which is—well, under siege, so to speak, does not function in quite its normal pattern."

"I do understand," he said in the grave manner Gaby and Aunt Emily referred to as his pompous voice, "that your difficult circumstances . . . two women living alone and unprotected in this city in time of war . . . All the more reason, I would think to avail yourself of the opportunity for an outing more suitable to the day."

"You mean church on Sunday?"

"Most certainly, unless"—indulgently—"you profess to be an atheist."

Oh dear, thought Gaby, he is giving her his saint-forgiving-a-sinner smile. Poor Lydia, her first holiday in heaven knows when, and Papa will intimidate her into coming with us.

She was just as surprised as her father when Lydia asked gently, "But is it a more suitable place for me to go, sir, when I do not believe in the trappings, the ceremony, and very often in the leaders who interpret God's way and God's words for me?"

"Is it not a form of conceit to fancy that *you* are a better judge of His will?"

"It may be so." Lydia spoke softly. "But I must believe what I believe . . . not what someone else tells me to be so. God is everywhere. For me . . ." With crossed hands, she pressed her heart . . . "I feel Him here. I do not have to seek Him out in a church full of well-dressed people, where so often He seems to me to be woefully absent."

Gaby stole a look at her father. He looked astonished, intrigued, vexed. Turning again to their young landlady, she decided that she had greatly underrated Miss Lydia Cathcart. Not only was she younger and more attractive than she had seemed at their first meeting; obviously, she was not the meek and submissive woman she had judged her to be two days ago.

Even as Lydia argued with the Reverend Mr. Foote, she was,

Gaby felt intuitively, as she eyed both of them, very conscious of him as a man. She tried to see her father through other than a daughter's eyes and remembered it was not that long ago, in their home in Massachusetts . . . the day she determined he ought to marry again . . . that she had acknowledged he was still a most personable man!

And then . . . *Dear Lord, I thank you!* she whispered, suddenly struck by an invisible bolt of lightning.

Here was the exemplary bride she had been seeking for her father. A woman intelligent enough to match her wits against his. A young woman, but not so young as to be easily subdued by his authority. A woman who could laugh and be gay, tease and torment him out of his tendency to pomposity.

She looked at Lydia almost fondly. *Perhaps, my stepmama-to-be,* she grinned to herself. She said aloud, "I have a proposal, Lydia. Do come with us now. Church will only occupy the morning hours, so you will still have all of the afternoon left to make merry. Perhaps, however, after church, we could find a respectable coffee house in which to argue about the service. Papa and I often do so. We disagree often, which I promise you can provide an invigorating discussion."

She cast a laughing look at her father. "I often take the opposite opinion to my true one for the sheer stimulation of arguing with Papa. I warn you, he is a skilled antagonist in debate."

Lydia cast a half-humorous half-defiant look at the Reverend Mr. Foote, who said, with a whimsical lift of his eyebrows, "Of course, if you fear to be beat, Miss Lydia . . ."

Lydia lifted a large furry muff from off the closet shelf and slipped her hands inside it.

"I know you spoke so only to provoke me into accepting," she told him crossly. "Very well, sir. I will go with you, but you had better prepare yourself afterwards for a fierce attack."

At the Anglican church Reverend Foote had been attending since his arrival in New York, the morning service was long and tedious. The minister spoke more energetically of George III than he did of God Almighty. Gabrielle was glad to note that Lydia was listening intently; she would be able to carry the brunt of any debate with her father.

Her own concentration, lamentably, wandered all too often into the byways and highways of her own mind. Her ears were filled, not so much with God's word as with the memory of curses, a whole long string of them, no doubt of military origin. She touched with her fingers the lobes that he had nibbled at; she curled her own tongue over the lips that his mouth had trapped into responding with such eager ecstasy.

Oh, God! she groaned and looked about in dread. To her relief, no one was observing her. She had not, as she had fancied for a moment, spoken aloud.

When they left the church, Lydia said, "Well, unless we are agreed—and I doubt it very much—my rebuttal may last longer than the service. I would like very much to invite you home to tea, but if we go back to Water Street now, I will spend the rest of the day serving and fetching for Mama and Mrs. Erskine, and I am loath to relinquish my holiday."

"You kept your part of our bargain, Miss Lydia; I shall keep the one my daughter made on my behalf. A coffee house it shall be." He hailed a passing hackney cab and bundled the two women into it. After talking to the driver, he entered the carriage after them.

When they arrived at their destination, Gaby could not believe her ill luck. Fraunces Tavern! Papa had actually taken her back to Fraunces Tavern!

She might have forseen it, she told herself numbly, while Mr. Foote was paying off their driver. It was the place he knew best, a logical choice, where (in his view) decent women might reasonably be safe from harassment.

Inside the tavern, the host, recognizing the Reverend Mr. Foote, escorted them to a table situated in a more private corner of the room. By refusing the seat he pulled out, stating her preference for another, Gaby was able to command a partial view of the entrance without being quite so open to view herself.

Lydia and Mr. Foote admitted to hunger and ordered a luncheon of mutton dressed with vegetables. Gaby, who was almost sick with apprehension, felt nauseated at the thought of food and requested only tea and some plain biscuits.

"Tea!" her father said incredulously when their waiter left with their order. "*You* have ordered taxed English tea, Gabrielle!"

"*Mea culpa,* Papa," sighed Gaby. "Please don't triumph over the fallen."

"You have never fallen in your life, my dear," he told her with brisk fondness and patted her hand. Then he turned to Lydia. "Well, Miss Cathcart. Will you start or shall I?"

The argument raged all during luncheon, and Gaby hardly heard a word. She sipped her tea, and from time to time, refilled her cup from the pot and took an occasional bite of a biscuit . . . and never once did she take her eyes off the entrance to the room.

Every time a British uniform entered, which happened fairly frequently, the bit of biscuit turned to an unpleasant weight inside her stomach and she held her teacup close to her face until the moment of danger was past.

She was almost beginning to feel quite safe and to enjoy for the first time in many years the taste of tea not made from garden herbs. She had even recovered so far as to consider ordering a pastry or a pudding, when a group of three officers came into the room, talking and laughing together. She had to be mad, Gaby knew, to believe that after less than half an hour in a hackney cab, she would remember both the voice and the laugh . . . but she did.

She had always felt in her heart of hearts that their encounter had a meaning and purpose in her life, but it was certainly not something that could be pursued under Papa's eyes. Papa! Oh, God! Imagine trying to tell Papa she had been made mad love to in a hackney by a British officer she had never seen before, a soldier enjoying the happy delusion that he was fondling his fairy godmother's gift of a whore!

By a small series of contortions that kept her back to the entrance of the coffee room but enabled her to take a fleeting, unendangered look at the three military men, she confirmed what she already knew: one of the three was Major Darcy Rhoads in all the doubtful glory of his scarlet regimentals.

Her father had just summoned the waiter to discuss desserts. Gaby leaned quickly toward Lydia.

"Please don't ask questions now. Just listen to me. Those three officers who came in and are being seated over there on the right. I have to get out of here and past them without being seen. I *cannot* be seen. Will you help me?"

"Of course," said Lydia, as though it was the most ordinary request in the world. "Don't panic, Gaby. Just follow my lead. Oh, dear!" she said more loudly, with a rueful glance at the Reverend. "I seem to have put my foot through my hem. I must go to the retiring room for a moment. Gabrielle, will you assist me, please. Mr. Foote, I shall leave the selection of my dessert to you. Pray surprise me." Both women stood up, and Lydia moved casually to Gaby's other side. "I hope your choice is superior to your last argument, sir," she added sweetly, "and also as easily demolished."

As she and Gaby walked together through the room, Lydia whisked her large plaid shawl from about her shoulders and extended it, as though shaking out its folds. It served as a perfect screen for concealing Gaby's face until they were safely past the entrance and standing in the back of the hallway.

"Th-thank you," said Gaby. Her teeth were actually chattering. "What shall I do? I must go home. I cannot wait here . . . or even in the retiring room. I might meet him when we leave the tavern with Papa. If Papa ever knew . . ." She shuddered. "I dare not take such a risk."

"Do you have any money with you?"

"No. I only took along enough for the collection box."

Lydia opened her reticule. "Take this." She pressed some coins into Gaby's hand. "Go outside and hire a hackney cab. Pay the driver extra for the waiting time. I will linger a while before I go back to the table to tell your father you were taken ill . . . nothing serious . . . a stomach complaint . . . your absence of appetite will confirm it. I shall tell Mr. Foote that I have secured a hackney and you are sitting in it, waiting to be conveyed home."

"Why can I not go home alone right now? You and Papa could stay."

"It would look decidedly odd for me to allow you to return home sick and alone," Lydia explained gently. "Your father would rightly be displeased. Do not be frightened, Gaby." Lydia pressed her hand reassuringly. "This plan will work. Go now."

There were no hitches in the carrying out of Lydia's simple scheme. Sooner than Gaby would have believed, they were all back at Water Street.

Once arrived, to lend credence to an "illness," Lydia went with Gaby to her bedchamber to help her into a flannel nightdress and tuck her up in bed. She then supplied a number of items indispensable to a young lady desiring to appear unwell . . . a pot of tea, a hot water bag, and several interesting bottles from an apothecary shop.

"I filched them from Mama's arsenal," she told Gaby gayly.

When the Reverend Mr. Foote came, with Lydia's permission, to visit his daughter in bed, she looked suitably wan but was able to assure him that she already felt much improved.

"Lydia has been *so* thoughtful," she said, lying back against her pillows, with her eyes half closed.

"Yes, indeed, I am grateful, Miss Cathcart, you have been more than kind."

Gaby's lashes fluttered down against her cheeks. She appeared to be asleep.

"We are strangers in a strange land," the Reverend Foote said soberly.

Oh, Papa, please don't get stuffy, Gaby yearned to say to him.

In the twinkling of an eye, the stuffiness dissolved. *Could there be such a thing as thought-transference?*

Mr. Foote took one of Lydia's hands between both of his and pressed it warmly. "We have met with extreme kindness in this very strange new land of New York," he said in a teasing way that both his listeners (though he was aware of only one) infinitely preferred.

Having won their approbation, he immediately set about losing it again. "Tell me, Miss Cathcart, have you lived long in this rather godless-seeming city?"

Gaby turned over in bed, muffling a groan. She foresaw that she might have to take an active role in this courtship if her father was to be guided into matrimony.

Once again, Gabrielle was quietly surprised at how capably Lydia Cathcart could take care of herself. When she wriggled about in bed again so as to peer out at them from under her lashes, Lydia was in the act of removing her hand from the gentleman's.

"Other than summers," she stated clearly, "which, before their deaths, we spent at my grandparents' farm in West Chester, in northern New York, I have lived my entire life in this city of New York, which I love dearly. Regrettably, the excesses of the British military have by no means improved the tone of our daily life."

Despite his moments of pomposity, the Reverend Mr. Timothy Edgar Foote was by no means deficient in intelligence or lacking in sensitivity. He recognized a snub when he heard one; he was also fully aware of the steel beneath the gentle rebuke.

As a minister, he had always retained the saving grace of recognizing error in himself as well as in others.

"I humbly beg your pardon, Miss Cathcart. I spoke carelessly, thoughtlessly, and my remarks were both ill-judged and unkind. I may never see Massachusetts again, but it is my home colony, the place of my birth. It will always be dear to me, and I would rush to its defense at outside criticism."

Very well done, Papa!

There was a short silence. Lydia could no longer meet his eyes.

"Am I not to be forgiven?" asked the Reverend with just (so Gaby declared to herself) the proper blend of humility and male assurance.

He had recaptured Lydia's hand, and she was only too uncomfortably aware of the pulse in her wrist. It was vibrating erratically at the exact place where his fingers gripped.

"Of course, I forgive you. I apologize for my own ill temper."

After a slight and silent tug of war, he relinquished her hand again.

"And may I hope for a continuance of the unfinished argument we began at Fraunces Tavern?"

Very speedy work, Papa!

"Certainly."

"When?"

"In a few minutes, if you wish, after I fetch a few things Gabrielle may need. I am still on holiday, remember?"

"Shall I come downstairs with you to your parlor?"

"Truthfully, we will have greater privacy if we use your sitting room up here."

Observing that he seemed rather taken aback, she teased, "We will leave the door open, sir, to protect *your* reputation. If we go downstairs to my part of the house, Mama and Mrs. Erskine might join us. Neither would take kindly to my contradicting a man of the cloth. As a matter of fact, they believe a woman should not contradict any man at all. You are, recollect, presumed to be the wiser sex."

"But not"—he laughed with boyish exuberance—"by you?"

Splendid Papa. Show her the man, not just the minister!

"Most certainly not." (Gaby suppressed a wish to giggle). "I hardly think you wiser only for being born a member of the male sex. Superiority is earned by one's nature, worth, and education."

My goodness, you can be a little pompous yourself, Lydia.

"In which case, Miss Cathcart," the minister said gallantly, "*you* are undoubtedly a superior member, not only of your sex but of the human race."

Several minutes passed in silence. Then Lydia Cathcart addressed Gaby.

"You may open your eyes and stop pretending to be asleep, Gabrielle. Your father has left."

Gaby rolled over and sat up. "That was as good as a play. Remember, you said that was what you wanted today. It's a pity we did not have any accompanying music."

"How unfortunate! If I had known you required music, I would have hired someone to carry my harp upstairs."

Gaby ignored the satiric tone but pounced on the statement. "You play the harp?"

"Yes."

"Do you play well?"

"Reasonably well. Why?"

"No reason," Gaby said blithely. "Except—"

"Except what?"

"My father is extremely fond of harp music . . . but only when the harpist is superior. He is most critical of amateurs who torture the strings under the guise of entertaining others."

"I shall ask him for a critique—if I should ever feel in need of one."

Gaby doubled up with laughter at this gibe. "Oh, we are going to get along splendidly, you and I."

"Gabrielle, what—"

She was not permitted to continue. "I realize I behaved very strangely," said Gaby, by way of diversion but also to express her genuine gratitude. "I appreciate your kindness more than I can say. I know I owe you an explanation, but—"

"You owe me nothing," Lydia interrupted very firmly, very finally. "You asked for my help, and I gave it. That is all. Should you feel any need of someone to confide in . . . that would be an entirely different matter. Mama always says—" She smiled faintly—"that I am closer-mouthed than a clam. It is true . . . or would be . . . about any confidence from a friend."

Eleven

The early post had included three letters inscribed in flowing capitals to the Reverend Timothy Edgar Foote. Two of the three gave evidence of coming from England. The third was from Williamsburg, the thriving colonial capital of Virginia.

Gaby's curiosity about her father's correspondence was diluted by her perplexity about one of her own two letters. She recognized at once her aunt's handwriting on the one addressed to Miss Gabrielle Foote, but the other was directed simply and starkly to G. Foote, and there was no marking of any kind to indicate that it had arrived through the postal service.

Rather strange, thought Gaby, slightly tearing G. Foote's letter in her eagerness to discover the sender. There was neither salutation nor courtesy ending attached to the brief and tantalizing message written out in oversized block letters:

IF PYTHIAS FURTHER WISHES TO ASSIST OUR NOBLE CAUSE, ON THE COMING WEDNESDAY, BETWEEN THE HOURS OF NOON AND ONE, THE POET WILL STROLL THROUGH THE FLY MARKET, AT THE SOUTH END OF QUEEN STREET NEAR TO HANOVER SQUARE. WHEN HE PAUSES AT A STALL TO CONSIDER THE PURCHASE OF A BASKET OF LOBSTERS, THE HANDLE OF SAID BASKET BEING ADORNED WITH ONE RIBBON OF BLUE AND ONE OF WHITE, THE CORRESPONDENT WILL TAKE APPROPRIATE MEANS TO MAKE HIMSELF KNOWN.

Having read this remarkable message over at least three times, Gaby folded it very small and thrust it into the pocket of her apron. Then she opened her aunt's letter, which for the most part was bright and cheery, offering little snippets of news, none of which Gaby would fear to share with her father or anyone else, should it fall into the wrong hands. One piece of news, in especial, she imparted to Mr. Foote at once.

"Oh, dear! Oh, my poor Elsie! She has—well, thank God, she is over the worst of it, recovering from a congestion of the lungs. But, Papa"—Gaby smiled rather impishly at him—"so much for my chaperonage. Aunt Emily does not think she will be fit to travel before the coming of spring."

To her surprise, her father heard her out in frowning silence. She had expected him to be more regretful about this temporary loss of Elsie's services as a chaperone . . . unless he was thinking, perhaps, that Lydia . . .

"Have you received troubling news, Papa?" she asked, with a pointed glance at the letters spread out before him on the table.

The frown lifted from her father's face as he looked across to her with an air of pleased excitement.

"Rather an embarrassment of riches, I would say. Each of these letters"—he tapped the topmost one with his middle finger—"contains an offer of employment."

"Em-ploy-ment?" Gaby stammered. "But Papa, two of your letters are from England, and is not the third from Virginia?"

"Exactly. I had not wanted to speak of this before. It would have been premature to plan when naught might come of it. Even before we left Massachusetts, however . . . shortly after the tragedy at Lexington and Concord, to be precise . . . I began to send out enquiries regarding opportunities elsewhere. In the event that I were forced—as eventually, I was—into exile, I did not want to lead the idle, useless life of so many exiles. Indeed, I could not afford it. This tutorship in Williamsburg"—he tossed aside the letter from Virginia—"I would not consider since she has joined her sister colonies in rebellion against our King."

"But *England!* You are willing to go thousands of miles away to a foreign land?"

"My dear Gabrielle." He rose from the table and took his daughter's icy hands in his, urging her closer to the fire in their sitting room. "England is not a foreign land. It is our home, our mother country, our natural refuge."

"Not for me!" said Gaby, putting her still-cold hands against her burning cheeks. "Whether it be Massachusetts, New Jersey, New York, or any of the other states—they are states now, Papa, not colonies—my home is here in America."

Seeing his grief at her outright declaration that this rebellion of children against their royal sire, this war between brothers extended so particularly into his own family, Gaby tried to regain her lost composure.

She asked softly, "Is there a position for you in England that you are inclined to accept, Papa?"

"I have been offered a teaching post at a boys' school in Winchester as well as the opportunity to serve once more as a minister, which, I confess, remains the first wish of my heart."

"But I have heard that ministers from America are not being cordially welcomed to English shores by their British brethren, who are concerned for the danger of their competition."

"This appears to be sadly true and most un-Christian, but it is also the reason why I rejoice doubly about this offer. My cousin and yours, Gaby, though you know him not, Joseph Hadley-Foote, who lives in Hertfordshire, is a lifelong friend of the chief gentleman of the area, Sir Horace Sidwell. It appears that the minister of their parish is not likely to live out the year, and Sir Horace holds the gift of this living. He wishes to retain it for his own fourth son, who is only a child of six. I could hold the living until the boy is of an age to take holy orders. What happens after that period, should I still be alive, I am perfectly content to leave in the Divine's all-giving hands."

Gaby smiled up at him, although he could see that her eyes were brimming over with tears.

"My beloved daughter." His own voice was so husky, she

could barely make out the words. "I would never coerce you. Are you unwilling to come to England with me—even for a trial period?"

"It is not so much England . . . Did I not stay in New York so as not to be parted from you? It just happens, Papa, that England is not *my* future. I have not told you of this before because I did not want you to think that I was making any sort of sacrifice by remaining with you, but Aunt Emily wishes me to come back to New Jersey to learn farm management of her and her agent. She intends for me to one day inherit Hillpoint, both the house and the estate."

"My dear Gaby, pray do not tell me of this piece of good fortune with such an apologetic voice and in such an apologetic manner. I have never needed or expected any bequest from my sister . . . there are not many years between us, after all. If I gave the matter of a future inheritance so much as a thought, I would most probably have considered that one of Emily's and my many nephews might be named her heir. It is now plain to me, however, that I would have greatly erred in this assessment. I should have realized that she could not have chosen a more ideal candidate than you—so plainly a young woman after Emily's own heart . . . intelligent, lively, hard-working, confident, capable . . . Oh, I could list any number of qualities, even some lesser ones that go with such a nature. Both of you so quick-tempered, impetuous, sometimes foolishly so, implacable to those you disdain and ever loyal and bountiful to those you deem your friends."

Gaby promptly burst into tears.

Her timing was ill because Lydia had just appeared in the open doorway. After one quick look of dismay, she prepared to withdraw.

Gabrielle called out, controlling herself, "Lydia, come back. Nothing private is going on here. Indeed, there are matters that we must discuss with you."

Although Lydia returned, she did not come all the way into the room but hovered in the doorway, like a butterfly poised on a flower, prepared to take instant flight.

"Do come in and sit down," Gaby urged her. "I will get a crick in my neck if I have to keep looking up at you."

The Reverend Mr. Foote added to his daughter's persuasion by going to Lydia, taking her gently by the arm and obliging her to come in and be seated near the fire between his daughter and himself.

"Actually, we are rejoicing—however contradictory Gaby's tears may seem—about some extreme good fortune that has come to both the Footes," the Reverend said with unaccustomed playfulness. "My daughter has been named as the heir to my sister Emily's fine estate in Princeton and proposes to make her future and her home in New Jersey."

"While Papa," Gaby said, watching Lydia quite closely, "has received the offer of an excellent living in the county of Hertfordshire."

"Hertfordshire." Lydia turned from Gaby to ask Gaby's father, "Do you mean Hertfordshire in England?"

He smiled, slightly amused. "It is the only county of Hertfordshire I can call to mind."

Lydia stared at him in blank amazement. Then her eyes rounded in dismay and her lower lip began to tremble. Then she, too, burst into tears, confirming Gaby's quiet conviction that her friend was in love with her father.

"I'm sorry," sobbed Lydia. "It is extremely silly of me. There is just so much change going on. You see, I will probably leave New York, too. My mother is anxious for me to sell *this* house and move to Philadelphia, where my aunt lives. We would share her home, her company, and all expenses. But"—with a fresh burst of tears—"I don't want to go to Philadelphia. I don't much like Aunt Eulalie; she would provide companionship for Mama, not for me. She is dreary and small-minded and so—so lachrymose . . . commonplace, too, but Mama," she sniffed, "says it is selfish of me to think only of myself. She says it is an *un*married daughter's duty to take care of her old and ailing mother and aunt, which is exactly what I would be doing, even though they are both healthy as horses. If I am compelled to share a house with them, they will undoubtedly both outlive me. And I do not *want* to wait for my reward in Heaven, which Mama says I will have. I am alive *now!*"

She gazed at Gaby reproachfully as her friend began to giggle.

"It is easy enough for *you,* Gaby. *You* are not one and thirty and living with a mother who never neglects to mention two or three times a day that you have not snared yourself a husband."

Exerting a strong effort to look serious as well as to appear quite sober, Gaby said in a no-nonsense voice, "Lydia, the solution to your problem is simple. One, send your mother off alone to Philadelphia to live with your Aunt Eulalie. They can always hire themselves a nurse or an extra maidservant. Two," she added with an air of piety, "take unto yourself a husband."

As Lydia cast her a look of combined shame and burning reproach, Gaby smiled across at her father. "Papa, can you call to mind any gentleman who is ideally suited to be Lydia's husband?"

The Reverend Mr. Foote stared at his daughter, first in amazement, then in comprehension, and last, very thoughtfully.

Lydia had covered her face with her hands and was sobbing quite audibly. Her tears crept between her fingers, streaming along her knuckles and all the way down her arms.

Gabrielle stood up and said decisively to her parent, who had not quite recovered from his shock. "You know that *I* will be happy in New Jersey with Aunt Emily, and when the war is over, I shall visit you in England. It would sadden me greatly, however, to send you there alone; and I would also grieve about Lydia's living so put-upon in Philadelphia. If the two of you went together to Britain—how different it would be! How happy your situation!"

She turned at the door to mention softly, "Mama would rejoice for you, you know. She would never want you to live without love the remainder of your life."

Then very firmly, very improperly, she closed the door and left them alone together.

Twelve

Within minutes of Gaby's precipitate departure from the sitting room, Lydia and the Reverend Mr. Foote came to such a complete understanding that less than an hour later Mrs. Cathcart was applied to and joyfully gave her consent to an almost-immediate marriage.

She did afterwards shed occasional tears that her daughter (together with her daughter's income) would hereafter be appropriated by a husband rather than a mother; but on the whole, she was well satisfied with the event.

A spinster daughter, however useful, must always be a reproach to her mother as having failed them both; and her own income, though less now without Lydia's contribution, would go much farther if she shared expenses with Eulalie. Then, too, she must confess (which she did only in the recesses of her own heart) Eulalie was more companionable than Lydia.

Her daughter tended to have odd humors and often sat silent and dull of an evening. Her sister was far easier to exchange sly barbs with and derived as much pleasure as Mrs. Cathcart in tearing reputations to bits over innumerable cups of tea!

A letter of acceptance went out to Hertfordshire, agreeing to accept the terms of the ministry until Sir Horace Sidwell's son attained his majority. Lydia's lawyers were then applied to for the drawing up of proper settlements; and a separate attorney was engaged by Mr. Foote to ensure that his daughter, too, would now receive her own income directly.

Then there was the sea voyage to England to be arranged for and numerous preparations to be made for a simple wedding.

The house on Water Street was in such a state of turmoil and confusion that—although questions might be asked later—it was quite easy for Gaby to slip away on Wednesday to keep the appointment that had been suggested in the message to Pythias.

Unclear as to whether she was expected to buy the lobsters mentioned in her mysterious letter, Gaby provided herself with a covered basket. She grasped it by the handle with both gloved hands, which were trembling so with nerves, she was glad that she had something to hang onto.

It was a cold day for the prescribed stroll, and she hoped her correspondent would not take it amiss that she preferred to walk fast and briskly from one end of the Fly Market to the other.

When she could see no one with a beribboned basket of lobsters, she purchased some apples and potatoes, as an apparent reason for her presence, then paused to admire a sample of cabinetmaking. On once again reaching the south end of Queen Street, she rejoiced to see a stall heaped with all the varieties of fish that New York rivers and harbors offered, including a barrel of fresh lobsters. Prominently placed in the middle of the stall was a basket containing two especially lively specimens with flailing claws. A gay bow of blue and another of white were attached to the handle of the basket.

A woman of medium height and medium years presided over the stall. She was soberly dressed in a gray dress covered by a dark cloak.

Gaby walked purposely toward her. She indicated the basket, not the barrel. "Your lobsters are very fine, ma'am. Are they as plentiful and cheap as the lobsters in my own state of Massachusetts?"

The woman smiled and spoke gently. "Lobsterbacks—that is, to say, lobsters, are cheaper and more plentiful in New York now than any other city in America."

Lobsterback being an even greater term of contempt for the

British soldier in America than *redcoat,* Gaby recognized the second signal that she had come to the right place.

She must give an appropriate answer.

"Even for the poet Pythias?" she inquired so softly she could not possibly be overheard.

"Thee speaks for Pythias?"

"I know the mind and heart of Pythias better than any other person."

"Then if thee will exchange thy basket for mine—let me first remove the ribbons—I will tie up these nimble fellows so they do not escape from thee. There is a message meant only for Pythias lying beneath them. Perhaps thee will not mind the exchange of a few pennies as well; even lobsters cannot be purchased without some small cost."

Both women smiled at the double-meaning that could be deduced from this last remark as Gaby accepted the basket and handed over a small coin.

When Gaby returned to Water Street, she first took the struggling crustaceans out of her basket and palmed the folded bit of paper underneath them. Then she went directly to the kitchen to give the lobsters to the housekeeper-cook, Mrs. Gershon.

"Thank you, miss," Mrs. Gershon said rather doubtfully. "Perhaps I could make a good creamed bisque of these. Mistress says if I serve up lobsters one more time, she is liable to turn into one of the pesky creatures."

Making her escape, Gaby ran up the narrow curving flight of steps from the kitchen that also led to the second floor. She encountered two new young maids along the way, both carrying linens that were no doubt being sewed for Lydia's hope chest.

In the privacy of her own bedroom, she disposed of her outer wear, then walked over to the window to read the message that had been hidden under the lobsters.

Block lettering again and a simpler message:

FROM NINE TONIGHT UNTIL HALF-PAST THE
HOUR OF TEN, A HACKNEY WILL BE WAITING ON

THE CORNER OF WATER STREET, NEAREST TO YOUR RESIDENCE. COME ALONE. YOU MAY ANSWER THE DRIVER'S RIDDLE.

After tearing the message into bits and sprinkling these in back of the logs she would set afire later, Gaby washed her sooty hands, dried them carefully and joined her father in their sitting room.

He sat peacefully reading and looked up at her with such a vague, sweet smile, she felt quite sure he was unaware that she had been gone from the house.

"There is no denying this is a man's world," she said to him with pretended severity. "The whole house is in chaos; everyone is hard at work . . . cooking, sewing, stitching, embroidering, decorating, drawing up lists—and you," she punned laughingly, "who sew and stitch not, but will surely reap, sit idle here. Poor Lydia, such a do-nothing husband as I have contrived to hand over to her. I pray she won't reproach me later on."

"I pray she will not either," said her father so seriously that Gaby, fearing such humility might lead him into a state of pomposity, promptly reminded him, "Oh, Papa, you know I was not speaking in earnest. Lydia could not be happier. Surely you know she is besotted about you."

"I love her, too," said Mr. Foote, apparently astonished that this was so. "I never thought . . . after my dear Annabel . . . I never dreamed there could be any other woman in my life but her. You know, do you not, Gaby, that part of me will always belong to your mother?"

"*I* know, Papa," Gaby responded quite seriously, "but do *you* know how important it is that Lydia not be given knowledge of it, too? It is not easy to become a second wife when the first one was so beloved."

"What are you trying to tell me, Gabrielle?"

"Mama's miniature portrait that you carry with you still . . . her spinet and spinning wheel at Aunt Emily's . . . some little ornaments you gave her . . . I have seen them in your bedroom when I dust it and set it to rights. Give them up, Papa. Say goodbye to Mama and to the past, too, when you leave America. Your future is with your new wife. Do not cloud it with remembrances she cannot share. Through a long spinsterhood, she has already been made to feel inadequate as a woman by her mother. If *you* have only half a heart to give her when you are wed, then *you* will complete the process. Let her reign as queen in your affections, Papa, and you will indeed reap a priceless harvest of love."

Mr. Foote sat lost in thought for several moments when Gaby had finished with her long speech. Then he smiled at his daughter, a smile of both pride and affection.

"Your mother would be quite pleased at the woman her daughter has become, never more so than at this moment. I cannot disagree with anything that you have said. It has been selfish folly on my part to believe that I can hold onto Annabel and have my dear Lydia, too."

He pressed her hands fondly. "Later tonight, after we have supped, I will bring your mother's things to you."

He left the sitting room almost immediately, and Gaby regretted nothing she had said until a few minutes past nine that evening, when she was pacing up and down in the sitting room, cursing her own stupidity.

She had come away an hour ago from the downstairs parlor, but her father was still there with the Cathcart women. If he stayed too late with them, all her fine plans for the evening were undone! Mr. Foote was so scrupulously exact that, if he did not find her waiting for him in their sitting room, most assuredly he would seek her out in her bedroom to give her, as he had promised, all the little possessions that had formerly belonged to her mother.

She was forced to remain in either of the two rooms until he came to redeem his promise. There was no way she could disappear from the house, alone, for several hours in the evening. Even the most trustful father could not be blamed for demanding an explanation!

Fortunately, before her peace was utterly cut up, Gaby heard her father's footsteps. He went immediately, as she had expected he would, to his own bedchamber. This gave her the opportunity to pat her hair into place, resume her white muslin cap, and to sit down on the rocker with a pillow slip to be hemmed in her lap. The flush in her cheeks had also died down before she was joined by the Reverend Mr. Foote.

He carried an octagonally shaped, handsomely carved mahogany box in his hands. As Gaby instinctively stood up, he held it out to her.

"But Papa," she said, "the box is your own. My—"

"Yes," he interrupted her, "my great-grandfather brought it from England, and my own father gave it to me when I became a minister. I have always used it to hold my dearest treasures. "I want *you* to have it now, Gabrielle," he told her tenderly. "Your mother's miniature, her wedding ring . . . the bow on her wedding bouquet . . . all her little bits and pieces . . . are inside."

"Thank you, Papa, I shall treasure them always, the box no less than Mama's things."

He folded her in a brief hard embrace, then quit the room hastily, while Gaby sat down again and allowed herself the brief luxury of tears—but only until she heard the closing of his bedroom door.

Thirteen

There was no time to weep. Gaby wiped her face with a sleeve as she hurried to her own room to change her shoes for sturdier boots, to slip on her warmest cloak and wrap an old wool muffler over her head and ears.

She threw the key to the front door, and some money into a reticule, but with the house still astir, she thought it more prudent to creep down the rear stairway and exit the house by way of the kitchen.

The expected hackney was waiting at the corner, but a fine mist was falling, and in spite of a lantern light across the room, she was unable to see the driver very well.

"I believe you are waiting for me, sir?" she said, looking up at him.

"Mebbe I am, mebbe not. Does ye know the answer?"

"The answer to what?"

He removed his tricorn and scratched his head. "It's by way of being a riddle," he said in a grudging voice.

Gaby waited in an agony of impatience.

"What riddle?"

"Well, I'm supposed to say this bit of a po-em by this fellow Pie—Path—"

"Pythias. For the love of Heaven, the name is Pythias."

"Mmm, that sounds like the one. I reckon you are in the right of it. Well, anyhow, this po-em, it begins like this." His voice seemed to change both in timbre and quality; it even sounded educated. Gaby listened to a far different manner of speech than she had heard previously as he recited in quite an easy manner:

> Beware
> You who dare
> Try so hard to subdue us . . .

"I hope," Gaby said with asperity, "that you have derived enjoyment from making a May game of me. That 'po-em,' " she mimicked, concludes like this

> The way
> We reply
> Will long make you rue us."

"That's it, miss, if you haven't gone and gotten it right straight off, then my name ain't—whatever it is. Hop in, miss, hop in, we have no time to waste here."

"In that case, I wonder that you wasted so much," Gaby told him in exasperation as she wrestled open the door of the waiting carriage.

Once seated inside, she was treated to a rather wild ride through the streets of New York, bounced back and forth on the leather seat and once even jolted off of it and onto the floor.

When the hackney finally came to a halt, Gaby struggled out of it, her temper in shreds. The driver pointed with his whip to a row of steps leading to the door of a commodious-seeming dwelling. "That's it, miss!" Then he whipped up his horses and was gone.

There was a large brass knocker on the door, but Gaby had no need to use it. The door opened even before she reached the top step and the lady of the Fly Market, looking even more Quakerish, in unadorned gray and a simple muslin cap, bade her come in.

She followed her hostess down a long hallway to a small parlor. There could not have been a greater contrast to the two of them than the lady who was standing there, with one dainty blue-shod foot resting, manlike, on the fireplace fender, revealing a shapely ankle clad in a pale blue stocking. She was small and trim, her exquisite figure exquisitely garbed in an obviously expensive gown of flowered brocade with a blue satin underskirt and lacy petticoats. Her powdered hair was twisted high on her head with every puff and curl and decorative device that current fashion dictated. Her lips were not pink but such a rich deep red, there could be no denying that they were painted.

Gaby quite longed to see the rest of her face, but she could not. The lady—if she was a lady—went masked.

When their Quaker hostess firmly closed the door and the three of them were shut in together, the lady of fashion spoke up rather sharply, "I thought it was understood we wanted only Pythias to come tonight. You must be the schoolgirl who spoke for him at the market?"

Gaby darted a reproachful look in the direction of her Quaker hostess.

"I am *not* a schoolgirl," she declared indignantly, "however much I may seem to *you*"—turning to the lady of fashion—"to be one. I dress as I do because I am the daughter of a New England minister. As to my age . . . In less than a six-month I will be one and twenty. As to my qualifications for this meeting: I did not ask to be invited. *You* requested me to come here because I *am* Pythias."

"I don't believe it!" Behind her mask, the lady of fashion was sputtering with merriment.

"And I, ma'am," said Gaby, already in the mood to catch fire, "am perfectly indifferent as to whether you believe me or do not. In fact, I am quite convinced that I have fallen among a pack of lunatics. First you, madam, with your messages and your lobsters. Allow me to inform you that I have had more than my fill of lobsters, whether boiled in a pot, broiled on a hearth, or worn on the backs of swaggering soldiery. Then—at your behest, mind—I am taken on such a mad ride that I quite feared for my life . . . all for the amusement of that idiot who fancies himself in the role of bucolic buffoon. And now this—this woman, in her fancy gown, with her painted lips, presumes to tell me that I am not who I am. Well, I happen to be Pythias. I adopted the name for my poems to avoid giving pain to my father, who is a loyalist. I do not give one single damn whether or not I have convinced you of the truth of my identity, but I am going home now!"

As she stalked toward the door, the lady of fashion moved swiftly ahead of her. "Indeed, Pythias, we do believe you," she said coaxingly. "Please do not be angry any longer. I must tell you that, firstly, it has always been taken for granted—perhaps because of the Greek name—that Pythias was a man. The original mistake was not made by us but by our superiors."

"Superiors?"

"We do not know them by name. The fewer who do, the better," said the Quaker lady with unruffled calm. "That is why this lady remains masked."

"But not you?"

"Thee may call me Mercy. As the go-between for so many others, it is important that I be known and can be reached in case there is urgent need."

"I should like to know, madam, what you are a go-between for?"

"An excellent question. All your questions"—she nodded her head in approbation—"have been sensible and prudent, too. It is our duty to deal as much as possible with the British in order to collect intelligence for the use of the American Army. In short," she concluded, no less tranquil than before, "we are spies, my dear, and we had hoped to enlist Pythias as one of us."

The lady of fashion once again gave her merry trill of laughter. "That is why I pretend to be a chère-amie; and your driver, who greatly enjoys his role-playing, is a merchant turned actor or an actor turned merchant, we are none of us quite sure which."

"What did you have in mind for me, ma'am?"

"Pray call me Mercy," said that lady again. "I was read out of meeting long ago, but I am a Quaker in my heart and mind still; I mislike formal address."

"Well, then, M-Mercy, what am I to do?"

"I am afraid—nothing—except, I pray, keep silent about this night if you are not to endanger us all."

"But why?" Gaby argued. "I am a patriot. I am Pythias. I want to help."

"If you had indeed been a man . . . you could have gone among the soldiery as one of them . . . as a peddler . . . in any one of many different guises."

"But"—Gaby pointed rather rudely at the masked lady—"she is not a man."

The masked lady shrugged. She said rather bitterly, "Ah, but I am considered both beautiful and charming by the officer class of the British Army . . . also, since I am American-born, not a *true* lady, whose feelings or reputation must be safeguarded. In fact, I am rated as a piece of merchandise, highly beddable. Many men vie for my favors, and amorous men are seldom wise or discreet."

There was a long pause.

"I see," Gaby said thoughtfully. "I might have been considered of use were I either a man or a woman—that is, to say, an *attractive* woman."

"An attractive woman of poor reputation," the masked lady hastened to remind her.

"But a dowdy schoolgirl," Gaby countered swiftly, "is of no possible use to you?"

"Not one who lives with a father who is both a loyalist and a man of the cloth."

"My father is being married in two days' time. Three days after the wedding, he and his wife will leave for England."

"And you?"

"I had planned to return to my aunt's home in Princeton. She—my aunt supports the patriot cause and, before the army retook most of New Jersey, she furnished intelligence to General Washington and other of his officers."

"It would be wise," said the masked lady, "if you did exactly as you had planned to before tonight. Go home to your aunt, Pythias, and help our cause with more of your clever poems. You wield a mightier pen than most men do a sword!"

"Try to forget," Mercy added in a kind, firm voice," that any of the three of us has ever met."

"Your actor-driver," Gaby pointed out coldly, "took himself away when he let me off. Am I expected to walk home alone? I do not even know where this place is or how to get back to Water Street."

"My man-servant will fetch the driver," Mercy reassured her. "You are not so far from home, as you think. He took the long way round to confuse you . . . just a precaution, my dear." Then, "there is herbal tea." She waved toward a table. "Pray both of you, help yourself."

Gaby marched over to the table without further invitation. She felt very much in need of a cup of good hot tea, entitled to one, as well. There was also a basket of sweet rolls on the table. She selected one sprinkled with cinnamon and another with a sugar glaze.

She ate and drank, ignoring the masked lady, who presently said, "I am truly sorry, I did not mean to offend you."

"Then you succeeded admirably without making the attempt."

" 'Tis a very chancy—a very risky business, spying."

"And you are competent to engage in it, but not I?"

"Sometimes it is not so much that one chooses the profession as that, by chance, the profession chooses one."

"And it chose you?"

"It chose me . . . and in a way that I hope will never happen to you. Good-bye." She put down her teacup and headed for the door. "I hope—most truly for your own sake—that we two may never meet again."

Then she was gone.

Gaby waited a full half-minute before following after her. There was a lantern on the table in the hallway, just as she remembered. She opened the front door to cold, swirling darkness but by lifting the lantern high, she saw what she had wanted to see. The shop sign of a baby in its cradle hanging high over the steps, and below the pictured symbol, in smaller lettering. *Mercy Enough Godwin, midwife.*

By the time Mercy returned to the parlor to tell her that the driver would be waiting in five minutes, the "dowdy schoolgirl" was most innocently drinking tea.

Fourteen

A friend—who had attended the Yale School of Divinity during the same years as the Reverend Mr. Foote—officiated over his wedding at St. Paul's Chapel.

Immediately following the ceremony, an elaborate breakfast, insisted on by the bride's mother, was held at the Cathcart residence. The house had been denuded of most of its furniture, the pieces Lydia's mother had not shipped to Philadelphia having already been sold and removed.

All that remained were the contents of the dining parlor and some extra chairs, Gaby's bed upstairs, and Lydia's in the downstairs chamber. Open boxes on the floor served as drawers for clothing.

By late morning, the last guest was gone from the house and Lydia and her mother were exchanging tearful adieux.

"Oh, my dear daughter, you are to live in England and I in Philadelphia. Who knows if we will ever meet again in my lifetime?"

At this mournful query, Lydia joined in her mother's prolonged fit of weeping; the bridegroom looked about him in wild discomfort, and Gaby decided that subtlety would not avail any one of them.

"Nonsense, Mrs. Cathcart, we are not living in the ancient times of the Vikings or Phoenicians. England is no farther away than a six-to-eight-weeks' sea voyage. Who other than you will Lydia want when she is expecting your first grandchild?"

Mrs. Cathcart's tears magically stopped flowing and Lydia's, too. The mother pursed her lips, mindful of the future possibilities to domineer inherent in grandmotherhood. Lydia blushed quite becomingly, cast a fleeting look over her mother's shoulder at her new husband, and blushed even more brightly than before.

Without quite knowing how the process was speeded up, the carriers hauled out the last two trunks, final good-byes were said in the vestibule; and only the Reverend Mr. Foote went out into the cold to hand Mrs. Cartwright into the carriage that would take her on the first stage of her journey to Philadelphia. He tucked a lap robe about her and another around the housekeeper, who had chosen to remain in the service of her mistress. He promised patiently, as he had done a score or more times in the last few days, to be good to her little girl.

"Thank You, Lord," he addressed his Creator in genuine gratitude when the carriage was lost to sight.

"Heavens, what a shambles!" Lydia said, as the three who were left surveyed the dining room in some dismay. "Let me just slip out of my gown into something sensible, and in no time at all—"

"In no time at all, Stepmama Lydia," laughed Gaby, "with me supervising and the two maidservants working, all will be set to rights and fit for the new owners next week."

Still laughing, she put out her hands to shoo away Lydia and her father. "Now, go!" she ordered. "The courtship and wedding are done with; the honeymoon has officially begun. For the next two days I do not expect to see or talk with either of you. The maids will not be here after tomorrow, mind, so you had best get your meals at a coffee house or tavern."

However fine and noble this determined direction might sound to the newly married couple, Gaby felt guiltily aware that it was intended primarily to serve her own purpose. She, no less than they, wanted to be alone; her need might be considered even greater.

Within days she must be on her way home to Aunt Emily in Princeton or starting life in a new—what had the masked lady called it?—a very chancy, a very risky business.

After bribing the maids with a little extra money so that the two happily took on the work of three, Gaby ran up to her bedroom and carefully removed her gown.

As Lydia's sole attendant, at Lydia's loyal behest, Gaby had worn the most dashing gown she had ever owned . . . but not yet the gown she wanted it to be. It was impossible for her to wear the planned-for garment in the presence of her father.

The Reverend Mr. Foote might not be much aware of the niceties of female dress, but even he could not have been blind to some slight differences in a gown suitable for a minister's daughter and one that resembled a courtesan's delight.

After taking down her hair and fashioning it into a severe knot at the back of her neck, Gaby slipped into one of her only two old gowns not yet packed away. It was dull and gray, with no delightful swish of taffeta petticoats, only one of serviceable muslin. She wished she had not also packed her crocheted lace collars and starched organdy fichus, then shook her head ruefully.

Papa was right. *All is vanity* could quite easily become the rule of one's life. And her objective must not be vanity for its own sake but only as the means she must employ to achieve a certain end.

When she left the house on Water Street a few minutes later, she walked to the corner so that no one in the house would notice that she was hailing a hackney. Not that such observance seemed likely. The blinds were down and the curtains drawn in the room she knew to be Lydia's. So she and Papa must . . .

Gaby shook her head at the rush of blood to her cheeks. Of course, they were in Lydia's room, making love. What a laggard lover she would consider Papa if they were not! But it was one thing to fancy a certain event from a distance, quite another to acknowledge that it could be happening—*must* be happening at this very minute!

Unbidden, as so often happened, words that hardly seemed to be her own, shaped themselves into a pattern in her mind, mingling—would Papa think it profane of her?—with the more sacred words of the wedding service.

> ... our bodies
> Bare and twisting,
> So entwined and entangled
> Truly we might have been one ...

Shamed to be thinking *so* of her own father and his bride, she stepped out onto the road and waved her arm to signal imperiously to a hackney that had almost driven past her.

"I want to be taken to the offices of your largest newspaper!" she snapped out to the driver who pulled up short for her.

"That'll be Mr. Gaines' *loyalist* weekly." In case she did not correctly interpret the satiric tone in which he uttered the word *loyalist,* he spat a stream of tobacco juice well past his horse's head.

"If his is the most prominent newspaper and carries advertising, yes," said Gaby meekly, "I would like to be taken there."

"So long as you pay, missy, where you go is your own business," he acknowledged grudgingly.

"How extremely kind of you to say so," Gaby retorted, climbing up into the carriage.

What was it in the air of this city, she wondered, bowling decorously along, that turned every New York hackney cab driver into a contentious debater against those who earned him his livelihood?

When they reached the shop whose sign proclaimed it to be *The New York Gazette,* the driver spat a few feet beyond his own last effort as Gaby counted out the fee demanded.

She then handed him another coin. "This," she told him grandly, "is for your political opinion."

"Didn't give none."

"Oh, yes, you did," she answered with a pert smile and a pronounced wink as another arched curve of brown spray landed, this time squarely on the horse's rump.

"Well, I'll be double-danged!"

"Not," said Gaby sweetly, "if you turn to prayer."

The apprentice in the printer's shop found nothing lacking in the appearance of the young lady in gray. She was so very pretty, so helplessly appealing as young ladies ought to be, and so in a fret about the advertisement she had most unfortunately thrown away.

"Last month I think it was, but I'm not quite sure. I fear I am not a very orderly person."

"We keep a file of the back issues for just such circumstances," the apprentice soothed her. "If you will just step back here and sit down—" He pulled out a wooden chair set near to a long worktable and rubbed both lightly with his own billowing white shirtsleeve—"I will bring you the files a month at a time."

Gaby looked up at him, wide-eyed with wonder.

"What a very good notion, to be sure! I wonder that I did not think of it."

His flat, bony chest puffed out with pride. He almost stumbled over his own feet, hurrying to the back of the shop.

As each new file was brought and another taken away, Gaby offered him a gracious smile with each thank-you. She carefully turned page after page, reading over the claims of each advertiser, whether conveyed in a few lines of print or in the more expensive box notices with an illustration.

Concentrating her search on someone soliciting business as a midwife, she almost passed over the precious tidbit of information that she had been seeking.

The subscriber, living at the sign of the Baby in the Red Cradle, just opposite the Cabinetmaker's on Beekman Street (the portion that some in New York call Chapel Street), takes this method of informing the Public, that she intends to make Grave-Clothes, and lay out the Dead, in the Neatest and most Respectful Manner. She is informed that a Person in this Business is much needed in your City, and hopes by her care and Diligence to give Satisfaction to those who favour her with the carrying-out of this Melancholy Duty.

Gaby's initial excitement over the "Sign of the Baby in the Red Cradle" had subsided as soon as she realized that the responsibilities connected with internment were being offered, not a midwife's. She skimmed hurriedly through the rest, even the name, and was on the next page before fully realizing what she had just read. She turned back the page and her heart leaped in joy to see the name of the signatory, Mercy Enough Godwin.

Not precisely an ordinary name. Mercy, yes, but Enough?

Gaby replaced all the papers, as they had been brought to her, so that, when he came to put the file away, the young man would not have the slightest notion which advertisement had been of such great interest to her.

She then retied her cloak and went to the front of the shop to thank the printer's apprentice effusively and make some small purchase by way of compensation for his time and effort. She considered a copy of *The New England Psalm Singer,* which her father would surely like. Just in time she remembered that his marriage was intended to bring more lightness into his life and she chose instead a play, which she had heard was rather daring—*The Rivals,* by Mr. Richard Brinsley Sheridan.

In bed, with a new young wife beside him, and a grandchild promised to bring Mrs. Cathcart over the seas from Philadelphia, Papa might be a great deal less prissy in the future than he had ever—even with Mama—allowed himself to be in the part of his life that was past.

Fifteen

On the second night after the wedding, Gaby was persuaded to have dinner with her father and Lydia at the City Tavern. Although it was a popular eating place of the occupying British, the possibility that she might encounter Major Darcy Rhoads seemed fairly remote.

After the period of time that had passed since their half-hour encounter, it seemed highly probable that she might not live on in his memory in quite the same way that he did in her own. This thought, which should have consoled a minister's daughter, aroused so very different a reaction that Gaby found herself further incensed with everything and every*one* British.

Lydia did not have to do much urging. Gaby was quite hungry; and with her father and his wife leaving by ship quite early the next morning, it would seem a little overpunctilious if she not spend these last few hours with them.

Unfortunately, when a bowl of thick chowder was set down before each of them and in the center of the table a loaf whose aroma announced deliciously that it was fresh from the oven, Gaby lifted her spoon, only to find that her appetite had fled. There was a solid lump in her throat and an even larger lump in her stomach. The very sight of food was repugnant.

She put down her spoon again, moaning, "Lydia, I owe your mother a most profound apology."

"Were you discourteous to her?" Mr. Foote asked in some surprise, but his more intuitive wife understood at once.

"I know," she said to Gaby, tears glimmering in her eyes. "I owe her one, too. I thought she was being overly sentimental . . . there was so much else on my mind . . . but when it came to the point of parting . . . Oh, dear! We did not even go on comfortably together much of the time, but she—she—she is my mother. Saying good-bye to people one loves is the very devil—and you need not take me to task, Timothy"—she rounded fiercely on her husband—"for my mode of expression."

"I was not about to," that maligned man said mildly. "We are all under great stress."

Gaby, who had been half-crying, and was now half-laughing, managed to choke out, "Stay on your guard all the same, Lydia. He once gave me a really hard whack on the bottom for saying something even less reprehensible to a visiting clergyman from Boston."

"You forgot to mention to my wife, in your zeal to promote her independence," the Reverend Foote said dryly, "that a moment before you spoke, you had knocked off Mr. Scully's cherished frock hat with a well-aimed snowball."

As they all smiled, Gaby picked up her soup spoon; Lydia picked up hers.

"I have never had a friend I loved as dearly as you, Gabrielle," Lydia said softly.

Both dropped their spoons again; both began to cry.

The Reverend Mr. Foote reached down and took one hand of each. He held the two hands in plain sight on top of the table. "My dear girls—my dear young ladies," he amended as they both glared at him. "Unless I am to figure in this hostelry as some kind of monster of depravity, you will really have to start acting as though this is a celebratory dinner we are having, not some sacrificial offering I am requiring of you. You, my wife"—he turned smilingly to Lydia—"you, my daughter"—he stroked Gaby's hand gently—"are my two dearest objects in life, and I refuse to believe that this is good-bye but only farewell for a while. We are all beginning a new chapter in our lives. Our trust in God and our faith in each other must be such that we see these chapters as beginnings, not as endings. Lydia and I are leaving for England, but England, as you so rightly pointed out to Mrs.

Cathcart, Gabrielle, is only a sea voyage away. And who knows? The madness and the cruelty that are now rampant in America may—they *must* one day end. Perhaps when that time comes, we will be able to return to our country.

"As to your future, Gaby," he went on, "I cannot conceive of any reason that you will not be content, nay, more than content with my sister. She and you are indeed two of a kind. But should circumstances change, you have all the necessary papers regarding your income from your mother's inheritance; you can always apply to the attorney we engaged if you have a shortage of funds. Should there be an alteration in your planned future, whether on your part or on Emily's, however, know that wherever we may be, there is always a home for you with Lydia and me."

"Are you trying to say, Papa," Gaby half-sobbed, "that if I commit all seven of the deadly sins and break most of the Ten Commandments, you will nevertheless receive your prodigal daughter at any time and take her into your home with love and rejoicing?"

"Of course, he is," said Lydia staunchly.

"Just so," said Mr. Foote.

Gaby wiped the last of the tears from her cheeks with her fingertips and again picked up the soup spoon. "I am suddenly hungry," she said buoyantly. "Let us eat before our chowder gets quite cold."

It became a merry meal for the three of them, after all, partly owing to their joint determination and partly to the effects of a bottle of light wine, which the Reverend Mr. Foote felt confident the Almighty would understand was in the nature of a healing potion for his womenfolk.

He had not counted on the aftereffect of a small amount for himself, which was so physical in nature, they had barely stepped into the house when he was bidding Gaby good-night and hurrying Lydia off to their chamber on the plea of extreme fatigue and the need to rise in the morning far earlier than usual.

Left alone, to wander upstairs to her own room, Gaby did an odd sideways dance step. She provided a soft singing accompaniment and enjoyed the gentle swaying of her skirts.

She still felt wonderful when she reached her room, even strangely happy. She was also completely undaunted by all that she must do before—like the two downstairs—she had earned the right to climb virtuously into her own lonely bed.

First, she unlaced and slipped out of her gown and laid it flat on the counterpane of her four-poster. The large basting stitches were easily snipped in two with her embroidery scissors. She had deliberately used the large stitches, making them strong enough so the dress would hold together for the period of the wedding. Luckily, they had held for tonight's dinner, too.

In a matter of minutes there were half-a-dozen separate pieces of the gown scattered over her bed. Each piece needed only to be reversed and then all the parts stitched together again. Then she would have the dress she had intended all along.

The masked lady had chosen a pattern in which blue predominated. Preferring to compete rather than imitate her, Gaby had chosen pink. The gown she had worn as Lydia's only attendant was of fine damask, dusty rose in hue. Cut low in front, but not so low as to shock her father, it had owed much of its appeal to her own fine figure as well as the richness of the cloth and charming little rows of organdy ruching along the sides and below the elbow sleeves.

Now the former lining of the gown had become its outside, the dusty rose damask had been turned into the lining. Gaby used large stitches again to baste it all together strongly enough to endure for the next few hours of wear. After tonight, she would take it to a seamstress to be properly restitched.

Gaby held up the finished product, to study it, front and back. Never, she felt sure, had a more beautiful gown ever been created. She certainly did not believe that its equal had ever been worn by the daughter of a modest minister from Massachusetts. The exotic design of the cloth had come from India by way of England. The stitches in the silk were so fine, so delicate, they appeared to be a print rather than simple needlework. The fine chain stitches and French knots were worked into an elaborate floral pattern, with small colorful butterflies hovering among the exquisite pink flowers with their pale green leaves.

Trembling with eagerness, Gaby laid the gown on her bed. She washed her hands and face and upper body with cool water in which she had dropped some lilac salts. She had remembered that the light sweet scent of violets seemed to cling to the masked lady.

She took off her wool stockings and drew on the fine pink silk ones, whose price had seemed so shockingly high to the country-bred Gaby. She had all but walked out of the millinery shop without them until she indicated her need for long gloves and shoes in matching pink as well as a bonnet. The price had been adjusted accordingly.

Dressing oneself in the latest fashion, unaided, Gaby soon discovered, was not an easy business. No wonder fine ladies needed maids, if a husband was not available. First came the petticoats; then she had to fasten on the panniers in just the right way to accommodate the draping of her gown with its double underskirt.

She had to breathe deeply and rhythmically in order to lace her bodice so as to emphasize—without revealing outright—the topmost half of her bosom. She had forgotten that the removal of the organdy ruffles would lower it by more than an inch. But she took comfort from the remembrance that her locket, threaded through a velvet ribbon, rested just at the juncture of her breasts. She was quite unaware that this called attention to a highly pleasing part of her anatomy, rather than the reverse.

When she was fully dressed, the final touch, the fitting touch, the most necessary one to complete the picture she meant to present, still lay in layers of papers inside the bandbox in which she had brought it home from the costumer's shop in lower Manhattan.

Removing the paper, one sheet at a time, so that not a hair would be pulled out of place, she drew the fashionable white dress wig from the box and carefully set it—as the shopkeeper had shown her how to do—just above her own head, then over it, and finally gave it a gentle tugging-down. She felt all around it with her fingers to make sure no stray tendril of her own hair had managed to escape.

Between the jamming of her breasts in a bodice that now seemed too tight and the cramming of her own hair under the padding of her wig, she felt ridiculously top-heavy.

She took a walk around the bed and discovered that the pink shoes pinched. The fashionable long gloves were so tight a fit, they would surely split before the night was over.

"No man could ever be worth this!" she proclaimed aloud.

A land, however, might be . . . a land and something even more unsubstantial . . . a new concept of freedom.

In spite of her distress and discomfort, in spite of the guilt she was feeling at the plans her father's daughter was setting in motion even before her father was out of the house, she was also experiencing a sense of great exhilaration.

How she longed to see herself, all of herself from the pink of her too-tight shoes all the way up to the fashionable silliness of her high wig. Its poufs and pompadours and flowered ornaments on which tiny butterflies perched, were so exactly a match for the silk of her gown, she had been unable to resist it.

The only large mirror in the Cathcart house had been shipped to Philadelphia in the carrier's cart. The framed fragment hanging on her wall was obviously a broken piece from a larger mirror, but it was so small that Gaby could only see her face and two side curls in it. The side curls looked oddly detached, and her face seemed unnaturally pale. It had not a single feature, Gaby decided, suddenly despondent, that could induce any British officer to be so unwise and indiscreet as to disclose to her information that would be of any value.

But she had gone this far and she would not retreat! Her state of simmering excitement threatened to boil over at any moment. Snatching up her cloak, Gaby wrapped herself in it and then, slowly, carefully, drew the hood all the way over her wig.

The house was still and quiet. Gaby knelt to pull from under the box on the floor a sheaf of papers that contained her shifts and stockings. She stuffed the papers into an oversized reticule made of bits and pieces from the rose damask. She slung the reticule over her wrist and took her chamberstick, with its single candle, to light her way along the hallway and down the stairs. In the downstairs hall, she blew out the candle and felt her way past Lydia's bedroom—the only point of danger, she felt—but her fears were groundless. Her father and her friend were deep in the exhausted sleep of lovers, and little short of a mule team driven right past their bed, was likely to awaken them.

Once out of the door, Gaby walked to the rear of the house and out into the next street, where the hackney she had prudently hired much earlier in the day was waiting. The driver was even standing at the open door of the carriage to let down the steps for her.

"Began to think you wasn't coming," he grumbled.

"I paid you to wait," she pointed out.

"Not the full price."

"You will have earned the full price when I reach my destination, not one single minute before," Gaby told him tartly. Really, these New York drivers!

This one, at least, helped her up the steps and actually touched his cap in a gesture of respect when she gave him the direction on Beekman Street.

Nevertheless, during the short ride, she dismissed the notion she had first entertained of having him wait for her. She must think differently than she had ever thought before; she must look at the world through different eyes. It would only draw attention to the house on Beekman Street at the sign of the Baby in the Red Cradle to have a hackney waiting for so long a time as to lead to speculation by curious neighbors.

On arrival she paid her driver and went quietly up the same six steps she remembered. From a pocket in her cloak, she took a silk mask cut like the blue lady's and fitted it over her face.

This time Mercy Enough was not expecting her, and waiting with the door open. Gaby had to lift and then drop the brass knocker, which she did not do too forcefully, hoping a more vigorous effort would not be needed.

In only seconds, she heard sounds of movement inside the house, and in less than a minute, the door swung open.

As soon as the Quaker lady saw the masked figure, she opened the door wide.

"My dear, I thought thee were acting at the theater tonight," she said as she closed and locked the door after her guest entered.

"Are we alone?" Gaby asked in not much above a whisper.

"Save only my little maid Jenny, and she is asleep in her attic."

"May we go into the parlor? I do not like to speak out here in the open."

"Thee is wise, but let us go to the kitchen instead. It is warm from the beehive oven. I have been baking my week's supply of bread, and I just put the kettle on for tea."

"What a lovely new gown, my dear," she said with genuine admiration. "When I was a girl, I had such a taste for finery like this"—she fingered a fold of the silk with a light, loving touch—"I was not altogether sure I was made of the proper stuff to be a Quaker. And now, when I am no longer accepted as one by my brethren, I prefer my grays and blacks . . . only for myself, of course. I understand that a lovely woman like thee longs for such clothes."

"Do you think"—Gaby was still half-whispering—"it is unnatural that I combine my longing with the needs of my country?"

"Not at all. I consider it, in fact, most natural. My dear," she added, pouring out the tea, "I am still troubled in my mind. Thee never comes here without forewarning, unless at my request. Thee does not seem thyself, somehow, and now I distinctly recall that thee were advertised to act in a performance tonight."

"If," said Gaby in her own voice, loosening the mask and then removing it entirely, "I have managed in these few minutes to convince you that I am the lady who was with us both some nights ago, it is no longer necessary to hide myself. As you see, I am not a dowdy schoolgirl tonight, ma'am . . . Mercy, if you prefer. Am *I* sufficiently pretty, do you think, to be of use to you—and to my country?"

Sixteen

At the house at the sign of the Baby in the Red Cradle, Gaby pressed for an immediate verdict from Mercy Enough Godwin. The Quaker woman, gentle, soft-spoken, firm as steel, insisted her unexpected guest sit down with her in the kitchen to eat a biscuit dripping with honey and drink a cup of tea.

"Thee must understand, it is not solely a question of thy being alluring to men," she explained patiently. "If it were, I would be eager to enlist thee this very moment. Thee must know thee are not at all pretty in an ordinary way. Rather," she added thoughtfully, "there is a fresh, vibrant radiance about thee that would appeal to any mortal man, not only lonely soldiers. There is this, too"—as though she were stating the merest commonplace—"in spite of the dress and appearance thee presents as a woman of fashion and experience; yet thy loveliness contains an element of purity, of . . . Oh, there is no denying thee would be to men as the sweet nectar of a flower to a bee."

"Well, then?"

"First of all, the decision is not mine alone to make. Whatever thee may think"—she smiled faintly—"I am but a small cog in a rather large wheel."

"But your own opinion will carry weight with the other parts of the wheel, will it not?" Gaby asked shrewdly.

"Ah, thee thinks things through, that is good. We knew Pythias had to be a person of intelligence, but there are times when common sense is more important. I would be interested to know how thee managed to find thy way back here after our subterfuge in bringing you."

Gaby laughed delightedly. "I am so glad you asked. I was longing to boast just a little of how cleverly I contrived it."

She described in detail how, after the masked lady left, she had taken the lantern and gone out to look at the sign of the baby in the red cradle, then of her trip to the printing office to find a newspaper advertisement for a midwife's services.

"When I came to your notice about grave-clothes, I almost passed it by. But there was your name. And it is, as you said of my appearance, not at all ordinary. Which, by the way," Gaby asked in genuine curiosity, "of your professed professions is the true one?"

"Why, both," Mercy replied. "It would be inappropriate if I were not adept at both. Such a slipshod mistake might easily lead to the discovery of my third profession."

"Third? Oh! Oh, yes, I see. The—the spying."

"Yes," said Mercy. "The spying. Does the word make thee uncomfortable?"

"Perhaps just a little. I mean, it does not sound at all *noble,* as for example, when one says I am serving my country."

"War is not noble, killing is not noble, spying is not noble, but there are times in our lives and in the course of human events when one does what one feels called upon to do by a higher force than self-interest or personal inclination."

"Oh, I truly do thank you," Gaby said fervently, and smiled with such brilliance that Mercy Enough blinked. The minister's daughter had moments of sheer beauty.

"Thee are more than welcome even though I am not quite certain why I am being thanked."

"When I was getting dressed in these extremely uncomfortable clothes, I was trying to decide why I wanted to do what I was about to propose to you that you allow me to do . . . and now you have put it into the proper words, and I am grateful."

Mercy nodded as though confirming an opinion of her own.

"If, after all the effort you have made, we decline your services, what will you do?"

"Exactly as I meant to do before, and will do afterwards even if you use me for a while. I will return to my Aunt Emily Van Raalte's home in Princeton, New Jersey to learn farm management of her."

"And what will you tell her of your visit here tonight? Of the previous one? Of me . . . and the masked lady?"

"I will tell her nothing. Those meetings never took place. I met no such people."

"Ah!"

"Have I passed some kind of trial, ma'am?"

"When thou hast, thee will know it."

Gaby lowered her eyes meekly. There was a brief silence, which was not broken till she reached out for the oversized reticule and took out the sheaf of rolled papers.

"Ma'am, I mean, Mercy. While I was devising various plans these last days, I could not help but think often of the fact that your—your group's interest in me stemmed from an interest in the poet Pythias. But that was my man-guise. As a woman—well, I am not an actress like the masked lady; and *you* have two professions . . . It seemed to me that, if I were to live in New York, I must have some*thing* distinguishing about me. So . . . you see . . . there are these other poems I write. They are very different, not political at all. No one else has ever seen them . . . except my mother . . . when I was much younger. The ones I showed her before she died were not so open. They had more of a fairy-tale quality; they were not quite so—quite so—"

"Quite so what, my dear?"

"Amorous," said Gaby faintly.

"So *what?*"

"Amorous." The word this time was said more loudly, more firmly, almost in a tone of defiance. "There are enough for a thin volume. I have decided I will call it, *Amorous Verse by a Lady of New York.*"

"They have not yet been printed?"

"No, as I told you, I have never permitted them to be seen. They are . . . some of them are very frank about personal . . . physical emotions. Back home in Massachusetts, or even in Princeton, it would have been as much as my reputation was worth to have it known that I wrote such stuff. Here, in a British-occupied city, however . . ."

"Ah!" It was a loud, prolonged sigh.

"Oh, you *do* see! I knew you would!" Gaby exclaimed jubilantly. "If I am to become someone that the officers are intrigued by, there must be something, besides mere appearance, to make me stand out. After all, New York is full of lovely women! A small edition of the poems could be printed—I would pay for it myself, if it is not too expensive. Then, in a short while, when I have attended a few parties—your masked lady could secure me invitations, could she not?—it might be whispered about that *I* was the Lady of New York who had authored them."

Mercy's hand went out. "May I see?"

"I will leave them with you tonight, if you wish."

"That would be necessary." Mercy Enough nodded gravely. "But I would like to read a sample from some of your amorous verse now."

"Oh, please, not with me s-sitting here," Gaby stammered. "I would find it mortifying."

"Very well." Mercy handed back the papers. "You read one to me, please. Perhaps one of the shorter ones."

"Me! Read aloud to *you!"*

Mercy Enough Godwin nodded gravely, and Gaby realized suddenly . . . all that had gone on between them before was minor skirmishing; this was a real trial. If her claim to fame in New York became these poems, she could hardly blush and stammer like a schoolgirl whenever they were mentioned!

Gaby accepted the papers and leafed rapidly through them. She stopped at a page and looked straight across at Mercy. "This one should be short enough. I wrote it just the other night, when my father and his bride were sleeping downstairs. I call it 'Loving.' "

Her voice was clear and cool; the only sign of her embarrassment was a slight tinge of red in her cheeks:

> The full moon of the midnight sky
> Shone through the window
> On our bodies,
> Bare and twisting,
> So entwined and entangled,
> Truly, we might have been one.
> And later, much later,
> Spent with the splendor of our love,
> We lay in repose,
> Handfast, eyes closed,
> Happily bathed together in the new day's sun.

Gaby raised her eyes. "Will that be enough, Mercy?" she asked impassively, then realized what she had said and could not help laughing. "An unintentional pun," she said. "Not enough, Mercy; I mean, Mercy Enough."

Mercy Enough's eyes twinkled at her merrily. "Read another short one, if you please."

Gaby turned a few more pages and took a sip of tea. "This one is titled 'Substitute.'"

> I embrace the down pillow
> I hold like a lover,
> It is all I may have
> Until I discover
> If the tale of male kisses,
> Of well-bedded bliss is
>   False or quite true.
> Oh, my love, my love
> Take me
> My love, my love
> Slake me
>   At present—with pillow—

> I have to make do,
> Not that it stills
> My fierce yearning for you!

Mercy Enough said quietly, "Thee are a virgin?"

"Yes, I have never been married."

"Thou art thinking as a minister's daughter," said the Quaker lady dryly. "The two, spinsterhood and virginity—even in prim New England—do not necessarily go together. Pray leave your *Amorous Verse* with me; I would like to read more. I believe you are right. Thy face, thy figure, and the right garments—such as tonight's—combined with the awareness that you are the writer of poetry of an erotic nature could easily make you irresistible to many a British officer. How well would you be able to handle their importunities, yet still retain thy virginity? Your country does not require thee to play the whore," she finished matter-of-factly.

"I have had my suitors in the past, not a great number, but enough to make some judgments about men. I doubt if they are any different . . . American or British. There will be those perfectly content to be seen with me in public, to show me off to others as a tribute to their own prowess with women, for their own vanity. There are others who will only want a sympathetic ear to listen to their troubles. There will be the married ones who I may truly claim to find it hard to resist, but I must because my own moral code will not permit me to have a liaison with a married man."

"And the handful who do not fit into any of these categories and will continue to importune you? There will always be those."

"Yes," said Gaby, "there probably will be. One must then regretfully tell each one that one's final choice is the other man; and he is both jealous and possessive, not at all inclined to share his *inamorata* with another. In such cases, a man usually removes himself gracefully from the scene, quietly, too. They seldom wish to advertise their failures. If necessary—in the event of someone who persists—I will do the removing for him."

Mercy Enough Godwin stood up, smiling faintly. She pointed to Gaby's papers. "Whatever the outcome, these will be returned to you. Sit and have another cup of tea while I fetch a driver for you. He will be in front of the house in ten minutes."

She turned back at the kitchen door.

"What is thy full name, my dear?"

"Gabrielle Forsyth Foote, but I seldom use the Forsyth because it is my mother's family name. The Forsyths thought Mama lowered herself by marrying my father, and I think—in his heart—he resented them. Why do you ask? Does it matter?"

"I assure thee little Gaby Foote is a charming child. But if the Lady of New York who wrote *Amorous Verse* ever becomes well known in our city, she ought surely to have a more exotic name to suit her exciting temperament. There is rather an elegant ring to Gabrielle Forsyth-Foote."

Seventeen

At home—after her father left Massachusetts a few hours ahead of a possible tar-and-feathering by overzealous Sons of Liberty—then later in Princeton and, lastly, in New York, Gaby had experienced the heady excitement of being as much in charge of her life as any woman could ever hope to be.

The two days after she stood on the dock, waving farewell to Lydia and her father (whose competent measures for sending her back to New Jersey must be cancelled) she felt abruptly catapulted back in time, as though she had been caught up in the center of a hurricane and was being whirled round and round by unseen forces.

Apparently Mercy Enough Godwin was in close (and immediate) touch with the cogs of the Wheel she had mentioned the night before. Gaby returned from the dock, dispirited, tired, a bit tearful, but as soon as she let herself into the house, she saw an envelope lying on a piece of carpeting at the entrance.

The letter, which had obviously been pushed under the door, was addressed in a bold, flowing hand to Mrs. Gabrielle Forsyth-Foote. Instinctively, she sensed that it was not Mercy's handwriting, which she would wager any amount (except that Papa considered the most innocent of wagers to be sinful) was likely to be neat and precise, not like Mercy Enough Godwin's heart, more like her orderly mind.

Surely the use of that "more elegant" name, together with *Mrs.,* indicated acceptance of her as a part of the Wheel!

She broke the seal on the envelope and, in her eagerness to read its contents, a fingernail as well. It said:

Dear Madam,

In view of the sacrifices suffered for his loyalty to the Crown by your esteemed father, the Commissioner has seen fit to interest himself in your plight. I am pleased to inform you that an apartment of two rooms has been assigned to you at 133 Queen Street. You are to be lodged in a space built into the attic after the great fire; but it is my hope that the inconvenience of being housed up so high may be compensated by the greater privacy of your situation.

There are three or four officers' wives living below you and several more on the first floor. All the residents are entitled to the use of the kitchen and a single sizeable parlor, which serves as both dining and drawing room.

Your own apartment is eligible for your removal there at any time after half-past noon of the present day.

Yr. Hmbl. Obdt. Servant . . .

Gaby studied the name very closely but could not make out the identity of her humble obedient servant. The ill-written signature had most probably been deliberately made illegible.

"Mrs. Gabrielle Forsyth-Foote!" she said aloud and whirled around and around until she was as dizzy as she was delighted. "I am part of the Wheel. I am—good Lord!" What she was now must never be spoken of, not even to herself. From now on, she must assume that the very walls had ears.

She read the note over again. An apartment in the attic where only she would dwell. The writer was quite correct. A steeper climb to her room was a small price to pay for the luxury of such privacy!

Half-past noon. Suddenly she could hardly wait, not only to start her new life but to be quit of this house, which had been full of life and laughter only the week before and now seemed so dreary and desolate, to say nothing of freezingly cold.

She ran upstairs to her own room and started a grand blaze in the fireplace. No need to be frugal about the extra logs; she had only herself to consider these last few hours.

She had just begun the last of her packing by laying the silk gown across her bed when a loud knocking sounded on the front door. It was hardly likely to be someone for her, so Gaby poked her head out the window to save herself a trip downstairs and send the unknown away.

"May I help you?" she called out.

The young woman standing on the doorstep looked up. "Mrs. Forsyth-Foote?" she asked.

"Yes," admitted Gaby after a few seconds of stunned silence.

"I was sent by the milliner's, ma'am, to take your measurements."

"From the milliner's," Gaby repeated foolishly. "Oh, yes, of course, the milliner's. I will be down in a moment."

When she opened the door, the young woman—a girl, really—dropped a shy curtsey and did not step inside till she was invited.

"Would you mind coming upstairs to my bedchamber?" Gaby asked. "It is the only warm area in the house. There are no fires in the other rooms because I am moving to different lodgings today."

"Oh, no, ma'am, I would be glad of a fire. It was quite a long walk."

"I am sorry to have brought you out on such a cold day." Gaby apologized as the milliner's girl followed her up the stairway. She had already become so involved in her part, she felt as though she really was responsible for having done so.

"I don't mind at all, Mrs. Forsyth-Foote. Truly. It made for an agreeable change. And Mrs. Sedley understood that, what with moving and the wedding and all, you could not come in yourself this one time. But she was eager—we all were—to get started on your order. The fabrics you chose are so lovely, it will be a pleasure to work on them. Oh, my!"

They had just entered the bedroom, and Gaby thought the pleased exclamation was about the fire. It wasn't. The girl had gone straight to her bed and was fingering the gown laid there almost reverently. "India silk!" she said ecstatically. "What a beautiful design!"

"Yes, isn't it?" Gaby glowed with pleasure. "It is quite my favorite of—of the materials I selected," she finished boldly. "As a matter of fact, if you would not mind, I would be obliged if you would take this gown back to the shop with you. It is only basted, as you see, and I want it stitched and ready to wear as soon as possible. I will send you in a hackney at my expense, of course."

"Oh, no, that won't be necessary, ma'am." There was a touch of wistfulness in her voice as she declined. "I don't think Mrs. Sedley would be best pleased to have you put to the expense of a carriage for me."

"Then you must tell her that *I* insisted . . . because I do," Gaby said firmly. "I would not want such delicate silk to be exposed to the elements. It might come on to rain. The way the sky looks, there might even be snow."

"Very well, ma'am," the girl answered dutifully, but Gaby saw the smiling pleasure in her eyes. A hackney ride would no doubt make another agreeable change for her.

"Let us go nearer to the fire if I must take off my dress," she proposed as the milliner's assistant opened a small work basket that she had carried over her arm. She took out a narrow strip of cloth for measurements, a paper of pins, and a small notebook and pencil.

She knelt at Gaby's feet. "Do you like this length for all your hems, ma'am? It is your decision, of course, but the present fashion is that they be just the least bit shorter."

"By all means, let us have an agreeable change for *me,* too. Before this, propriety has been my main concern since my father is a New England minister."

"Oh, New England way," the milliner's girl said innocently.

"I wondered at the strange way you pronounce some of your words."

Gaby, who had found a constant source of amusement in the varying accents of New York, could not help laughing as she removed the dark drab gown she hoped never to wear again.

She did not explain her laughter, and the milliner's assistant did not ask questions, except those that related to her work. A tedious twenty minutes followed for the new Mrs. Forsyth-Foote, who longed to be doing something more active than standing, turning, lifting her arms, lowering them again to her sides, and having the size of her waist, her breasts, her hips, her thighs and her height each verified at least three times before being finally written down in the notebook.

"I am finished, ma'am."

Gaby reached thankfully for the gown she had hoped never to have to wear again. She could hardly go without it or one quite similar, till some of her new gowns were made up.

"When is my fitting to be?" she asked a little awkwardly, having no notion where Mrs. Sedley's shop was located. She did not relish the prospect of another trip to the offices of the *New York Gazette*.

"Oh, your friend wrote it all down for you," the girl assured her.

Her omnipresent friend again! Gaby reached out a hand for the notebook. "You will need my new direction. Let me write it down."

"Oh, your friend gave us that, too. On Queen Street, is it not, at"—she turned back two pages—"yes, here it is, Queen Street, at Number 133."

Really, thought Gaby, half-entertained, half-exasperated, this Wheel rolls along with incredible smoothness, considering that the streets of old New York are almost all cobbled. If I am not careful, I may wake one morning and find I have been supplied with a genuine *Mr.* Forsyth-Foote to lie beside me!

And the man who lies beside *me,* Gaby vowed to herself as

fiercely as though she had actually been commanded to take a husband, will never be of anyone's choosing but my own.

The milliner's assistant left quite happily, with Gaby's silk gown turned inside out and folded carefully over her arm, and the money for a hackney tucked under the notebook inside her workbasket.

Gaby finished her packing and then threw all the odd bits and pieces of her possessions into the smallest of the boxes. As she made a final survey to make sure she had overlooked nothing, in the single drawer of her nightstand, she discovered the copy of *The Rivals,* bought as a good-bye gift for Lydia and her father.

Oh, well, she decided philosophically, as she carried the book down to the kitchen, it will amuse me instead.

She poked around in the cupboards in search of food for a late breakfast or an early lunch. She would eat and read until it was time for her to move to Queen Street.

If Mr. Sheridan's play was as daring as she had heard, no doubt she would appreciate it more than the newly married couple, who had other pleasant ways to occupy themselves aboard the ship. Just now, it would make the time till she could leave for Queen Street pass faster and more pleasantly for her.

Eighteen

From the day she moved into her rooms at 133 Queen Street, the life of Mrs. Gabrielle Forsyth-Foote was full of experiences entirely new to naive young Gaby Foote.

Membership in a private library where all the latest books from England could be borrowed . . . extravagant purchases of ornaments she had never owned before . . . lace-edged fans and beaded reticules . . . shoe roses, delicate flowered scents, and wispy silk scarves.

She was invited to afternoon tea with British wives who regarded most Americans as provincial traitors, except, of course, the wealthier and more prominent loyalists who had fled to New York.

Gaby would hardly have understood how to go on in this extraordinary new life of hers if the unknown patriotic group for which she worked had not frequently intervened in her life.

After providing her with a dwelling space, Mercy Enough's Wheel (as Gaby had named it to herself) next bestowed a very solid benefit in the person of Mrs. Penelope Rogers, a genuine lady's maid.

The new lodgings consisted of two spacious rooms, and Gaby immediately determined to use the larger of the two for her sitting room, as in the Cathcart house.

Only hours after she removed to Queen Street, a vigorous knock sounded on the door of her bedroom. She opened it to Hezibeth, one of the parlor maids, and next to her a stoutish pleasant-faced woman.

The parlor maid sketched the scantiest of curtseys. "The lady's maid you was wishful to interview is here, Mrs. Forsyth-Foote," she informed the new tenant.

Fortunately, Gaby had already learned an important and necessary lesson of her new profession . . . to think first and speak afterwards. She resisted her immediate impulse to deny that she desired a lady's maid, receiving as reward a letter directed to her in the familiar bold script of her *humble obedient servant:* only this time he (or she) claimed to be Mrs. William Thos. Smith.

After watching Hezibeth clatter downstairs, she made sure the door was tightly shut. "Please sit down." Gaby indicated an upholstered chair.

The woman settled her substantial form into it and looked about, quite at her ease, while Gaby hastily scanned the contents of the letter.

It was her pleasure to inform any persons who had need of the information, Mrs. William Thos. Smith stated firmly, that Penelope Rogers had been in her service as a lady's maid for more than five years and was leaving said service through no fault of her own. The writer was leaving the city to make her home with a sister in the extreme northern part of New York Colony.

Penelope, Mrs. Smith declared effusively, knew everything there was to know about taking care of a lady's wardrobe as well as a lady's appearance. She was honest, hardworking, sewed and mended beautifully, and was not above helping out in other ways—such as bed-making, when a chambermaid was unwell.

Gaby sat down in the rocking chair and looked across at Penelope, whom she estimated to be in her mid-forties. She was a woman of unusual height and weight.

Gaby read the last line of the recommendation for the second time. *Penelope is of cheerful and amiable disposition, but her special genius lies in the dressing of hair.*

The prospective employer looked doubtfully at Penelope, whose own graying hair was pulled back from her forehead and fashioned in a far-from-becoming bun beneath her muslin cap and unadorned black bonnet.

The lady's maid smiled slightly as she uttered a gentle reminder. "It is my duty to make my mistress—not myself—look elegant."

Gabrielle's cheeks turned quite red at this bit of thought-reading. "I must confess," she murmured awkwardly, "that I am not accustomed to having a—a personal maid. I have . . . until recently, my home was a country village, where the very notion would have been frowned on. I—I—to tell the truth . . ." Nervousness made her slight laugh rather shrill . . . "I don't know a thing about proper wages or—or anything. Would you expect to live here or—?"

"That flibbertigibbet who brought me up told me there are beds for any number of servants in a room that connects with the kitchen. If you prefer—for reasons of privacy it might be better—I could set up a trundle in your sitting room, which would not discommode you, since, naturally, I would never retire before I had helped undress and put you to bed."

"I have undressed and put myself to my bed—unaided—these dozen years or more!"

Penelope Rogers smiled slightly at the look of shocked revulsion on her prospective employer's face. Then she took note of the stubborn chin and said quickly and kindly, "But Mrs. Forsyth-Foote, it is necessary that you fulfill the role of a fashionable English-type lady now."

Gaby hesitated. Was there any hidden meaning in those words? Was Penelope Rogers an active part of the Wheel, as the handwriting on the letter and the emphasis on privacy seemed to indicate? Or was the knowledgeable maid only meant to teach the mistress how to go on?

No matter. Gaby folded the letter carefully. Obviously, she was intended to accept this woman into her employ.

"What," she asked almost resignedly, feeling once again swept up by a hurricane, "do I call you . . . Miss or Mrs. Rogers?"

"A British lady would call me plain Rogers, without any such dignity as Miss or Mrs., but since you are an American, Mrs. Forsyth-Foote—even though loyalist—I should think plain Penelope will do us fine. Besides, ma'am, 'tis the only one of my names that never changes," she added with an unexpected flash of humor, "it having been my fate to marry and bury three husbands in the last twenty years."

During the next day or two, Gaby acquired the part-time services of three more servants. Hezibeth, for a very small sum, would fetch and carry and do in-house errands. A chambermaid, for a slightly higher fee changed linens, laundered clothes, and cleaned out her rooms. Lastly, she agreed to pay the cook-housekeeper a handsome sum to include her when she cooked and served meals to the British officers' wives.

Gaby also elected to eat in the combined dining-and-drawing room with all the other women. Her personal preference would have been a tray in her apartment, but her own wishes were of no account. She could hardly refuse such an excellent opportunity for possible friendship and gossip with the wives and daughters, the widows and mistresses of the British military.

On the whole, the ladies at 133 Queen Street proved to be a cheerful, convivial lot. Two of the widows, Gaby soon realized, might truly deserve that designation. It was polite as well as politic to accept whatever label each chose to affix to herself.

After all, Mrs. Gabrielle Forsyth-Foote, who flaunted her mother's modest wedding ring, had never been wedded, bedded, or widowed!

It was not in the least difficult, she discovered, to field questions about herself. The English ladies, living their life of near-luxury, were abysmally ignorant about America and Americans.

Nevertheless, Gaby had determined never to make the mistake of underestimating any one of them, and she strove to stick to the truth, whenever possible. Always in the forefront of her mind was Mercy Enough's admonition. Aunt Emily's, too.

This work they did was deadly serious. The British had spies of their own. Unlikely people situated in unlikely places.

Had not she herself, in a dizzyingly short space of time, been demure-seeming Gaby Foote, daughter of a Massachusetts minister; Pythias, the rebel poet; a masked member of the New Jersey Regulars who punished wife-beaters; and the whore (so he thought) who had commandeered Major Darcy Rhoads's hired carriage?

Who could deny that she was Mrs. Gabrielle Forsyth-Foote, daughter of a respectable New England clergyman now on his way to the mother country, and the widow of a long-suffering loyalist landowner whose property had been confiscated by the rebels?

Within a few days, they were all following the lead of Major Barnes's wife, who called her, even to her face, totally unaware of the condescension, "the dear little American."

Gaby gritted her teeth, smiled her dear little smile, and allowed Mrs. Barnes to instruct her in the niceties of piquet.

"I always longed to learn," she confided to a group of them, as they sat around the parlor table, "but my papa was so set against it—a minister, you know, and in *New* England. They regard card-playing as one of the seven deadly sins."

The Englishwomen shuddered together at such barbaric deprivation and liked "dear Gabrielle" all the more for her disarming gratitude. They reminded each other—when she was not by—that, provincial or not, she had the wardrobe of a lady of fashion, apparently no lack of money, and spoke "almost like an English lady," without the awful accent of so many of her countrymen.

Still, almost a full week had gone by, and neither at breakfast nor over teacups or across the card table had she heard a single word or fact worth sending to Mercy Enough Goodwin.

She had not been invited to a single evening party, where soldiers were to be found.

"Patience," she could almost hear Mercy Enough saying. "Be patient, my dear."

Patience—alas!—permitted her mind to dwell far too often for comfort on the one identity it was imperative that she forget . . . that outrageous little hussy Emily Washington, who had come near to losing her maidenhood in a hackney!

Nineteen

Penelope's private manners to Gabrielle had soon become as easy as Gaby's own. In public, of course, she exhibited the respectful, formal propriety that an Englishwoman would have expected between mistress and maid.

One rainy afternoon, therefore, Gaby was greatly surprised to have Penelope invade the drawing room, unasked, and dressed in outdoor wear. Four of the women sat at the inevitable card table; she herself was part of a gossiping group sitting near to the fire.

Penelope walked directly to Gaby and bobbed a curtsey. Gaby accepted this cue. Her eyebrows lifted. She tried to sound properly haughty. "Yes, Penelope?"

"I'm back from the printer's, as you requested, ma'am, to make my inquiries; and it turns out that he is beforehand." She produced a slender, paper-wrapped parcel from underneath her voluminous cloak. "Mr. Gaines said as how he hoped it was bound to your satisfaction."

"Oh! Oh!" Gaby accepted the parcel eagerly and pinched it as though to be sure of its contents. "My book!" she breathed reverently, seeming to be unaware of all the curious eyes directed at her.

She returned the package to Penelope with apologetic air. "Break the string, do, woman!" she ordered imperiously.

Penelope bent her head and bit her lip to keep from smiling. *I must warn her not to look ashamed when she acts like a proper bitch.* She broke the string easily with a single tug of her strong right hand, then handed the package to Gabrielle, who appeared to be admiring the soft whiteness of her own slender fingers.

As the maid left the drawing room, Gabrielle was tearing off the paper wrapping in a way that would have horrified the frugal soul of Miss Foote of Massachusetts, where blank paper was treasured in every household.

"Is it a new title?"

"Is it from England?"

"Is it a novel we will all enjoy?"

"Not some prosy sermonizing essays, I hope?"

From the very depths of her diaphragm, Gaby fetched a lengthy breath. *Let the play begin.*

"The book," she said clearly, holding it up, "is called *Amorous Verse.*"

"Amorous Verse!" repeated Mrs. Torrington, her eyes all a-sparkle. "My word, that sounds promising."

Mrs. Robinson craned her neck for a look at the spine of the book. Gaby obligingly turned it her way. Then she opened it to the title page. "No, not England. The author is listed here as a Lady of New York."

"Do read us one," urged Charlotte Gray, the least self-important of the British ladies and the one Gaby liked best.

Gaby felt none of her old shyness about reading her romantic verse aloud. Was she not now—like the lady in blue—an actress?

She turned the page. "The title of the first poem is 'Loving.'"

> The full moon of the midnight sky
> Shone through the window
> On our bodies,
> Bare and twisting,
> So entwined and entangled,
> Truly, we might have been one.
> And later, much later,
> Spent with the splendor of our love,
> We lay in repose,

> Handfast, eyes closed,
> Happily bathed together in the new day's sun.

"Oh, how delicious!" tittered Betty Arbuckle, the youngest and silliest of the wives.

"Humph!" It was impossible to interpret Mrs. Barnes's grunt. Interest? Disgust? Perhaps surprise? Square-shouldered, buxom Mrs. Barnes did not have the appearance of a woman whose body had ever been entangled fondly with any man's, but there were five little Barnes children at home in England to prove to Gaby that she must be wrong.

Mrs. Torrington stretched out her hand. "Oblige me, dear Mrs. Forsyth-Foote. I would like to read the next."

Gaby gladly handed over the book, and once more the card players paused in their game to listen more attentively.

" 'Fidelity,' " squeaked Mrs. Torrington. She coughed, cleared her throat, then read rapidly.

> Faithful I will be to you
> Faithful always—always true
> I'll love you much
> I'll love you long
> While your own love proves as strong.
> However, such fidelity
> Is not yours without a fee
> Not a coin and not a kiss
> The payment you must make is this—
> None but *I* may give *you* bliss!
>
> If, by any chance, somewhere
> You see a face that is more fair
> Or a figure whose design
> Is built more beautifully than mine,
> Bid your heart to slow its beat
> Bid the rest of you—RETREAT!

> Because if—even once—you stray,
> Together ne'er again we'll lay.
> *She* may be ready for flirtation
> *My* pride demands
> You shun temptation.
> So run, my dear,
> Speed straight away
> To love me on another day.

"You read too low and too fast, Mary," Mrs. Barnes said unexpectedly. "Now Mrs. Forsyth-Foote has a pleasant carrying kind of voice."

"Then, by all means, let Mrs. Forsyth-Foote do the reading," Mrs. Torrington said languidly.

It was time, Gaby decided, to speed up this spying process; and the two-minute interlude of Mrs. Torrington's recital had given her the necessary time to make a calculated move.

"I accept the office of reader," she said laughingly, "provided there is one ommision. I cannot bring myself to read 'Fulfillment' aloud."

"Is that the next poem?" Betty Arbuckle jumped up from her chair and hurried over to Mrs. Torrington, who still held the book. "Let *me* read it. I don't embarrass easily," she boasted.

Gaby said, seemingly without realizing her blunder. "No, 'Temptation' comes next. 'Fulfillment' is the next to last poem."

"How do you know—?" Charlotte Gray saw where her question was leading and shut her mouth abruptly.

"Dear me." Mrs. Torrington ruffled through the pages of the slim volume. "Fancy this. Our dear Gabrielle has guessed correctly about 'Fulfillment.' It *is* the next to last poem in the volume . . ." She read it in silence and then looked up, laughing lightly. "It is fortunate we are all wedded women here. I am afraid 'Fulfillment' would not be altogether suitable for virgin ears."

Gaby blushed violently in sudden awareness that she, the poem's author, possessed the only virgin ears present!

Her blush was happily misunderstood.

"You have read these poems before!" Betty Arbuckle made it sound like an accusation.

"But did not your maid say she had brought the book fresh from the printer's for you?" Mrs. Robinson puzzled.

Mrs. Sherman, without turning from the card table, ventured an opinion. "I would hazard a guess, Mrs. Forsyth-Foote, that you have read the entire volume before."

In the silence that fell, they all stared at the blushing Gaby, who looked the very picture of guilt. Then two of the ladies spoke at once.

"Humph!" said Mrs. Barnes.

"You all forget Mrs. Forsyth-Foote is American-born." Charlotte Gray tried valiantly to aid her new friend. "Naturally, she must know many more ladies of New York than we do. You are probably acquainted with the writer of this book, are you not, Gabrielle dear?" she prompted, plucking the volume out of Mrs. Torrington's hands and returning it to Gaby.

"How very kind . . . and I must add, enterprising of you, Mrs. Gray," returned Mrs. Robinson rather spitefully. "You have saved your new friend all the trouble of having to make up her own explanation."

"Charlotte was indeed most kind," said Gaby with quiet dignity, setting her book down on a table. "She has my gratitude, but I require no defense. I do not feel anyone here is entitled to any explanation of anything I say or do. I freely and gladly acknowledge that I am acquainted with the poet and that my opinion of many of the poems was sought by her before she sent it to the printer's. Now, if you will excuse me, ladies . . ."

She walked out of the drawing room, stately as a duchess, carefully neglecting to take the book with her. They watched her go up the stairway, spine still erect and head held high. When she reached the landing and disappeared from view, eager hands reached for the book and the first poem turned to was 'Fulfillment.'

Perfectly aware of the tumult going on in the drawing room, Gaby ran up the second flight and burst into her sitting room, where Penelope sat in the rocker, placidly knitting. Gaby collapsed into the chair opposite and gave way to silent convulsions of laughter.

Penelope looked at her mistress in silent sympathy. "All went well?" she asked after a while, when Gaby was quiet but still rubbing away tears of merriment.

"Exceeding well. You were superb, Penelope"—she began to giggle—"but so was I! I would wager any sum they all have their heads together over my book and are reading it cover to cover, starting, of course, with 'Fulfillment.' "

"I dare say, you are right," said Penelope, as composed as though they had not advanced a great step forward.

Gabrielle's smile was full of mischief. "Did *you* read 'Fulfillment,' Penelope?"

"Yes, indeed. I read the entirety of your book in the print shop while Mr. Gaines assisted another patron."

"In its entirety!" Gaby scoffed. "You mean you skimmed through it."

"With all respect, Mrs. Forsyth-Foote," said Penelope, her voice prim and proper, but her eyes glinting with amusement, "I read each poem all through and with the utmost attention. " 'Tis a way I have and never thought to wonder why when I was young, it seemed so natural. When I look at a page of writing, the words seem to leap right out at me. They stay here forever—" She tapped her forehead with her thimble finger. "When I grew older, I often asked my first husband—a godly, church-going man—why he thought I had been given such a needless gift. He said to me over and over' "—she dropped her knitting into her lap—"He said to me, 'Penelope, you are in the Lord's hands. In His own good time, the Almighty will tell you what He has in mind for you to do.' " She shook her head wonderingly. "And now it's two more husbands and another two years since I was last widowed and the Lord has surely shown me."

"Then you *are* an active member of the Wheel?"

"The wheel?"

"I call the midwife's group . . ."

"Hush, child. We must believe that even the walls here may have ears."

"I am whispering."

"I know . . . but it is wise to err more on the side of caution than less. Speaking of which . . . I think it would be best to place two upholstered chairs facing each other with a table between to hold knitting and some skeins of wool. Thus, if anyone enters the room suddenly, or without notice, it will appear that I have sat down to assist you with your knitting yarn, not to chat like friends. Most of the help here is American, but the ladies are British, and British servants among the gentry are trained to enter a room without knocking."

"How terrible!" Gabrielle frowned in revulsion. "I could not endure such lack of privacy."

Penelope did not answer, but just looked at her, and Gaby rose to her feet.

"Oh, very well." She sighed deeply. "I can. I will. Shall we move the chairs now?"

Each one shifted a large chair around, so they were opposite and near to the fire but far enough apart to permit both of them to stand and to sit without knocking their shins on the legs of the game table they placed between them.

Penelope put several balls of wool and an extra bone knitting needle on the table, then sat down in her chair and resumed knitting.

"Your poem 'Fulfillment,' " she mused. "I must admit it surprised me."

"Oh?"

Collectedly, and quite low, Penelope recited,

> No, stay, love,
> I'm here where I would be
> A-top you
> Riding on your knee.
>
> Oh God, love,
> I am about to burst . . .

> You're jesting
> Of course, I did—and first!
>
> Cry out, love,
> Cry long and loudly, too.
> What joy if
> I Could but enter you!
>
> Alas, love,
> Since it is not to be,
> I yearn, love
> Return . . . and enter me.

"For a virgin—which our mutual friend assures me you are, Mrs. Forsyth-Foote, you seem strangely learned and intuitive."

"Dear Lord, you do have an extraordinary gift of memory recall! As to myself, my mother thought it was a sad mistake to send girls into marriage completely ignorant about its physical aspects. She felt they should be educated about the . . . the niceties of the marriage bed and h-how the carnal act might be engaged in for pleasure as well as procreation. She knew of too many girls who were terrified on their wedding night and endured needless agony because they were unprepared and their husbands were often not much wiser. She believed pleasuring one's own self both before and during marriage was not sinful or why would God have created us as he does."

"Your mother sounds most remarkable. She must have been a woman of great sense and sensibility."

"She was. She—" Gaby swallowed the lump in her throat. "Penelope, did you really read 'Fulfillment' only once?"

"Only once, I promise you, Mrs. Forsyth-Foote. I think, Gabrielle—" Her mouth turned up at the corners—"the man you wed one day will be a most fortunate gentleman."

Twenty

As quickly as he stocked them, copies of *Amorous Verse* by a Lady of New York flew off the bookshelves in Mr. Gaines's print shop. A discreet notice in his prominent loyalist newspaper, the *New York Gazette,* announced an early second printing.

The identification of the "Lady of New York" became known even more speedily. Soon invitations to luncheons and tea parties, theater and evening parties began to pour into the house on Queen Street.

Gaby sat at the tea table one afternoon, holding seven hand-delivered notes.

"But I don't even know these people," she said with pretended bewilderment.

"What does it matter?" said Mrs. Torrington. *"They* know *you."*

Gaby stared at her blankly.

"I mean," Mrs. Torrington amended her statement, "they know *of* you."

"Oh, Mrs. Forsyth-Foote," Betty Arbuckle tittered, "what's the use of pretending? Everyone in this city knows the Lady of New York is *you!* You'll be invited everywhere," she added somewhat enviously.

"Why not attend and enjoy yourself, Gabrielle?" Charlotte Gray suggested to her friend. "You can't mope around the house by yourself forever."

"Humph!" uttered Mrs. Barnes and then added, surprisingly, "Mrs. Gray is right, you know."

"We live in a practical world," said Mrs. Torrington, seemingly to no one in particular. "It is apparent from your elegant dress"—she aimed this barb directly at Gaby—"that you are no longer in mourning for your husband—the gentleman, I presume, who made you so well-informed. Surely you would like to become acquainted with some of our brave *British* soldiers . . . a cut above your American variety, I would venture. Undoubtedly, you will find one at least who can—if you intend to write more verse of an amorous nature—further your education. Or, perhaps, you may be the one to further *his*."

Gabrielle shook her head slightly at Charlotte Gray, who gave every indication of being about to deliver a stinging rebuke to this bit of malice.

"Why, Mrs. Torrington, how gracious of you to remind me," said Gaby easily. "I am a great believer in learning for both sexes. Yes, indeed, you have convinced me. I believe I will accept most of these invitations. If you will excuse me, I must mend my pen and send out replies. I do hope I have a sufficient supply of fine paper." She held out the notes in her hand. "These are of such superior stock."

She ran upstairs to her sitting room, where Penelope sat, busy with her inevitable knitting.

"I told Mrs. Torrington—spiteful cat that she is—I planned to accept most of these invitations. Do you think I should?"

Penelope put down her knitting, accepted the handful of notes and carefully inspected each one, pronouncing her final verdict in one succinct word. "Excellent."

"*Should* I accept them all?" asked Gaby again as she slouched with unladylike ease in the chair facing her "maid."

"By no means . . . we must show great particularity," answered Penelope as she divided the notes into three separate piles. "And these"—she pointed—"are most definitely *no* . . . just as these"—she pointed again—"are most definitely *yes*."

"What about those in between?"

"The perhapses. We will take a day or two to consider; and I may consult . . ." She coughed delicately into a man-sized linen handkerchief tucked in her sleeve. "We must decide which—if any of them—may be fruitful."

"And on what," gurgled Gaby, "do you base your very definite decision?"

"The good they will do those we serve."

"Then, I think, *perhaps,* dear Penelope, you had better explain to me both the whys and the wherefores of yes, no, and in between."

"The best of these invitations"—Penelope indicated the *yes* pile—"is from Mrs. Loring."

She pronounced the name so impressively, Gaby expected her to elaborate further. She did not.

"Mrs. Loring," Gaby repeated. "I have heard her name mentioned several times, I believe, but I know nothing about the lady."

"The most important bit of information about Mrs. Loring is that the one thing she cannot rightly be called—despite pretenses to the contrary—is a lady. She is American and a loyalist. Her husband—a truly wicked man—has been appointed to the lucrative position of Commissary of Prisoners to the Army in New York. This position is his compensation for being cuckolded—apparently with no ill-will on either side—by General Sir William Howe."

"You mean the la-... Mrs. Loring is General Howe's mistress, and her husband profits by it?"

"She is indeed; he does indeed. And although"—she lowered her voice even more than usual—"her husband is detested for his cruelty to our poor captured soldiers and sailors, truth to tell, General Washington ought to be grateful to the wife. General Howe is completely under her spell. He neglects military duties because he much prefers her bed to what one can only presume to be a less energetical battlefield," she concluded primly and took up her knitting again.

Gaby wiped away tears of laughter. "You are a constant refreshment to me, Penelope. You appear so puritanical and proper, and you make your far-from-proper remarks with such composure."

Penelope smiled her usual decorous smile. "The highest-ranking officers are to be found at Mrs. Loring's evening parties . . . as well as wives, mistresses and older daughters; in short, a veritable garden of oysters. Many pearls can be plucked from such gardens as these, especially when the ladies sit together after late supper while the gentlemen remain at table, drinking prodigious quantities of port. If there is dancing afterwards, or you merely engage in a tête-à-tête with a soldier in his cups, much can be learned. Remember all you hear of such conversations to relate to me, even the most ridiculous of rumors. I will deliver the information. It will be the chore of others to separate the wheat from the chaff. And, Mrs. Forsyth-Foote," . . . She hesitated. "There is something I have been meaning to mention. It is most unlikely, but if ever *I* should be taken up, then *you* must be properly horrified that I am uncovered as a patriot. Not only must you disavow any knowledge of who and what I am, you must also express anger and disgust for being imposed on . . . and, of course, you will cease making contact with anyone else unless you are so instructed. I put the reference I gave you from my last employer in your dressing table drawer." Her eyes positively twinkled. "Keep it always."

"But, P-Penelope . . ."

"It is, as I said, a most unlikely contingency, but should it occur, those are your orders. Will you carry them out?"

"Yes, ma'am." Gaby sniffed. "But I—I don't want—"

"Nor do I, my dear," said Penelope, briskly matter-of-fact. Then she turned the discussion. "Now the reason for declining these two invitations is that the little you might learn would not compensate for the type of people with whom you would come in contact. Your friends and associates among the British and, more specifically, the American Tories, must be of the highest social standing. Selectivity will give you importance. The hostesses whose invitations you accept ought to feel themselves honored."

Gaby started giggling. Soon she was laughing out loud. Presently, she slid from her chair to the floor, her mirth uncontrolled.

When she recovered enough to wipe her eyes and desert her

prone position to kneel beside Penelope's chair, her voice was still far from steady.

"Forgive me, dear *dear* Penelope. Indeed, I was not laughing at you, only at the notion that I . . . oh heavens, I mustn't start myself off again; but when I consider that a short time ago I was a Massachusetts minister's dutiful daughter, with the stricter members of the congregation occasionally objecting to a scarlet ribbon in my hair. Then in just a hair's-breadth, I was in New Jersey, transformed by day to Aunt Emily's sweet little niece and going out at night, dressed in male attire, taking turns with near a dozen other women at flailing—with a right good will—the flabby naked bottom of a wife-beater. Lastly, almost overnight, I settled in New York, supposedly a Tory widow . . . despite a minor circumstance. I have never been wedded or bedded.

"It seems incidental that I truly am the author of *Amorous Verse*," Gaby admitted after a thoughtful pause, giving Penelope *her* turn to smile. "I never meant my poems to be considered—as they are—*salacious*. Salacious enough to bring me both praise and fame. So much praise and fame, in fact, that I honor lords and ladies, as well as high-born gentry and generals' whores, by accepting their invitations to dine and dance or join theater parties.

"Well . . ." She walked toward her wardrobe. "So be it. Let our own performance begin. You will have to advise me often about wardrobe, Penelope. And I am expecting," she reminded her saucily, "my lady's maid to give ample proof of that special genius Mrs. William Thomas Smith spoke of in the dressing of my hair."

"You may be sure I will, mum," said Penelope parodying behavior frowned on by American servants—an English maid's subservience.

Gaby swooped down on her and kissed her cheek impulsively, then gathered up the invitations. "You will have to critique my replies, too, I fear. I am unaccustomed to having my presence solicited at any formal occasion with quite such pomp and circumstance."

Twenty-one

> The moment after
> I heard laughter
> My heart told me
> I soon would see you.
>
> *More Amorous Verse*

After much discussion between the two, both mistress and maid decided that the Lady of New York should make her entrance onto the New York scene at Mrs. Loring's evening party.

They wanted to flesh out her portrait of a woman of the world in a gradual way, so Penelope agreed to her wearing the gown that Gaby suspected would always be her sentimental favorite.

She now had many elaborate costumes in her wardrobe. In British New York, a different type of garment was indispensable for each separate activity, walking, carriage rides, afternoon teas, suppers and evening soirees. Still, the dusty pink brocade with the organdy ruching that she had worn as attendant to Lydia at her wedding would always remain the wondrous one, the loveliest gown she had possessed until then. She found its inverted form of India print with fine chain stitching and French knots especially dashing.

In this gown she had been accepted by Mercy Enough for a role in the Wheel's activities. In this gown she had reaped the rewards of an education begun long ago in a small Massachusetts town by a mother who did not believe that a woman was merely an appendage to the male head of his household.

She need not accept the part of being only someone's daughter, raised to be someone's wife and to eventually complete the cycle by bringing forth children to give her identity as someone's mother.

In New Jersey Aunt Emily had indoctrinated her further. She had shown her that an unmarried woman sometimes had the power to be as independent as Mama, more so if she was a woman of property. She could own as well as manage lands and farms. She need not just cry out against injustice and ill-treatment but could exact retribution, partly to punish but also to prevent further abuse.

In this vibrant city of New York, she had received the greatest acceptance of her own personal worth. As well as being Pythias, secret patriot poet, she was an acknowledged woman of letters . . . famous . . . perhaps infamous, but very well known.

Even more incredibly, she was now considered an accepted link in an important chain, the burgeoning intelligence network that operated at risk and clandestinely in English-occupied New York. As much as any soldier, she served under General Washington in what was no longer a skirmish but full-scale combat to wrest the former thirteen colonies from the greedy fingers of Great Britain.

When her hired carriage arrived at Mrs. Loring's house, it had to line up behind three others. The opposite side of the road was similarly choked. After Gabrielle descended the carriage steps, she let down her skirts. A moment later she was forced to raise them again in order to mount the stone steps leading up to the red-brick Georgian residence.

The door was flung wide in welcome and a butler rushed forward immediately to offer solicitous help in the removal of her cloak. He waited expectantly and it took Gaby several seconds to realize why.

"Mrs. Forsyth-Foote," she said languidly, as though it was

absence of mind rather than lack of *savoir-faire* that had caused her to neglect to state her name for him to announce.

"Mrs. Forsyth-Foote!" he called out in an impressive bass voice. Immediately an elegantly clad lady came forward to say gushingly to Gaby, "My *dear*, at last! We have been *panting*, absolutely panting to make the acquaintance of the Lady of New York. Your book is *so* titillating, I read it from cover to cover at one sitting. More than once, I promise you."

She covered the lower half of her face with a fan of ivory sticks and black lace, brown eyes sparkling wickedly across at her guests. "Your poems are so *very* naughty, my dear, and so *very* delicious."

She lowered her fan and slapped it playfully across Gaby's knuckles. "Just see how everyone is staring. I did myself. We all expected you to be somewhat older than seven or eight and twenty."

Thank you, God. Thank you, Penelope, for the cosmetics and insisting on this atrocious wig, rejoiced Gaby, smiling with genuine delight at her hostess, who chattered on, "How unfair of you to be not only beautiful but younger. Dare I introduce you to Sir William? I warn you, my dear. He is taken."

The slap of the fan was not quite so playful this time. "Is there any *other* gentleman you would like to meet? I will most happily bring him to you."

Gaby fingered the small pink heart patch at the corner of her mouth. "I have heard too much of Sir William Howe's devotion to believe I could ever represent a danger to the lovely Mrs. Loring," she said in a husky voice, her smile and the words as well all combed with honey. "As for bringing a gentleman to me . . . I would rather prefer to look the field over and make my own pick. Is it not better for the innocent dear to think he has approached me of his own accord? I have always believed it starts the relationship off on a much better footing."

Just behind them the butler announced, "Captain Lord Francis Rawdon," and Mrs. Loring squeezed Gaby's hand and gave her a small push forward as she whispered quickly, "I do, indeed.

Good fortune then, *dear* Lady of New York . . . but remember, no poaching."

Her hostess hurried to greet the new arrival and Gaby advanced a few steps. There was so much noise and bustle in the drawing room just ahead of her, it was ridiculous of her to believe that somewhere to the left of the entrance way, she recognized the sound of one particular man's laughter.

Mere self-delusion because of one hackney ride, however unforgettable; one rather prolonged session of kissing, however ardent; and—oh, yes, one non-encounter at Fraunces Tavern.

There were so many British officers in New York, so large a number at this very house, she must not look for *him* around every corner, nor indulge in what was merely wish fulfillment.

She stood in the hallway, admonishing herself to be sensible. Once again, she heard the laughter and, no longer even *trying* to appear prudent or restrained, Gaby followed to where the laughter led.

She arrived at a large crowded parlor. In the far corner a middle-aged woman—with a wig to rival Gaby's own towering structure of powdered curls and puffs and pompadours—sat idly plucking the strings of a harp in no particular harmony. She was listening to the earnest conversation of a soldier half her age who stood over her, one hand placed intimately on a bare plump shoulder.

Across the room Gaby saw a stunning oak harpsichord that made her mother's spinet, hidden now in one of Aunt Emily's attics, appear more like a toy. At any other time, Gaby would have rushed over to examine the instrument more closely . . . even sit down and pick out a simple tune. Annabel had instructed her, and she sorely missed music.

Her main objective tonight, Gaby thought with a flash of humor, as she stood outside the music room, feeling somewhat at a loss, was presumed to be patriotic rather than melodic. Not only the cacophony of sound confused her. She was also bemused by the bewildering array of silk, satin and brocade-clad ladies chattering away to what seemed a swarm of soldiers, their red and blue uniforms liberally ornamented with gold.

Light feminine laughter mingled with heartier male tones.

For one fleeting, panicked moment, Gaby wanted to run away . . . no . . . rather she longed to see familiar faces and find herself in any familiar place . . . Aunt Emily's . . . Papa's study . . . even the house on Queen Street.

She forced herself to stay right where she was, deliberately taking long deep breaths. Remember who you are and why you are here at Mrs. Loring's tonight, she scolded fearful little Gaby Foote. After all the trouble taken on behalf of Mrs. Forsyth-Foote, all the time and money spent, she would never be able to live with the shame of having abandoned her first difficult assignment and forfeited the trust placed in her by Mercy Enough and the Wheel.

As Gaby's resolution revived, she heard him laugh again. Her head swiveled round ever so slightly. Although he was not standing so as to confront her directly, she had no trouble in picking him out from among a group of four men.

Impossible to forget that nose, which, on what seemed a long-past morning, she had considered a bit too long and slightly supercilious. Studying it now, she confirmed her own past judgment . . . but could not help calling to mind (with a fiery blush) how competently that nose had dealt with buttons and bows and ties that impeded access to tingling flesh.

She could still taste the lips that had so easily reduced her own lips to putty; and although she could not see them now, she remembered that even the shadowy interior of a hackney had not dimmed the vivid color of unusually deep blue eyes.

The blood drained from Gaby's cheeks at the dawning of a single self-evident fact.

The Wheel's sole reason for preparing her to be at Mrs. Loring's tonight was to further her solemn and sacred duty to meet British officers or American loyalists from whom any useful bit of information could be culled. *She,* from the very beginning of her stay in New York, had been deceiving herself as well as Mercy Enough and a host of other unknowns.

True, she was heart and soul an American patriot, determined to play her part in liberating America. Hypocrite that she was, however, her heart, not her head had dictated tonight's mission.

All along she had secretly hoped, prayed, *intended,* if she could, to ferret out one particular British officer . . . and not for love of country but for . . .

Oh, dear God, thought Gaby, who was Parson Foote's Bible-raised daughter, *I was seeking he whom my soul loveth.* Then, *No, no, one cannot love on the instant a chance-met stranger, an enemy stranger who mistook me for a fallen woman!*

Seconds later, the Gabrielle who was much more her mother's forthright, impulsive daughter treated this argument with the contempt she knew it deserved. *It is useless to say that I cannot do what I have already done!*

She loved him.

So be it!

It might be highly improper and foolishly impetuous, ridiculous as well as reckless, and certainly calculated to bring future heartbreak. Still, once she had acknowledged the truth to herself, she felt strangely at peace.

An officer standing near the harpsichord tried to catch her eye; she studiously avoided looking at him. A lieutenant near the window seemed inclined to join her; she turned away.

If I must choose a man as my first source for information, why should I not choose one who interests me rather than one who does not?

Recognizing—at last—the jolt of her heart and other symptoms for the sickness of love, she stood patiently in the doorway, her eyes fixed on him.

There was no doubt in her mind that soon he would come to her . . . she was willing it to happen.

Suddenly he became still, talking and laughing with his companions no longer. He leaned forward and put the glass he held on a table within stretching distance. And then, just as she had known would happen, his electrifying glance boldly challenged Gaby's. She tilted her chin up impudently and stared right back, unaware that the fire in her sooty dark eyes betrayed her interest.

In a moment he was standing before her, his body blocking the door. His quick glance took in her left hand (Mama would approve this use of her wedding ring, Gaby felt sure). He was able to bow and address her correctly.

"Good evening, madame."

"Good evening to you, Major," said Gaby, quite proud that there was not the slightest tremor in her voice.

A strolling couple wanted to leave the music room, and he made the duo's egress possible by flattening himself against Gaby. At once this three seconds of proximity brought to her mind the heated, repeated excitement of their shared hackney ride.

"Your voice tells me that you are an American."

"And yours . . . even without the uniform . . . that you are not."

"I assure you that I did not mean to disparage Americans. I admire your countrymen and regret that circumstances place us against one another. When all is said and done, we are Englishmen—and women."

"Then you are more charitable than I, sir, for I was born and lived most of my life in Boston. My husband's chief estate was not far from Concord where the first blood of this war was spilled. I am both angry and resentful to have been uprooted by rebellion, dislodged from my home by politics."

"New York is your home now?"

"So long as the British Army is here to protect me."

"Then I take it your husband is in one of the loyalist brigades?"

"No," Gaby said bluntly. "I am widowed."

Their eyes met and clung. An unmistakable message had been given and received.

"My dear Matthew was some twenty years my senior," she added gently, "too old, too untrained for military service, but since he was an outspoken loyalist, all our properties were confiscated by the rebels, so here I am a refugee; and I will be poor, I fear, until the Crown rules rightfully again."

"You are blocking my way, sir," said a testy voice behind them.

As they both moved out of the way, the major extended his arm, suggesting, "Let us find a more convenient and comfortable place to become acquainted."

Gaby placed her hand lightly on his arm. As they moved along the hallway, she glanced fleetingly upward and was surprised by the strange expression on his face. Even though she knew there could be no happy ending, her own heart leaped with passionate love.

Then, of course, she understood.

During their carriage ride, she had been Emily Washington, a whore.

Tonight, he had been instantly attracted to her; but at Mrs. Loring's, what was she but another American widow, much like her hostess in character? Attractive. On the catch. And, if the situation was to her advantage, wanton.

Disappointment at what she was, still mingled with desire. He had two alternatives . . . to woo her in a very different way or decamp with all possible speed.

Little Gaby Foote would have liked to scratch out his eyes—his damned mesmerizing blue eyes—for what he was thinking. Mrs. Forsyth-Foote would lend her smiles and charming ways and seductive manners to advance the flirtation.

Twenty-two

> Most women would make a bid
> Just as I did
> For a brief time of happiness.
>
> *More Amorous Verse*

Although they walked arm in arm, Gaby became aware, when they arrived at a green and white striped sofa in a curtained enclosure, that she had, in actuality, been led. Overhanging velvet drapes lent an air of privacy—even intimacy—to the corner.

In her mind, she ticked off the significance of certain facts.

One, he was familiar with the house. *Libertine!*

Two, he knew of the existence as well as the direct way to this charming retreat, an indication of his having used it before. *Lecherous lobsterback!*

Three, she had already been designated as a woman who would not raise any question of decorum about being one-half of a snug little twosome. *Pigeon-brained Briton!* she reflected, restraining her inclination to slap him. Glacially calm, she left the opening gambit up to him.

He obliged her immediately. "If you have been living in New York for some time, I cannot understand why I have never met you before tonight."

"Why are you so certain that you have not?"

His answer proved as disappointingly predictable as her question. "Do you really believe that any man, having seen you once, could so soon forget?"

"I think," Gaby parried quite sweetly, as she tilted up her chin, dark eyes gleaming with challenge, "that on such occasions sincerity goes out the window and a gentleman is prone to say anything a lady wants to hear."

He laughed delightedly. "You would make an excellent soldier, ma'am. Straight on the offensive. Never retreat."

"There are so many restrictions placed on us, we women must, of necessity, make war in our own way," said Gaby, now demure.

"I doubt then that there are any words of my own, convincing enough to make you believe in *my* sincerity. Perhaps you will be less distrustful of an Elizabethan poet's."

With barely a pause, and as though reciting poetry was the most ordinary pastime for a soldier, he leaned back, speaking softly:

> There is a lady sweet and kind
> Was never face so pleased my mind
> I did but see her passing by
> And yet . . .

He paused and looked across at her inquiringly. Gaby, had listened to the astonishing words with her heart taking wing; yet it was Mrs. Forsyth-Foote, perforce, who replied to the uniform of the enemy.

"I see I must believe in your sincerity since you were honest enough to omit the final pledge."

"You know the poem?"

"Yes, Major, we *can* read in the colonies; I know the poem."

"And yet . . . I love her till I die."

"I thank you for the vow . . . but shall not hold you to it, sir."

"Not *sir*, if you please, definitely not *Major*. I don't wish my rank to put such distance between us. Rhoads is my name, Darcy Rhoads."

"I am Mrs. Forsyth-Foote."

"And does not Mrs. Forsyth-Foote have a given name?"

"Certainly. It is Gabrielle, but my position . . . my widowhood . . . demands certain formalities. Men can afford to be cavalier about the conventions. Women cannot. Regretfully, it must be Mrs. Forsyth-Foote."

"I am yours—however unwilling—to command, but it is difficult to make one's eternal pledges of devotion to a Mrs. Forsyth-Foote. Does it not strike a discordant note even for you? Dear Mrs. Forsyth-Foote, bewitching Mrs. Forsyth-Foote, *yet will I love her till I die.* Even in my own ears, I do not sound convincing. Now the name Gabrielle has infinite possibilities. Close your eyes—magnificent eyes they are, too, if I may be permitted the opinion. Of a Gabrielle one might easily say, 'Her gestures, motion, and her smiles—' "

"I know, I know. 'Her wit, her voice *your* heart beguiles'; but it is still Mrs. Forsyth-Foote."

"Very well, Mrs. Forsyth-Foote, I hear and I obey, but I still think—hell and damnation!"

"I beg your pardon."

"No, I am afraid I must beg yours for speaking so, but I was taken by surprise. I suddenly realized the context. I knew from the first your name sounded familiar . . . and the reason has just come to me. Mrs. Forsyth-Foote. Are you not—?"

He paused, but Gaby chose not to help him out.

"I have heard—" He spoke only after she allowed a full minute of silence to slip by. "I have been told that Mrs. Forsyth-Foote is the Lady of New York who has written a book of poems called *Amorous Verse.*"

"Many people in this city," said Gaby enjoyably, "believe the same thing. Do you?"

He studied her thoughtfully for a moment. "I believe in either possibility. You have the spirit to be making a May game of everyone by allowing them to believe what is not true . . . but also the spirit to have written a book that has set all of New York on its ears." He finished with entire good humor, "My poor efforts to woo you with poetry must have entertained you vastly."

"Major—very well, Darcy, if you prefer, since we are alone—you must do yourself more justice. No one in an officer's uniform—or even out of it, now that I think back—has ever wooed me with poetry. I assure you, it is an exceedingly potent device. Very soothing to one's self-image. Flattering, too. In fact, almost unique. It gives me quite a different impression of you."

"That one can be a fop as well as a soldier?"

"Not at all, sir. Rather, I admired your courage. You were not ashamed to be yourself. You felt poetical and you gave rein to the fancy, at the risk of possible ridicule. Now in my eyes, *that* is true valor and exceeds the boldness needed to take a man into battle."

"Gabrielle . . . Gabrielle . . ."

Just the sound of her name, spoken twice in a husky undertone, and Gaby felt control of the situation and of him slipping away. She was unsurprised at what happened next. From the very beginning, *this,* too, was intended to happen!

This was the act of being not-so-much-taken as snatched into his arms. She saw devils dancing in both blue eyes just inches away from her own. Then there was no distance at all and only one reality. His two hands held the back of her head in an iron grip . . . and he kissed her . . . and kissed her . . . and would doubtless, if not rebuffed, have continued to kiss her the whole night through.

After a period of complete self-indulgence, Gaby finally and fiercely summoned the strength to pull away and push him back to his side of the couch.

"For heaven's sakes!" she said. "Haven't you any sense? This is a public room. Someone, *any*one could happen on us at any moment."

He was breathing hard and fast but managed to chuckle. "Is that your only objection?"

"I can hardly say I minded," Gaby snapped, "after participating so enthusiastically in your sport. Nevertheless, the other objection holds true."

"It was not sport."

To avoid his eyes, Gaby contrived to make a long fussy business of patting the curls of her wig into place and straightening her skirts.

"Don't pretend you did not hear me, Lady Faint Heart. And I *am* surprised a woman of your mettle is now unwilling to look me in the eye! I said that kissing you was not sport, and I spoke the truth. I kissed you because it seemed the most important and desirable thing in the world for me to do at the time. Because from the moment I looked at you across the room, I knew the inevitability of what would happen. And do not tell me it was an *un*shared thought because I detest liars. We both experienced the same emotions. We both knew it was not mere sport. Now admit it to be so or I vow I will hold you here and kiss you until we attract everyone in the house to the scene, and *that,* I promise you, would certainly be the talk of the city come tomorrow."

Gaby looked deep into both blue eyes. "It was not sport," she said, "and I *am* the Lady of New York. I wrote *Amorous Verse* and I love Elizabethan poetry."

It was a while before he stopped eating her up with his eyes. "Why did you tell me?" he asked presently, the eyes now half-shuttered.

"Because"—she managed not to wince—"you hate liars and . . ."

"And?"

"You would have ferreted out the secret for yourself."

He laughed and took one of her hands and pressed a swift kiss into the palm. "Virtuous by necessity," he said buoyantly. "And an honest woman for all that. Your price is above rubies, my dearest Mrs. Forsyth-Foote. Now, having returned my kisses with an ardor I appreciate more than I can say, will you not give me the lesser but nonetheless much-desired privilege of calling you Gabrielle?"

"I will take it under advisement, *sir,* and render my decision at another time."

"Tomorrow, perhaps? Will you lunch with me? Dine with me? Perhaps go to the theater? Any or all of the above?"

DARCY'S KISS

Gaby shook her head, smiling in slight derision. "Your military duties must be quite arduous. How do you keep up your strength?"

Very good, Gaby. A neat and spontaneous effort at getting information.

"Now, now, my sweet, such mockery does not become you. Winter is with us, and the war—as it is fought here—will have to wait on better weather."

Disappointing, but at least, I tried. I think I am beginning to get the hang of it.

He stood up and held out both hands to help her to her feet. The moment she was upright, she moved quickly away from him.

He laughed softly. "Never fear, my love. At the moment my intentions are of the most honorable or rather *must* be honorable for lack of any other possibility. Since we may not kiss, perhaps we should resist temptation by repairing to the supper room."

He held out his arm, murmuring, "We would more or less be substituting one sort of appetite for another."

Gaby had never felt less like eating. Reaction to all of the evening's emotions had been, to say the least, unsettling. She felt decidedly queasy.

"Thank you, no." She was about to add that she planned to leave at once, then stopped, aghast at her own incompetence. Penelope and Mercy Enough had made it quite clear that many hours and many full days and evenings would be spent without producing any news or facts of value. Seemingly wasted time should not trouble her since the merest rumor might have value.

Even so—to come home from her first foray into the world of spying with nothing more to offer than her belief that Mrs. Loring would brook no competition where Sir William was concerned . . . how humiliating!

She hardly proposed to mention that Major Darcy Rhoads kissed as competently on a couch as in a carriage!

"I must excuse myself for a few minutes. If you could get me something to drink when I return . . ." Her hands fluttered toward her waist. "Something to ease my . . . me . . ."

He withdrew his arm so as to be able to look down at her more directly. "Gabrielle, are you unwell? Forgive me, I did not mean to go so far with my teasing. My Uncle has always said that one of my jokes would get me into serious trouble one day. Have I tormented you too much?"

The forbidden name sounded all too sweet in her ears. Gaby gathered up her scattered wits; and her determination not to be overset produced its own cure. She gave him a bright shining smile.

"La, sir, you have a strange notion of me—an entirely false and misleading one, I might add, if you think a little friendly teasing would have such an effect on me. Rather, I would be planning my revenge. We have both tilted at windmills as well as at each other this night, I believe, to our mutual enjoyment. If anything distresses me, it is too tight lacing and the excitement of the evening. I passed the first eighteen months of my mourning in great seclusion. I must accustom myself again to crowded rooms and such continuous noisy conversation."

She put out one hand to him and he pressed it warmly in both of his. She saw a certain look in his eye and slowly shook her head. "No salutations in public, Major Rhoads, not even gentlemanly kisses on the hand." She withdrew it gently. "Let us rendezvous in the music room after you fetch a plate for yourself . . . and for me, a beverage and perhaps some biscuits."

She spent a few minutes in the retiring area designated for the ladies and then made her way back to the music room. It was not so crowded as before. A trio of young officers stood near the long windows, talking with great animation. An elderly couple sat together near the fire, not talking at all.

Gaby made her way over to a handsome rosewood harpsichord. It was near enough to the lieutenants, without unduly attracting their attention.

She touched the keys softly, straining to hear anything that might be significant.

"I tell you it was a damned disgrace. Opportunity . . . victory itself was in our grasp. We had the entire rebel army stranded on

Long Island, ours for the plucking. Any other general would have been court-martialed for failing to press his advantage. He permitted . . . no, he practically offered that devil Washington and his motley crew safe passage out of Long Island. Now he stands over us on Harlem Heights, crowing!"

"I have heard it said that Sir William has too much sympathy for the damned rebels. *Englishmen like us,* he's been heard to call them. If they were like us, we would not be in this Godforsaken country!"

"Lower your voices, both of you. For God's sakes, have you forgotten where we are? Such accusations should not be aired in public."

The soldiers looked about hastily. The elderly couple appeared frozen in the same immobility; and Gaby calmly turned the page of the music stand in front of her and bent to the keys, playing a little louder.

"Speaking of courts-martial," added the peacemaker of the group, "Lord Francis was telling me of the vastly entertaining ones they have on—I think it was—Staten Island. It appears the maidens hereabouts have a great objection to rape and do not bear it with the proper fortitude."

"I can understand objection to rape from a common soldier or a sausage-eating Hessian, but how can such coarse provincials not be honored when anyone above sergeant's rank condescends to dally with them?"

"Ah well, there will be plenty of little British bastards born of this war."

"But they will grow up to be big bastardly *Americans.*"

"Not after we win the war and bring this wretched land to her knees."

Twenty-three

> I was stricken with a sudden strange ailment . . .
> Although it had never come on me before
> I somehow knew
> There existed no antidote
> For such sickness of love as I felt on the instant
> Only you!

Gaby continued to sit at the harpsichord, apparently absorbed in her music and impervious to everything going on around her. This business of being a spy was more complicated than she had realized.

She was trembling with rage and dared not reveal it. She must sit, looking sweet and insipid and unaware when she would have liked to break something heavy over each beastly British head. She longed to be able to rant and scream and swear.

Was it possible Darcy Rhoads talked like that when he was in company with his friends? As though Americans were inferior beings, as though rape was of no particular consequence; and a girl was not a person but a thing, to be used, brutally violated and then made the object of crude jests.

No, impossible. Her instinct could never have betrayed her so! She could not have lain happily (twice now) in the arms of a man who shared even a like thought or feeling or expressed the point of view of the trio of uniformed thugs who had discreetly discarded political discussion and were now whooping with laughter as they described the physical assets of American females, not knowing there was one in their midst.

As soon as Major Darcy Rhoads stepped into the room, holding a single glass, while a servant followed with a round mahogany tray that bore another glass and several plates of food, he both saw and heard his junior officers. He bade the footman set the tray on a game table nearer to the fire and crossed swiftly to Gaby.

"If you will excuse me just for a moment," he addressed her quite formally and left before she could answer.

The lieutenants were not mindful of his presence until he spoke.

"Gentlemen—though the word seems hardly to apply in this case since your discourse, as well as your manners, belong more to the barracks or a street brawl than to a private party. If you cannot hold your liquor, you should not drink. If you cannot act so as not to disgrace the uniform you wear, you should perhaps consider another profession. I suggest you take leave of our hostess now. Kindly report to headquarters tomorrow promptly at eleven. Ask for Major Rhoads."

In total silence, the junior officers almost bolted from the room. The elderly couple nodded their heads in unison at the Major and he bowed back. Gaby jumped up from the harpsichord bench and hurried to meet him halfway, both her hands held out. He took them in his and pressed her fingers hard, but it was a most pleasant pain.

"Oh, thank you, thank you. I was furious. I wanted *so* badly to confront them myself, but it would have made a frightful scene. I am, after all, American, no matter where my sympathy lies in this quarrel with the mother country."

Totally true, Gaby, no lie there!

He threw back his head and laughed aloud. "Shall I summon them and lend you my sword? I would not want to frustrate a budding Boadicea."

"No, indeed. You vanquished them single-handedly. It was a

masterly speech. Will they be shaking in their polished boots tomorrow at eleven?"

"If they are not, they very soon will be."

"Good! I would hate for you to be too lenient. If you are to be found at headquarters tomorrow," she added, amazed at her own ability to dissemble, "I see that Sir William does occasionally require your services?"

"Occasionally."

"What would you have done had I accepted some of your invitations—ones that interfered with military duty?"

"Thrown myself on the mercy of Sir William."

"Who occasionally forgets military duties, too?"

"No, no, my dear, you are not going to embroil me in any discussion of that hot potato. Come, my wine is going flat, hot food is getting cold and cold food warm. I brought a little brandy to settle your stomach and nerves, or whatever it was that ailed you, but you seem to me to be quite healthy and glowing."

"Happily true, but let us pretend otherwise! I have never tasted brandy, and I would like the experience."

"One's first sip of brandy . . . a notable event. Here is your glass. Clink it against mine—so—and we will drink a toast to your eyes."

"Not to my magnificent eyes? I am disappointed."

"I stand corrected. To your magnificent eyes, Mrs. Forsyth-Foote."

"To your blue ones, Major."

He pulled out a chair for her and then sat down in the one opposite with the game table between them.

As she raised the glass to her lips, he reminded her hastily, "Take small sips at first . . . it is heady stuff for the unaccustomed."

Gaby tipped her glass slightly and barely lapped her tongue in the brandy. Major Rhoads smothered a smile.

"It's strong," she said, "but rather fruity. How strange. Not at all what I thought it would be."

"I chose peach brandy. I am sorry that your first experience is disappointing."

Gaby took a tentative sip. "Not exactly disappointing. I think perhaps"—she looked at him questioningly—"it is an acquired taste?"

"I would say so," he agreed gravely, holding out a plate. "Would you care for a biscuit?"

"Thank you." Gaby selected one and nibbled at it, then absentmindedly took a hearty swallow of the brandy.

Her eyes watered, her mouth stung, her throat burned and delicious heat invaded her body.

"Heavens!" she said to him happily. "That *was* a notable experience, thank you, Major Rhoads."

"You are more than welcome, Mrs. Forsyth-Foote."

"Tonight," she offered grandly, "you may call me Gabrielle."

"I will be more than happy to do so, if you still give me leave when the effect of the brandy has worn off."

Gaby looked at the small amount left in her glass and drank it down. "When will that be?" she asked him.

"Well, keep in mind"—he studied her thoughtfully—"that I am not an expert judge of ladies in their cups—but I should say no more than a quarter of an hour."

"A quarter of an hour." Not very long, but belatedly she remembered one of Penelope's cautions.

"As Mrs. Forsyth-Foote, you must sip a little wine now and then, but never overmuch. Let others drink and talk. You must drink sparingly; your purpose is to listen. You endanger others, not just yourself if you do not guard your tongue."

Oh, dear Lord! My first night out as a spy and I have had too much to drink.

"Be careful whom you trust. Be always on your guard. Be seemingly friendly to anyone you meet casually, in the military or where you live, but always be wary—even of yourself."

Heavens above! I am an abysmal failure. This man—this enemy officer has only to look at me, and my heart turns over. He smiles, and my heart spins. He takes my hand and my heart leaps up. He sounds too British and my heart plummets.

"I think," said Gaby, pronouncing each word precisely, "that I must go home immediately."

"Good God! What have I said? What have I done?"

"Not you," she answered. "I am thinking of me. A woman may express very foolish notions in a quarter of an hour's time. I do not," she concluded with great dignity, "wish to appear foolish."

"My dear Mrs. Forsyth-Foote." He had risen himself and rounded the table. His hands were on her shoulders, pressing her down in the chair. "A less foolish woman than you I have yet to meet. If you need reassurance still, then you remain altogether silent while *I* talk of many things, some foolish, some that are not. If my tongue lags—which it seldom does—you can always ask a question that requires a long answer."

Having been easily persuaded, Gaby sat down again and so did the major. He took out his pocket watch and set it on the table.

"I will pay strict attention to the time," he said with the utmost seriousness, though she could detect a smile behind the words. "Let me speak first of you. You are an enchanting woman, Mrs. Forsyth-Foote, and I an enchanted."

"Thank you," said Gaby faintly.

He shook his head. "Such courtesies as thank-you to any comment of mine are not required. We will consider them said. You are a captivating woman, Mrs. Forsyth-Foote, and I am captivated."

"Th—" began Gaby, then remembered and held her tongue.

"The variety of your moods . . . your wit . . . your charm . . ." He paused for an instant to consider them all. "Your eyes, as I believe I have mentioned at least once this evening, are magnificent, in terms of shape and color; but even more remarkable is their look of bright inquiring intelligence. Your conversation—except now and then when you remind yourself to be more correct, a tendency I deplore—has the added spice of that same intelligence. Is there anything more you would like to know about yourself?"

Before Gaby could utter a word, he answered his own question aloud. "Rhoads, old boy, is there any other part of her you should describe?"

"Good Lord!" he then said to Gaby. "I haven't uttered a word about your beauty. I suppose most women would want me to do so?

"But then"—now he appeared to be arguing with himself—"she is delightfully unlike most other women." He pondered a moment. "Not *that* much unlike. I had better put it to the test."

The major looked squarely at Gaby. "You may answer just this one question of mine," he told her. "Would you care to discuss your beauty?"

"I—if *you* wish to," she said cravenly.

"Very well, then. The fact is, I would never call you *pretty*. Pretty is a paltry word. No woman of distinction should desire any such trifling description as that she is pretty. And yet . . ."

He pushed back his plate, planted his elbows casually on the table and rested his chin in his hand while surveying her face and neck. "Yet you are not precisely beautiful."

Gabrielle, who had never in her life believed she had any claim to be called a beauty, was affronted by this opinion, although she said not a word but held her lips tightly together.

With difficulty, suppressing his laughter, he continued his summation. "The true beauty of your face lies in the harmony of *all* your features rather than the perfection of each separate one. It mirrors your emotions; it is lively and animated. You took my arm when we walked because it is the custom, but you no more needed it . . . you, so vital and vibrant, hardly need a man's assistance to guide your footsteps. And, in conclusion, Madame Gabrielle Forsyth-Foote, I cannot believe that Divinity did not play a large part in the fashioning of your figure."

He dropped his elbows and lifted his fork. "Only seven minutes to go, but I am in need of sustenance. And my throat"—he lifted his wineglass—"is considerably parched. I suspect that *I* am considerably high-flown while you are the more sober of the two of us; but if I am intoxicated, *you,* not the wine must be the cause. May I help you to some of this shrimp . . . or perhaps the cold lobster . . . before I serve myself?"

"No, I thank you," said Gaby primly, and it was her turn to suppress a smile. "Around Boston way, it used to be said that we had in our colony a surfeit of both lobsters and lobsterbacks."

He helped himself to a generous portion of the shellfish. "Now that," he said, "is exactly what I mean. One wonders—perhaps, even fears, but never knows what you are going to say next. You enjoy sticking pins in a man's pretensions, do you not?"

"In anyone's . . . man or woman," said Gaby with false innocence. "Have we many minutes to go? I seem to be coming down from the clouds."

"Another three or four. Would you like to ask some questions? I promised that you might."

"Yes, I would. Just as soon as I try these apple tartlets you did not eat. Mrs. Loring's pastry chef must be superlative."

He watched, tenderly amused, as she nibbled all around the crust rather like a child, saving the succulent fruited part in the middle for last.

"My question is this: What is your opinion of rape?"

"I beg your pardon."

"Rape. As a member of the sex that is the aggressor in such matters, what is your opinion of the forcible violation of a woman—against her will—by a member of the enemy army fighting her country?"

"There can only be one opinion for a man of decency." His slow-burning anger began to come to a boil. "It is a dastardly, cowardly, brutal and criminal act. By any chance, is your real question whether I condone the rape of American women by British soldiers and Hessians?"

"I suppose so."

"I thought perhaps it might be; and since your quarter of an hour is up, we can now quarrel without any limitations on speech."

"Is it necessary for us to quarrel?" Gaby asked naively.

"If you did not know—without asking—the answer to such a question, then most certainly we *are* going to quarrel. I was marveling at the great strides forward in our acquaintance we had made in just one night, dismissing the usual boring persiflage of small talk."

"I must ask you to forgive me," said Gaby in a very small voice, "but, you see, the lieutenants—the ones you dismissed—they were talking *so* . . . I can't even begin to describe my feelings. They laughed merrily about the *honor* for a provincial woman of being violated by an officer. They boasted of all the little British bastards who will be born of this war. I was quite ill with rage. It made me wonder for a moment if I had chosen the wrong side."

He took her hands across the table. "If you forgive my temper, which is sometimes hasty, then I forgive you for not understanding what manner of man I am. We all have our moments of doubt, many uncomfortable moments about the rights and wrongs of this war. I cannot leave my regiment in the middle of a fight in America, however dubious I am about the cause that brings us here. As soon as duty and honor permit, I intend to resign my commission and prepare myself for my future life. My uncle wrote in his last letter, how much he wanted me to be home at Ashford Hall to begin my education as a landholder."

"Why an uncle?"

"I cannot even remember my mother, she died so young, and my father followed her when I was only ten. My father's elder brother Lord Percival Ashford, has been father, mother, guardian and friend the greater part of my life."

"You spoke of being a landholder. Is your uncle without children of his own?"

"His first wife died in childbed. After twenty years of marriage to Aunt Charlotte, his second countess, there have been no children. Before I left America, my uncle pointed out to me how very unlikely he was to beget a son of his own. He was grateful, he said, for the blood tie that made me his heir because I had always been a son to him in affection."

"What a kind, sensitive way to express his feelings!" said Gaby with ready sympathy.

The major nodded agreement before saying quietly, "The changing life of the army, the excitement of the unknown suited me very well at one time, but I will more than welcome the next stage of my existence. I want stability in my life now. I like to think of my children growing up, as I did, as my father and uncle did, at Ashford Hall."

He smiled ruefully. "I used to snicker at the portrait gallery, where any number of the Earls of Linley and their countesses and children hung row on row; and now I think I must indeed be approaching my sober years because I think of the gallery quite fondly."

"Your uncle's wife . . . has she been as fond an aunt as Lord Ashford is an uncle?"

"Despite her disappointment about not bearing sons, she has always been more than kind."

"But not, perhaps, loving?"

"She is not *un*loving, but she has a shy nature and it is hard for her to show affection even where she feels it strongly."

"Often, when I hear the British ladies in our lodgings on Queen Street speak of their growing years, I am amazed. English gentry's way of life seems incomprehensible to me. It certainly does not promote loving relationships between parents and children. Nurses, nannies and servants in their earliest life. Next, governesses and tutors, and later far-away schools. Brothers and sisters leading lives so separate, they hardly know one another . . . or their parents."

"In that, too, I was fortunate. My father kept me by him after he lost my mother and later he supervised my education himself. My uncle hired tutors and set up a small school for me at Ashford Hall. My best friend was his estate manager's son. We went to Cambridge, I to enjoy myself, he to study law, under my uncle's patronage."

He said thoughtfully, "I never gave it much consideration—my own life was so different—but I dare say you are right." His eyes rested on her warmly. "Certainly, I would not have liked to be as little acquainted with my family as any number of my friends are to theirs."

"Major." Gaby stood up. "I have had a delightful evening, but this time my wish to go home is a very real one. I am so weary that I will either fall asleep or begin to bore you. I should like to leave before you come to the conclusion that you were previously too lavish in your praise of my company . . . as well as my person."

Immediately, he was on his feet, too, smiling at her with such tenderness, Gaby had to blink back tears. He did not utter a single one of the platitudes men are likely to keep in stock for use at such times.

Instead, he came to her and offered his arm, which this time she accepted gratefully. As they walked to the front hallway, he spoke low but distinctly:

> I did but see her passing by
> And yet . . .
>   and yet . . .
>   and yet . . .

Twenty-four

> On our short hackney ride
> Poor Emily was so beguiled
> This sheltered Massachusetts miss
> Fell in love at just first kiss.
>
> *More Amorous Verse*

On learning that she had arrived at Mrs. Loring's house in a hackney, Major Rhoads offered to escort her home. When Gaby insisted that it was not necessary, he stifled all her objections with a single piercing look and a single spoken word. "Hush!"

As though I were a child, Gaby told herself, while another part of her brain dictated a very different message. *In his eyes, you are anything but a child.*

A footman was sent to flag down a hackney, a maid to fetch her cloak. There were good-byes to be said. Major Rhoads expressed his thanks to Sir William, who stood inches away while Gaby was expressing courteous thanks to her hostess for a most enjoyable evening.

She was staring at the general of all the British forces with a somewhat horrified fascination when Mrs. Loring said to her in a sly little whisper, "So Major Rhoads is the pick of the field. Well done."

"He is personable and quite pleasant company," Gaby answered low and calmly.

"And the fact that he is heir to an English earldom is unimportant?" Sir William's mistress trilled. "Well, good fortune to you, dear Lady of New York. I think you have chosen wisely; and I hope we will have the pleasure of your company soon again. We are very social in this city, I assure you. Some of my other guests quite long to meet you, but I heard from many that the major could not be pried from your side."

Uttering the other commonplaces exchanged on such occasions, Gaby took her leave of Mrs. Loring, thankful to be finally out of the house.

A few minutes later, having given Major Rhoads her direction, so he could relay it to the coachman, Gaby was almost overpowered by a sense of having experienced all of this before . . . but, of course, she had.

She was penned inside a hackney with a British officer . . . not *any* British officer but this particular one. Her hands and feet were chilled, her heart was thumping erratically, and all her senses were concentrated, all her being consumed by this one man.

It was startling, yet somehow not unexpected to have him reach over unceremoniously to take hold of her and deposit her "where you belong, my very dear Mrs. Forsyth-Foote."

"Where she belonged"—not unsurprisingly—turned out to be his lap.

It had all happened before . . . the breathless kisses . . . and the exploration of anatomical parts. She had never known till the previous carriage ride in his company that they were rare sources of delight.

Oh, dear Lord in Heaven! While his hands were busy with her lacings, there he was again, using that long nose of his to deal with clothing that impeded any effort to become quite familiar with bare flesh.

Without remembering quite how it happened, she was off his lap, flat on her back, and he was lying half across her, his blue eyes blazing away at her with an emotion even the inexperienced Gaby could recognize as passion.

He wanted her . . . here and now!

"Oh, my God!" A faint moan escaped the lips of Parson Foote's well-bred, well-brought-up virgin daughter. *I want him, too!*

"Please stop. Please sit up." Her hands, trying to thrust him off, were not a convincing repudiation, but her words were something in the nature of a bucket of cold water emptied over their heads. "We will arrive at my lodgings in five minutes."

"Hell and the devil confound it!" he roared, as Gaby was released from the body that had pinned hers down.

Tears came to her eyes. Release did not spell relief . . . she felt cold and alone, bereft and deprived.

Darcy was sitting up, his face shadowed. "When will I ever learn?" he asked bitterly.

"I—don't understand."

"Well, if you don't," he snarled, "you are more milk and water and less flesh and blood than I thought."

"Indeed?"

"I suppose I owe you an apology, but I am not exactly in an apologizing mood. I have already been humbled enough."

"Humbled?"

"Yes, humbled. For one, I should know better than to start something which common sense tells me that I do not have a prayer of finishing. Two, I seem to share hackneys with more than my share of nubile women in this blasted city. Are *you* going to disappear, too, and never be seen again?"

Gaby had gotten herself more or less neatened up and was sitting very upright. "Is that what happened to your previous lady?" she asked with a touch of disdain.

"Yes and no."

"Indeed?" Not so much haughty as condescending. "I was not aware the two could go together."

"She disappeared. That's the *yes*. The *no* is that she wasn't my lady. To be specific," he added glumly, "she was not a lady at all, just an enticing little chit who probably found someone bet- . . . but that's neither here nor there."

"Were you trying to avoid the use of the word *whore* to spare my tender sensibilities?" asked Gaby icily.

"I take it you are trying to tell me that your sensibilities are not that tender?"

"Yes."

"Very well then, Mrs. Forsyth-Foote. On a morning that now seems eons ago, I shared a carriage ride with a lovely American minx, who I *almost* made love to. She was—since you claim to prefer plain speaking—not exactly a whore, but something . . . somewhere in between . . . and a very snug armful for all that."

Gaby bit her under lip, and the hands concealed underneath her cloak turned into claws.

You smug, cocksure Englishman. She is so well-remembered you cannot recognize her when she is in your arms. What's in a name? Emily Washington. Mrs. Forsyth-Foote. By either name, a momentary diversion for a soldier.

"And I?" she asked aloud. "Am I something in between, sir, that you consider *me* fair game in a hackney, too?"

"Don't be a fool!" he snapped at the same moment the carriage stopped. They sat still, looking at one another. "The next time I try to make love to you, I shall choose more suitable surroundings."

She recognized the storm signals in his eyes and had not forgotten his admission of a hasty temper, so she knew it was rather daring of her to ask. "Because I am something in between or because you hope for a more fortunate outcome?"

It was hard to distinguish each word because his upper teeth were scraping against the lower, but the gist of the message was unmistakable. "Mrs. Forsyth-Foote, you are trying my patience."

Gaby wished she had Mrs. Loring's lace and ivory fan to cover the lower half of her face. It would have made her smile more flirtatious, her speech more effective. "How distressing for you, Major Rhoads. The thought of your anger has me all a-tremble, of course."

To her surprise and pleasure—there was no spice, she had always thought, to a man without a sense of humor—after one fiery glance, the teeth stopped their scraping and he laughed both long and lustily.

Gaby allowed him his enjoyment while she sat, quiet and rather passive.

"What are you thinking about?" he asked presently, wiping his eyes with a fine linen handkerchief.

"I was planning to buy a fan when I shop tomorrow . . . cream lace, I think . . . yes, I believe I would prefer cream to black."

"A fan! Why in the world would you sit beside me making plans to purchase a fan? What has that to do with you and me?"

"More than you might think," Gaby murmured.

The sense of humor showed signs of slipping.

"I will buy you all the fans in New York if you will be kind enough to stop going on about them."

"Thank you, sir, but I doubt it would be *comme il faut* for me to accept such a personal and extravagant gift as all the fans in New York . . . or even one."

"You accepted my kisses and I don't believe *they* were more proper than a lace fan!"

"Accept!" Gaby repeated, righteously enraged. "You *inflicted* your kisses on me, sir."

A smile tugged at the corners of his mouth. He leaned against the carriage back, arms folded. They had neither of them noticed that the hackney driver was waiting patiently in front of the dwelling on Queen Street.

Presently, Gaby uttered a little sigh. "Not true," she admitted. "I did accept them. If I had truly wished to, I could have stopped you at any time."

He took her hand and brought it to his lips, then gently restored it to her lap. "I said your price was above rubies," he told her caressingly. "Remember always in our relationship that unshared passion is empty and there is no zest at all in unwanted kisses."

"What relationship? No, don't tell me."

"Very well, minx I will not. Perhaps it will be *you* who tells me."

Gaby's color heightened at this outrageously self-satisfied opinion.

"You are getting your nubile New York women confused," she

said tartly. "Minx was the in-between woman who disappeared from both your hackney and your life."

"Well, praise God, *you* cannot disappear from my life. The Lady of New York is much too public a person. Have you noticed, by the way, that this conveyance has stopped? I presume we have arrived."

At his casual command, the driver waited while he escorted Gaby up the steps. "I shall take note of the way you are greeted. A servant's greeting is always a good clue," he added confidingly as he escorted Gaby up the steps.

This servant's greeting was completely American as to voice and familiar manner. "Bless me, Mrs. Forsyth-Foote, if you are not as fine as a new-minted sixpence. I was that provoked, I did not get to see you leave. The ladies can hardly wait until tomorrow to hear all about your evening."

Gaby turned to the major and held out her hand. "Well, sir, do I live here?"

"The most skeptical of men could not doubt it. Will you dine with me tomorrow night at Fraunces Tavern?"

"Fraunces." Gaby's eyes were suddenly alight with laughter. "Certainly, sir." she said. "I think fate has always intended us to sup there. I am told it is one of the finest public dining places in New York."

"I think, perhaps," he said in a voice meant for her ears only, "fate intends a good deal more for us than just one dinner."

He looked at her lips longingly, then kissed her hand.

"Is seven too early for you?"

"No, I am a countrywoman. I prefer to dine early. At home seven would have been considered sinfully late. Good night, Major. I am obliged to you for escorting me home."

"And I am obliged to you," he said gravely but with devils dancing in his eyes again, "for a great deal more."

Twenty-five

Late that night Gabrielle and Penelope sat near to the sitting room fire, sipping from steaming cups of untaxed English tea, while discussing Mrs. Loring's supper party.

Except in the omission of certain episodes with Major Darcy Rhoads—which appeared even more shockingly intimate on review than earlier in the evening—Gaby told all, with a faint air of apology that it should be so little.

Penelope held up her fingers. "You have told me a great deal more than you realize.

"Item one: A high-ranking British officer is unhappy about this struggle, which he considers a *civil* war . . . brother against brother. He is anxious to resign his commission.

"Item two: Three lieutenants—officers, too but rather more lowly—are dissatisfied with General Howe's passive conduct of the war and they despise the Hessians, their supposed ally.

"Item three: The manifest contempt for American women . . . provincials, unworthy—probably carries over to equal contempt for the men. American Tories—no matter how loyal—are bound to resent this more and more.

"Item four: There seems to be a great deal of complaint in the officers' rank because of nothing to do.

"Item five: The British command regards war, in a climate like ours, as a seasonal business."

Penelope flexed the fingers she had used to make her points. "Whether of high rank or low, whether on one side or the other, the attitudes and feelings of the men who fight in a war are exceedingly important."

Gaby said worriedly, "But much of what I told you was mere gossip."

"Some of our most important information begins as gossip," Penelope soothed her. "Do not fret, my dear. It is sifted . . . sieved . . . checked and compared by higher authority before it is ever acted on."

"You have done well for your first time, Mrs. Forsyth-Foote. Nothing to take one's breath away," she added rather dampingly, "but enough, combined with other bits of information, to contribute to the whole on which others make the decisions whether to act or react."

Reassured, if still slightly puzzled, Gaby went to bed and dreamed of a hackney dashing along the Boston Post Road. The road was made entirely of fans and the sole occupant of the hackney was herself . . . but Major Darcy Rhoads, mounted on a dark horse, galloped alongside her carriage.

In the morning she went down to breakfast as usual with the other women and wives. Since they questioned her with great spirit, she found herself discussing every aspect of Mrs. Loring's gown, her ornaments, her manners and her attachment to Sir William Howe. They were even interested in her table . . . how it had been laid . . . what foods had been served . . . how many servants waited.

Finally, Gaby threw up her hands. "No more, I beg you. Surely you don't think I spent the evening counting her servants. She seemed to have the usual number for such an establishment."

"How *did* you spend the evening then, my dear Mrs. Forsyth-Foote?" asked Mrs. Torrington. "Surely not in an exchange of confidences and counsel with Mrs. Loring?"

Her seemingly languid voice betrayed both envy and malice, which Gaby responded to with sweet smiling ease.

"My kind hostess was far too busy. She was entertaining a vastly large number of guests. She was so kind as to introduce me to some of her more interesting guests."

"Officers?" Charlotte Gray.

"Ladies or gentlemen?" Betty Arbuckle.

"Betty, do not be a fool," advised Mrs. Torrington spitefully. "Surely you don't think our ravishing Lady of New York spent the evening at an *American* harlot's house getting inspiration for more poems from the *ladies?*"

As though Mrs. Torrington had not spoken, Gaby addressed the younger woman directly.

"I must confess, Betty, that I met more officers than I can remember . . . just the usual small talk with most of them, but very agreeable they are, I confess once one gets accustomed to the odd English accent, as I have done"—she looked around beamingly—"with all of you."

Some of the women laughed, several looked indignant. Charlotte Gray coughed, Mrs. Barnes uttered a single "Tallyho," and Mary Torrington turned crimson with rage.

Gaby ignored all these symptoms. "I did, however," she went on, grateful for the opportunity, "meet one especial gentleman, who was kind enough to escort me home. A Major Rhoads."

"Darcy Rhoads?"

"I believe so, Mrs. Barnes."

"Good man. Good family." Her eyes were kind, but Gaby sensed a warning.

Betty pounced. "Oh, Mrs. Forsyth-Foote! Do you think he will call on you?"

"I have no idea."

"Surely you want to see him again."

"I surely do . . . and I shall. We are dining together at Fraunces Tavern tonight." Gaby rose from the table. "Now, if you will excuse me, I must tend to some letter-writing to my dear father and stepmama in England."

She ran up the stairs to her apartment, laughing at the thought of Lydia's face if she had heard herself labeled a stepmother.

When Gaby's letter was completed, she put it aside for Penelope. How it was achieved, she did not know or wish to know; but the letter, when it arrived in England, would appear to have been sent from New Jersey while Papa's and Lydia's to her would mysteriously arrive by way of New Jersey.

As she affixed a seal to her letter, Penelope entered the sitting room with a milliner's box in her hands. "I have your new bonnet, Mrs. Forsyth-Foote."

"What bonnet? I haven't purchased a new one lately. I have enough to last me till the turn of the century."

"Is there a note?"

"Perhaps inside."

Gaby took the box on her lap and opened it. Lying on a bed of soft cottony cloth was a calling card. *Major Darcy Rhoads.* Who else? She turned the card over.

Not time enough before eleven (if I am to win your further approval by properly tongue-lashing a trio of ill-mannered loutish lieutenants) to buy you all the fans in New York. I hope a baker's dozen will do.

There were thirteen fans in the box. The two women spread them out on the bed. Each fan was wrapped separately. Each fan was exquisite. They had ivory sticks, bone sticks and wooden sticks. They were of lace and sandalwood, shimmering satin, fine silk and heavily embossed flowered paper. They were English and French, Chinese and Spanish. They were new fans and antique.

"My stars!" said Penelope, shaken out of her usual calm. "Do you realize there is a maiden's dower here?"

Gaby was stroking a lace fan in her lap with her left hand and using her right to create a fluttering sound in the air and release the scent of sandalwood.

"I must give them all back, must I not?" she asked dolefully.

"Do you know why—on very short acquaintance—you should receive such a gift?"

Gaby hedged. "Not exactly." Then, "Oh, well. I suppose it was because of our conversation during the ride home after we left Mrs. Loring's." She forestalled Penelope's question. "I know I must be more specific. Let me think . . . Although we talked together easily, there were two, perhaps three times when we were briefly silent. He teased me because my thoughts seemed far away, and I said I was thinking of fans . . . which I was. She—Mrs. Loring had an absolutely beautiful one, black lace and ivory sticks, and she would unfurl it *thus* . . ." She demonstrated—"then hold it *so*. Very enticing it was . . ."

"Yes?" prompted Penelope with admirable patience.

"I really think he was piqued that I did not say I was thinking of him. Men," she said with the air of one imparting rare information, "are quite strange at times."

"I have often observed it," said the widow solemnly, and Gaby looked at her, surprised, then went off into peals of laughter, leveled mostly at herself. "Oh, dear," she choked, "talk about coals to Newcastle—here I am, an unwed virgin explaining men to a woman who has had three husbands."

"Just so. Now about these fans . . ."

"Oh, dear, oh dear. I'll do whatever you say, Penelope," Gaby told her mournfully, "though I don't know how I will be able to bear returning them. Look at the ornamentation on this one, and do you see how these dear little naked nymphs are embroidered into the pattern?"

"What are your intentions regarding this man?"

"To stay on friendly terms and milk him of all possible information."

"It seems to me he is interested in a great deal more than information."

"Why do you think so?" asked a very small voice.

"My dear Gabrielle, use your head. You only met him last night."

Gaby's head was drooping slightly so Penelope did not observe her violent blush, as she continued, "You appear to have spent the greater part of your evening with him. He escorted you home; and tonight, you will be observed having dinner with him at one of the most popular eating places of the British officers. Two encounters in a bit over twenty-four hours, one planned and one unplanned."

Gaby blushed even harder, which this time Penelope noted.

"Between these meetings," she pursued, "he takes the time and trouble—to say nothing of the huge expense—of selecting and sending you a treasure house of gifts. Unless this man is more a saint than any man I have ever met, these fans were not intended only to seal your friendship."

Gaby sighed agreement.

"There is, however, a second alternative."

Gaby's head and her spirits both lifted.

"Serious courtship," said Penelope. "Marriage. Only you can say whether there is any possibility that he has a wife in mind."

"Of course, he doesn't seek a wife," said Gaby wretchedly. "At least, not here in America with someone like me. Neither the true *me* or the one I am pretending to be. He is the heir to an earldom."

"Which means—?"

"He seeks diversion with one mistress rather than a succession of whores."

"Mrs. Forsyth-Foote is not expected to be any man's mistress." She spoke rapidly to give Gaby a chance to regain her composure. "None of us are expected to go against our nature. Why, it has not once been suggested that I take a fourth husband, although I have no objection at all if a good man presents himself. I like being married."

A quick, kindly glance told her that Gaby was again in command of herself.

"As I read the situation, acceptance of these fans would be a subtle sanction of his plans for you. What is your opinion?"

"The same."

"Would you like me to consult Mercy Enough?"

"Not yet. Perhaps tomorrow. Perhaps not at all. Would a one- or two-day delay matter, do you think? I would like to speak to him first. When I return the fans, it must be in a manner that does not give offense. I want to hold onto the acquaintance."

Twenty-six

My heart leaped
With passionate love
That I knew was forbid . . .
This first love
This sweet love
This pure love of mine must be hid

from *More Amorous Verse*

A few minutes past seven in the evening, when Major Darcy Rhoads assisted Gaby down the steps of the house on Queen Street, she was observed with great interest by a number of the English ladies crowding an upstairs window. She was pleasantly surprised (as were they) to find, not a hackney, but a handsome private chaise, its driver standing in the road to let down the steps.

The major handed her up into the chaise, then followed. "Now you sit in your corner, while I sit in mine, and we will observe the proprieties," he said firmly.

"How admirable! How proper!" Gaby marveled. "What a difference the right kind of carriage makes. Is it only in a hackney," she asked innocently, "that you cannot practice self-control?"

"I have—if I wish—great self-control in any kind of vehicle, which is why your ears remain unboxed, my pretty poppet. I give you fair warning—do not try me too far."

"*That* from the gentleman who told me *pretty* was a paltry word and any woman of distinction would reject it out of hand. Have I sunk so soon in your opinion?"

He gave her a laughing glance. "You are a devil in verbal combat, my dear Mrs. Forsyth-Foote, or may it be Gabrielle for the duration of our short journey?"

"For the duration of the ride," Gaby conceded graciously, "but please to remember I become Mrs. Forsyth-Foote the moment we reach Fraunces Tavern."

"For the period that you are Gabrielle, may I be Darcy? In England a boy is so seldom called by his first name, he sometimes forgets it."

"Darcy," said Gaby, "I—"

"And you pronounce it so delightfully."

"Darcy," Gaby began again, "I have never received so prodigal and precious a gift as your thirteen fans . . . one for each of our colonies, that was a charming notion. I fear, however, all thirteen must be returned to you."

He eyed her coldly and moved a little closer on the cushioned seat.

"Why?"

"I consulted a friend of my mother's—mine now—on whose mature judgment I rely. She explained to me what I already knew in my heart to be true but did not want to acknowledge to myself. There are three reasons for you to bestow such a munificent gift on me."

"Am I to know them?" he asked after an uncomfortable pause.

"She said the fans *might* be a gift to seal our pact of friendship; but if that were so, you must be a saint. Unfortunately, she does not believe in saints."

"And the second?"

"They were a suitable gift if you intend to ask my hand in marriage, an even more unlikely possibility than your sainthood since a future earl would never choose as his countess a provincial American whose dower depends on the outcome of this war."

"And the third option?"

"The simplest and most plausible explanation. You want me

as your mistress . . . and a mistress accepts anything and everything . . . then asks for more."

"Your friend is certainly correct about my sainthood, and I would very much like to continue as your friend. You are a stimulating companion; you have charm, wit, intelligence . . . but to be constantly in your company and not want more would be impossible."

"So that brings us to marriage," said Gaby softly.

"You said it yourself, Gabrielle. An English earl is seldom given the luxury of marrying where he wishes. His wife is chosen for reasons of family background such as breeding and estate. He can only hope devoutly that she gives him strong sons and does not bore him too much in her bed or at the breakfast table. When we are better acquainted . . . I had planned to write to my uncle . . . about you. I owe him so much, it would be painful to go against—"

"And just where are we to get better acquainted?" Gaby interrupted mockingly. "In your bed—or mine?"

"Gabrielle, for the love of heaven—"

"Major Rhoads—"

"Darcy," he reminded her automatically.

"I am sorry, but I have lost my Darcy mood. Major Rhoads you are, and Major Rhoads you will continue to be! I beg you, do not write to your uncle on *my* behalf or on your own regarding me. I would not for any amount of money agree to marry a man who had to ask his uncle's permission to have me for his wife. Good God! Can't you English understand the way Americans think? You had better learn fast if this damn war is to be won. The very thought of being an English countess freezes the blood in my veins. I want my own land, my own estate, my own customs. Believe me, if you ever succeed in attaching me, it will be as your mistress, not as your wife. One arid marriage is enough in any lifetime, and I have already had mine!"

"We have arrived at the tavern," Darcy said in a strained, mortified voice, "but I suppose you would prefer to go home."

"Go home!" Gaby showed him an astonished face. The brilliant eyes were full of laughter. Her face looked happy and glowing. "No, indeed. You enticed me out of my warm, comfortable lodgings with the promise of a dinner at Fraunces Tavern. It would be most ungentlemanly of you to deny it to me when I am famished. You need not be embarrassed," she assured him kindly. "You can send a messenger tomorrow for the fans, and we need never mention this again."

When they were seated in one of the more private corners of the tavern, they spent a great deal more time than usual discussing numerous selections on the bill of fare. When their long-suffering waiter finally went off with their order, they faced each other across the table.

Suddenly, both burst out laughing.

"Oh, dear, if you could have seen your face!" Gaby recalled enjoyably.

"I should have known. We have been acquainted not much more than twenty-four hours, and you have managed to shock and enrage me at least once on the half-hour."

"Only because you British think you are God's gift to the world," Gaby explained earnestly. "Someday you may have to accept a different judgment from the rest of humanity. After all, the whole of your island could be tucked away in a corner of New York, with plenty of room to spare."

"I wonder sometimes," he said thoughtfully, "why, feeling as you do about America and the British, you are one of us."

Stupid, stupid Gaby, the intelligence agent reproached herself, before saying in a calm and equally thoughtful way, "I wonder sometimes myself. Certainly it would have been the smoother path. It was no easy thing to flee my house—not that it wasn't about to be confiscated—to be reviled in my community, estranged from my friends, and disowned as family by many of my blood."

She shrugged. "I could not help myself nor deny my ancestry. I was brought up by my father in the belief that I was English before I was American and my loyalty was owed to the British throne."

"I had not thought of this war in such terms before. It must have been hellish—I beg your pardon—for you . . . and many others."

"In many ways," Gaby said quietly, "it remains hellish. I—we Americans who sacrificed so much to stay loyal—except for a prominent handful—are not really accepted here in New York as the equals of our cousins from across the ocean. Rather, we are considered a very inferior sort of Englishwomen and men. We are good enough to pay taxes and bring riches to your isle, but brethren we are not!"

He gave a few moments' consideration to Gaby's passionate outburst, then admitted ruefully, "I suppose we are a bit inclined—we British—to walk as lords of the earth."

"More like those great fearsome monsters reputed to have strode this land long before it was invaded by Europeans. Rapacious!"

He laughed, giving Gaby time to decide that she had perhaps expressed a bit too much fellowship with her own countrymen. It might be prudent to retract a little.

"To conclude this sorry subject—my husband, after our marriage, completed my education in loyalty. So behold me,"—she threw up her hands—"a sorry victim of indoctrination by the two men in my life. And also," she observed wryly, "take note that neither one of my instructors is around to help me in my sorry predicament."

"Are they both dead?"

"Yes."

"I am sorry."

Gaby looked across the table. "The devil you are!" she said quite deliberately. "A husband or a father would be very much in your way. Sir William has paid a handsome price to buy off *his* lady's husband. I doubt you would be willing to do the same. A ménage à trois, even with the lover living under a different roof would not appeal to a man of your pride."

He looked quite thunderstruck. "Why do you think so?"

"I know you."

"You *know* me?"

"Yes."

"In twenty-four hours?"

"Yes."

"You find me so transparent?"

"Not at all."

"Then why—what—explain yourself?"

"It is quite simple, Major Rhoads, if you will put your mind to so simple a process as rational consideration. First, accept the premise that my Scottish great-grandmother was *fey* and her gift, in lesser form, has been handed down through the generations."

"And the second?"

"Second," said Gaby with the utmost composure, "is that we are—you and I—in the process of falling in love."

"Your wine, sir."

The waiter presented a cork and the major waved it away irritably. "Just pour," he said hoarsely, never taking his eyes from Gaby's face.

He pounced again as soon as they were alone. "You were saying—?"

"That we are on the verge of falling in love. We have not gotten all the way there, mind. We still have time for one or both of us to draw back . . . but there is a certain—what is that word for the galvanic substance Mr. Benjamin Franklin has experimented with?"

"Electrification, I think," he offered, "though I would not take my oath on it . . ."

"No, I seem to recall . . . Electrification is the word. A kind of fiery connection between us that is also incredibly strong . . . I feel the pull whenever I am with you. Have you not felt it, too?"

"Yes." The curt syllable was followed by a muffled oath.

"Are you upset?" she asked with an air of surprise.

"Upset. Why should I be upset? Why would I want to deprive you of the pleasure of driving me out of my mind?"

The waiter arrived with two steaming bowls of chowder.

Darcy was prepared to continue where their conversation had broken off, but Gaby said, "No, no, we can argue after we finish our soup. Doesn't it smell delicious? Chowder loses something of its flavor if it cools too much."

He seized his soup spoon and wielded it like a sword. The spoon as well as the soup was spicily hot. It burned going down his throat and he blistered both lip and tongue.

His eyes watered; he could scarcely speak, but she could read in his eyes (which were burning, too) how greatly he longed to wring her neck.

Pausing just seconds to swear, he grabbed his wineglass and drank its contents in a single long gulp, not noticing the disapproving stare of an old gentleman at the next table, who was clearly shocked that wine was being quaffed like ale.

Gaby disposed of her soup daintily, but the major pushed his bowl away. "Thank you," he said. "I think I prefer mine cold."

After the bowls—one empty, one full—were taken away, he pounced again.

"How can you be so sure we are *falling* . . . and have not already *fallen* into love?"

"We are not the most cautious pair in the world, you and I," said Gaby, serious now. She looked directly at him and spoke with friendly candor. "We do not want to take the last fatal plunge into deep waters and final surrender."

The tension seemed to go out of him suddenly. "Suppose there is nothing I so much desire as to take the plunge. Suppose I look forward to deep waters and final surrender."

"It would not be wise."

"Wise for you or wise for me?"

"For both, I fear."

"Every time I think of you as indomitable, you become lady Faint Heart. We have both been play-acting at love and the play turned serious too soon. True?"

"Perha- . . ." Gaby hesitated, sighed, then acknowledged, "True."

"In that case," he told her boldly, "I suggest that we get on with the third act, the better to arrive at a happy ending."

"Therin lies the problem." She shrugged. "I see little hope of a happy ending."

He reached out to her across the table, then took back his hands as their waiter appeared, his tray heavy with dishes.

Gaby closed her eyes briefly. "Oh, that aroma! If it tastes even half as good as it smells . . ."

"Duckling with orange sauce for the lady." He set the plate with duck in front of Gaby and juggled three small side dishes onto the table, followed by the sauce boat.

He was waved away by the major as soon as he received his lamb cutlets, Long Island potatoes, two plates of greens and one of pickled baby onions.

Plying his knife and fork with great vigor, he addressed her, "Now, ma'am, you were saying . . ."

"Oh, come now, Major Rhoads, why should we spoil this delicious meal with foolish brangling?"

"We need not. Brangling is unnecessary. All we have to do is quickly come to an agreement."

"Which is?"

"To plunge into deep waters and thoroughly enjoy the bath."

"I am not yet willing to do so."

"Is that a yes, a no, or"—he grinned—"something in between?"

"Any one of them." She closed her eyes, continuing to chew. "This is marvelous," she said, with her mouth full.

"Gabrielle Forsyth-Foote, let us understand one another. Interpret the working of your own heart in any way you wish, but do not try to read mine. I will decide if and when you and I are in love. When that happens, I . . . again, not you . . . will decide what to do about it. Now behave yourself and try not to open your mouth unless you are putting food into it. We will both enjoy our meal a great deal more if we do not cross swords while we are eating this very expensive food."

"I shall behave, sir, if behaving consists of silence."

With a great effort of will, he manged not to reply; and for the next quarter of an hour, only smacking sounds of appreciation were heard.

Twenty-seven

> For I played a game
> With a deadlier aim
> Than choosing a lover
> And it meant I might choose
> To use
> Any man for my cover.

The next morning Gaby reported the events of the previous evening while Penelope was dressing her hair. "Nothing earth-shaking," she said modestly, "mostly grumbling about the British command's prosecution of the war. There was conversation I overheard on a trip to the necessary and back. I left my handkerchief behind as an excuse to go back a second time."

Penelope nodded approval of this subterfuge.

"There were two officers . . . both captains. The gist of what I heard was that British intelligence had secured—they called it ferreting—a preacher . . . a healer, too, like the one in Boston, with valued connections in the American military."

"Healer . . . preacher in Boston," Penelope mused. "That would be Dr. Church."

As the lady's "maid" nodded in satisfaction, Gaby added caustically, "And, of course, anyone I was introduced to or eavesdropped on was talking of our 'primitive country.' They regard New York as the only oasis of civilization in America. Naturally, of course, even *this* city is inferior to London."

"Let them think what they will," Penelope said dryly. "The

greater their surprise when we throw them out of our primitive country."

Gaby laughed. "Faithful Penelope. A thousand like you, and General Washington could send half his troops home."

Penelope's face softened. She seemed to be looking back down the years. "My husband, Will MacGregor—he was my second, we had ten years together—used to say the same. 'You are a bonny fighter when you have a cause, Mistress MacGregor.' And," with a touch of complacency, "so I am."

With a sigh and a smile, Penelope started plying Gaby's brush again. As soon as her hair was fit to be seen by the critical ladies downstairs, Gaby joined them at breakfast, where close questioning obliged her to regale everyone with details of her first dinner at Fraunces Tavern and then listen to their observations about her host.

Opinion on the major was quite divided. Two thought him extremely handsome; another two said that his looks were utterly undistinguished. The majority agreed with Mrs. Barnes, who had a slight acquaintance with him, that he had a pleasant, open countenance and carried himself well.

Only Charlotte Gray had the courage to ask the question that was in all their minds.

"Will you see him again?"

"We are to go to the theater in two days' time," said Gaby with great delight. "Fancy it! I have never seen a play acted out by professional performers."

"I cannot conceive of the misery of such a bland existence as yours has been," said Mary Torrington with a fastidious shudder. "No wonder you long so much for British rule and British ways."

"Quite right, we do, Mrs. Torrington. But you must also remember British manners. We could do very well without them. Regrettably, American-born loyalists who have risked all they possess for their duty to the Crown have been appalled by the lack of common courtesy we are treated with in New York because our speech, our dress, and our backgrounds do not suit the exacting taste of the English."

A paralyzed silence prevailed for twenty seconds after this stunning put-down. Then several women began speaking together while Gaby calmly and quietly finished her breakfast.

"I think I have made an unnecessary enemy among the British wives," Gaby confessed ruefully when she returned to Penelope.

On hearing of the breakfast scene, however, her fellow-spy was comfortably reassuring. "It appears to me that you acted very naturally. With that type, a soft answer never turns away wrath. It just makes her meaner. Nevertheless, Mrs. Forsyth-Foote"—her voice became slightly severe—"you cannot afford the luxury of a temper to lose. Your every word, your gestures, smiles and frowns, all of your actions belong to the Wheel, of which you are a very small cog."

"Yes, Penelope," said Gaby meekly. "I will try. No, not just try. I *will* remember."

Penelope gave a grunt of satisfaction and Gabrielle asked the question most on her mind. "Would it be possible for me to see Mercy Enough today . . . or perhaps tomorrow? I could go to her late at night as I did before," she offered eagerly.

"However slight . . . it is a risk. Such risks must not be taken lightly."

"I know that," said Gaby softly, "and I would not ask if I did not think the meeting was of . . . It is a matter of importance, I think. To me, to her, to you . . . all of the Wheel."

"I can only promise that a message will be sent and you will have an answer as soon as may be."

Shortly after this brief exchange, Penelope left the house on a number of errands. Gaby came out on the landing and called after her down the stairs, "You will not forget to match up my scarlet ribbons and—oh, come back, come back. Here are these horrid, sermonizing essays to be returned to the circulation library. Do you hear me, Penelope?"

"Yes, mum," the maid called up, at her most stolid, attempting to flatten her comfortable bulk and a bosom of formidable proportions against the stair rail so that Mrs. Barnes could pass by ahead of her.

When she reached the top stairs, she accepted the "horrid" book with a grim little smile. "It is no small matter for a woman of my weight to climb extra stairs," she wheezed.

"Oh, Penelope, I'm so sor—"

Penelope's pinch nipped her apology in half.

"Yes, ma'am, I will look out the newest novel for you," she said loudly and again plodded down the stairs, with Gaby's "horrid" book tucked beneath her arm.

She did not return until teatime when Gaby was gossiping with the ladies. On seeing her pass through the hallway, Gabrielle called out to her and Penelope approached the tea table.

"I found an exact match for your ribbons and a play as well as a novel, but I have sorrowful news as well. Your mother's friend, Mrs. Howell, has died."

"Died! Mrs. Howell?" Gaby played for time, "But—"

"I met her housekeeper at the market, laying in provisions for callers. I knew you would wish to be informed, and she so blooming when you saw her only weeks ago."

Thus prompted, Gaby answered, "I can hardly believe this news. She appeared to be in good health."

"It was a sudden seizure. She was playing piquet with friends when suddenly her head dropped forward on the table and she was gone. This was two days ago. A pity you were not informed sooner, but I knew you would want to pay your respects to the family."

"Oh, yes, thank Heaven you found out in time. Do go up and see if I have anything suitable to wear."

As Penelope left the room, Gaby said to the room at large, "After eighteen months of mourning, I threw away every stitch I owned, vowing never to wear black as long as I lived."

Mrs. Barnes was presiding over the tea service. Gaby turned to her. "Ma'am, if you would be so kind as to pour another cup of tea for me and . . ." She paused, almost seeming to ask for Mrs. Barnes's kindly suggestion.

"Perhaps it could be laced with a bit of brandy for your shock.

Stevens," she called to her own maid, who went at once to the sideboard to get the brandy.

"Thank you, ma'am," said Gaby to Mrs. Barnes as she accepted the cup from Stevens.

"Was she a close friend, my dear?"

"Was she a near connection?"

"Oh, no, it is not really a *personal* loss," said Gaby. "Rather, because my mother spoke of their friendship at school with such affection, I have always regarded her more fondly than our actual acquaintanceship calls for. In memory of my mother . . ."

She allowed a lingering silence to say the rest and, having sipped just a small amount of tea, aware of her equally slight acquaintance with brandy, she rose from the sofa.

"I had better decide with Penelope what I should wear."

"How sad that your clothes for the theater must wait," said Mrs. Tarrington solicitously.

"Thank you, but they need not. However real my regret, I will not be in mourning."

With a sweeping curtsey to all, she left the room and ran swiftly upstairs to Penelope, enveloping her in a great hug from behind.

"Dear, *dear* Penelope, you have contrived something, I know you have."

"The family of Mrs. Howell hired Mercy Enough to lay her out. When your request reached Mercy, she told me how you might communicate without your going to her home. Tomorrow she will be at the house to prepare food to be served after the burying. She is often asked on these melancholy occasions to do so. So many guests come to eat as well as to mourn."

Gaby stifled a giggle. Sounds of mirth—if anyone was about outside—might be considered unseemly. But she realized—with a sudden easy confidence and comfort in her new profession—a giggle could readily be turned into mournful hysterics.

Imagine it! Me! Gaby Foote. A minister's daughter from New England. And now a spy!

Twenty-eight

> If, to take my love,
> I had to slake my love
> And become a fallen woman . . .
> Then . . .
> Fall I must!

Dressing for her mourning call the next day, Gaby wriggled into a lace-edged shift and then sat upon the bed to pull on a pair of stockings imported from England, marveling as she still did at their silky texture. How would she ever be able to go back to heavy cotton or wool?

When she was no longer employed in intelligence work and returned to Hillpoint Farm, perhaps she could persuade Aunt Emily to indulge both of them. Just for parties and their Sunday best, of course.

She tried not to remember that the end of the war and her return to Hillpoint included a final farewell to Major Darcy Rhoads (who might not even be in New York by then). British soldiers surely fought some of the time!

She must try not to think of it. She would not dim present happiness with anticipation of sorrow. Penelope had once advised her, "In this business of ours, we must think only of what is happening now. Tomorrow will take care of itself."

The first woman who caught Gaby's eye when she entered Mrs. Howell's drawing room was Mercy Enough in a gown nearly the same color as Gaby's own, but much more severe. No lace fichu at her neck, no organdy cuffs to her long sleeves, no embroidered handkerchief to sop up tears. Most of the other ladies were applying them while Mercy Enough handed round cups of tea and little sweet cakes.

There were five ladies, not counting Mercy Enough and herself, but only one gentleman. He was portly and middle-aged and wore an ill-fitting wig. His bulbous nose and cheeks were those of a man who imbibes too freely, and his coat of bottle green, and embroidered yellow vest were unfortunate choices for a man of his complexion.

Gaby took the only unoccupied chair in the room, which was hard-backed and quite uncomfortable; and the ladies all paused in their weeping to look at her expectantly.

"I am Mrs. Forsyth-Foote," Gaby obliged them. "Mrs. Howell and my late mother were school friends many, many years ago."

The ladies commenced weeping again, and the gentleman approached Gaby, whose lack of loud lamenting he seemed to appreciate.

"I am Mr. Prescott, Mrs. Howell's lawyer," he said abruptly. "Are you known by any other name? There is no bequest in her will for a Forsyth-Foote."

"Nor was one expected," said Gaby with the utmost calm. "Mrs. Howell, as I said, was a friend of my mother's. We have not met above a half-dozen times in my life, but when I heard of her death, I felt that I must pay my last respects. It was a gesture made more out of sentiment for my own dear mother."

During the course of this speech, Mercy Enough had left the room with an empty silver teapot. She returned with it full and set it on the tray.

"There is plenty of cold meat and cheese, although"—for just seconds Mercy's eyes sent a silent signal to Gaby—"there is no staff to prepare, as the housekeeper and cook are too greatly afflicted. If any of thee wish I could serve a cold collation in the dining room."

Several murmuring voices conveyed the information that a cold collation would not be unwelcome.

Mr. Prescott made no pretenses. He rubbed his hands together and said heartily. "Most kind of you, ma'am. The truth is that I am devilishly sharp set. And—not for the ladies, of course—but a little port with my beef would not come amiss."

As Mercy Enough turned to leave the room, her eyes flicked once again toward Gaby, who rose from her hard seat and called out, "May I be of service to you, ma'am, if there is no other help in the kitchen? Truth to tell, I would rather have some task to busy me instead of waiting here in this melancholy way."

Mercy Enough turned back, her expression serene as ever. "That would be most kind of thee. I will be glad of an extra pair of hands."

The kitchen quarters were constructed in the old Dutch style, separated from the living quarters and ten steps down from the hallway. With no one there except their own two selves, a more private meeting place could not have been devised. Even if someone came down to the kitchen, steps would be heard on the hardwood floor overhead or, if that failed, clattering down the stairs.

A side of beef, a roast duck and a boiled chicken sat on the long trestle table, facing the beehive oven.

"How good are thee at carving, my dear?"

"Not good at all, I fear. Papa always did it at home or Elsie."

"Then I will cut the meat and thee will sit here, near to me, and slice the cheese. There are several large wheels in the curing room through the open door."

Gaby went through the door and came back, staggering under the weight of a half-wheel. Mercy Enough had a cheese knife ready, although she made the first cut to ease the task.

"Now let us work side by side, while thee tell me, keeping thy voice low, why this meeting with me was so necessary."

"There is something I want to do . . . something which may require your permission. I think what I really want is your blessing."

"The something," observed Mercy Enough not unkindly, "has caused thee to blush most violently."

Gabrielle had given much thought to the explanation she proposed to make. It would be brief, but extremely lucid. She would present her facts in a composed matter-of-fact way.

Instead, "Very soon now, I feel quite sure that Major Rhoads is going to ask me to be his mistress."

"Dear me!" said Mercy mildly, continuing to cut paper-thin slices of beef. "Are thee worried that thy refusal will in any way damage thy ability to work for us?"

"N-not at all."

The kitchen was delightfully warm from the beehive oven and the fire on the hearth, but neither accounted for the flush of heat throughout Gaby's body or the need to wipe her dewy face with the dainty handkerchief more suited to tears.

"Then wherein lies thy problem?"

Gaby paused in her hacking at the much-abused cheese. "I don't want to refuse him," she said ever so softly.

For the first time in their conversation, Mercy Enough put down her knife.

"My dear Gabrielle," she said, "I told thee when thee embarked on this enterprise that thee did not have to sacrifice thyself in this particular way on thy country's behalf. Thou art of value to us but not—believe me, we will find other sources among the officers. The ladies of the military, as thee has discovered for thyself, spill out plenty of private information they have gotten inside their bed curtains. Many a tidbit spoken of at night is passed on ignorantly over teacups the next day."

She picked up her knife again. "Indeed, dear child, this did not require a private meeting between us, always a slight risk. Thee could have spoken to me through Penelope."

"No, I could not. You *will* not understand me," said Gaby wretchedly.

"Thou had best clarify the situation then and tell me what it is I will not understand."

"I don't want to refuse him."

"Ah. Is this for personal or professional reasons?"

"I love him . . . I want him . . . for the short while it is bound to be. When I return to my aunt in New Jersey, I may marry or

I may not. The freedom of my own land, unfettered by male domination, seems very sweet to me."

"Aside from being . . . in a sense . . . thy employer, I speak as a much older woman to a younger, as a woman of experience to one who has practically none. I am a widow and a midwife. I serve in two opposite professions, bringing new life into the world and preparing both men and women for the grave. Will you listen to my sober counsel?"

"I will listen," said Gaby, "but I do not think I will like your counsel or heed it."

"It is still my bounded duty to give it . . . while you cut your cheese."

Gaby picked up the knife, smiling faintly.

Mercy Enough started spreading her beef slices on a platter.

"Go home to thy aunt in New Jersey as soon, as quickly as thee can. Thy heart will ache for a while. Thee will know a period of grief and regret. Then, not soon, but sooner than thee thinks, thy heart will be whole again. Then, if a man comes along—and believe me, Gabrielle, another man *will* come one day—thee will be able to give him, not only the whole of thy heart but also the purity of thy body."

"It is sound advice, wise advice; it would be everyone's advice, but it will not do for me. Long ago, my mother said to me that some women can love a number of times . . . like, well, like Penelope. She seems to have felt great fondness for her husbands, all three of them. She appears to have been loyal and loving and faithful to each one."

When Mercy Enough turned to speak to her, Gaby held up her hand. "Please," she said. "I think I know precisely what you are about to say. Is it not this? You would remind me that Penelope continued to love so long as she had an object. When each husband died, she grieved and wept and, after a while, put aside her grief and looked about for someone else."

"Exactly."

"I think Penelope is a wonderful person," Gaby assured Mercy earnestly. "I have come to love her dearly, but I am not like her.

I think I am like the other women Mama spoke of. She said that for such women, no matter how many years pass by, no matter how many husbands they take . . . or even lovers . . . there is only one man enshrined in their hearts forever."

"And for thee . . . Major Rhoads is that one?"

Gaby lifted her chin and looked straight into Mercy Enough's eyes.

"I believe so."

"And after how many meetings did thee reach this conclusion?"

"Weeks before I met *thee,* Mercy Enough, I met Darcy Rhoads. Our first encounter came barely minutes after my ferry crossing from New Jersey. It was freezingly cold, and my portmanteau grew heavier by the minute. I walked from the river to the Broad Way so that I might get a hackney. The first one I hailed—actually I commandeered it, not realizing the driver already had a passenger—all I could think of was getting out of the biting cold."

Her face softened in remembrance. Her voice grew less brittle. "I threw my portmanteau onto the floor and sank down on what I thought was the seat, and which turned out to be his lap! *I* jumped like a scalded cat, and *he,* not understanding American ways, very much mistook my being there. A girl alone . . . under such circumstances. He thought I was a woman of easy virtue and"—for the first time casting her eyes down—"I did not contradict his misjudgment. It was—I was enjoying myself too much, if *thee* must know."

"Dear me," said Mercy imperturbably. "Thee need not sound like a child caught with his—or her—hand in the cookie jar. It is not *my* place to chastise thee for any wrong-doing, but was there any?"

"Well, after a while I got into difficulty about keeping up my pose. In the end he was so persistent in his attentions that I agreed to have dinner at Fraunces Tavern with him on Tuesday next and when he asked my name, all I could think of was Aunt Emily's." She laughed a little, remembering his face when she supplied her last name. "I also said Washington, because it, too, was the first name that popped into my head."

Gaby sighed deeply. "Naturally, I had no intention of meeting him, nor did I. I admit I had some regrets about it, but ... but ..."

"Thee need not explain further. I understand thy buts."

"Strangely, I did go to the tavern one afternoon with Papa and Lydia. He was courting her then. I was horrified that Major Rhoads might come in and recognize me. The interior of the hackney was quite dark, it's true. Still, I was wearing my own hair down to my shoulders, without the powder, paint and patches, to say nothing of the fashionable wigs worn by Mrs. Forsyth-Foote. I doubt Papa, himself, would recognize me now before I spoke.

"To my misfortune, he *did* come into the tavern with some fellow officers, but, luckily, Lydia helped me to leave the room without attracting his notice. Mercy Enough." The sheen of unshed tears glimmered in her eyes. "From the first, without my even realizing it, my heart went out to him, but you must also believe this. Pythias wrote her poems many months before she knew of the existence of Major Darcy Rhoads and she did not become less a patriot when she turned herself, with your help, into the Lady of New York. Nor is she less determined to serve the Wheel because of meeting and giving her heart to a British officer. You must know—or, perhaps, you do not, that my aunt in New Jersey works there as we do here. I will inherit her lands one day. It would be in my own interest to bring peace to this land and victory for America, even if I were not heart and soul for this cause of ours."

She paused for breath while Mercy, tranquil as ever, waited for her to be done.

Gaby surprised her. "Do you not see?" she asked with passionate intensity. "I intend to betray the man I love for the cause of American liberty. Dear God, am I not betraying him as I speak to you? There will come a day when he returns to England, perhaps never knowing how much I cared or how greatly I deceived him. I hope so ... but it is still less important than our work. If

I were to know positively at this moment that one day he would curse me for my treachery, despise me for duplicity, and turn away from me in our scorn and disgust . . . *still* I would use him to aid our cause. *My* heart and *my* honor were pledged to my country long before they were pledged to him. There is a poem . . . I know it well, but I cannot think of the lines . . ."

Mercy Enough said, "I believe thee refers to a poem by Richard Lovelace.

> I could not love thee, dear, so much,
> Lov'd I not honor more.

Why so surprised, child? Because I am Quaker and sober in appearance, dost think I have not the same heart or passions of any mortal woman? Put down the knife, Gabrielle. Thy hand trembles; thou art in distress."

Gaby's hand was indeed trembling. With sudden revulsion, she cast down the knife and and walked away from the strong aroma of beef and cheese.

She folded her arms on a spice shelf and rested her head upon them. "Must someone else be convinced," she asked huskily, "or is the decision yours to make?"

"There is one other, but" . . . as Gaby lifted her head . . . "upon such matters as this, that person is likely to accept my decision."

"And have you decided?"

"Even though I believe with all my heart that thy allegiance is safely, securely ours, I must pray on it and consider whether thy present circumstances suit us better than a liaison with thy major."

Gaby frowned a little. "I do not understand."

"It is customary, when an English gentleman sets up a mistress," explained Mercy Enough, imperturbably as ever, "that he install her in a house in solitary splendor. If you left Queen Street, we might lose valuable bits of gossip from among the women there."

Gaby came back to the table and picked up her knife, hacking away at the cheese almost blithely.

"If that is his intention, I shall refuse. A respectable American widow may be *suspected* of dalliance, but if I—" She paused dramatically—"the author of *Amorous Verse*, went to live in a house with him, I would soon have the reputation of a Mrs. Loring. How could any man"—she put down the knife again to resort to the lace handkerchief—"how could any man who loved me propose such a scheme?"

"It is thy love of play-acting, not thy lack of skill, that may undo thee one day, my dear Gabrielle," said Mercy dryly.

Twenty-nine

"Gabrielle," Mercy Enough spoke softly and from the heart. "It is not too late. Even now, thee may draw back from this. There will be no disgrace in it."

"Not to *thee* but to *me!*" said Gaby, taking deep breaths to calm herself. Her face was more pale than usual. Her eyes darted about, watching every move of Mercy's.

The guardian of the Wheel went over to a cupboard and came back with a small bottle of wine and a glass of water. She poured the wine halfway to the brim and brought it to the padded table where Gaby half-sat, half-lay.

Gaby sat up all the way and drank the wine eagerly. Every drop. "Oh, but that's good, my mouth was so dry. May I have more?"

She was given a smaller amount this second time and even less the third. By the time Mercy bade her, "Lie down, my dear," her head was in the clouds. Lying down seemed a most sensible thing to do.

Mercy had covered her with a soft, light flannel blanket, which she now folded back from the bottom. Instinctively, Gaby drew away.

"This is an herbal salve; it will not hurt. Rather, it will give thee ease."

Gaby unclenched her hands and closed her eyes and did not open them again until the scorching stabs of pain she experienced during the next few minutes was over.

"There," said Mercy, again busy with her jar of salve. "The

hurt is over. Thee will experience some discomfort, perhaps only for a day or two, a little soreness." She folded a square of linen into a small pad and handed it to Gaby, who uttered a sound that was somewhere between a grunt and a snore.

"I can't imagine," she said disdainfully, "how men could take pleasure—as I've heard and read that they do—in *that*."

"Many do not. No compassionate man could take pleasure in inflicting pain on a woman he loved; but it is nature's way that this particular pain must precede much later pleasure."

"Umph," said Gaby, unconvinced, then closed her eyes again to stop the walls and ceiling from circling all around her. "With a hey nonny no," she said sleepily, "I think I may be . . . lessee, in my *cups* was the way he said it, to-tal-ly in-e-bri-ated, Mercy . . . Mercy . . . what's the rest of that name? Oh yes, Mercy Enough . . . enough what? I don't want to be rude, but Enough is a rather strange name for parents to inflict on a poor, defenseless baby."

"Many have the same thought," Mercy acknowledged, "but I rather enjoy it and so did my dear mother, who was often, even as I, reprimanded for her frivolous turn of mind."

She took a warm wool plaid blanket and spread it over Gaby, who snuggled underneath it, purring like a kitten. "Mmm, that feels wonderful . . . warm . . . and cozy . . . Enough, enough what?"

"Progeny," said Mercy Enough, merrily.

"Pro-geny?"

"Descendants, Gabrielle. The children of one's children. When the midwife bade my father come into the bedroom, where I had just been born, he kissed my mother tenderly, then directed his eyes toward heaven and petitioned the Almighty with great fervor. 'Lord, thou hast been bountiful in entrusting so many of thy children to my care. But, forgive my presumption if I remind Thee that these souls are also mouths that require to be fed. For a farmer, one son followed by six daughters is more bounty than I need or deserve. In God's mercy—enough!' "

"My mother," Mercy continued, "was giggling . . . much as

you are now, Gabrielle. To the scandal of the midwife, she kept repeating, 'In God's mercy . . . enough.' And then it suddenly struck her. 'That will be her name!' she cried. 'Mercy Enough.' At that point, my father thought that perhaps they should both forget their lively bit of humor, but she was a stubborn one, my dear mother, and in the end, she prevailed. 'If, for nine months I can carry her and then go through labor,' she said, 'I ought to at least have the modest privilege of determining what she should be called.'

"So, Mercy Enough I became. Mercy Enough Penner. After I married, I settled even more comfortably into my changed name. Mercy Enough Godwin."

"They go well together," Gaby admitted after a comfortable drowsy pause.

"Your eyes are closing, little Gaby. Sleep then. It is the best healer, God's gift of refreshment for the mind, as well as the body."

Several hours later, fully dressed again, Gaby sat on the table, her legs hanging down and her ankles primly crossed. She was crunching on a scone and sipping herbal tea.

"This is delicious," said Gaby, her mouth full of scone, "and I have almost come to prefer the herbs to the tea we drank before our fight for independence. At Queen Street, the tea is made much too strong."

"I do not wish to hurry thee, but I think it best thee leave now. The last customer has left the shop and thee will take thy new shawl and bonnet with thee, vowing thee could not bear to be parted from them. Thy new gown will be sent on later."

"But why all this charade?"

"If thee has spent several hours shopping, it is better that thee have something to show for thy time when thee arrives home. A carriage is waiting for thee. On the way to Queen Street thee will make a brief stop at Mrs. Howell's for your final call of respect to her family."

"Oh, Mercy, must I really?" Gaby wailed. "I'm tired and I want to go home."

"Nevertheless, you must do it," said Mercy, gently but inexorably. "It is often the smaller details rather than the more complex ones that trip one up."

"I am so comfortable here," Gaby said. "No British ladies to cater to or appease, no importunate lover trying to scale my defenses, no one to please except myself. For this night—and this night only—you are speaking to me of heaven."

Mercy Enough helped wrap her in her hooded cloak. "Just one more look," she said and darted ahead of Gaby from the back of the shop to the front, then as quickly returned. "No, no one save the shopkeeper.

Suddenly frightened, Gaby hung back. "Mercy Enough, there are so many things I want to know . . . I *need* to know. It's not enough, is it, to be no longer a maid?"

"My dear, what I did this noon does not alter thy condition. Thou art a maiden still."

"But that's it . . . I am *too* much a maiden. I don't know any of the things I should know as a married woman, much less a widow. I can hardly question *him*. Are there not skills a woman of my supposed background should be familiar with?"

"We have not time now, but it is a problem that has been discussed. You will ask your questions of Penelope. She is more experienced even than I," Mercy Enough said cheerfully. "I have had but one husband; she has had three."

"Only one husband?" Gaby turned back to look at her inquiringly.

"Only one."

"And he?"

"He died young."

"Recently?"

"Long ago."

"Very long ago?"

"Yes."

"I see."

"What dost thou see, O wise one?"

"One love, one man only. You agreed because of that, rather

than the force of my own supplications—which puffed me up with conceit, I must admit. You agreed out of the understanding that comes with experience."

"Thee is quite right, but the force of thy supplication was most powerful, too, and stirred up a host of fond recollections. Now come, we are dallying too long. Remember, thou hast Mrs. Howell's to visit, too."

Gaby's long-suffered groan was pitched quite low as she followed Mercy to the front of the shop.

Only the shopkeeper was there, seated on a high stool and making count of papers of pins. She slid off her stool, then handed over both a parcel and a bandbox to Gaby, with a respectful curtsey, which Mercy graciously acknowledged. Gaby—Mrs. Forsyth-Foote again—merely inclined her head.

"The coach is at the curb," Mercy directed in a low voice. "God go with thee, Gabrielle."

Without looking back, Gaby's posture, her entire demeanor changed as she stepped out to the street.

Her coachman had descended to help her up the steps of the chaise.

"Do you know the direction of Mrs. Howell's house?"

"That, I do."

"Very well then, but not too shocking a pace, if you please." She settled back among the cushions and tucked a worn rug around her legs, reflecting that it was rather enjoyable to be allowed to speak and act without concern for others—even while she blushed at the rudeness of such self-consequence and conceit.

They arrived at Mrs. Howell's house both too soon and too late for Gaby's taste. The sooner she arrived, the sooner the visit was over, and she would be done forever with the hypocrisy of being a dear family friend.

She breathed a sigh of relief as she left Mrs. Howell's, and so attuned was she to her play-acting now, that, as she crossed the threshold of the Queen Street house, she literally braced her shoulders, relaxed her expression, and slightly changed the timbre of her voice.

What she could *not* change was the flush of her cheeks and the glaze of her eyes. Charlotte Gray, passing toward the parlor, noted them at once.

"Mrs. Forsyth-Foote, are you unwell?" She stood on tiptoes to permit her to touch her friend's forehead. "Oh my, you *are* fevered, I think."

All in a minute, it seemed to Gaby to be true.

"I don't feel very well," she admitted, "but I thought . . . well, you know how tired one gets shopping . . . and then I had to pay my last respects to Mrs. Howell's family. The house will be put up for sale tomorrow and with housing at a premium ever since the great fire, no doubt it will soon pass into other hands."

She gripped the rail of the stairs. "Heavens, how weak I feel. The stairs . . ." She sank down on the bottom one, clutching at the rails.

Mary Torrington came down the steps and at once inquired what had overset "the little colonial." Gaby felt too wretched to say anything; it was left to Charlotte to explain.

Although she managed to keep her distance in fear that whatever ailed the American widow might be infectious; Mrs. Torrington took the prompt steps that were indicated.

"You, there"—to a passing maid—"fetch Mrs. Forsyth-Foote's maid down at once. Her mistress is not well and needs assistance."

In no time at all, Penelope was there, gently urging Gaby to her feet. With Penelope's arm about her on the right, Gaby held tightly to the left rail and laboriously climbed the stairs, never so glad as when she reached the top. The parlor maid followed in their wake with Gaby's reticule, parcel and milliner's box. It seemed also her allotted task to become a cushion for them to fall onto in case they tumbled backwards.

When the maid had been made happy with a small coin kept on Gaby's writing desk for just such purposes, Penelope followed

Gaby through to her bedroom to find her lying crosswise on the bed, still wrapped in her cloak, with only her shoes kicked off.

"My dear Mrs. Forsyth-Foote, are you truly unwell?"

"It seems so," said Gaby, sitting up and pulling the weight of her own long hair back from her face, irritably swatting at specks of powder.

"I hate powdered hair," she said peevishly, as she had said any number of times before.

"I will brush it out," Penelope soothed, "just let us get your gown off first."

Gaby slid to the floor and allowed herself to be undressed like a child.

"Your powdered hair by day," Penelope pointed out, "and your towering wigs by night are the most perfect disguise there could be. Sometimes, I cannot tell one fine lady from another between the absurdity of attaching patches to their faces and snow white wigs or powder to achieve the same aspect. Such foolishness! Do they not realize that all too soon nature will deal with their complexions and time will whiten their hair without any cosmetic aid?"

Penelope pulled a flannel nightgown over Gaby's head. When her mistress's head emerged from the neck, she was giggling rather hysterically.

"You were n-never a Quaker were thee, Penelope?"

"No indeed. I like my creature comforts far too much," said Penelope placidly. "Why do you ask?"

"At times, you sound so like her, I cannot help but wonder."

"Not I!" Penelope denied. "Mercy Enough Godwin is a woman of rare goodness and grace."

"Thou art the same."

Red color stained Penelope's skin, beginning at the crossed knot of her neckerchief and climbing fast over the whole of her face.

"Such nonsense," she scolded fondly. "Now, climb into this bed and I will fetch thee a posset of my great-grandmother's. It is health-giving and an aid to sleep . . . but first . . ."

She crossed the room and came back with Gaby's leather writing desk, which she set upon her knees.

"Have you forgotten, you were to be dining with Major Rhoads again? You need write very briefly. The kitchen boy can deliver it to British headquarters."

Gaby said something under her breath which would have shocked Papa to his very core. She hoped he had heard it already from Lydia. Then, she took a sheet of paper from inside the box and scribbled on it without much thought.

Dear Major Rhoads,
 I must beg to be excused from our dinner tonight as I find myself unwell.
 Not only would I make a sadly dull companion, but I fear I might also spread the contagion.
 As soon as I recover, I will be most pleased to renew our engagement.

Yours Truly, etc.

Gabrielle Forsyth-Foote

Thirty

"Dear me," said Gaby mockingly, looking about her, "when you say 'obscure,' you definitely mean obscure. I have not, since I arrived in New York, seen anthing *more* obscure than this inn . . . or is it dignified by the name of tavern?"

Major Rhoads took her by the arm and hustled her unceremoniously through the door of the inn/tavern.

"Call the place what you will," he said. "I'll be happy if the food is good—as it is reputed to be—and it is—or so I have heard—and the common room is not crowded with my fellow officers tumbling over their heels to be introduced, and you"—he looked at her sternly—"are making no effort at all to rebuff them."

There was a brief amnesty while they were greeted by the innkeeper and showed to their table comfortably near a sputtering fire. The fire was quickly given the improvement of a heavy log and a few good kicks.

"I do know how to be quite rude now from lessons learned after I arrived in New York, but I must confess," Gaby told him charmingly, "that I was educated by British ladies, not my own provincial people."

"If you think to entangle me in a quarrel, ma'am, you are far out in your calculations. This dinner was supposed to have taken place a full week ago, and"—he looked at her searchingly—"you really were ill."

"If you are looking at my hollowed cheeks and the shadows under my eyes, pray do not mention them. There was no disguising them, I knew, when I looked in my mirror; you do observe, I hope, that my maid did marvels with the rouge pot." She learned forward across the table, "Is not my color good?"

"Your color. yes. Your manners, no. So please, lean back and stop trying to seem a colonial hussy. You don't quite have the knack of it."

Gaby leaned back. Her breathing was quick and labored. *Stupid, stupid,* she admonished, herself blinking back tears, *you stepped outside your part.*

Very well, then. Let *him* supply the conversation.

Their host brought the bill of fare to the table. "We have mostly fish and lobster and a good stew, but if you prefer, Captain, I can offer—"

"The gentleman is a major," Gaby interrupted. "That's much more exalted than a captain."

The gentleman found Gaby's foot under the table and pressed down hard on her shoe.

The lady promised breathily, "I will behave."

The innkeeper apologized and was pacified and asked to repeat the names of the dishes available.

"What I was just about to say, Ca—Major, was that I have some prime lamb . . . fit for a king, it is, if I say so myself."

"You are a veritable worker of wonders, if you speak truly. Where on earth did you get it?"

"I had to pay the earth for it from one of the parcel of cowboys that got it up north in West Chester County. Run off a full herd they did, one even said they got it from Van Cortlandt Manor. No more than he deserves," he said righteously, "with him commanding one of the rebel regiments."

Gaby—about to explode with anger—gripped her trembling hands together underneath the table. The major and the innkeeper came to an agreement about their dinner, with Gaby parroting "yes, yes" to everything suggested.

"I will be delighted to sink my teeth into a good piece of mutton again, but could you," the major asked his guest, "make anything of our good host's explanation?"

"Certainly," Gaby drawled, Mrs. Forsythe-Foote again. "Mr. Philip Van Cortlandt—though I am sure he must have a much higher rank by now—is descended from one of the old Dutch patroon families who first settled along the banks of the Hudson River. He is one of the largest landholders there, and one can only assume he is strong in his beliefs—however misguided—because, in taking the rebel side, he has much to lose by this war and nothing to gain."

"I would suspect so," Darcy said soberly. "I confess that since I have been in your country, I find much more to admire than I expected I would. And I am as much puzzled by what keeps some Americans loyal to the King as by what makes others revolutionaries."

"I know," said Gaby, softly, "I, too."

For all too brief a moment in time, their eyes met, *his* glowing and alive with love and passion, hers naked with longing and then regret.

"I know it must have been hard to forsake your home and your people," he said excusingly, "but remember always that you had to follow your conscience, Gabrielle."

Gaby looked across at him again, heartened by this speech, though in a far different way than he assumed.

"Thank you," she said softly. "It was kind of you to understand and remind me. It is quite true . . . I had to follow my conscience. Now, did our host say anything else that needed explaining?"

"Who—or what—are these cowboys?" he asked comically. "I confess I never heard the term before."

"They are a group of partisans given the name cowboys because mostly they steal herds of cattle from up north in New York State and bring them here to the city to sell to the supply masters, who are proud profit-making defenders of British America. The truth is—not surprisingly—that they confiscate herds in the name of the British Army, securing them with force and intimidation, and they have not a shred of loyalty in them. They sell to the highest bidder, hence the British occupying force. In this year and at this time, who is wealthier?"

"War makes strange bedfellows."

"It does indeed," said Gaby, her sense of humor getting the better of her once more as she contemplated what strange bedfellows she and Major Darcy Rhoads were like to be one day . . . rather, one night.

Goodness me, that was one point she had forgotten to take up with Penelope. Was it always and only done at night? Did one look . . . or merely feel? Did one speak or perform silently? Heavens above, if she was not more thoroughly educated on such points as these, she would seem like the veriest amateur. As a widow, the one thing she dared not be was virginal. She would ask Penelope as soon as she got home.

Major Darcy Rhoads blinked in surprise at the brilliance of her smile as she reassured him, "Lest you feel too guilty about the cowboys who deal with your army, you might consider the skinners."

"Skinners?"

"Yes. Another partisan troop who operate in the same territory as the cowboys, but also cross the river from time to time, for marauding raids into New Jersey. There, they look in on patriots' homes or, truth to tell, in any homes or barns they happen upon. They get their name from Colonel Skinner, who was in the American Army for a short stint. When his first enlistment was over, presumably he realized that scavenging was far less dangerous and far more rewarding."

"War—"

"I know," said Gaby. "It makes strange bedfellows."

"That was not what I was about to say," he told her with great dignity, "but it will do for the moment. Do you know that even in this dim room, not improved by the glow of these pitiful candles, your eyes are two points of light, brilliant as stars?

"Yes?" he uttered a little impatiently to the servant boy hovering at his elbow, just as the stars took on an added sheen.

"Master wants to know . . . do you be wanting something to drink?"

The Major turned toward Gaby. "Wine, perhaps, or a little sherry?"

"Thank you, nothing just now. If that delcious aroma coming from the kitchen is our dinner, I do not want to drink anything at all that might diminish the taste. Later, perhaps."

The major nodded understandingly but ordered ale for himself and dismissed the boy.

"Gaby, the last week has been sheer hell, I missed you so. I never knew I could yearn so achingly, so unbearably for anyone as I did for you. Were you informed that I stormed the house on Queen Street at least twice? The first time I spoke to your Penelope and she refused to let me go upstairs to see for myself that you were really ill and not pretending."

"Why would Penelope lie about such a matter?" asked Gaby laughingly.

"I did not accuse her of lying on her own behalf. Only that *you* had bade her lie for you."

"And why would I do that, sir?" asked Gaby at her most demure.

"Because you delight in tormenting me, shrew, that is why!" he retorted.

"What overcame all your doubts on the subject?"

"Mary Torrington heard me upbraiding your—er—Penelope, and came to the vestibule to tell me not to make a fool of myself."

"Her you believed."

"Her husband is in my regiment. A thoroughly good fellow; he deserves better than that spiteful cat. She thinks the whole command should be in love with *her!* If she admitted that a possible rival for universal admiration was ill, then that lady must, indeed, be quite ill."

"So the next day," Gaby purred, "you sent me the one fan to still your guilty conscience."

"I sent it because . . . damn it, woman, you know full well why I sent it."

"And the other fans? One a day so long as I was a-bed. Were they sent by way of remorse, too? Or as offerings for my improved health? If you wish to return all thirteen to me, I may have to take to my bed again for at least a fortnight."

He uttered an incoherent sound. It was lower than a lion's roar but louder, much, much louder than a pig's grunt.

"I beg your pardon." said Gaby innocently. "I did not quite catch what you said."

"I said"—he pronounced each word with the utmost clarity—"that as soon as possible, I intend to strangle you."

"Oh, is that all?" Gaby waved one hand airily. "I would appreciate being strangled *after* the lamb, not before, if you please. The prisoner at the bar should derive that much satisfaction before final sentence is passed, should she not?"

"At the moment, no."

She reached down into her lap, then her hand came up with one of the fans, unfurled . . . silk, with an intricately embroidered Chinese pattern, all of it hand-stitched in exquisite detail by a true artist.

The fire on the hearth was now blazing enough to justify Gaby's slow, rather sensuous fluttering of the fan before her face.

"I love my fans. I am only sorry that I feel compelled to give them back to you a second time. Except this one, of course. Since flowers are out of season, *one* fan to comfort my illness can be justified—but one only. To my own regret even more than yours, Major Rhoads, the others will again be returned."

"Not," said Major Darcy Rhoads, future Earl of Linley, in a hoarse, impassioned voice, "if you would consent to be my wife."

Gaby came out from behind the fan, furled it again, and returned it to her lap.

"Did you say what I think you said?"

"Your hearing is excellent, and your understanding powerful. You know exactly what I said. It is customary for the lady in the case to make a reply."

"I know it is customary," said Gaby ruefully, "but I was taken by surprise. I had expected the question to be quite a different one."

The appearance of the host with the major's ale, followed by the serving boy with a heavy tray loaded down with dishes, forced a temporary truce.

They both sat, silent and hostile, while their main course and the side dishes were placed on the table. The innkeeper gave his last admonition for them to enjoy the meal and finally took himself off.

Gaby took up her fork and knife and helped herself to a small piece of lamb.

"Mm," she said. "God forgive me, since I know from whence it came, but this is truly delicious. Do eat yours," she urged him, "surely you don't want to spoil your dinner. We can quarrel in the greatest comfort after our meal. Who knows? You may even be in a less belligerent mood by then."

"I strongly doubt it," said Darcy, but Gaby was amused to see that after a few swallows washed down with ale and a little poking and trying of several side dishes, he looked and sounded a good deal more cheerful.

"Tell me what has been happening in New York this past week," she said to him, smiling. "I would have been totally unaware had there been a plague of locusts or even the end of the war. I seemed always to be in a half-sleeping state and when I was awake, I read no news sheet or anything morally uplifting or dull, only poetry or novels. Poor Penelope spent a great deal of time finding me new literature and making all manner of possets, none of which were approved by the doctor. She tossed away all the remedies he left, declaring them to be rubbish."

"Your servant disposed of your medicinals without permission?"

"Not any servant. Penelope. I inherited her from my mother, who had her as a child," Gaby explained outrageously to the man who hated liars.

"Ah." His face cleared. "You mean your nurse. Yes, they do rather insist that their nurslings are still two feet tall and in need of a swat on the bottom."

He looked across at her, slightly frowning. "I had not realized your cold was severe enough to require a doctor."

"Penelope again," said Gabrielle carelessly. "My every sneeze or sniffle is an infectious cold, and should my eyes water, too, then I most likely have an inflammation of the lungs."

Inwardly, she was cursing herself for having told the first unnecessary lie about Penelope. Mercy Enough was quite right. Her reprehensible sense of humor, rather than a matter of more import, would one day be her undoing.

"Now, tell me, I beg, what has been going on in the city since last I saw you."

"There have been two new plays at the theater, one Shakespeare, one farce, but I saw neither. There was a cockfight near to Bowling Green which ended in a brawl. While it was going on, someone of great good sense made off with the cocks—undoubtedly for the dinner pot. Many of the participants were jailed, but had to be freed for lack of evidence. Do not fret," he said kindly, "nor look at me with such disfavor. I did not attend."

"I *am* glad," she said impulsively. "To set two cocks at each other, like gladiators in the Roman empire, and let them peck each other to bloody death." She shuddered. "To think in civilized nations it is called a sport!"

"Well," he said whimsically, "it is just as well we agree, for after that description, if I had been inclined to attend, I no longer would be." He beckoned and the serving boy came at once. "Pray, take away these plates and what is left of the meat."

He saw, as well as Gaby, the boy's furtive glances at the hefty portion of lamb still remaining. "No, leave the meat and call the innkeeper here to me."

The innkeeper hustled over to them importantly.

"What can I do for you, sir? I trust you enjoyed your meal?"

"The lamb was delicious," murmured Gaby.

The major spoke right over her.

"Sir, I want that youth of yours to eat the remains of our meat."

"Certainly, sir. I'll send him to the kitchen this very minute."

Gaby was just about to say that once in the kitchen, the lamb would be otherwise disposed of, when Darcy shot her a glance of steel that closed her mouth at once.

"I would rather I had the pleasure of seeing him eat with my own eyes. There is a table back in that corner where he will disturb no other patrons of which"—he looked about him—"you do not have as many as you should, considering the quality of your food and the superiority of your cook."

The landlord bent almost double. The major bowed. The landlord backed away, bowing each time he caught the major's eye. When he exited through double Dutch doors, using his substantial behind to open them, Gaby no longer had to restrain her laughter.

In a trice, the boy was back with their leftover lamb and a fork. His eye dropped shyly, but he sat in the corner and attacked his meal with a zest that plainly proclaimed his hunger.

"Oh, I love you when you are like this, not Britishly stiff-rumped," Gaby said ringingly, then put both hands up to her hot cheeks as she realized what she had said.

She fanned herself vigorously then fell to laughing again.

"Stiff-rumped," he repeated. "Stiff-rumped. Now, there's a fine expression . . . so imaginative . . . so full-bodied . . . so colorful. What—I almost fear to ask—are you trying to convey by describing someone as British and stiff-rumped?"

"Well, if you really want to know . . ." She paused provocatively although her cheeks were scarlet. "Are you *sure* you do?"

"I am not only sure, I demand to know."

"It means stuffy and patronizing and dreary and full of conceit. It means talking as though you have a large piece of candy in both cheeks. It means arrogant and patronizing and full of your own importance. It means—"

"Mea culpa! Enough! Enough!"

At which Gaby started sputtering again and had to sip from the glass of sweet liquor that had ended her meal, but this time she was prudent and did not lie about what amused her. She took care not to mention there even existed such a person as Mercy Enough Godwin.

Thirty-one

They were closeted in the coach, just the two of them, traveling back to New York City. For all intents and purposes, they might have been alone. Obviously, Major Darcy Rhoads, future Earl of Linley, had come to this conclusion, for he moved much closer and turned, facing her.

Although Gaby had been rather expecting some such gesture, she was taken by surprise at the vigor with which she was plucked from her seat and laid across his knees, her ridiculous powdered wig almost touching the floor.

She was helpless in the matter of close contact and fond embraces, and he took full and ruthless advantage of her predicament. She *could* object to his kisses, of course, but as soon as she opened her mouth, both to repel and reproach him, he would fall to kissing her again.

After a while, it seemed better to yield him his simple victory and make no effort at all. She would lie where he had placed her, limp and lifeless, she decided, and utterly ignore the proceedings.

This high-minded decision was more easily made than kept.

Her heart and her body were at war with her resolve. There was such comfort, such strength, such excitement to be found in his arms.

His kisses were honey-sweet, but breath-taking as well. It was humiliating to realize that she would be happy if the kissing never stopped, but went on and on . . . on and on . . . .

She could see his eyes for a few seconds when he paused to

gather her to him more firmly. His nose was almost touching hers, and his eyes glittered very strangely.

"Passion," she whispered below her breath. So *this* was what Penelope had meant when she discussed passion.

Of course. It was obvious he wanted her, with more than love, which was wonderfully exciting. What she found *not* quite as wonderful, not quite so exciting, and certainly not cause for exultation, was that *she* wanted *him* just as much.

She had thought that physical love would be quite pleasant, a mutual pleasure-giving and pleasure-taking experience.

It had never once dawned on her that when their love was confirmed by the delights of sharing the same bed, all this confused rapture would not be satisfied. For as long as they enjoyed being together . . .

In whose bed, Gaby? her treacherous voice asked of her equally treacherous mind. *Yours or his?*

"I love you. I want you to marry me," Major Darcy Rhoads murmured against her lips, then stopped only long enough between his kisses to say it aloud so she could hear him.

After the fourth time of saying it, he grew somewhat impatient that his participant in Eden kissed back but never said a word.

"For God's sake, if you can kiss, why can you not speak? It's simple to remember, just three one-syllable words. *I love you.*"

"I love you back," said Gaby sadly.

"Good progress. Now try again. Four words this time. Equally easy. *I will marry you.* Or perhaps, *I will marry you, beloved.* Too strong? Then, try this one. *I will marry you, Darcy* . . . the beloved bit can come a little later."

Gaby laid her hand in his. "Where would we live?"

He started at her, taken aback.

"In England, of course."

"Of course." She shrugged, palms upturned indicating a wry certainty. "I took it for granted that England would be your choice. What I meant was, where would our home be?"

"At Ashford Hall in the County of Norfolk."

"With your uncle and his wife?"

"Certainly."

"And what would I do?"

"Do? Good Lord, any number of things. I am sure Aunt Charlotte would be delighted to have you take some of the burden of running the house off her shoulders."

"But I don't know how to run a household of such proportions."

"It would come to you gradually. Remember, too, you would have time for your reading and writing. Have you ever learned how to ride?"

"I once had a donkey cart."

"A donkey cart! That's not riding. Lord, girl, you haven't lived until you feel good horseflesh between your legs!"

"And I suppose," said Gaby helpfully—*dear Mercy Enough, please forgive me*—"you between my legs, as well? That would take up a good bit of my time at Ashford Hall, too?"

She met his astonished gaze, her own eyes limpid and full of laughter.

"Gabrielle!"

"Well, would it not?"

"You are damned well right, it would!" he retorted, snatching her back for a quick, hard kiss, then setting her down again as before.

"Then, too, we would spend some of the winter months in London, where you could enjoy theater-going, fine restaurants, or dancing parties, if you wished. Art shows, theater, concerts, something for every taste.

"There would be children, too, I hope," he continued, to Gaby's tender amusement, in some confusion.

"Ah, yes, future little lords and ladies."

"But if it should not be—as with my aunt and uncle—there are other branches of the family. I would not—it would not distress me."

It was necessary to stop him. The supposings were getting out of hand.

"It sounds like a delightful prospect for one very fortunate woman, but I regret . . . I am not the one."

"Why not?"

It was a very natural question. What irritated Gaby was his tone of voice. Indulgent. Patronizing. Head-of-the-household—not taking a woman's attitude seriously but condescendingly prepared to humor her until his goal was achieved.

"Why not?" he repeated. Less condescension. More irritability.

"I am American. My life is here, my roots are here. My lands—when the war ends—are here . . . and I would hold them without any man's domination. I would—I will hold my estate in my own right. I intend to manage it, not be merely the wife of the owner with no rights at all but those he gives to me. I will read, I will write, I will ride my lands, keep my own accounts, deal with my manager and determine what money should be spent. And, yes, I will continue to go about in my donkey cart, but in memory of my time in New York and of *you*, Major Rhoads," she finished gratefully, "I would choose someone who knows good horseflesh to buy me a mare so I may ride over more of my acres in one day."

"I have never heard such claptrap in all my life!" he thundered at her. "Whoever had the raising of you showed too much forebearance, girl. He should have spoken less and used his hand more."

"Typical man's attitude!" Gabrielle spat out. "If persuasion doesn't work, barter it for violence."

"Violence! The fact that you are unshaken, unbeaten and your ears remain unboxed proves what a high rate of tolerance I possess toward anyone so spoiled and unreasonable as you are!"

Gaby looked at him thoughtfully and allowed another full minute to go by before she spoke.

"You have given what, from your point of view, would be the usual reasoning. If *I* accept that as the case, I can understand why you *genuinely, honestly* feel that I am unreasonable. We come from very different backgrounds and have been reared in totally opposite ways, destined for utterly unlike futures. When first we met, you made it quite apparent that dalliance was the only thing on your mind. I accepted an attitude that completely matched my own. Think how fast you would have run if you suspected *then* that I was trying to attach you seriously. If you are honest, tell me truly, how you would have behaved! If I am not much mistaken, you would have fled for your life."

Concluding that she would be silent the entire drive back to the city, unless she had an answer, he grudgingly admitted, "It *is* true."

He looked at her searchingly for some sign of rejoicing or triumph and saw in her face only a great sadness. Aside from his fortune, face, and manly person, the future earldom had always been his trump card.

For the first time, it occurred to him that the course he had set for himself could not now be taken for granted. It was not a matter of persuasive arguments to reinforce his stated goal and the might of his present wealth as well as what he would one day inherit.

His own peculiar and particular love had no desire to be a countess!

Honors and estates meant nothing to her . . . or, at least, they meant nothing to her when they were to be found on the other side of the Atlantic Ocean!

He felt his first pang of fear that what he wanted so much, so achingly might be out of reach.

How could an Englishman fathom the workings of a mind so utterly alien? A woman of rare quick intelligence, with disdain for what most women desired, a woman who thought herself equal in spirit and strength to any man alive. A woman who intended to manage her own affairs instead of collapsing in bewildered helplessness on the nearest available man's shoulders.

"Which is?"

"I said once . . . I say it again . . . you would be far more likely to succeed in attaching me as your mistress than as your wife."

His lids half-shuttered over the fury in his eyes. "Pray oblige me by explaining your twisted logic," said Darcy, in a voice that should have given her pause. "You think me worthy of a casual affair where only the saisfaction of the physical senses is involved? I do *not*, however—in your view—fit the standards you have set for the man you mean someday to marry?"

"You make it sound a little harsher than I intended," Gaby

protested a bit weakly, "but basically—" She paused for a moment's consideration. "Basically," she repeated, stroking his nearest arm while smiling up into his dark, fierce eyes with an air of light-hearted encouragement, "it does seem to sum up the situation."

A moment later Major Darcy Rhoads, future Earl of Linley, an officer in his Majesty's Army, by all standards of birth and breeding an English gentleman, could hardly believe that he had so completely lost control of himself!

Impossible to accept—much as *she* deserved it—that he had soundly boxed first one ear, then the other, of a saucy, presumptuous, *ungrateful* American minx without the sense to recognize the singular honor he had bestowed on her by his offer of marriage!

"Gabrielle," he said huskily, "I cannot give you up. I will not give you up. How can I? I love you."

"I love—I *think* I love you, too," Gaby said, painstakingly in earnest, "but there is more than love to consider, is there not?"

"Of course there is," he agreed impatiently, "but surely where there is love, there can be compromise."

Gaby shook her head. "By all means," she said. "Tell me of possible compromises. Would you resign your commission?"

"Gladly. Tomorrow, if I could. Like my general, I have not much stomach for waging this war against those I consider Englishmen rather than enemies. I cannot, however, resign in the middle of a war without bringing disgrace on my name."

"So much for the first compromise. Now . . . as to the second. Would you give up England and live in America?"

"You know that I cannot, surely you have understood always what my future is meant to be."

"So much for the second compromise. We would live in your country, not mine; in your uncle's house, not in one that is ours."

"There is a comfortable dower house on the estate. If I asked, I feel quite sure that Uncle Frank would be delighted to furbish it up for us."

"Please, Darcy, please, I beg you to say no more. It is impossible, it is hopeless. Why can you not be satisfied with *my* compromise?"

Thirty-two

He had apologized at length and been repeatedly assured that there was nothing to forgive.

"For the love of Heaven!" Gaby said at last. "Let us be done with all this! How often must I repeat that I bear you no ill will? My mother and father were driven to doing the same a few times, though not"—she choked slightly on her own laughter—"in their cases for anything *I* proposed to do. They were kept busy enough with what I had already done."

"Has it never occurred to you," he snapped, "that you are subject to inappropriate fits of laughter? I would find it stranger if they had *not* laid hands on you. I can quite understand normal parents being roused to a point past bearing by a daughter of your willful, perverse, contrary and uncontrolled nature."

Gaby pretended to droop. Her posture, her downcast eye and trembling lower lip all qualified her to pose as a statue of dejected womanhood.

"I believe it is exactly what did happen," she said, looking at him with great sad eyes. "How else can I explain their willingness to marry me off to my husband when I was only seventeen?"

"*Is* seventeen considered too early a marriage age in the colonies? It is not so back home in England, provided the head of the family consents."

"No, it is not too old," Gaby sighed. "At the time of my marriage, however, I could not know *that;* but I grew to recognize it was not too wise to match a widower, forty-five, with a virgin of seventeen."

"Good God!" He calculated quickly. "Your husband was twenty-eight years older than you?"

"Twenty-eight and . . . pretty much an invalid. It would have been wiser of him to hire a nurse. She would have answered his needs far better than an unruly, tempestuous young wife."

"Did you know . . . did you realize . . . for God's sake, were you never husband and wife?"

"Why, certainly. In his own good time, a month after the wedding, he ordered the housekeeper to bring two glasses of wine up to his bedroom. When she left to get them, he bade me follow."

She put one hand up to a cheek that was burningly hot. *Dear Lord, Gabrielle, you should have gone onto the stage.*

"It was humiliating," Gabrielle, the actress, said softly. "I could hear the servants snickering in the kitchen. I felt as though the whole evening was intended to be performed especially for them. And it *was!*" She cried out passionately, actual tears springing up in her eyes.

"When Mrs. Bevins came up with the wine—she brought the whole bottle not just two glasses, which I was glad of later. He did not mean to hurt me, you understand, but after a while, he said there was no avoiding it, I *must* bear my woman's burden. Then, he hurt me in earnest and it was so undignified and so unpleasant, and my legs ached so, there was no bearing it . . . but I had no choice, he said. I *must* bear it, it was woman's lot and I must do my duty and bear him sons, which his late wife had failed to do."

"Did he abuse you?"

Gaby said slowly, "It seems so long ago . . . it's as though it all happened to someone else in a different life. As husbands go, I later realized that William was not unkind, certainly not overly demanding. We had a repeat performance about two times every month. He would keep better track of my monthly courses than I did and expressed his displeasure that I was not carrying his son, as though I had a choice!"

"Did it not ever occur to you that *he* might be the one at fault, if fault there was?"

"No, never. I knew very little about such things and he took no pains to educate me. After two years of constant monthly disappointment, our doctor talked to me alone one day. A condition of my husband's made it unlikely, if not quite impossible, that he would be able to give me a child."

"Did you say anything to your—to Mr. Forsyth-Foote?"

"No, it would have been too cruel. William was not a mean man or uncaring. He was merely obsessed—as many men are—with siring a son. Knowing it was no fault of my own, I could afford to be generous. Each month, I would listen to his laments on the subject and hang my head and pretend to grieve at having failed him."

When Darcy would have spoken, she put up a hand to stop him. "I can't say that it was the ideal life, but on the other hand, it could have been much worse. Aside from his obsession, William was considerate and agreeable. He was more generous than most husbands I had heard of, and he cared not how much I spent. He purchased a harpsichord for me—English-made—and some of our happiest evenings were when I played and sang. He purchased all manner of trinkets for me. Orders went out to his booksellers in London. He never limited the time I spent amid my books or devoted to my writing. He even gave me leather-bound volumes in which I could do 'my versifying.' "

" 'My little Gaby is a poetess,' " he would say to visitors, patting my hand. At such times, I felt like a cherished lapdog with a jeweled collar held always on a tight rein. My owner was tolerant, I received all the sustenance I needed, but there was always that rein to pull me back if I tried to wander. I was imprisoned by my collar (however big the jewels) and my jail might be luxurious, but it still kept me confined."

"When did your husband die?"

"Three—nearly four years ago. He had a paralysis of some kind on his left side from which he never really recovered. He lost most of his power to speak. Naturally, he did not—he could not. Our marriage, as such, ended. I took care of him with great help from Mrs. Bevins and a woman of the neighborhood, who was often hired by family members when such sickness puts too much of a hardship on all the rest. He continued as he was for about eighteen months. Then, very quietly, in his sleep, he died.

"I received calls from nieces and nephews and cousins who had not been much in evidence when he was healthy and of middle age, then later a husband with a young wife, who might yet conceive. They came scurrying round for the reading of the will and it was, as wills often are, disappointing to many. I, who had hoped only to have an inheritance of a size to make me independent, was suddenly a rich, land-holding widow.

"Then, there truly was a large gathering of the bees around the honey pot. My, how they buzzed about me, lapping at the honey and trying to dip their spoons into it and the money-pot, too."

"It might not have been for your inheritance," he said stiffly. "Did it never occur to you that your person might be an object of desire, too?"

"Now and then, it passed through my mind, but only briefly. Once I had known the power of owning my house and furniture, my lands, farms and my fortune, every single cow, sheep, chicken, every blade of grass, every bale of hay, there was no going back. Mine and mine alone. It was absolute, incredible riches, more than I had ever dreamed of achieving."

She looked at him very straightly, "As a man, you never have experienced the awful hopelessness of a woman's lot now and forever, aware she is only a pawn in a game played exclusively by men, and subject always to their rules. I no more intended to have that happen to me again than I proposed to try to fly from a mountain top down into the ocean below."

"And you never did?"

"No, I never did. Unfortunately, however, my glorious life of freedom was much too short-lived. Before my first year of widowhood was behind me and six marriage proposals been rejected, the politics of the nation forced me to make a choice. As you know, my husband and my father before him had taught me that the ultimate political duty of an Englishman or woman was loyalty to the Crown.

She shrugged. "So behold me. The fortune and farms and the estate were about to be seized; so I fled to New York with money and jewels and a trunk full of clothing and a box full of my verses. I prepared myself to wait out the war in comfort till the inevitable English victory would put me back in full possession."

She gave him a twisted smile. "This shameful secret is one I confess to you and you only. I am loyalist not for the Crown, but with an eye to my own interests. Do you find that disillusioning?"

"No, only human."

He reached out and touched her gently, first on her cheek, then on her shoulder.

"Have you never been with any man other than your husband?"

"I took a lover during my early widowhood when I found out that I—experienced certain yearnings. He was the son of a farmer with more abundance of money than most, also of sons. Seeing that Thomas had no bent for farming, his father was able to humor him in a rather ambitious wish for a boy of such background. He was going to divinity school at Yale, which is in our Colony of Connecticut."

"Were—was it—pleasant for you?"

"Yes." She smiled, remembering. "Yes, indeed."

He knew his pang of hot jealous anger was as unreasonable as it was unwise. He could not bring himself to comment pleasantly, so he did not comment at all.

"I think he knew no more than I did of how to go about the business. We were as innocent and ignorant as a pair of bumbling puppies romping about in the barn at night and discovering with delight that we were made quite different. At least *he* discovered it then; I had been aware of it before."

She smiled reminiscently. "It was a good romp for the sweet-scented springtime that it lasted. When he had to return to Connecticut, to become a minister while I stayed at home to manage my property, I was able to remember our time together with the greatest enjoyment. I still do, but the difference now is that he is a chaplain in a Connecticut regiment, as he feels God ordained. I have no notion what God has ordained for me. For the present, I am landless."

"Gabrielle, you know nothing—not one thing at all—about married love as it can be, as it should be, between a man and woman in love. It is difficult to believe that, lacking experience, you are so wonderfully warm and passionate a woman. Marriage would open up a new and wonderful world of ecstasy for you."

"You may be right," Gaby admitted, "but I choose not to put it to the test you suggest. Once married, there would be no way of retreating if I—or you—or both of us proved to be wrong. My compromise seems to *me* to be in every way admirable. After all, we could both walk away if we did not like the experiment. One cannot walk away as easily from the married state."

"You impudent little hussy! What you actually intend to do is try me out for size. If I come up to your expectations, then—only then—you may consider marriage."

"You have the same option that I do." Gaby pointed out. "If you are disappointed in how the relationship between us fares, you may run as far and as fast as your legs permit without once looking back and without any tie to bind you."

She smiled frankly up at him. "Can I say fairer? Most men in your position would consider it an enviable choice."

"I am not most men."

"I am not most women."

"So be it."

"You *do*," said Gaby enjoyably, "have the most original turn of expression."

"And you," he riposted, "have a most original turn of mind."

"You only say so because you cannot bring me to heel."

"Never, *never* have I wanted to do that!"

"You may not think so, but you do, my dear, you do."

"I challenge you to provide the evidence."

"Having sowed sufficient oats and reached the age of responsibility, you find that your own hearthstone beckons more alluringly than a different bed each night. You are prepared to settle down with one woman only although I am not certain what *only* means in your mind. You yearn for little ones at your knee doubtless for not too great a period either."

"I have had my *affaires*. What man on earth my age and in my circumstances has not? Does it not occur to you that it is *you*, not my years that have changed me. I have been in lust before . . . many times, I admit . . . but never in love. It . . . is altogether amazing. One night, there I was, wholly heart-free and looking about me for some source of amusement . . . Oh, never fear, from the very first, before we exchanged a word, I never thought of you as amusement. Rather, I thought myself incredibly fortunate. How many men and women, strangers one minute, exchange a single glance and know that what they feel is forever."

"Forever?" Gaby repeated almost mournfully. "Why must you insist on a lifetime pledge of love? My dear Major, you insist on the impossible."

"Improbable, yes. Impossible, no.

> Yet change she earth or change she sky.
> Yet, I will love her till she die."

"Dear, *dear* Darcy, you keep quoting the wrong poet. Mine says . . . 'You get no more of me. Come, let us kiss and part.' "

" 'My true love hath my heart.' "

" 'Hasty marriage seldom proveth well,' " Gaby capped him.

" 'Her gestures, motions and her smile,' " he interrupted.

" 'Her wit, her voice, my heart beguiles.'

"Gaby," he urged huskily, "I am a soldier, not a poet. From my heart, I love you. I want to marry you, not just share your bed now and then for a short period of passion. I don't *want* to leave you to go home after we make love. I want home to be wherever we both are. I want to go to sleep with you in my arms and wake up to find you there beside me in the morning. I want to have breakfasts with you, and dinners. I want to read with you in the evening and sit comfortably in an armchair while you play the harpsichord for me. I *do* want to have children about the house. I promise we will bring them up ourselves, not thrust them always into servants' care or send them off too young to school."

"You make it sound so simple, so easy."

"Because it is."

"Not for me."

With a sudden change in technique, he leaned back with an air of nonchalance. "Never fear; I will give you the opportunity to grow used to the notion that your life is not completely your own any more."

"And you do *not* call *that* an attempt to curtail my liberty?"

"Certainly not. My life, too, is not exclusively my own. I have given it into your keeping."

"But I don't want it," Gaby wailed.

"A pity, but there's nothing you nor I nor any other person can change what has already happened."

Gaby turned away from him. "I do not want you to say another word to me. I want time to think!"

The last twenty minutes of their journey were driven in complete silence.

When they reached the house on Queen Street, the major descended the carriage steps first and then handed Gaby down. He escorted her up the stairs.

"Marriage," he whispered just before the door opened. "Marriage or nothing."

"Me," she said. "All of me but a wedding vow."

Thirty-three

A not-unfruitful week followed their mutual ultimatums.

Gaby went to the theater with a young lieutenant who had never dreamed the famous Lady of New York would deign to accept the invitation stammeringly delivered at a concert two nights before.

The lieutenant proved to be a gold mine of information for those in the rumor-and-intelligence business.

Yes, he believed many complaints about Howe's conduct of the war must have found their way to England.

Yes, several of the higher officers were determined not to waste another summer of sport at country estates in New York. Assuming, he added wryly, that summer ever came to this benighted land. However, the general would probably be superseded at his own request.

Yes, he had heard from several sources that colonial paper money would soon reach the lowest value. The English pound had always been preferred, of course, but colonial notes would continue to sink. A set of rascals—some saved from the gibbet—were in New York even now and had begun the business of making damn clever forgeries for this very purpose. His friend, Captain Percy had seen a bank note himself. The British plans for distribution of great quantities of colonial counterfeit money could wreck the American economy, with consequences of the most serious to the fledgling country. Damned funny way of waging a war, if you asked him.

Gaby began to play him a bit. He was a small fish, to be sure, but his information appeared sound. One small question here. One small question there. The lieutenant, who knew much—fortified by a good deal of wine which he failed to observe Gaby had asked for, but he drank—told all.

Mrs. Loring's next evening party was Gaby's earliest opportunity to seek out Captain Percy and flirt with him in a playful manner that made him feel the very devil of a fellow with the ladies. She was able to coax a few details out of him that appeared to confirm the lieutenant's information about a counterfeit scheme.

Penelope listened to all the bits and pieces Gaby managed to discover and relayed them to the proper source (by what method Gaby neither knew nor cared to know). Her lady's maid reported back to Mrs. Forsyth-Foote that Mercy and the Wheel were delighted with her intelligence but had warned again that she must take care. Too many direct questions could lead to her own undoing.

During the eight days since their sumptious supper at the "obscure" inn, she had neither heard from nor seen Major Darcy Rhoads (no matter how hopefully she looked about for him at private parties and in public places).

On the eighth night Gaby attended a late supper in the City Tavern hosted by Major Barnes and his wife. All the ladies from the Queen Street house had received invitations, and where there were no couples, single gentlemen had been included to make their numbers even.

She had been dashing about so much lately with other officers that the observant Mrs. Barnes was among the few to notice that Major Rhoads was her escort of choice. She had placed them side by side at the supper table.

When they were seated, Gaby smiled into Darcy Rhoads's enigmatic eyes. She held her silk fan from China in a manner copied from Mrs. Loring, slightly extended and covering the lower half of her face.

"La, my dear major," she observed playfully, "it seems an age since we met. Whatever have you been doing with yourself this last se'ennight? Not deserting the social scene for the military, I hope? Why, if you did so, you would have all the eligible women of New York weeping into their lace-trimmed kerchiefs. Indeed, I would have joined them myself, if I had not been sure I would dine and dance with you sometime soon. Plenty of bachelors in this city, but so few *eligible;* the supply is halved even by more if one leaves out the handsome men, the rich, and those too scrupulous about their military duties—dull fellows. Why, only yesterday at the breakfast table, I was saying to Mary Torrington or, dear me, could it have been Charlotte Gray? At any rate, it seemed to her, too, that the supply of eligible men should be greater considering how many military men—"

She broke off with a slight gasping sound, her response to the hand that, under cover of the table, had pinched her inner knee quite hard.

"If you do not put an end to your play-acting and talk like a woman of sense, I vow I will do much worse than that. If you ceased talking altogether, it would be an improvement."

Gaby said not a word for at least two minutes . . . not because she was in the least intimidated by these threats as because of a sudden thought that had occurred to her.

This was not the first time that he had teased her about her play-acting or mentioned casually the tendency she had to play a part.

It meant she had indulged her own sense of fun too unwisely. This was one of those traps that Penelope had mentioned over and over (herself a little bored with the repetition) could betray the prideful. Such traps were like great yawning pits of quicksand, ready to trip up the unwary and swallow them with a few sucking gulps.

"Good God!" said Darcy. "Have I overset you for so little cause? Your spirits usually rise in proportion to the challenge. Surely, I have not subdued *you* with a single admonition and just one slight pinch."

"Quite true," said Gaby semimockingly. "If I *do* seem more

subdued than usual, I beg you to believe that it would never be for so paltry a cause as your disapproval."

"I seem to have mentioned before," he said, with his hand still under the table, now plaiting her fingers in his, "that you are a devil in combat."

"So you have. But then"—she unfurled the fan again—"you have said a great many things to me, dear sir, that are eminently forgettable."

The plaited fingers turned into talons. His were much stronger.

"Peace," she said breathlessly, then, "My God, that hurts. Damn you, Major, I surrender."

He released her fingers at once. "I surrender, too," he said quietly.

"I beg your pardon." Her fan slipped to the floor as she turned to face him.

"In the battle of the ultimatums, I yield the victory to you. It is not the relationship I would have chosen, but—since you will not accept my hand in marriage, *I* accept *you*—if you are still of the same mind—as my mistress."

"Excuse me." She gulped audibly. "I seem to have dropped my fan."

Immediately after this explanation, she slid off her chair and dropped onto her knees and vanished under the table. Two seconds later, he followed her.

"In the best circles of society," he said, ever so courteously, "a gentleman is supposed to perform this small service for a lady."

"Which should prove to you," said Gaby blithely, "how unfit I am to be a high-born English wife."

"You could always learn," he suggested. "I have noted many times that you do not lack intelligence."

"How vastly kind—how vastly flattering... I have never been praised so highly before. My fan—are we not forgetting my fan? Both of us crawled under the table in order to recover it."

"Yes. The sooner, the better, I th—"

"Damnation! Here it is under my left knee, just as I was thinking that the floor of this dining hall was uncommonly rutted. Will you get up first or shall I?"

"If you are so set on propriety, *I* will get up first and seat myself. You may count to ten and then follow with the fan."

"A well-thought-out scheme. But, before we carry it out, another first . . ."

They were still kneeling, each with their hindquarters bumping the other side of the table, their faces remarkably close. He lifted one arm in order to bring her even closer.

They kissed . . . and they kissed . . . and then they kissed some more. They might possibly have gone on kissing until the meal was done and it was time for the ladies to leave the table, if a gentleman, uncrossing his legs and trying to cross them in the opposite direction, had not accidentally aimed a fairly strong kick at Darcy's rear.

Gaby held both hands over her mouth, stifling a fit of giddy, girlish giggling which was most unlike her. The space below the table was rather too cramped for his attempts to rub his posterior with one hand.

"I'll move back so as to give you more space. Then . . . Dear God in heaven?"

"What now!" It was intended more as a sign of his frustration than as a real question.

"That man, a little behind you and the woman," Gaby whispered, "is he—are they—doing what I think he—they—are doing?"

He managed to screw his neck around so he could look where Gaby was pointing. He surveyed "that man" briefly and pronounced his conclusion. "Yes. He is, she is, they are! Now ma'am, get back to your seat in a hurry."

"No," Gaby said mulishly. "I want to *see*. I have never—"

He stretched as upright as he could and loomed over her. "Gabrielle." Each word seemed to be drawn from his mouth with a pair of pincers. "Get back in your chair this moment or I will strangle you with my bare hands."

"Oh, very well!" said Gaby, deeply displeased. She turned from him, reversing her position so she could stagger upright.

Even for a British officer and gentleman, the target she was offering him proved to be irresistible. He whacked it . . . not too hard . . . one might even have called it more of a caress than a whack.

The effect on Gaby was galvanic. At the intimate touch of his hand, she gave a small leap that landed her a bit higher than she needed to go. Instead of crawling out from under the table, she hit it with the side of her head.

She grabbed hold of one leg of her chair, crawled out, scrambled up and got into her seat. Looking around, she saw no discernible sign of interest from anyone at the table. Those attacking their food (mostly men) like lions feeding on gladiators were far too absorbed by their supper. Others (mostly women) picking daintily at their plates were too busy carrying out their sacred duty to seem delicate and small of appetite.

No one appeared to have noticed the duo's leaving, much less their return. Both sexes had absorbed such prodigious quantities of wine, they were tipsily unobservant.

"I had no notion that you were so strait-laced," Gaby said haughtily. "Perhaps we should reconsider our agreement."

"I am not strait-laced. If you mean you have decided to be a wife, not a mistress . . . fine. I am agreeable to hearing your arguments for the exchange of posts."

Gaby paid him no attention. Her eyes had wandered far down the table. "That's *them,* isn't it?" she hissed. In a swift movement of his own hand, he grabbed her arm and held her hand down on his knee so she could not succeed in pointing.

"Yes," he hissed back. "Do me a tremendous favor and keep your mouth completely shut."

Gaby, hungry now, was delighted to observe that somehow or other—perhaps fairy servants had been at work—her plate was full.

"Major R . . . Darcy . . . whatever I am supposed to call you now, this is simply delicious. Do try some."

He looked over at her plate. "If you will take the trouble to pause for ten seconds, you may notice that *my* plate is sadly empty."

"Oh, to be sure . . . how shockingly selfish of me not to notice and share." She turned slightly in her chair and beckoned to a formidable six-foot footman with a distinctly boyish face.

He came almost at a gallop.

"Young man," she cooed—he was probably the elder of the two of them—"Major Rhoads is quite hungry. Actually, one might even say he has an *enormous* appetite. Would you fill a plate and bring it back to him?"

She smiled bewitchingly and he lost whatever hold he had on his senses.

"Yes, ma'am, sir, I would be hap- as s-soon as . . . excuse me, please."

"He forgot to take my plate," the major said sardonically.

"Oh, silly you." She tapped his elbow lightly with her folded fan. "I am sure that he will find another one in the kitchen."

"I am quite certain he will. And probably fall and break it hurrying back to earn another flirtatious smile."

"Me! Are you accusing *me* of flirting?"

"Yes, *you,* witch woman."

"I have noticed," she told him confidingly, "that hunger takes some men that way. When your appetite is satisfied, no doubt you will have recovered your sunny disposition."

"If you utter even one more *double entendre* about my appetite, either singular or plural, it is likely to be satisfied underneath this table on that extremely uncomfortable floor, and possibly before a host of onlookers. You may not be the only lady present who drops her fan."

Gaby gasped, blinked her eyes very rapidly and fanned her red-hot face, not at all flirtatiously.

"And *that,*" said a low voice close to her ear, "my dear Mrs. Forsyth-Foote, is what is known as bringing the war into the enemy's own camp."

The footman came to her rescue by whisking the empty plate

from in front of the major and replacing it with one that was piled high with meat and vegetables."

Even while he did so, his adoring eyes never left Gaby's face.

"Cook says these are all the best things, mum . . . I mean, ma'am." Even a whispering voice could not conceal the nasal twang of New England.

"I am sure the major will be satisfied."

The major nodded agreement.

"Yours is a Boston voice, young man, if ever I heard one," said Gaby.

"Braintree, ma'am, so you're not far off in your guess."

"There's no mistaking those broad A's. Ah, the home of John Adams and his dear wife Abigail, so you are a loyalist?"

"Never call me that, ma'am." He straightened up with dignity. "I'm as rebel as the bunch who emptied the tea in Boston Harbor. Truth to tell, I was one of those there Indians."

"But what are you doing *here,* then, a footman and in New York?"

"I was captured in the fighting at Long Island ma'am, and they had us all lined up with others to be rowed over to the *Jersey*, that British prison ship in the East River. Never mind what it must be like on board. The stench is carried on the air and across the water from miles away. That smell, ma'am. It was like to make me lose me my breakfast."

"Then, this spit-on boots bastard of a British officer, he picks out me and one of my mates, Dickie Mullins, and he says with that snooty way o' speaking they have, how's we could take our choice, being both of us over six feet in our stockings which is what—for no reason on God's good earth I can think of—a footman is required to be. Either—they says—you can be a footman in a military family or prisoners on the *Jersey*."

"Gaby," the major glanced her way and said, "you are beginning to attract notice. I suggest this young man bring us champagne in the parlor when our supper is over."

His eyes, as he spoke, met the Braintree boy's, delivering a message. The footman gave a brief nod and moved off, careful not to glance at Gaby again.

"My dear girl," said the major after swallowing a mouthful of cold beef, "in English households, it is not considered *comme il faut* to engage in personal conversation with the servants during a meal."

"Oh, thank you," said Gaby, looking at him all wide-eyed innocence. "I never knew that before. Do you see *now* how unequal I am to be the mistress of a nobleman's household? Just think how mortified you would be if you took me to Windsor Castle?"

"Windsor Castle? What the hell—never mind. I know you are about to make some point."

"I should think it would be obvious to you," Gaby told him with seeming sadness. "There are so many matters, just sheer everyday manners about which I would not be—as you put it—*comme il faut*. Imagine your chagrin if, just when I was supposed to make my curtsey to royalty, I was found discussing politics with a footman who I found a great deal more entertaining than the King of England. You must admit I would be a sore embarrassment to you."

"More like," said Darcy, his shoulders shaking, "a great entertainment."

"Here, yes . . . in England, no."

"How very wise and profound you are, my dear Gabrielle."

Gaby poked distastefully at her plate, her appetite quite gone. She suddenly felt quite melancholy and did not know why.

Darcy glanced at her once or twice before speaking. "What troubles you, my dear?"

"I think, perhaps . . ." It suddenly came to her in a rush. "It was his accent. The dear, familiar, not altogether lovely accent of Massachusetts. No matter that he is now a footman . . . he fought for what he believed in. *I* ran away with plenty of money and my tail between my legs, to live a life of comfortable luxury in New York. He made me feel—oh, I don't know—ashamed, I guess. I don't belong here."

It was not play-acting. She had never been more sincere and, most strangely, this speech served her better than the finest performance she had ever put on for his benefit.

Her clenched right fist lay on the table. With his left hand, he covered it and unfolded her fingers one by one.

"Gaby," he tried to comfort her, "I know in spite of your witticisms and air of languor that you are sincerely torn apart by the divisions in your country. As much as any Englishman is able, I do understand. I hurt for your hurt. I pity your inner conflict. When you are in distress about the choices you made, remember this one thing: a woman as well as a man—when she has to take sides in any conflict—not only should—she *must* make the choice her conscience dictates."

Gaby looked up at him. Her eyes were full of gratitude. Her unclenched hand was still enclosed in his, but both hands were under the table now, away from curious eyes.

"I must make the choice my conscience dictates," Gaby repeated so softly he had to strain to hear the words.

"And I hope one day," he said just as softly, "that your conscience will dictate that you take permanent refuge in my arms as well as in my house. I want a wife, not a mistress, but for the present, I will take you on whatever basis I can get you."

Thirty-four

They were standing together near the fireplace when the footman sought them out with two glasses of champagne on a round pewter tray.

The major took one glass and handed it to Gaby.

"Your name and rank?" he asked the footman.

"Corporal Isaac Purdy, 1st Massachusetts."

"It is obvious to you," Major Rhoads said, his eyes fixed on the American corporal, "that I, too, am a spit-on-boots bastard of a British officer, possibly with the same snooty way of speaking, but I have just a few questions for you. You chose being a footman over incarceration on the *Jersey*—a choice any man can understand. If a second choice was offered, what decision would you make? Safety as a footman or being exchanged and returned to your regiment?"

"God's truth, you can't be serious! Serve as a lackey in this plastered hair with fleas and nits nestling in it and the constant confounding itching so I'll likely scratch through to my brains one day. By God, sir, I would rather freeze my butt off with my comrades or go hungry in Massachusetts or anywhere else they speak good old American. You get me exchanged, sir, and I'll kiss your boots and polish them with my own spit, kneeling before you."

"You need not go to quite such extremes at that," drawled the Major while Gaby chortled into her champagne. "Mind you, I cannot promise, but I will do my best."

"God bless you and yours forever," said the footman fervently, giving the second glass to the major and swinging the tray down at his side.

His deep bow was for the English major, who was so human as not to appear British at all. He gave Gaby the lightest of smiles as he took himself off.

"So much for infatuation," said the lady to the major. "I pray yours for me is not as brief, sir."

"Not sir, not Major. Darcy. From now on—unless you choose to be more formal in public—never again are you to call me anything but Darcy."

"Very well, *sir,* I am yours to command."

"If you think I am not capable of teaching you a lesson, lovely Gabrielle, you may think again. I am willing to do it here at Major Barnes's supper party as if we were alone. And, now that you have reminded me of the possibility, at Windsor Castle, as well. *Comprends-tu?*"

"I comprehend very well, *sir,* and I am all a-tremble with fear."

"Gaby, you are trying me sorely."

Gaby swallowed a little more champagne and looked at him directly, then bent her head a little. "I speak and act as I do because I am a little nervous."

"You!? Nervous?"

"Well, of course I am!" Gaby said indignantly. "Do you think I become a mistress every day in the week?"

"You have an alternative."

"Oh, don't be absurd. Mistress or wife, I still will be going to bed with you."

He looked at her so tenderly, Gaby wanted to weep. This love business was a very tricky thing. It roused the senses and muddied the brain, just when clear thinking was important.

Why in the world should she want to dissolve in tears because this one special man looked at her with love and longing.

"You must find a place where we can meet," she said in a businesslike way.

"I have already bought a house."

"A house! How in the world did you find a house? They are at a premium since the great fire."

"Rank is not without privilege," answered the major casually. He grinned down at her. "Money is the greatest persuader of all."

"That sounds immoral!"

"Would you choose to come to me in my bachelor's lodgings? Or prefer that I visit your lodgings on Queen Street?"

Gaby shuddered. "Heaven forbid!"

"It is a very pleasant little house, in a quiet cove, with an embankment at the rear which leads down to the Hudson River."

"How lovely," said Gaby happily. "Will you be there often?"

He stared. "I shall live there with you."

Gaby had discussed this matter with Penelope and learned of Mercy Enough's feelings. The gossip at the Queen Street house was too valuable to give up. If she and Darcy moved into a house together, she would be cut off from too many sources of intelligence.

"I cannot move into a house with you, Darcy. Pleasant as it might be"—she looked up at him, with eyes so expressive of her love, he took her champagne glass and his own and set them on the nearby tilt-top table and put both hands lightly on her shoulders.

"Dear God, how I love you, Gabrielle!"

"I know."

"How can you possibly know?"

"By the way that I love you."

"Will you go with me to *our* house tonight?"

"Yes."

"Are you sure? It is not too late for us to marry first."

"I am not ashamed of loving you. I am not ashamed of the choice I have made. Remember, *you* are the one who always insists one must make the choice dictated by conscience."

In the hush and crush of the leave-taking and offering courteous thanks to their host and hostess, the major and his about-to-be mistress were able to leave together without anyone taking notice.

It was a twenty-minute ride to the little house down near the river. They sat, handfast and silent—both of them (for very different reasons), overwhelmed by what was about to happen. There was a cheerful light in the window as Darcy helped her down from the carriage. He spoke a few words to the coachman, who then drove off.

"I have bought the carriage from an estate sale, and the coachman has agreed to stay on in my service. He will always be available to take you up or bring you home when I cannot do so. There will be no embarrassment, Gabrielle."

"Thank you," she said. "That was kind of you."

"It was not kind," he said almost savagely. "You are the woman I love and desire. Do you think I would not shield you in any way I could?"

"Please, don't be angry with me. Oh, dear, I think I am about to cry."

"I will take you home this minute if you have changed your mind. But for God's sake, decide and end this agony."

"Oh, damn, it wasn't because I was afraid . . . it's because I'm so full of love, I can't bear it . . . and I'm a little afraid, too, but not because of changing my mind. Suppose"—she stopped on the path and looked up at him with big, troubled eyes—"suppose I disappoint you."

"Disappoint me how?"

"In bed, of course."

"Why would you disappoint me?"

"Because," she reminded him nervously, "I am not very experienced."

"You were married four years and also told me there was one, an energetic, if not very expert, lover.

"Yes, I know. *I* told *you* . . . but perhaps you missed the *significance* of all I said. I was with much too old a man, my husband, and one who was much too young. The truth is, I know very little about . . . well, a mistress is supposed to be extremely knowledgeable, is she not? I am afraid of making a fool of myself . . . and . . . and not measuring up to your standards."

"In that case, my dear, my darling, my absurd little American, I have no fear. You see, I—I must confess—*am* experienced and if you cannot educate me, then I promise that *I* will educate you. In fact, my love, I will be delighted to undertake your schooling." He held out his hand, and she took it. "Let us go into our house."

The room upstairs that he led her to was brightly lighted. The furniture was mostly of oak, with a few birch pieces that were solid as well as handsome. Gaby ran her fingers across a wardrobe. "No dust," she commented.

"I have a housekeeper who will supervise the cleaning . . . only when you are not here. There will always be some fresh bread and cold meat and cheese and good New York apple cider, which I have been informed is the best in any of the thirteen colonies."

"In any of the thirteen states." The word *state* was spoken very emphatically. Then, remembering her supposed loyalist leaning, Gaby laughed. "You British constantly need to be taken down a peg or two; and who but an American would dare to do it?"

She walked resolutely over to the huge four-poster bed that she had been doing her best to ignore.

With her back to him, she felt much braver, but she gave a great start when he came close, holding her from behind as he asked tenderly, "Gabrielle, would you prefer me to leave for a while or may I remain here and watch you undress?"

She turned about in his arms and looked up at him, startled.

"Watch me! Why would you want to watch me?"

He took hold of one of the four posts and laughed so hard, he had to lean against the bed to support himself.

"Why would I *want* . . ." He fell to laughing, then collapsed again. "My dear, my darling, if you are forced to ask such a question, you truly are inexperienced. Your husband was indeed, too old and your lover much too young. You know nothing . . . nothing at all worth knowing. The undressing, love, is part of the numerous exquisite pleasures that come before final fulfillment.

It is quite exciting for a man to let his fancy rove while he watches a beloved woman slowly and sensuously remove her clothing."

"I have never undressed before anyone," Gaby said naively, "except, my mother, of course, when I was a little girl. But it's not the same, I suppose."

"No, darling," he answered gravely, "not at all the same. With some men and women, it is even regarded a great pleasure if the gentleman assists with the undressing."

"Truly?"

"Truly."

"What you are really trying to say," said Gaby wisely, "is that you would like to undress me?"

"Yes," he said solemnly. "In fact, I would gladly serve as abigail for the taking off of every garment—shoes and stockings included—that you have on."

"I will consent to . . . to pleasure you in the matter of removing my clothes provided you will do something for me."

"You may have half my kingdom, girl."

"No, this is serious."

"Then I will be serious, too."

"I want us both to pretend that this is my very first time of . . . of . . ."

"Loving."

"Yes, thank you, of love. I want to be able to feel that I have never done this before, which, in one way, I feel I haven't. I want you to teach me to love in the way that you would if I was your bride. A frightened virgin bride on her wedding night. That's what I want to be. Someone in love but scared because everything is so unknown. She wants kindness and understanding as well as love."

"You shall have all three, I promise you."

She gulped a little, looking down at her shoes. "And can you . . . would it be too hard for you to pretend that there has been no other man in my life?"

"Agreed," he said quietly. "And shall we expand that just a bit?"

"I—suppose," looking up again but sounding rather doubtful.

"Let there be no other man after."

Her face lit up, her eyes a-glow.

"With all my heart," she pledged. "No other man after."

And with that, Darcy reached for her, and they embarked on a long and passionate embrace. His hands wandered about her person, intimate in the extreme, and sometimes even shocking.

It seemed a long time before he released her, and now she had to clutch the bed post because her legs were so unsteady, she knew they would never support her. The post would hold her upright until she regained her balance.

"Oh my! I certainly liked that," she said so fervently that Darcy had a difficult time holding back laughter.

"But why," pursued Gaby, "did you do that little flicking motion of your tongue across my lips?"

"You did not like it? Then, let us banish it from the course of study. Everything I do is meant to be part of your education."

"In that case, you may do it again, if it pleases you," she offered graciously. "Later on, we can weed out the parts that are . . ."

She floundered about in her mind and was grateful when he came to her aid.

"I think," he said helpfully, "that you would like to learn each bit of knowledge so that you can accept or reject it later on in the—er—proceedings. That is, as much as one can reasonably expect of your first lesson."

"Thank you."

"You are quite welcome. Now, about the tongue—"

"As a matter of fact," Gaby confided, "I rather liked the sensation of having your tongue just touching my lip lightly . . . It gave me a delightful, shuddery kind of feeling. But that one time, when your tongue pushed against *my* tongue, I did not like the sensation at all. If you want me to be quite honest . . ."

"I want you always to be quite honest."

"Well then," confessed Gaby, "it did not strike me as a healthful thing to do . . . and one hardly feels romantic while indulging in an act that may do harm to the health."

"It would be," Darcy said solemnly, "absolutely fatal to romance. We will never . . . accidentally . . . touch each other's tongues again. Anything else?"

"No, everything else, I recall, was quite enjoyable."

"Good. Now come with me"—he held out his hand—"to the bed."

"So soon? We have hardly begun—"

"My dear girl, I hope you do not think that once I have you on a bed the preliminaries are over and the serious love-making starts." He studied her bent head and downcast face. "I see. It was exactly what you *did* think. You were quite right in your previous judgment. Neither husband nor lover appears to have been skilled in the art of love."

Gaby lifted her face to his. "The *art* of love," she repeated. "It is truly an art?"

"The most passionate and consuming of all arts."

Gaby considered a moment, then, to his astonishment, she laughed out loud and joyously.

"Teach it to me, please. I long to be passionately consumed and passionately consuming. It sounds the most pleasant art form I have ever heard of."

And it was.

Thirty-five

Darcy lay on his back, with his hands folded under his head. His eyes were still closed. She studied him carefully and was relieved to see the movement of his chest—good, he was breathing.

Gaby had curled herself against him like a kitten, loving the proximity of his body. He smelled differently, somehow, but it was a wonderful smell, a man-smell probably . . . or, perhaps, just a making-love smell. She would ask him . . . a little later . . . when he opened his eyes . . . when she was not so lethargic . . . when she was not so altogether languorous herself . . .

In the middle of her decision to consult him, Gaby's eyes closed, too. When she awoke again, Darcy still slept. The still, deep sleep of total exhaustion. Poor darling, he had done most of the work. *She* was bubbling over with energy and delight.

She put one hand on the nearest of his bared shoulders and wondered if the correct and modest thing to do now was to put on her shift or some other article of clothing that would cover up part of her own bareness.

The trouble was—she squirmed even closer against him—she enjoyed her bareness. For that matter, she was enjoying his bareness, too. Body against body, skin against skin.

Incredible that she could have been terrified of the consummation that, recaptured in memory, had been the most blissful experience of her life.

The marvel of it had begun the moment she sat down on the edge of the bed. He had knelt in front of her to remove each of her shoes. After the shoes had been tossed to a far corner, his hand slipped under her overskirt and petticoat. Slowly, tantalizingly, he held onto a foot while his hand made a slow progression all the way up her leg. When it reached the summit it sought, he was able to dispatch a garter (which he flung away, too) and then slip inside the stocking, which he had peeled off her leg in the same leisurely way, so that, to her own bewilderment, she suddenly wanted to cry out, *Hurry, hurry, get on with it!*

Why she felt as she did—why she wanted more from him—much more—she did not know. The urgency of her desire was utterly bewildering.

After shoes, garters and stockings were disposed of, he seemed perfectly content to give his entire attention to her legs. Each one, in turn, received the benefit of having the instep stroked, the toes nibbled quite gently, and the ankles caressed and kissed.

Just when it seemed to her she could not bear another minute of such bittersweet torment, he laid her back on the bed and then stretched himself across her. It was only farther along in her education that she realized he had used the strength of his hands and wrists so she would not feel his full weight.

"Dear God," she heard him mutter, "how is a slip of a girl like you going to carry me?"

The question was one of the many puzzles of this strange, wild night that she stowed away in her memory to consider later.

There was something deliciously wicked about his next attack on her senses.

With her overskirt and petticoat still on, he managed to keep his hands under them, touching only vulnerable places, investigating here, there, everywhere. The shocking intimacy of it left her paralyzed, unable to protect herself from his lusty onslaughts, dubious about whether she *wanted* to protect herself.

She became excited, and he quite frenzied.
She soon became inflamed, he was already impassioned.
She became flustered, he was fiery.
She felt pangs of dismay, but he was determined.
She was finally aroused to the same pitch as he.
She never remembered how Darcy did it. Magically, he was

naked and so was she. Both splendidly bare and frantically eager, they were ready for rapture together. Clutching each other in wanton abandon, they rolled over and over the bed.

She was whimpering and he was moaning.

"Someone is screaming."

"Yes, my wild, unschooled love. The someone is you."

She was indignant. "I never scream."

He was indulgent. "You were never loved."

Thirty-six

The weeks and months fly by for lovers . . . but for spies, they often drag.

"I don't know what I am going to do," Gaby confessed miserably to Penelope one morning. "He keeps pressing me *so* for marriage, and his uncle keeps pressing *him* to sell out and go home."

"I am amazed," said Penelope, in her usual calm way of dealing with momentous matters, "that you have not considered a very simple solution to most of your problems. Let him leave the army, marry, and go home to England with him."

"Penelope, how can you even suggest I do such a terrible thing?"

"I see nothing terrible—nor does Mercy—about marrying the man you love. We will not be at war with England forever, remember, and your father is there, after all."

"Yes, indeed, the father who is presumed to be dead. Don't you think it would require a great deal of explaining if that father came onto the scene, hale and hearty, and married to a much younger woman?"

"Hm," Penelope mused. "It would take a deal of explaining."

"Besides which," Gaby asked indignantly, "how can you believe that I would ever leave the Wheel in the lurch? Do you think so little of my promises? I swore to Mercy, when I first asked to be a part of it, that I would never put my personal life before the Wheel's interest."

"My dear," said Penelope kindly, "circumstances alter, resolutions change. We are talking *not* of the next few years, but of your entire life."

"Quite true, and my entire life is bound up in this new conception of our freedom from England. You know that to be true, Penelope. Was I not Pythias long before I came to New York? My inheritance is in New Jersey, so is my life. Even if I wished to marry Darcy, and damnation, part of me yearns to do just that, the fact remains, there is no possibility that I can."

"You seem to have considered your options rather seriously."

"Of course I did. Good God, Penelope, you and Mercy know I am not some flibbertigibbet spinster trying to catch a man. How could I even do so? By telling another mountain of lies? He hates liars. He would not forgive me lightly. The truth would injure his man's pride most grievously. He would never forgive my using him as I have all too freely done." She parodied a piteous confession. 'Darcy, it is true that I sometimes went through private dispatches you had with you, after you fell asleep, but I loved you even while I did it.

" 'Many times, when you wished to be alone and so did I, I urged a social life upon you so that I could milk your friends of gossip and trick them into honest answers. I would betray your interests any time I had to if it was for my country's need.' "

"It would indeed be difficult to find a solution. On the other hand, not impossible. As for the Wheel . . . no one is indispensible, Mrs. Forsyth-Foote, not even"—she patted Gaby's shoulder to take the sting from her words—"not even you and I, nor Mercy Enough, nor any of the others."

"Penelope, you have had three husbands. You understand the working of men's minds more than all of us. Darcy loves me. He loves me truly. I think he might ultimately forgive me the lies, the betrayal, the pretenses . . . I don't think he would forgive my making a fool of him. In my own mind, I did not; but in his mind, I fear, that is how he would always regard what I have done."

Penelope considered for a moment, while she hefted the brush with which she had been untangling Gaby's own hair.

"Yes," she sighed finally, resuming her brushing, "men are very prickly when wounded in their pride."

"Besides which," said Gaby stoutly, "there is the matter of my own pride. I do not want to live with a man who has 'forgiven' me when I believe that I did nothing for which I need to be forgiven. You know me well, Penelope. Do you really believe I could ever be a properly humble penitent?"

"No, my dear, I can't imagine it for a moment." She heaved a deep sigh before adding, "I shall tell Mercy Enough my opinion when next I have the opportunity. I daresay you realize, too, that there is an extremely romantic heart beating under Mercy's Quaker gray. She has been trying to convince herself, as well as us, that there could be a happy ending to this love story."

"There *is* a happy ending," Gaby declared stoutly. "I shall have known a deep and true love and been grateful all my life for it. When the war is over, I will feel proud all my days for having played some small part in making a single nation out of thirteen unruly, rebellious colonies. I shall live all my years after the war with an aunt I dearly love and admire, who will train me for my future as a landowner, and I shall work all my life for the cause of unruly, rebellious women who want only for themselves what their men want for this land."

There was silence between them for a few minutes, while Penelope continued to comb and brush.

Presently, Gaby sighed. "Oh, by the by, I suppose I need not report to you that another simple soldier has confided to me, with the solemn mien of one who is divulging news of great secrecy that General Howe will soon be embarking with his main command for Philadelphia."

Since any man or woman on the crooked, cobbled streets of New York or in the many coffee houses was well aware of the general's intention, Penelope only smiled. The Wheel had received its initial information on the subject, almost as soon as the decision was made at British Headquarters.

"I think," Gaby continued, "it is why my major is so urgent. He has no real fear for my safety here, while he is away with the army, but he would feel a little less uneasy about me if I could be his loyal, legal wife, under the protection of *both* armies."

"It is a rather sound notion," Penelope said, tipping her head slightly to the right, one finger on her mouth in a way she habitually used when she was deep in thought.

"No, and no again," said Gaby decidedly. "As his mistress, I will give the Wheel all my local cooperation; but to *marry* him and then use that marriage for his country's undoing is an act of infidelity even I cannot contemplate."

"Very well." She sounded much too meek to be Penelope. Gaby twisted around and looked up at her with great suspicion.

"I mean it, Penelope!"

"I know you do, Mrs. Forsyth-Foote." Penelope smiled broadly. "I merely wished to discover the boundaries of your love for him, your allegiance to us."

"It may not appear so to you, nor to Darcy, if he knew all there was to know about me, but I do have an honor of my own."

"I know you do, child." Penelope bestowed a rare kiss on Gaby's cheek. "I even have a rather muddled one of my own. But with three husbands, I had neither chick nor child. I find myself adopting you for that role, which Mercy would not approve of either. Although I agree our allegiance belongs to the Wheel, I find myself more and more inclined to wish for your permanent happiness with Major Rhoads. You say nothing of it, but I know you are making a considerable sacrifice."

"Dear Penelope. Thank you, but I chose sides long before I met Darcy Rhoads; and after I met him, please believe, I entered into the bargain with Mercy Enough, then you, in the full knowledge of what I was doing. I would be far more happy if Darcy remained in total ignorance of who and what I am than discover the truth and learn to scorn and despise me. Himself, too, if it comes to that. I could not bear for him to be filled with self-hate, never sure during the time we were together how much I loved him. That," she finished sadly, "would be the canker in his peace when we parted, much more so than just believing I did not love him enough to share the life of his choosing."

* * *

"I know it must be a matter of importance or you would never have arranged for me to come to you," said Gaby, as Mercy Enough took her plain black bonnet and laid it carefully on a sideboard in the pantry.

"Yes, Gabrielle. We must discuss the next phase of our operations and decide the extent of your involvement in it—if any."

Gaby's brows mounted her forehead. "Indeed?" she said icily.

"Dear child," said Mercy with a softer smile, "no one of us doubts your capability or your support, but the shifting of Howe's present base to Philadelphia makes that area of strategic importance just now."

"I could go to Philadelphia if I am needed there," said Gaby eagerly, then she drew back and was quiet a full five minutes, looking into her own treacherous heart.

"No," she said presently, "it is better that I do not go. Major Rhoads will soon be there, and I know that when I asked about Philadelphia, I thought more of being reunited with him than of my work. I am looking for him, even before he departs."

"Thou art a brave child."

"I feel myself to be decades older at times," said Gaby, conscious of a great weariness of both body and spirit.

"Have thee given any thought to resigning—quite honorably—from this service thee enlisted in and have done so well by? A tired agent is a danger to all, and so is a discouraged agent. Unless thee are with us, body, heart and soul, thou canst not give us the unquenching, unquestioning service that is our need."

"I think I can," said Gaby carefully. "I am despondent now, I confess, because tomorrow I will see him for the last time before Howe and his army embark. Darcy tried to pretend otherwise, but I knew he was angry at our last meeting because I did not promise to commit my life to him. I do not know how he will feel tomorrow. Torn between his love, I suspect, combined with the same resentment. I will go wherever you choose to send me, Mercy Enough. I will yield any judgment of my own to the service of you and the Wheel. If it means I never see Darcy again, so be it. I can bear no more scenes, no more of my inclination at war with what I believe is my first devotion."

Tears began to roll down her cheeks. She talked on through them. "I knew that eventually there would be sorrow the day I sent the first poem by Pythias to our town newspaper, in defiance of what my father's wishes would have been."

Mercy Enough handed her a handkerchief from her pocket. Gaby wiped away her tears and their conversation continued. "If God has any part in such a wicked man-made thing as war, he sent me to Aunt Emily's for a purpose. Up until then, the only sword I had wielded was my pen. It was she, a woman alone, subject to no will but her own, who taught me that women need not sit meekly by and do the bidding of their men-folk. Mercy Enough, why are you laughing when I have been pouring out my heart to you?"

"Forgive me, child." Mercy fetched the kettle from the hob behind the fireplace and poured out cups of tea for both of them. "It was the concept—sincerely spoken, I am quite sure—of thee, sitting meekly by while thee does as thy men-folk decree. There is not a submissive bone in thy entire body, my dear Gaby."

Gaby gave a sputtering little laugh. "Well, perhaps you are right, but what you said of me, I would say of *thee*. You may dress soberly and walk sedately, but you are no shrinking violet, Mercy Enough, any more than I am."

"That is true, Gabrielle, painfully true. I, too, confess to the sin of pride. Let me suggest something to thee. Have thy farewell with Major Rhoads, and once he is gone . . ."

She paused tactfully and Gaby said it for her. "And that chapter of my life is over and done . . ."

"Exactly. Then thee will consider carefully, very carefully for several days and inform Penelope of thy decision. If thee wish to go home to thy aunt in New Jersey and forget Mrs. Forsyth-Foote ever existed, it will be arranged. If thee wish to continue in this deviant branch of General Washington's service, thy rooms on Queen Street will be kept for thee—in case of thy future need—but thee may be sent elsewhere, perhaps only for a while. No, Gaby, I am aware thee long to know where that 'elsewhere' is, but it is better thee do not know, if thou art *not* to serve."

"I suppose you are right." Gaby sighed deeply. "Sometimes, Mercy Enough, I wish that *thee* were not so everlastingly, tiresomely right all the time!"

"If I am that, I must wish it, too, Gabrielle. One may appreciate the precise, the perfect, the pedantic, but seldom is it loved."

"No one could not love you, Mercy Enough."

"I thank thee, dear Gabrielle. Now, finish thy tea and get thee gone. Take as long as thee wishes to come to a conclusion. Thy decision must be the right one."

Thirty-seven

Their love-making had always been vocal, if incoherent, but on this night, they surpassed themselves. Though it was slightly on the chill side in their house on the river, sweat poured down both bodies as they clung together.

No doubt, the coming separation was part of it, but neither could get enough of the other, and they fell asleep several times, only to wake an hour or two later, ready to fulfill their need again.

Darcy made love to her, unhappy that they would be so long apart, and frustrated that he had not wrung from her what he most wanted—the promise of marriage. Gaby was in even worse case. She knew only too well that he and she might never meet again. She wanted a lifetime of loving in just a matter of hours.

Both fell into uneasy sleep, but at Darcy's last waking, he looked at his pocket watch lying on the nightstand and turned to put one arm around the sleeping girl, all too aware of how little time they had. How much younger she looked when she wore her own hair, and it drifted over the pillow, cloudlike.

She looked so much younger, so very innocent, utterly unlike the woman of fire and passion who had shared so many long nights of love. Nor did her face give any clue to the stubborn woman who unaccountably refused to marry him. Sometimes, when he looked down at her, a tiny flicker of remembrance stirred his brain. It came and went so quickly, so fleetingly, he had no idea just who he had remembered or what. The girl in his arms was a unique blend of personalities.

Gabrielle, the delightful companion, lovely and desired; the wanton Grabrielle; the aggravating, headstrong, willful Gabrielle. All three had challenged him deeply, wormed their way into his heart to be kept there forever, but refused him his heart's desire. Half the women in England would have accepted him, not for himself, but because they desired to be the future Countess of Linley. Only *she,* this outrageous American widow had spurned his proposals and she was the only one he wanted.

He cuddled Gaby close in his arms and, looking down, saw that her eyes were open.

"It's morning?"

"Yes."

"How soon must you leave?"

"In an hour."

"Will the carriage take me to the dock with you when you leave?"

"Please, don't come. It will be a mad scene. I don't want our good-byes spoken in public before a large throng of onlookers. I prefer some decent privacy."

Tears welled up in Gaby's eyes, even as she strove for enough control to quip, "I think you mean *in*decent privacy."

"So I do," he said, kissing away her tears.

There had been enough fire and passion during the long night. This time, they kindled no fires. They came together slowly, leisurely, lovingly, like a man and woman who had loved long and knew each other well.

He stroked her with his hands, with his mouth, and whispered of love in her receptive ear and asked in return and received from her like pledges of love and faithfulness.

"Damnation!" he said, as she moved onto her back and he slid over her so they were face to face. "I believe if I had a chaplain here this moment, I would induce you to marry me."

"Probably," she sighed.

"Do you know how maddening you are?"

"Yes. Kiss me."

"I'm damned if I will. Why should *you* be the one to have things all your way?"

"My way?" said Gaby indignantly. "I'm in your house, in your bed, and half of New York knows about it. What's my way about that?"

"It was all done without a wedding ring."

"For you or for me?"

"For you, of course."

"Why should *I* wear a ring and you not?"

"Because any damn woman I ever met, till I came to this country of stubborn, opinionated people, prizes a ring above all."

"I don't happen to be another woman."

"Tell me something I don't know."

"Darcy . . . Darcy, please . . . We have so little time. Even if it's just banter . . . I know it's part of your love-making, but there's so little time . . . you haven't gone . . . and I'm already missing you more than I can bear."

He settled his full weight on her and she bore the burden gratefully. It felt so good. So achingly marvelous.

"Darcy. I love you. Please promise to remember always that with all my heart and soul and this body you are squashing like a flapjack, I love you. If the time ever comes when you doubt it, believe your heart, not your head."

"Silly girl," he whispered in her ear. "I know you do, which is why I occasionally want to wallop you."

"Knowing I love you makes you want to wallop me?"

"Yes."

"There are ways and ways of loving," said Gaby with a droll look up at him. "I would appreciate another way, if you don't mind."

"At your pleasure, madame."

"At yours, sir."

"Roll over."

"Yes. No. Kiss me, kiss me, kiss me."

He kissed her and she kissed back. It was a long, loving kiss and their joining was the same, quiet and filled with tenderness.

"Stay here," he said a little later as he eased his way out of the bed.

* * *

"Is that where you want to remember me?"

"Where else?" he asked, loving her gallantry. "By the way, I put the house in your name. The papers are in the wardrobe. I prefer you stay at Queen Street, rather than alone here, but in case of need, it is here and it is yours."

Incapable of speech, Gaby nodded.

"There's the direction of the housekeeper too, if you want her services."

She bobbed her head one more time.

"Close your eyes, my love. Think of me."

She closed her eyes obediently and he kissed each lid. She thought hard of him. In a little while, when she opened her eyes again, he was gone, and the wave of desolation that swept over her was a foretaste of what was to come.

Darcy was to prove too sanguine and Gabrielle too despondent about when or if they might ever meet again.

In May of 1778, General Sir Henry Clinton succeeded General Howe and brought his army back from Philadelphia.

During most of that year, Gaby had lived in Setaucket, one of the many harbor towns along Long Island Sound. The entire area had been a British outpost since the American defeat in 1776, when Long Island fell under the governance of the British.

Setaucket, like so many cove towns, was half-enemy, half-American. The difficulty sometimes was in knowing one from the other—distinguishing friend from foe. When Mercy Enough gave Gaby her assignment, she emphasized that would be one of her main problems. The handful of agents she could trust were made known to her. To all others she met, male or female, if she erred, it must be on the side of caution.

Friends, neighbors and relations had divided on this question. "Even families," Mercy had sighed. "Thus, it is in a civil war."

"Thee will have a set of three rooms at the home of a prosperous farmer. His is one of the rare homes that appears to have remained neutral, probably due to having only daughters in the present generation. However, do not trust even *this* information from *me*. One never knows."

"But Mercy, dear Mercy, what is my excuse for staying with them? And why are they willing to have me?"

Mercy's eyes twinkled merrily.

"For the oldest reason in the world."

"Ah," said Gaby. "Money."

"Ah," Mercy agreed. "Money."

"But you said he is prosperous?"

"He is also," she explained, "originally from Connecticut."

"Oh, a Yankee." Gaby nodded wisely. "That explains all. I wonder his house is not crowded from cellar to rafter with paying guests."

"He had three daughters, who all married during this last year and are now scattered with their husbands from Rhode Island to Pennsylvania."

"Three daughters. Three rooms. How do you keep all these bits and pieces tucked neatly away in your mind? And in what guise, Mercy Enough, have you foisted *me* on *them?*"

"Thee are troubled by nervous complaints and the air of New York did not agree with thee. Thy doctor recommended the sea air, a more tranquil atmosphere, and less rich food and wine."

"Good God!" Gaby groaned. "How could you do this to me Mercy? I can imagine what kind of creature they expect me to be."

"Then thee will be a pleasant surprise for them, though not," Mercy warned, *"too* pleasant a surprise, Gabrielle. It is better to establish that thee are wealthy and pampered and notional; it widens the scope of your activities without raising eyebrows if you do not always act according to fixed custom."

Gaby nodded. It made—as Mercy Enough always did—good sense.

"Penelope?"

Mercy shook her head sadly, knowing what a blow it would be to her intrepid operative. "A fine lady's maid would be out of place on a Long Island farm. She would cause undue speculation.

Thee will have much more need of wool in winter, cotton in summer, and stout boots instead of dance slippers."

"And a powdered wig would have me laughed off the island?"

"I fear so."

"Thee need not fear," said Gaby waspishly. "I will be glad to be done with pompadour wigs and powdered hair once and for all, but I shall . . . I shall miss Penelope quite dreadfully."

"I know, my dear. And she is grieved to be losing thee. She loves thee as a daughter."

"Do I lose you too, Mercy Enough?"

"Thee has no further need of me in this new service."

"Thee are wrong. I am losing all else, it appears. I need *thee* badly."

"I expressed myself wrongly. For thy work and mine, we no longer need each other here in New York. My love and good wishes will always be with thee, dear Gabrielle. And I will pray for thee that when the war is over, thee finds peace and happiness."

Gaby tried to answer her but could not, her voice was too choked.

"Take this paper," said Mercy Enough. "Sit here near to the fire till the names and directions are fixed in thy memory. This is thy litany. Recite them every day, twice a day, however often thee need to remember. Then, throw it on the fire and make sure it is reduced to ashes. I will be upstairs in the bedchambers for twenty minutes. Will that be enough time?"

Gaby glanced at the paper. "M-more than enough."

When Mercy returned to the kitchen, Gaby's eyes were reddened, but the paper was burned to black embers and she was able to recite the whole of its contents to the sober, middle-aged spy who she had suspected sometimes of being the head—not just a worker—in one of the espionage rings in New York City.

"There is only one thing more," Mercy Enough said gently, "and this sacrifice may be hardest of all for you—or, perhaps even impossible, I must know if it is . . . If you question it, even the least bit . . ."

"Why did you bring me so far," Gaby interrupted painfully, "when you knew that this, of all things, would be most difficult of performance? You are going to speak to me of cutting off any contact between Major Rhoads and me."

"I think it best if he not know you have left New York while he is in Philadelphia. If you correspond, let your letters be farther and farther apart and then gradually cease."

In her effort to keep her voice quite steady, even to Gaby's ears, it sounded bitter and astringent. "Major Rhoads, in spite of being British, has reasonable intelligence. Do you think he will be unable to detect the difference between a letter directed from this city and one posted on Long Island?"

"All your letters will come first to me, and I will see to their safe sending. His will be dispatched to me before ever they reach Queen Street, and then from me to thee. I regret—it is only fair to tell thee—that these letters must be read carefully by others. We cannot relax our vigilance to save thy finer sensibilities, Gabrielle."

There was a slight pause. Then, "You must have been a terror at Meeting, Mercy Enough," said Gaby ruefully.

"Some sinners," Mercy said complacently, "were wont to quake before me."

"Even as I."

"Thee are no sinner, my dear Gabrielle. Thee are a woman I love and admire—and whether anyone ever knows of it or not, thee deserve the thanks of a grateful nation." She folded Gaby in a fond embrace. "God be with thee, my dear, now and always."

Thirty-eight

Any place without Darcy was bound to seem a wasteland, Gaby admitted drearily, the day after she arrived in Setaucket. So, if she was going to be unhappy, she might as well be unhappy in Setaucket, on Long Island, where the air was unpolluted as well as freshened by a stiff salt breeze from the Harbor and Conscience Bay.

Although the island was a part of her country that had been foreign to Gaby's experience, it was not that different from New England's shore. It permitted her to be comfortable in an old familiar way. Stout leather shoes for walking along the shore and up inclines of rock and sand. Comfortable dresses suited to such walks. She wrapped herself in a cloak and tight-knit wool shawls that it was needful for her to buy at a shop in the town. Such workaday accessories had not been part of Mrs. Forsyth-Foote's wardrobe.

Best of all, was the dressing of her hair. It was luxurious by its very simplicity, to have it combed back from her face and tied with a simple ribbon. When the wind blew strong, it was a pleasure she had all but forgotten, to have her hair streaming behind her back, long, tangling and meshing together.

She loved to remember how he had hated her powdered hair and wigs. At night in bed, sometimes during the day, too, she thought with a remembering smile, he had played with the soft masses of her hair, as though it had a life of its own.

"I love the soap and garden smell of your hair," he would say often and sometimes when Penelope had knotted up her hair during the day for the itching, overperfumed, gluey mess that fashion decreed, she had thought of Darcy and lowered her head so Penelope would not see her small, secret smile.

Mr. and Mrs. Turner, the farmer and his wife with whom she boarded, were a plain, solid couple who were never likely to become bosom companions—which was all to the good. They were kind as well as brusque, however, and had a care to her needs. Gaby took her dinner with them, but not her breakfast, which was left on a tray, since she was no longer in the custom of rising at six in the morning. Promptly at eight would come a knocking at her door, and when Gaby, yawning and sometimes even cursing a little under her breath, padded to the door, Mrs. Turner would be gone, but the tray on the landing made its own statement.

Her duties at Setauket were light in comparison with New York. She was to be smilingly polite to all the natives, as well as to anyone from the British garrison.

At the same time, she was to keep a certain distance from all, so she would not become involved in personal relationships.

On receiving this order from one of the six names that had been on Mercy Enough's list, Gaby had exclaimed "Pray, how am I expected to do both, sir?"

The grizzled gentleman, a whaleboat captain from Stamford in Connecticut, noted for his lightning attacks on British vessels in Long Island, followed by swift retreats with the spoils of the British ship, answered rather sheepishly, "Damned if I know, ma'am. Begging your pardon, I'm only passing on a message from above."

"Well then, tell whoever is the damn fool who gives us our orders that this latest one is quite contradictory."

He tipped his hat. "I'll do that, ma'am," he said genially. "Don't suppose it will do any good no-how, but less'n the British sink me on the way home to Stamford, I'll deliver it, and Captain Abraham Cabot stands by his word."

Whenever Captain Cabot or one of his men came to Setauket, she passed on any drifting bit of information she had acquired, and received directions to relay to some of the others in her group, as well as packets of money for paying expenses.

She did not need the money, herself; she had a great deal of her own. When she looked in the wardrobe of the house near the river, Gaby found much more than the deed to the house.

The deed was there, to be sure, a packet of 500 pounds, English, and a copy of his will, in which she was named as his sole beneficiary. There was a letter. She read it once, twice, thrice—and during the whole of the next year, seldom a day went by without her feasting her eyes and her heart on the treasured words, though she knew them by heart.

Gabrielle, beloved Gabrielle, dear, sweet, stubborn Gabrielle. These words are for our parting, not at all in the nature of a final farewell. I am going only to Philadelphia, where there is no fighting. I suspect that we will be given over to the same frivolity that distinguished our operations in New York.

If you were with me, I would be overjoyed (and keep a minister handy for another of your more yielding moods).

Since you are not going to be with me, all I can pray for is a speedy return. My dearest of dears, I never believed that I could love a woman as I love you.

I am yours more than I am my own, Darcy.

Gaby well knew that her first letter to him would be read by others, but she made up her mind to pretend otherwise. He deserved a letter meant solely for him, and the devil with the readers of other peoples' letters, who ought to be ashamed of themselves.

My dearest, my only Darcy

I hate Philadelphia (where I have never been), but it is the place where *you* are and *I* am not, so I can only say as Macbeth did—or was it his Lady?—"Out, damned spot! Out, I say!" Not that I wish any harm to Philadelphia or its inhabitants. It is only that—exactly like you—I am hostile to any city which houses only one of us.

I am yours, too, beloved

Gabrielle

When she finished her letter to him and cried over it just as copiously as she had over his to her, though it was neither wise nor prudent nor true, she could not resist adding one small *post scriptum: I pray you will have your minister handy when we meet again.*

As the weeks passed, Gaby had so much free time, it became a burden. Exchanges of messages with ship captains and shopkeepers took only so many hours in a week.

She could not help Mrs. Turner around the house or offer to do light chores on the farm, having established her reputation to all but agents as a sweet but silly woman unaccustomed to doing a hand's turn of useful labor.

She was forced—she who hated sewing with a passion—to always have a bit of sewing about her. She was making baby clothes, she explained, for her dear sister in the Hampshire Grants, about to have her first child at the overripe age of thirty-five.

She blushed with shame and confusion when Mrs. Turner gave her little knit garments. "I was saving them for my girls' needs, but there are so many, I have to spare. Cloth and thread are costly in the Grants, I hear, and needles so dear, they are hoarded carefully."

Gaby locked the door of her room one night and poured out all her feelings on the back of an invitation for a ball at the British garrison.

> The climate here is splendid, I have improved my health by being removed from the malodorous atmosphere for New York City, most particularly in this season. I have time and funds with which to pay my way and have struck up acquaintance with a varied assortment of residents here, who offer cheerful hospitality and enjoyable companionship.
>
> There is this to weigh, as well. If my duties add up so much as a half hour of every day, I would be much amazed. It is necessary that I write lying letters to my dear father

and his wife, in England, to my beloved aunt in New Jersey, to the man I love . . . wherever he may be. All this deceit, all the lies and broken promises would be endurable if I could take pride in my sacrifice . . . If I could tell myself, I do this because of what the Lord did for me when I came out of bondage.

Further, I can no longer disguise from myself the emptiness of my present life. I can no longer dismiss the possibility that I serve no useful purpose here. My presumed leader could struggle along quite as well without my puny services.

I am weary and tired of this nothingness, of false smiles and insipid conversation, of flirting with British officers, who snicker about my clothes and leather brogues, but become all respect when they hear my voice and realize I am not so much a farm maiden as I appear. There is, however, more than their truckling respect. Their attempts to lure me into odd corners (hay mows, barns, the stables, to name a few) for even though they realize, belatedly, that I am a lady, an *American* lady is not entitled to the respect given her English counterpart. Other than Mrs. Loring, of course. For a general's whore a more outward respect may be commanded.

Summing up all there is to say, I am sure you understand my determination to resign, and I would appreciate some acknowledgment of same. Until such acknowledgment is received, I shall carry on, but for a reasonable time only.

Gaby, who had written sitting up in bed with her lap desk resting on her knees, gave a deep sigh. When she was finished, she put the desk aside and leaned back against her pillows, flexing her hand, which was cramped from writing.

She closed her eyes, not to sleep, but to rest her eyes, and began to plan.

There was a letter from Darcy underneath her pillow . . . probably the last letter she would ever receive from him. And scrupulously, she had obeyed the Wheel's dictum . . . letters farther and farther apart . . . becoming less and less personal . . . and then ceasing.

This letter . . . slow tears dropped onto it as she read . . . showed how very successful she had been in obeying orders.

> *Are you out of your mind, Gaby or am I? Love and intimacy are supposed to go forward, not retreat. Once upon a time, I was your dearest, your only Darcy . . . and now you have the infernal impudence to demote me to dear Major. Once upon a time your letters were warm-hearted, impetuous, loving and they talked to me in the voice of my beloved Gabrielle.*
>
> *They were love letters, damn it!*
>
> *They were expressions of what we felt in our hearts but can only say now in our letters.*
>
> *Yours to me are cold and conventional; I might be only a slight acquaintance.*
>
> *Something is wrong between us. I know it is, but whenever I ask, you hide behind a barricade of insignificant formalities that drive me wild.*
>
> *If I had you here, I would shake the truth out of you.*
>
> *It is not that my man's pride is bruised—though it has taken a beating—but that we, you and I, loved as few ever do, and I cannot believe that mere distance has changed all that. Not when my own love for you burns bright as ever, and my wishes for our future are unchanged.*
>
> *Write to me again, dear, dear irritating Gaby. Tell me my fears are groundless. Speak to me as though you are in my arms.*
>
> *Tell me you love me as I love you—and will forever.*
>
> *Darcy*

Thirty-nine

New York was now only a city in which Darcy did not reside, so it was ridiculous of her to be excited, sensible Gaby admonished light-hearted Gabrielle, well wrapped in both a cloak and wool shawl, all the way from Long Island to Brooklyn.

Her scolding brought no change of attitude. She was excited . . . even happy, and happiness had been a long-time absent friend.

On reaching Brooklyn, she immediately asked where she could get a boat going to New York. It was near, just a few steps away. On the short ride, Gaby stood outside on the deck of the ferry, with the wind blowing her hair from under the shawl and billowing her petticoats and sending drafts up to her knees.

She was freezing; she was blithesomely happy.

When there was land underneath her feet again, she speculated as she walked how changed she was from that naive young girl, Gaby Foote, who had landed in this very place what seemed like years ago.

Since then, her whole life and even her character seemed utterly different.

She was on her way the last time to warn her father not to return to New Jersey. She carried a packed portmanteau, knowing her stay might be prolonged. She had never imagined, *could* never imagine that five minutes after she started walking from the docks toward the Broad Way to hail a hackney, she would find not only a hackney, but within it, the man she would come to love.

It was not cruelly cold as it had been then. There were such hordes of people, most of them shabby and—she pressed a lilac-scented handkerchief to her nose—in need of bathing. She was not lugging a heavy piece of baggage, and she could even see hackneys in the distance. Good. She must return to the docks in time to catch the last ferry back to Brooklyn City.

She secured her hackney easily and sat forward in it, after she gave the address of her dear house on the river.

She could not go in, she only longed to see it again and remember happier times.

She had been remembering them all too often since the brief exchange with her whaleboat captain from Stamford along the shore a fortnight ago. He looked at her, as they came nearer to one another, with none of his usual geniality. He would have passed by without so much as speaking, beyond "good morning," and a light tipping of his cap.

Gaby could not endure such suspense. She uttered a little cry of dismay and staggered.

"Oh, my ankle!" she cried aloud.

"Do you need assistance, ma'am?"

"No," bravely. "I am sure it's fine." As she said it, he whispered, "All operations to cease."

Gaby sat down on the rocks, with her back to him as she carefully inspected her ankle.

"No more messages," she heard behind her as the captain went on his way.

Since then, she had felt that she was living in a winter wasteland. No scrap of information received and none to give. How long would such a state continue? She could not bear the suspense.

From the vantage of the unbearable, she began to contemplate what might be possible.

Two days ago, she had begun to execute her own plan.

"I sometimes think that Setaucket is the most boring, poky, do-nothing place in this country," she complained over dinner, jabbing at a piece of chicken and then putting down her fork, chicken and all, and pettishly pushing away her plate.

Neither the farmer nor his wife commented, but just continued to chomp away at their own food with undiminished appetites.

"There's everlastingly nothing to do!"

"There is for them that don't mind putting their backs to a little hard labor."

Gaby suppressed a smile. *Good for you, Mrs. T.,* she applauded, but said aloud, heaving a great sigh, "New York was so gay. Parties and the theater, dances almost every day."

"Ain't that way now I hear," Mr. Turner said between mouthfuls, "except maybe if you're a British officer. Heard it's dirty and bad-smelling and overcrowded."

"Oh, no!" She pretended shock. "It could never be like that."

Mr. Turner used his index finger to dislodge a bit of chicken from his teeth.

"Got it firsthand," he said with great relish. "Tom Bishop up at the tack store. He were there only last week, getting supplies. Said you could have New York . . . he'd be happy never to see it again. Naught but a stinking cesspool, it was. Give him Long Island any time."

"But how could it change so," Gaby bleated, "in just a year?"

Mr. Turner shrugged philosophically. "War does strange things. Rich refugees from up north gittin' away from the cowboys and the skinners. Plenty of runaway slaves. British wives comin' by transport. Housing so almighty short, even some who held themselves pretty high is reduced to the street. Garbage and sewage everywhere. Packs of starvin', thievin' poor. If you're of a mind to do it, you can always take a boat to the city and see it for yourself. Me, I'd just as soon stay safe in Setaucket and take it on trust," he finished genially.

The meal was finished in total silence. Gaby had made her point; Mr. Turner had made his.

"Do you know what I have decided?" Gaby asked her hosts the next day. "I *am* going to go to New York and see for myself. I just can't believe that wonderful city has gotten as horrible as you say."

"You take an almighty lot of convincing." Mr. Turner smiled

at her and Gaby smiled right back. He glanced admiringly at her ankles when she lifted her skirts a trifle to get seated at the table. Mr. Turner liked his own plump, capable Maggie—she suited him fine—but there was no denying that Mrs. Forsyth-Foote showed pretty teeth when she smiled, and her ankles were something he didn't mind an occasional peek at.

The next day, by her own request, Gaby was wakened at five in the morning and summoned to breakfast at six. Then, because it was getting a little late, Mr. Turner drove his boarder to the docks in his farm wagon, so she would not miss passage on one of the rowboats that passed constantly between the island, Brooklyn and Manhattan.

At the time of day when she was usually still in bed in Setaucket, Gaby's hackney was rattling noisily along the wayfare that led to the house on the river. "Wait for me," she told the driver as she stepped down from the carriage.

She had the key to the house in her reticule, and her reticule was in a knit bag she had brought along in case she did some shopping.

Perhaps, however, she ought to knock. It would give the housekeeper a terrible start if she was in the house and Gaby suddenly appeared.

As she lifted her hand to the knocker, the door opened and a woman with two children clinging to her skirts looked at her in great surprise.

"May I help you?" the woman asked.

A British wife.

Gaby recovered quickly.

"I figure so, ma'am." She tried to sound Long Island. "Are you Mrs. Forsyth-Foote?"

"No, I am not," the woman answered in some annoyance. "I have lived here nearly a year, yet I keep getting inquiries about the woman. I wish she would tell her friends"—with a disparaging look at Gaby's flyaway hair and plain wool dress—"where she now resides."

"I beg your pardon, ma'am, I'm sure." Gaby backed away along the path, then turned and hurried to her hackney.

"Let me think a minute," she told her driver.

"Goin' to charge you the same as fer driving . . . takes up my time the same way."

"Very well. I shall pay for my thinking time, too," said Gaby tiredly, too worried to be amused.

She could not go driving past the house on Queen Street. Despite her unpowdered hair and drab dress, someone might recognize her, which no one should be able to do.

She longed with all her heart to go to Mercy Enough at the sign of the baby in its cradle, but that could put Mercy in jeopardy. If the captain's warning had meant the British were suspicious— even though she did not know what that suspicion might be—it might endanger anyone or everyone.

What she ought to do was go home—to Setaucket—this very minute and tell the Turners they were right about New York, it was as disagreeable as they had said.

But first, she ought to do a little shopping. The Mrs. Foote who resided with the Turners would certainly shop a little, no matter how or what the conditions were in New York.

She had used up a good deal of her "thinking" time when she was struck by a sudden notion.

"Take me to the Fly Market near Hanover Square. It's—"

"I know where it is, missie."

He whipped up the horse so swiftly she was thrown back against the cushions.

As he passed by street after street, Gaby was able to see and smell the evidence that New York had been desolated in the way Mr. Turner described.

Tears filled her eyes. It was so sad . . . like seeing a once-beautiful woman with her face painted, her skin mottled, wearing clothes and ornaments meant for someone far more youthful.

The Fly Market, at least, was much as Gaby remembered it from the day she first encountered Mercy Enough, although there were a great many children in raggedy clothes. They were so pale and skinny, their bones poked out from sallow skin. They looked near to starving, she realized in horror. Gaby scattered pennies and stray shillings among them and a trail like the Pied Piper's began to follow her. Presently she had to harden her heart and insist, "No more, no more"; and when that did not discourage them, she held tightly to her bag with the reticule thrust down to the bottom, bunching the cloth together and holding it in such a grip that it could not be wrested from her by one of the more daring boys or girls.

They finally gave up and she walked quickly to leave them far behind. As she reached the south end of the market, her steps lagged a little. This was almost the same spot where she had encountered Mercy Enough the first time, standing behind her stall with fresh lobsters to sell.

Oh, what she would not give to see dear Mercy Enough again. She paused, smiling mistily to herself, and prepared to walk on, then stopped again in the belief that what she saw could not be real.

There she was, Quaker-clad as always, neat and nice, smiling her usual pleasant smile. Mercy Enough stood behind a stall. There were two crates of lobsters on the ground, several poking their claws out of a basket on the stall table.

"Are thee in need of lobsters today, my dear?" said Mercy with the utmost tranquillity.

As she spoke, Gaby observed a man lingering at the next stall, inspecting fresh fish. He was too tall and erect to be a peddler . . . his eyes were on Mercy . . . his ears . . . most assuredly, he was listening to Mercy's conversation.

"My dear woman," said Gaby, her voice both loud and strident, "I live on Long Island, where these creatures abound as they do here. I sup on lobsters boiled and grilled and fried and baked, in chowder and in stew, even cold with garden greens. If I never saw—or tasted—another one, I would be quite pleased."

"Give gratitude to heaven then for thy good fortune," Mercy Enough said in her usual serene way.

"What good fortune is that?"

"Look at them." Mercy pointed to the crowd of children still dogging Gaby's footsteps from a distance. "What you disdain could bring them life."

"Ah," said Gaby, "a very good notion. I shall get rid of some of these pesky lobsters and give alms to the poor at the same time." She dug out her reticule and brought out a British pound note. "How many will this buy?"

"Very many."

"Good." Gaby hailed the children. "This lady will give you some lobsters and this gentleman . . ." She pointed to the peddler (who she would be willing to wager any amount was an agent). *Oh God, please God, let him not have evidence against Mercy.* "Give them half a dozen fish and some of these breads in the basket . . . no matter if they are hard, they can toast them."

She started passing money to the fishmonger, who looked sheepish as well as stunned. "Build yourselves a fire in one of the abandoned warehouses," she advised the children. "Cook them well and toast the bread."

Grabbing their booty, the boys and girls ran off, shrieking with excitement. The fishmonger addressed himself to Gabrielle. "You notice, they didn't bother to say thank-you."

"The Almighty thanks her," Mercy intervened. *"His* gratitude is infinite and everlasting. From where would children such as those learn proper ways? When they only know hunger and abuse, where would they have learned the niceties of etiquette?"

Gaby nodded to the "fishmonger" and looked deep into Mercy's eyes as she bade her an abrupt good-bye.

Shaking a little, she went on her way. At a stall where there were lovely knit garments, she purchased a fine, fringed shawl for Mrs. Turner, who would wear it proudly to church. Further on, she was able to find a pipe for Mr. Turner, and for herself, handkerchiefs and garters and stockings, not so much because she wanted or needed them, but to complete the picture of a lady from Long Island who had gone shopping in New York.

Forty

Gaby never could remember the hackney ride from the Fly Market to the docks, and then the two boat rides that returned her to Setauket, though clearly she must have spoken to a number of people in order to get herself home.

In spite of the bitter cold, she was glad of the walk to the farm. It gave her a little more time to compose herself.

When she came through the kitchen entrance, the Turners were seated at the trestle table having an early supper. Mrs. Turner jumped up at once.

"Just sit you down and I'll lay a plate for you, dearie," she said kindly. "You look plumb tuckered out."

"I *am* tired," Gaby admitted, "but not the least bit hungry. A friend I visited gave me a late tea, so I am still stuffed to here..." She indicated a point just below her chin.

What a facile liar I have become. When I am back with Aunt Emily, I must learn all over how to tell the truth... provided she is not deep in intelligence, too, and wanting my assistance.

She dug into the bag packed with her day's shopping and came up with the fringed shawl for Mrs. Turner. "I hope you will accept this as a little memento in appreciation of all your kindness to me."

"Why, thankee, Mrs. Foote." Mrs. Turner was plainly astonished that her boarder remembered her acts of kindness. "My! 'Tis the handsomest shawl I have ever owned." She threw it about her shoulders, preening a little. "Wait till folks see me in this."

"On Sunday at church?" Gaby suggested, smiling a little.

"Oh, my yes! Lottie Rawlins will be pea-green with envy."

"Now, wife," Mr. Turner's heart was not really in the reproach, especially after Gaby produced the meerschaum pipe for him.

"I will be swarmed," he said at least three times, "if this isn't the danged dandiest pipe I ever set my eyes on."

Gratified as she was by their pleasure, Gaby was so bone-weary, so surely troubled, she was afraid of bursting into tears.

"I think I will rest a while. Perhaps later . . ." She appealed to Mrs. Turner, "just some tea and biscuits."

"You just get some rest, m'dear," said Mrs. Turner in a motherly way. "Later, I will bring you a tray."

"Thank you."

Gaby climbed the two flights to her room, and as soon as she got there, tossed her cloak in a chair, pulled off her shoes, then almost fell on top of her bed, fully dressed.

Unless she was judging wrong—and she feared she wasn't—Mercy Enough had come under suspicion and there probably were others, too . . . Penelope . . . the actress . . . the coachman . . . God alone knew who else.

She did not fear for herself. It could easily be proved she had spent the last year in Setaucket in entirely blameless tedium; and there were plenty of island people (especially the Turners) to confirm that she had come there for her health and was a ladylike but useless sort of woman about the house.

Moving restlessly on her bed, she was struck by a sudden possibility. *Dear God, why did I not think of it earlier?* She need not stay on in Setaucket! With the Wheel in danger and operations closed, there was no reason—nay, it might even be better to leave.

She could not go back to New York. The beloved house on the river that Darcy had given her was gone . . . at least for quite a while—and she dared not return to Queen Street. Even if her standing there was the same as it had been as before, she could not be entirely sure . . . so it represented a risk. Besides . . . her eyes opened and shut several times before sleep overcame her. What was New York without the spice of her double life? What was New York if she must avoid Mercy Enough and not try to find Penelope?

Most of all, what was New York without Darcy? Dear, probably even-more-enraged Darcy than he had been in the letter he wrote to her?

Her father would receive her with joy, Gaby knew. Once he recovered from the shock and surprise of the confession she must make to him, he would comfort and forgive her. Lydia would be balm for her spirit.

But England was a long sea voyage away; and no matter how many Britons were in sympathy with Americans in this strife, England was still an enemy country!

She slept more than an hour, and when she awoke, Mrs. Turner was in the room, holding a tray.

"There now!" she said. "I was wondering, should I wake you—and you just awoke yourself. Here's your tea and some biscuits with honey and butter, and two fresh-laid eggs I just boiled for you. Fancy tea party or not; a body needs some good, plain food when she's all tuckered out. Can you manage if I put the tray on your knees?"

"Yes," said Gaby faintly. "Thank you."

The tray disposed of, Mrs. Turner lingered a moment. "I fancy you were upset about conditions in New York," she said shrewdly.

"Yes."

"Is it as bad as Bishop said?"

"Worse."

"Ah, well, that's war for you," Mrs. Turner said philosophically. "Men and their stupid quarrels."

She shrugged as she walked toward the open door of Gaby's bedroom, and Gaby called out to her, knowing that her heart had made the decision for her even as she slept.

"Mrs. Turner, I received several letters held for me in New York, which should have been sent to me here. My husband's mother is poorly and very much wants me to come to her. It is what"—she dabbed at her entirely dry eyes with one of her new handkerchiefs—"my dear Darcy would have wanted me to do, so it will be gratifying"—*Gaby, you hypocrite*—"to have someone need me again."

"Well, we shall be sorry to have you leave. For a lady," Mrs. Turner added, quite innocent of intent to insult, "you have been much less trouble than I imagined. But family is family; and, if she needs you, it is only right that you go."

"Th-thank you."

Hours earlier in New York, Gaby had been convinced that she would never smile again. Now, she had difficulty holding back her laughter. When the door closed behind Mrs. Turner and she heard the thump of her footsteps going down to the kitchen, she allowed her laughter full rein.

She laughed and laughed, with imminent danger to the tray on her knees; and after the laughter came her tears, a veritable waterfall.

She sobbed as she cracked her eggs; there was no need to add salt to them. She sobbed as she sipped her tea and poured honey over the biscuits.

I'm hysterical, said Gaby to Gabrielle.

I know, Gabrielle answered soothingly. *You are entitled to some small emotional indulgence.*

Small? I sound like a cat in heat.

You will be the better for it.

You sound so damn noble, I can't endure it. Gaby was decidely cross.

Very well, Miss. Solve your own problems. Gabrielle was gone.

After Mrs. Turner collected her tray, Gaby undressed, put on her warmest flannel nightgown and fetched her lap desk. She pulled little knit stockings on her feet, then got back into bed, fluffed two pillows behind her back, and set the lap desk comfortably on her knees.

She smoothed out, until it was almost flat, the piece of paper in which her new handkerchiefs and garters had been wrapped. Then she began her list.

What to give away.
What to take with me.

How do I travel to New Jersey without any single person having knowledge of Aunt Emily's name or my destination?

There must be no trails for anyone to follow. Gaby chewed reflectively on the end of her pencil.

Pampered, self-styled invalid, Mrs. Forsyth-Foote must disappear as completely from Setaucket as the effectively fashionable loyalist, Mrs. Forsyth-Foote, had vanished from New York.

Is there anyone I must contact? On the contrary. Those I wish to have speech with are the very last ones who should have speech with me.

She chewed on her pencil again.

Her expenses in Setaucket, like those in New York, had been paid for by the Wheel. She would have to ask the Turners if anything was still owed to them. Other than that, there would just be traveling expenses.

She had long ago spent all the money that Aunt Emily had pressed on her when she left New Jersey. The five hundred pounds that had been left by Darcy in her wardrobe along with his will, the deed to the house, and her precious love letter . . . was far more than the maximum sum she was likely to need.

By the time she snuffed her candles, she had penciled in all the answers to her questions. She had pretty much decided where and how to leave.

On awakening in the morning, she reached for the list on her nightstand to find out if the plans she had made in the evening seemed wise by the light of day. Happily, they did.

She slid down under her comforter again to stay warm and cozy. She would go to West Point in the New York highlands above the Neutral Ground, traveling by a private hired coach with her trunk half-full of Mrs. Forsyth-Foote's splendid wardrobe—not that she cared about the clothes per se, but each item was in some way connected with Darcy. The yellow one in which he declared her his little buttercup; the one cut so low at the neck, he had promised to ravish her on the spot if she ever wore it out again in public. There was the blue and silver brocade . . . "My

God, do you know how beautiful you are?" he had said the first time he saw it.

"That is love talking," she had teased him.

"Know then, my dear skeptic Colonial, that you are beautiful because I love you, which is a great deal better than I love you because you are beautiful."

She closed her eyes, reliving the dialogue.

"That sounds too profound for me."

"Then, accept my word for it."

"Your man's word."

"Of course." His eyes had dared her. "You know full well that man is wiser, stronger, in every way superior."

They had been in bed in the dear-loved house on the river. She would probably—deed or not—never see the house again. The silver and brocade dress so inspired him, he had just extricated her from it.

At his teasing challenge, she had knelt on his chest and was pummeling him with a pillow. He endured this treatment for as long as it pleased him to pretend to be at her mercy.

When the game became no longer a game, in a trice, he had reversed positions. She lay underneath him, and he was smiling fiendishly down at her, her thighs in the grip of his knees and, no matter how she jerked her head about, he managed to snatch kisses from her lips, and to shower them on her forehead and eyes, as well as the tip of her nose and the ticklish spots just behind her ears.

Oh, God, dear God, I don't want ever to forget, but someday there must be an end to pain.

She opened her eyes, awakened to reality, and conscious of the convulsive movements of her legs.

She threw back the comforter and the rush of cold air took care of the wonderful, painful memories, along with her body's yearning.

It was freezing cold. She scrambled into the clothes laid over the fire screen. Unfortunately, the fire was not yet lit, so dressing brought more than one shriek and a few curses too at the touch of chilled garments.

She was just tying up her hair at the back with a bit of ribbon when Mrs. Turner's perfunctory knock was followed so soon by her entrance that if Gaby had wished to keep her out, it would have been impossible.

Mrs. Turner looked at her boarder in some surprise. "Why, Mrs. Foote, you are certainly up and about quite early today."

"There is so much to do . . . so many plans to make," Gaby answered, a bit flustered.

Mrs. Turner whisked away a lace doily on the dresser and set down her tray.

"Why," she said, "I had not thought of it, but I expect you are right. Bless me, I'll be forgetting where my own head is next. There's your trunk and that great leather case of yours under the rafters. You will be wanting them down soon, I don't doubt."

"Oh, yes," said Gaby as though up until now, Mrs. Forsyth-Foote's trunk and young Gaby Foote's portmanteau had never entered her mind. "So I will. Please tell your husband . . . the moment he can spare a few moments, I would be obliged if he would bring them down from the attic to this room. They could be set in the corner over there"—she pointed—"out of the way, but close by hand when I start sorting and packing my clothes and linen."

"Oh, ay, never fear, he's got a stout back, has Turner," Turner's wife assured Gaby with simple pride. " 'Twill be no trouble at all. He'll have them down in a jiffy. I'll mention it when I go out to gather the eggs. Will you be needing a hand from me yourself, dearie?"

"Not at present, thank you." said Gaby, sounding properly grateful. "Later on, I expect that I shall."

"Will you be wanting the Sommers lad for a wagon cart to convey you?" Mrs. Turner asked more from curiosity than to oblige. "He's a good steady lad and won't drive you to distraction and give you palpitations by reckless driving."

"I'm not sure yet," Gaby hesitated only for seconds, then decided she might as well begin her cover story now, starting with the Turners. There was bound to be gossip and speculation. Let the news bruited about town be of *her* choosing, rather than fancied rumors.

"I am not quite sure how I will travel, Mrs. Turner. You see, West Point is such a far distance, I do not know even if I must sleep at an inn along the way. I have never been there before because the elder Mrs. Foote came to *my* home for the wedding, and we have not . . ."

She plucked a clean handkerchief out of her sleeve and, greatly to her own surprise, it was needed to mop up real tears. "We have not met since my husband's . . ." She hid behind the handkerchief, half-laughing, half-crying again.

"There now, there my dear, you will be a comfort to each other, I feel certain. Some called the senior Mrs. Turner crotchety, but I ended up real friendly-like with her before she got the consumption. I missed her like my own blood when she passed on to her reward."

Gaby emerged from behind the handkerchief, reasonably sure that her eyes were swollen and red.

"I think I will take a walk," she said. "The cold air will be bracing and I can plan."

Much as it hurt Gaby's frugal New England soul, she had also paid two months' rent in advance on an unseen cottage in a valley village near West Point. She would lay in a small supply of food, wait about a week and then start making her inquiries about transportation *out* of the area.

In about ten days after her arrival, she would have hired another farmer or farmer's son to convey her to an inn near Bear Mountain or Peekskill—whichever she decided was better.

During her stay at the inn—she need not make it more than a day or two—she was sure she could hire a coach to take her home to Aunt Emily's.

On the first day of coach travel from New York, she kept going over and over the plan in her mind. At night, sitting in bed, she pored over the only rough little sketch of New York and New

Jersey that she had been able to buy from an itinerant artist in Setauket whom she had bribed by allowing him to sketch her first.

The artist did so well that Gaby commissioned him to draw a second sketch. She would bring one as a gift for Aunt Emily and she would send the second one to her father in England when she was safe in New Jersey.

It was just a simple pen and ink sketch that no one in New York would ever have recognized as Mrs. Forsyth-Foote, but to Gaby's untutored eyes, it seemed very like the real Gabrielle Foote.

The sketch showed her standing sideways, with the wind whipping her hair into disarray and playing havoc with her petticoats so as to reveal more of her legs than was truly proper. Her head was turned to the side and she was enjoying her tussle with the wind and smiling at the artist, too.

The next few weeks were tiring and tedious, with both short and long stays at assorted inns and then the wretched little house at West Point. The only virtue of the period was that her plan functioned smoothly.

Three weeks and one day from the morning she left Setauket, she stepped into the carriage that would take her on the last lap of her journey home to Aunt Emily.

She had not slept well the night before . . . or for that matter, on any other night since she left Setauket. The relief of knowing she was almost home brought on another bout of the tears she had all too often indulged over the last month.

Wearied by the tears and even more by the strain she had been under, Gaby curled up on the cushions of the coach after a listless survey of the countryside. She was soon deep in the sleep of exhaustion.

Forty-one

She was not awakened by the jolt that shook the coach when it was brought to an unexpected halt. The door was yanked open and after a moment, closed as quietly as possible.

The lone rider remounted and indicated with a pistol to the driver to take the fork in the road that indicated Amboy, rather than the direct road to Princeton.

The rider rode ahead of the coach, with the reins gathered in his left hand and the pistol in his right, never wavering.

When Gaby awakened, she felt rested at first, then actually hungry. She had bought cheese, cold meat and spiced apple cider at last night's inn.

She lifted her basket off the floor, spread a napkin across her lap, and prepared to feast.

Two slices of beef folded into a chunk of bread made a wonderful beginning. She did not even try to pour the cider into a pewter traveling cup, but drank it in long grateful gulps from the jar.

She had just broken a piece of cheese off a larger slab and was nibbling on the smaller chunk, glancing casually out the window, when the worst of her nightmares came true.

British redcoats to the right, and what looked like an artillery park to the left. My God! How could she be in British-held territory? Princeton was American. It had been American ever since the glorious nine days and nights that began on Christmas night of '76, when Washington and his rag-tail army crossed the Delaware and overpowered the Hessians at Trenton. Then, notwithstanding enough British blunders to cap his success—he also defeated the enemy at Princeton.

Since that American victory, the only British presence in all of New Jersey—a small one—was at Brunswick and Amoby and certainly, British officers and men should not be walking the village green.

Could the driver have taken the wrong turn on the road?

Gaby pounded with her fists on the partition that separated them. He did not appear to hear her. She pounded again and cried aloud, "Idiot, stop this coach at once; you are going the wrong way."

She had shouted herself hoarse by the time the coach came to a jerky halt. What remained of her lunch had fallen to the floor. She trod it underfoot as she leapt up, seized hold of the door, swung it open and jumped down without waiting for the steps.

Her first furious look and words were for the driver. "You whoreson fool!" she spat out most reprehensibly.

A laugh from the rider, who still held his pistol, though it was no longer pointed—changed the direction of her glare.

For a long moment in time, they stared at one another speechlessly, and she could not at first believe her eyes. When they convinced her of the truth, the earth swayed beneath her feet and she swayed along with it.

With an oath of his own, the rider dismounted and in three steps he was beside her. He checked his pistol and slipped it into his belt before he took her by one shoulder, shaking her roughly.

"You are not going to faint!" he commanded, and then in a lower voice, "It is very unacceptable behavior for a spy!"

Gaby glanced up at him quickly and did not take any comfort from his expression. She did not fear for her safety . . . no matter what his anger, he would never give her away . . . but there were many ways to punish when love turns to hate. She was in no way reassured by the implacable look on the face of the man who had once loved her with all his being and worshipped her with his body. His look did not bode well for the foreseeable future.

Gaby stood very straight. "What now, Major?" she asked quietly.

"Not Major any longer. A plain Mr. will do, or perhaps," he added mockingly, "a respectful, *sir*. The choice is yours."

Gaby was never to see the coachman paid off and her baggage depart because the innkeeper came out and bowed deeply as he said, "Your room is ready for you, ma'am."

She needed time to think, to plan, to get herself out of this fix, but in the meantime, the wisest course was to follow him and gain herself some time.

She was shown to a small but pleasant room with blue and white checked curtains at the window, and a counterpane to match on the bed.

"Is there anything I can get for you, ma'am?"

"Yes, brandy!" At his look of surprise, she explained, "I am not feeling quite the thing; it may help settle me."

There was a fire lit in the fireplace, but it was not very strong. She shifted the fender, added some kindling and kicked at the logs. Shivering more with nerves than from cold, she stood there, toasting her icy hands.

The innkeeper returned with her brandy at the same time a servant boy arrived with her trunk on his shoulder. He tumbled it unceremoniously near to the bed.

"In that corner," Gaby directed, "and be more gentle, if you please, with my other boxes."

"Clyde, you donkey's hind-part," said the innkeeper, handing the glass to Gaby and frowning at his luckless servant, "how many times must I tell you how to set things down so's they're not damaged?"

Sorry that her ill-temper should have drawn his employer's wrath onto his luckless head—for which Clyde was not to blame—Gaby smiled at him ruefully.

When he brought up the rest of her belongings, she gave him a more substantial apology.

Grinning from ear to ear at the amount of the coins in his hand, Clyde ducked his head with a "Thank 'e, m'um."

As soon as she was alone again, Gaby took the single glass of brandy and gulped it down more like water than strong spirits. She was warm now rather than cold. She removed her pelisse, poked ineffectually at her hair—which was no doubt disordered—and felt the impulse to cry when she looked down at her drab gown and thought of the appearance she must present.

Seconds later, she was enraged at herself for crying. She decided against making herself more pleasing to the eye. She doubted if Darcy was in a mood to appreciate an improved appearance, and her own pride forbade any repairs that might allow him to believe she cared tuppence worth for his good opinion.

She continued to stand, beginning to feel the first reassuring effect of the brandy and wistfully wondering why she had not asked for another.

He would be coming any moment now. In fact—how dared she fancy the footsteps on the stairs were his? She turned her back to the fire and braced herself in a way that suggested she was ready for physical assault.

Darcy did not knock. He opened the door as though he had every right to enter her bedchamber uninvited—which he promptly did, then closed the door behind him.

"Don't you know better than to stand with your skirts so near the fire?" he asked harshly. "Or is it that you are less afraid to meet your Maker than to meet myself?"

Gaby put both hands to her mouth and began to laugh. At his outraged expression, she began to laugh much harder.

"I am delighted to find,"—though his expression was anything but delighted—"that you find humor in this situation."

"It's your fault"—Gaby hiccuped several times and had to pause in midsentence—"you were the one who taught me to drink brandy." He stood, rigid and disapproving until she was once more in control of herself.

"I know you have lots to say," she told him presently, "so you might as well say it now."

"*I* am not the one who needs to talk, *you* are. I believe you have a great deal to say, Mrs. Forsyth-Foote, daughter and widow of two loyalist gentlemen. Or is it plain Mrs. Foote of Setauket? Or perhaps, you have claim to a name I have never heard? Are you even Gabrielle?"

"My name is Gabrielle Renée Forsyth-Foote and the Forsyths were my mother's family, though I seldom used the name until I"—she smiled sweetly and curtsied—"as you so rightly said, I turned spy."

"Don't try my patience, girl."

"What right have you to question me? You are not—you say—in the army and I'm not *trying* to. It appears I just am."

"I have the rights of your former lover . . . of a former officer in His Majesty's Army . . . the rights of the man you made a fool of . . ."

"None of those claimed rights matter," said Gaby, fierce and prideful. He had not said *of the man who loves you* and *they* were the only words that mattered.

He took two strides forward, yanked her by the arm, pulled her in no gentle fashion across the room and pushed her down on the bed. Gaby sat, looking up at him in some confusion.

"Madame, you seem to be totally unaware of the fix you are in. You appear to believe—quite falsely—that you may give me orders and pert answers and throw tantrums. Nor is the consideration of your wishes of concern to me. In short, you have not the slightest bit of authority. If you will accept that I"—his teeth gleamed through an unpleasant smile—"control this situation, not you, we will both go on much better."

Gaby leaped off the bed in one fluid movement.

"You control *me!"* she spat. "That will happen the day a regiment of redcoats drain Boston Harbor and bring up your precious 342 boxes of tea as a gift for your king and Lord North."

He took her by the wrist and pulled her into his arms.

"I have never in my life laid hands on a woman. Don't drive me into breaking my record."

Gaby stood still, very content to be where she was. "Oh, I don't know," she drawled. "I can recall any number of times when you laid your hands on me . . ." She tipped her head back to look up at him, "and very pleasant it was, unless my recollections are at fault."

He shook her a little. "You know full well *that* is not what I meant."

"But it's the only laying-on of hands I want to remember."

He looked as though he was about to shake her again. Instead, he bent his head and kissed her.

What happened next began as an impulsive laying-on of lips. It continued for a short while as a slow-burning fire.

The earlier kisses were kindling which ignited beyond control. They were consumed by the blaze of their regenerated passion.

Forty-two

Gaby was swimming. Struggling against the tide. Something must be wrong. There were no tides in the creek back home, although sometimes, after flooding, unaccountably there were strong dangerous currents. She had been forbidden to swim there for safety's sake. Thereafter, quite naturally, the prohibited creek held a magic allure for the young Gabrielle. In summer, the sun dappling the ripples of water made it look so deliciously inviting. At ten, she succumbed to a long-resisted temptation.

It had been marvelous. Not the slightest hint of danger. Just the bliss of the cool, forbidden waters, from her neck down to her toes. Dressed . . . rather *un*dressed; only her shift had been left on . . . she was as near naked as made no difference at all.

The time went by only too swiftly. She had just climbed out to sit on the bank, planning to sit in the sun and dry herself, her shift, her hair . . . anything which would have given her away.

Unfortunately, a member of her father's congregation came by before she was fully dried and dressed. Knowing he would report her misdeed, Gaby confessed first. Her father had never—in Darcy's words—laid a hand on her, and she could see him struggling with the conviction that this time he must.

Abigail saw it, too, and took the task on herself. Her short, brisk paddling left a lasting impression on Gaby, not because it was severe, but because it was rare.

"Poor Mama, poor Papa," she murmured. "They hated laying hands on me."

"They have my deepest sympathy," the strong male voice seemed to be coming from far off.

"Water and no clothes . . . wonderfully free . . . not earthbound at all."

The drawling voice was closer to her ear. "Regretably, you are still wearing any number of clothes."

"The serpent in the garden of Eden," she mumbled resentfully.

"I suggest you open your eyes. You are in Amboy, not in Eden. One of us—I wonder which—must play the role of snake."

She wanted to stay here . . . there . . . wherever she was. She did not *want* to open her eyes.

With the greatest reluctance, Gaby did so.

A fearful mistake. She did not *want* to deal with realities either. The truth had to be faced.

He—Darcy was naked. Lying on his side, facing her . . . or perhaps summing her up, not with love and tenderness, but rather like a shopkeeper taking inventory of his stock.

She was the one dressed except for her stockings and shoes. When someone knocked, he had aimed her footgear quite accurately at the closed door. His voice must have been heard by anyone in the inn, as well as the stable. Perhaps even gotten as far as the British garrison.

When she tried to sit up, protesting, he had immediately and urgently flattened her beneath him again.

Oddly enough, his unashamed nudity and her comparative modesty did not have the reassuring effect that might have been supposed. Remembering all the events that followed those unbelievable torrid kisses, Gaby began to blush. She blushed as she had never blushed before.

There were so many things she had to blush about!

Could she really have spat out a mouthful of petticoats, managing, as she did so, to gasp, "You're suffocating me, you fool. Let me take my clothes off."

And he, the bastard!

"Sorry, I am pressed for time. You can suffocate or be strangled."

She tried bucking her entire body so she could free one of her awkwardly bent legs to kick him.

Not a good move.

He had grabbed an ankle in each hand.

"You misbegotten idiot, do you think I'm a circus performer?" And then . . . aware that she was moaning quietly, "You look like one at the moment," he said as he peeled the petticoat off her face, slapped her bottom in playful fondness and stifled further protest by throwing her underskirt over her head. But a moment later, he pulled it lower and reversed her position.

Without further attempts to arouse or appease her, *he* gathered her into his arms. *She* gathered him into her.

They were thrashing wildly about the bed. Their love-making had never suffered from restraint or inhibition, but this was the ultimate shamelessness.

"Oh, my God! Oh, my God! Oh, my God!" She remembered saying that, it seemed a score of times.

Darcy must have thought that *he* deserved more credit than was being given for her excess of gratitude.

"God's in His heaven, *I* am the one doing the work."

And she had said . . . oh, no, she could not possibly have said that . . . no and no again . . . she *had* been his mistress, she *had* been a spy, she *had* broken enough commandments to grieve Papa to the heart. She could never have instructed a British officer (to whom she was not married) how, and in what manner and at what speed, to please her in bed.

"Oh, my God," Gaby moaned, now not even aware she was speaking aloud.

"Your blushes are charming . . . almost virginal," Darcy said. "And your technique—I really believe—has improved. This interlude, I must confess, has been most enjoyable. Have you had many lovers since we were last together?"

It took a minute for the full impact of this monstrous insult to seep entirely through Gaby's consciousness. When, finally, it did, she swallowed painfully and grew quiet. She had always become remote and quiet, he remembered, when she was concealing some hurt.

He had meant to hurt her. For a long time now, he had felt a savage need to hurt her badly. He had longed for her to suffer even a small part of the suffering he had endured, thinking her faithless. His later conviction brought him comfort. She had never loved at all, but only used his passion to further her ends.

"Please get dressed and leave my room," said Gaby, haughtily turning her back to him. "You have had your revenge and may leave me to get on with my journey."

"Revenge!" he repeated incredulously as he left the bed and started to dress again. "You think I have had my revenge!" He added as crudely as he could, "You consider that an hour of robust swiving wipes out the past and makes us equals in the question of who hurt whom?"

She made no answer, gave no sign of having listened or heard him.

"I am fully clothed. You need not avert your eyes so modestly."

Gaby ignored him as she walked over to the door to retrieve her shoes and stockings.

"All I can say, madame," he added contemptuously, "is that you rate your charms far too high if you think this . . . this brief episode sufficed me. I am not yet done with you."

She was very much Gabrielle when she turned to face him.

"You know that I am . . . or rather, have been an American agent. My spying days are over. You were a British officer, but your soldiering days are over too. I suggest that without further attempts to harass one another, we say good-bye. For both of us, let the past be forgotten as soon as may be."

"A very neat plan. Do you think I am likely to agree?"

"Darcy," she said tiredly, "let us be honest with one another. I know you well enough to understand that, no matter how your feelings about me have changed, the past—our shared past—will not allow you to betray me to the hangman."

"True. I could not. When I returned to New York and eventually learned the truth, I was forced to resign. In good conscience and honor, I could not remain in the military and permit you to go free."

"So, that is laid to my account, too?"

"No," he said scrupulously, "I had intended to send in my papers in New York. Your letters were getting fewer and more impersonal. I thought perhaps there had been a misunderstanding . . . some trouble you would not tell me. I could not believe . . . I refused even to consider that you might no longer love me. Impossible—when I still . . . well, no matter . . . I stopped loving when I learned all."

"All," said Gaby. "I was wondering about that. How *did* you learn?"

"I will tell you . . . eventually. It will give us something to discuss on the long winter nights seated near the fire in the small drawing room at Ashford Hall."

Standing there, with her shoes in one hand, her stockings in the other, Gaby grew very still.

"I assume you mean Ashford Hall in England?"

"It is the only Ashford Hall I know."

"And you think *I* would go with you as your mistress!"

"Not as my mistress, dear Gabrielle, as my wife."

"If I refused you before, do you really believe that after this day . . ." Gaby half-turned, looking away from the bed, "anything short of hanging could induce me to marry you?"

"Yes, dear Gabrielle, I do."

"Stop calling me dear Gabrielle in that hateful way!" she told him sharply. "And tell me, if you please, the inducement you have in mind. For the life of me, I cannot think of one."

"Perhaps because you are no longer thinking as an agent. It is true the only harm I can do *you* is marriage; but there are others . . . oh, at least half a dozen others I would not have the slightest inclination to keep from going to the gallows. Our countries are, after all, at war. Half a dozen agents . . . six reasons why you will agree to marry me."

"Name them."

"Well, there is the lady who has the interesting professions that encompass the full circle of life. She helps bring the newborn into the world and prepares others for their departure. And, now and then, she sells lobsters for a local fisherman at the Fly Market."

Gaby's eyes remained painfully fixed on him.

"I do not believe," Darcy said judiciously, "that the lady's Quaker brethren, to say nothing of the military, would approve of a good many of her other activities."

Gaby crossed the room going right past him. She sat down on the side of the bed.

"Are you done?"

"Not at all. There is also your lady's maid . . . what is her name . . . ah, yes, how could I forget when so much of your beauty was a result of her art? Penelope. You were quite fond of Penelope, I recall. I remember your saying once that she mothered you."

"Then the third . . ."

"You need not go on," Gaby interrupted him. "I will marry you, if a marriage of mutual hate is what you want."

"It may not be as fulfilling as a marriage of love. On the other hand, it might be rather stimulating . . . we have just done quite well, coming together in hate rather than in love."

Gaby's tears ran unchecked down her cheeks.

Ignoring them, Darcy walked to the door, then turned to deliver a few more commands.

"I shall have a bath sent up for you. When you dress again, please put on a suitable gown. The one you are wearing should be put on the fire or given to a chambermaid . . . I prefer never to see it on you again. Have you retained your New York wardrobe?"

"Yes."

"Good. Then something suitable for a formal evening party, but not cut too low in the bosom, unless you can cover it with a scarf. The Presbyterian minister who has agreed to marry us knows you are a widow, but I believe he expects a certain decorum, as well as an older woman. If you can appear to be somewhat more aged, it would help. How old *are* you, by the way?"

Gaby looked up at him from half-closed eyes and smiled unpleasantly.

"I think that I, too, will save my answer for one of those long winter evenings in England. That is, if you truly intend to go through with this travesty of a marriage."

"The wedding is at five o'clock . . . in the church study. The minister's wife and daughter are our only witnesses, our only guests. We will forego certain proprieties common to love marriages and have the wedding supper in the private parlor of this inn, then leave tomorrow for New York. I would have shipped out earlier, had it been possible, but there is no packet leaving for England until Wednesday next."

He came over to her and forced her chin up. "If you have any thought of trying to get away from me in any one of those six days, I suggest that you put it out of your mind. We are instructed from the most righteous source that after marriage, a man shall cleave unto his wife and they shall be one flesh. You, my dear Gabrielle, are going to be cleaved unto as woman was never cleaved to before . . . at least till our ship leaves New York harbor."

Forty-three

It was hardly the wedding of a young girl's dream. The bridegroom's demeanor was blasé to the point of rudeness, and the bride kept her eyes fixed on the opposite wall studying a poorly sketched representation of the clergyman with his family.

His responses to the minister were surly, and *hers* indifferent. The Reverend Cole, reacting to the pervasive atmosphere of gloom, shortened the elaborate ceremony he had planned in gratitude for his prodigal fee in gold. He very much doubted that this odd pair would notice the lack of pomp.

Skipping half a dozen pages, "I pronounce-you-husband-and-wife-you-may-kiss-the-bride," he announced with the greatest relief.

"I don't need a kiss. Dear Lord, eleven!" Gaby said aloud in a tone of heartfelt disgust. She turned to the minister's wife. "You poor thing!"

"Eleven what?" asked Darcy in bewilderment.

The minister's wife smiled kindly at the former spy. "I like a house full of young 'uns," she said. "I used to get right lonesome, growing up like I did with neither sister nor brother."

"My Sairy"—the minister looked at her fondly—"is a wonderful manager."

"And God blessed us with one more since the peddler made that painting."

"Good God!" Gaby said. "Darcy," in a low voice to her new husband, "give her enough to buy toys and sweets for all the children. I will wait outside."

As she mended sufficiently to utter a brief word of thanks to the Reverend Cole, the minister's Sairy had the last word.

"It's heartening to see two young people so in love. Don't fret, love," to Gaby alone, though they all could hear her, "nothin' some honest talk and four legs in a bed can't untangle."

Darcy smiled. It was an honest-to-goodness the-way-it-used-to-be-smile. Her face was as red as any lobsterback's uniform, when Gaby fled the room.

They had walked over from the inn; no reason why she had to wait . . . *Dear Lord, I married him . . . I've been widow . . . mistress . . . spy . . . and now . . . It can't be . . . but it is. I am Darcy's wife.*

Her bridegroom caught up with her halfway to the inn. He slipped his arm through hers and said affably. "In England, upper-class ladies do not walk alone and without escort in an unchancy area."

"What is unchancy about it?" Gaby asked sweetly. "Everywhere I look, I see British soldiers. Surely"—in even more honeyed accents—"you cannot mean that any one of *them* might offer me insult."

The arm that was supposedly giving her minimal support clamped her own arm to his side. "I mean just that, madame, so my first command in this marriage is that you don't play your role of bewildered innocence with me. You will get the worst of it, I assure you."

Gaby's first impulse was to respond in kind (which he no doubt expected). She curbed her tongue and answered pleasantly, "But, my dear sir, did you not notice that the Reverend Cole became so flustered he forgot to request a number of the usual pledges. *You* were not required to love or to cherish me, and I have certainly not promised to obey *you*. Keep that in mind, Major, when you are tempted to issue a command."

"Oh, I shall, I shall . . . though, of course," with the greatest possible courtesy, "I feel certain that our interpretations of what is a command and what a request may be vastly different."

Gaby bit down hard on her lower lip and managed—just barely—not to reply.

"Quite a neat little ceremony, I thought," he observed chattily.

"Neat?" she asked incredulously. "You thought it was *neat?* With *you* acting more like a pallbearer than a bridegroom and *I* bored, not to mention angry *and* unwilling. Did you, by any chance, happen not to notice that the minister who united us was sorely distressed?"

"True, but on the other hand, *I* secured my objective and yours was denied."

"What objective?" She pulled her arm free from his. "What are you talking about?"

"We are married," he said quietly. "I am no longer soldier, you are no longer spy. I am no longer lover, you are no longer mistress."

"So?"

"So, madam, I am your husband and you now belong to me. In strictly legal terms—which are as binding in England as here in His Majesty's colonies—the lack of *obey* in the marriage service has no significance. You are my possession, my chattel, my very personal property. Also—when I wish you to be—my bed partner. What *I* already own or may receive in the future is mine, not yours. What *you* have or get is also mine.

"Now and forever, my girl, you are wholly mine. You have no separate standing in law, unless I choose to bestow it, but as long as you do my will, your life may be entirely agreeable. Defy me and . . . well, let us just say, you will suffer the consequences."

They were within a few yards of the inn when Gaby came to an abrupt halt. "I hope, Major, you are not too disappointed in the life you believe we will share. I am not any more intimidated by you now than I have been in the past. Your masculine strutting and preening would be laughable if it were not so pathetic!"

She had the satisfaction of seeing his eyes narrow and grow dark, in the way that had formerly told her he was holding a tight rein on his temper.

Pleased to have provoked him, Gaby started walking again.

As she reached the inn, two steps ahead of him, her arm was jerked back into his and she was forced to enter the frame building with every appearance of affectionate domesticity.

To pull away from him would only make them both look foolish, especially since, when they stepped over the threshold, the innkeeper, Mr. Gormly, bustled up crying out congratulations and pressing them to step into the small private parlor, where their wedding supper would be served to them.

"I could have done better if I had been given more notice," he lamented, as he brought them to a sideboard heaped with more fish and fowl than a half dozen guests could possibly consume, as well as a variety of pickled onions and beans and beets. There were also all manner of hot vegetables common to the season, soft rolls, spoonbread and a wheat loaf cut into chunks.

Looking over this inviting repast, Gaby realized she was hungry and did a mental turn about. She would delay deserting her bridegroom until she had eaten.

"My dear sir," she said to Mr. Gormly, "no apologies are necessary. I am amazed that you could have managed such a feast as this in so short a time."

He beamed with pleasure, then turned to Darcy and began to apologize again. "I have only beer or ale for you and for the lady, sir. You understand how hard it is in such times as these."

"Beer will do very well."

"And I," lied the lady, just to be contrary, "prefer ale."

Their host bowed himself out, returning in short order with a boy staggering under the load of a tray with two heavy pitchers and two pewter mugs. All three held their breath until the tray was set safely on the table.

"You can go, Ezekial," the innkeeper said to the servant boy in lordly fashion. "I will serve the lady and gentleman meself."

"For their very first meal together as husband and wife," said Darcy with a warming smile that begged the innkeeper's kind indulgence, "the gentleman would like to serve his lady himself."

It cut Gabrielle to the heart to see how quickly the smile vanished along with their host. Darcy then closed the door firmly behind him and strode across to the table.

He took one plate out of the warming shelf and started heaping food onto it.

"No onions for me," Gaby called out as he dipped a serving spoon into one dish.

"My dear girl." He half-turned, looking at her in sham surprise. "I am filling my own plate, not yours. I dare say you were misled by my little speech to our good landlord. I merely intended to speed his departure, else he would have hovered over us during the whole of this meal. I do not"—he turned back to the table of food—"like to be hovered over while I eat."

Evidently amused by her lowering look, he went on with his selection.

Gaby counted slowly to thirty to restore her calm. Having achieved it, she rose from her chair and sailed over to the serving table just as Darcy left it.

"Oh, how lovely!" she caroled, with a flirtatious look back at her husband. "How pleasant it is to choose my own food when dining out. I never mentioned it . . . after all, it would not have been *comme il faut,* but I have always detested having a tavern meal chosen for me by my escort, who often does not know which foods I favor."

She returned to him, carrying a plate heaped high. Having set it down, she returned briefly to the serving table to bring back a honey bun.

She then plumped herself down in her chair and pulled it closer to the table. She was seemingly interested in one thing only . . . how much and how speedily she could consume vast quantities of food.

She stopped munching only once, to say with fervent appreciation. "My, but I love to eat!"

"No one watching you," Darcy answered gravely, "could doubt it."

"Oh!" Then, "Do you mean, sir that my enjoyment is unladylike? I am sorry if it offends you. I do know from living at Queen

Street that high-born English ladies are prone to act in public as though they hardly eat at all. They do it, I was told, so as to be considered by the *stronger* sex as fragile, ethereal creatures. I, however, am a simple *American* and despise such silly affectation."

"Affectation," said Darcy smoothly. "You refer, I collect, to the fabrication of a counterfeit person meant to indulge some poor fool in such counterfeit emotion that he imagines it is love . . . Yes, I certainly agree with you, indeed I do. I despise all such falsity. I detest a liar."

It took all the willpower Gaby possessed to hold back her tears and answer calmly.

"My dear Darcy," she finally managed, without so much as a tremor in her voice. "Let us face one single overwhelming truth. There is a war going on in this country . . . and there is no neutral ground to be shared. We are enemies, you and I—political if not personal. You, on one side, I on the other. Would you have refused such service had it been requested by General Howe?"

"I do not know. Thank God, he never did."

"That is the difference between us. I *know* I would have accepted, even encouraged him to ask."

"How noble of you!"

"It was not noble!" she declared angrily. "I stumbled onto the first situation accidentally, and then I . . . you might say, I *solicited* further service to our United States."

"And who picked me as whipping boy?"

"I did."

"One honest declaration, at least, and by the by, in one thing you are mistaken. You and I are both political *and* personal enemies. If you think you are bound to me in marriage out of love, you will soon find out the truth."

"I already know it," she spat back. "And I think you are ignorant of the correct phrasing. It is not the bonds, but rather the bondage of marriage."

She pushed back her chair and stood up. "If you will excuse me . . ."

"I will not."

She blinked. "I am no longer hungry."

"I am. Sit down. I like company at the table."

"Then summon our host, the innkeeper. I am sure he would be delighted to oblige you."

"I choose your company. And yes," seeing her momentary hesitation. "I will bring you back forcibly if I must."

She looked across the table at the implacable face and cold eyes. He would do it, she decided, the misbegotten son of—

Gaby sat down.

"How wise of you," he applauded. "And how right in your conclusion. I *would* have carted you back and set you down in your chair. One thing, at least has not changed. I always thought you more intelligent than the generality of your sex. Your decision to stay with me just now certainly confirms it."

Gaby made no reply. He could bring *this* mare to the water trough, but the mare would decide when to drink.

She sat majestically in her place for the next half hour watching her companion eat. There was no conversation other than his occasional remarks about one dish or another that he thought particularly tasty.

"A pity you have lost your appetite. This roast is delightful. The most exacting gourmand in England would not be ashamed to serve it at his table."

Gaby, who had been staring longingly at the beef, did not respond.

"Who would have thought to find meat of this quality in such a provincial place?"

Gaby could not help herself. Just one short answer could not rob her of dignity.

"It undoubtedly came to this place by the usual means, theft! The cattle are driven toward the city by a group of cowboys, having been stolen from New York farmers, and then sold to the highest bidder."

"Fortunes of war, my dear."

His "dear" lapsed again into silence.

Just as she was calculating her chances for success in a bolt from the room, Darcy threw his cloth onto the table and stood up.

"Shall we go?"

Her head tipped a mere inch to indicate willingness, and Darcy was immediately beside her, offering his arm. Although she accepted, her fingertips barely touched his sleeve as they left the parlor.

The innkeeper heard them mounting the back stairway and rushed to inquire if they had enjoyed their meal. Darcy, who had eaten like an ox, was unsparing of compliment; Gaby, who had eaten so little, thanked him at length and effusively.

"It is time to retire, my dear Gabrielle." Darcy interrupted one of her more fulsome sentences. There was a wealth of meaning in his simple statement.

Mr. Gormly smirked, Gaby blushed, and Darcy smiled benignly as they continued up the stairs.

When they were both in her room, she slammed the door shut and turned to her bridegroom in a fury.

"I kept my share of the bargain. We are married. In return, you agreed to spare any of my friends you knew about who were in . . . in intelligence work. Now understand this. Our contract is fulfilled and you have been given all you may expect from me. You will not enter my room uninvited. You will not share my bed under any circumstances. You will—"

He picked her up and tossed her onto the bed. "Mrs. Rhoads, obviously you paid no attention to my statement of legalities. It is *you* who must understand I will enter your room whenever I wish, I will treat you just as I wish, and there is no way in hell that you can prevent me from entering your bed. Allow me, however, to reassure you on one very important point. When I am in your bed, it will not be for the usual reason."

As Gaby struggled into a sitting position, he eyed her with cool insolence.

"It goes without saying that you are a tempting tidbit, but not so tempting that I will take you when you are unwilling. I cannot think of anything more distasteful than a reluctant partner."

"But yesterday . . ."

"Yesterday," he said, "you were *not* unwilling. Far from it. If you do not lie as easily to yourself as you do to others, you will admit—not to me, only to yourself—that you were eager, even a demanding participant in our pleasure. Today—tonight is different."

"But . . . then . . . why m-must you be here . . . with me?"

"Because I do not trust you, my dear Gabrielle," he answered smoothly. "If I turn my back on you, you will do one of your neat little vanishing acts. That being the case, I will lie beside you tonight and all the ensuing nights that we are in New York and ensure that you do not make a bid for freedom while I sleep."

"I never thought of . . . I wasn't intending," she said stumblingly.

"Oh, yes you were, Mrs. Forsyth-Foote. Not so much because you want to get away from me as out of the blow to your pride at having been so bested. Really, instead of being infuriated with me, you should be grateful."

At the door, he turned back to her. "By the way, my dear, soldiers are light sleepers. They wake on the moment if someone so much as stirs."

He gave her a chance to reply, but Gaby remained adamantly silent.

"I will give you a short while to prepare for bed. I know your new-born modesty requires it."

Forty-four

True to his promise, Darcy climbed into Gaby's bed on the four nights following; and never once did he lay a hand on her, not in anger, not in desire, not in any emotion at all.

They stayed on in Amboy because—as he kindly pointed out—it was a much easier place to keep her always in view.

On the day they were leaving for New York, their hired chaise arrived for them just after dawn.

Gaby sat in one corner, quiet and yawning. Darcy sprawled out over two seats and kept up a constant patter of conversation.

"Very comfortable chaise. Much more comfortable than I thought it would be."

Gaby yawned again.

"Do you not want to know where we will lodge?"

Gaby sighed wearily.

"At Fraunces Tavern for just this one night. Our ship leaves New York Harbor on the next morning's tide. It is strange, but whenever I have taken you to Fraunces, there seems to be something that I am trying to remember."

Gaby swallowed nervously and Darcy frowned a little.

"I think we will be quite comfortable for your last night in New York. I gave sufficient notice so as to get pleasant quarters."

Gaby yawned once more.

"Good God!" he said. "Did you not sleep well? Oh, now I recall. You had a restless night. Occasionally, I felt your tossing and turning. What a pity! And I so comfortable. I had a wonderful night's sleep."

DARCY'S KISS

Gaby gave him a look of loathing and turned her body so as to deny him the opportunity of looking at anything except her back.

"There is an extra cushion here," he said solicitously, holding it out. "Perhaps if you tucked it under the other, you might be able to get some rest."

Gaby accepted the pillow from him only to fling it on the coach floor.

"My dear Gabrielle." He bent to retrieve it. "You must try to get the better of your crotchety ways. A mature woman cannot go through life giving way to tantrums whenever her will is denied. I say this," he addressed her back, "for your own good."

"If you do not want my tantrums," said Gaby wearily, "then let me not hear your voice. It grates on my nerves."

She curled up on the seat like a kitten, with her head against her own cushion.

Sleepless night, indeed. She had just endured four endless nights of proximity without the possibility of satisfaction. He was hers, she knew, if she could bring herself to utter the few words that granted him victory.

I want you.
I am not unwilling.
For the love of heaven, take me.
You, low, conniving devil, you are killing me.
This is torture.
No, not merely torture, it is hell.
You will not be able to hold out forever, Darcy Rhoads, British gentleman.
If it is the last thing on earth I ever do, I will get back at you.
I may hate you now, ex-Major Rhoads, but I achingly, everlastingly desire your body.

No, she *would* not, she *could* not yield.

Surrendering meant the loss of all personal power. She would indeed be his chattel, his possession, his bed partner and his victim.

Her head filled with contradictory emotions, her heart filled with troubled sorrows, she finally fell deep asleep. And while she slept Darcy stuffed a second pillow behind her head and covered her with a carriage rug.

She slept so deeply as not to feel the tender stroking against her cheek. She slept with the sweet innocence of a child.

A child! Who but he knew that her look of beguiling innocence was all pretense? Who but he, knew that the truth was not in her?

He drew his hand back and moved a few inches from her. He remembered the worry when her letters became farther and farther apart and then altogether ceased.

The time when worry became apprehension and apprehension turned to despair.

He had loved her. Oh, God, how he had loved and believed in her. There was a time when he had been willing to give up his future, his earldom, his country . . . all for her.

She had been so loving, so passionate, so giving in their bed play. Loving her had humbled him before his God. Surely, their rapture together had to be heaven-sent.

And then to return to New York to search for her, only to find . . .

He tried not to think of that wretched week after he discovered the truth—and he himself began to scheme.

If he had to tie her up with ropes and dump her down before the church to achieve it, his once adored, seemingly adoring girl, was going to be his wife!

By English standards, Darcy was almost abstemious. When he could no longer shrink from the body of evidence laid before him, he had taken to his bed each night with a bottle of wine or brandy to keep him company and induce him to sleep. Talk about restless nights, he thought bitterly. Madame Forsyth-Foote did not know the half of it.

Out of his misery and bitterness, there grew a powerful urge to make her suffer as he had suffered, to make her writhe in humiliation as he had writhed. It was a very properly biblical notion after all. He would exact an eye for an eye, and a tooth for a tooth.

He tried to hide from himself all inconsistencies in his reasoning. A voice of doubt within him kept on sticking pins into his flesh.

Good sleep, ha! He would lie awake at night, thinking, *I want her in my power; by God, I want her in my power.*

Why, Darcy, why? To have her in your power means you must find her and keep her with you.

I want to punish her. She deserves to be punished.

How, Darcy, how? You have never laid a hand on any woman. What is there left for you to do but rant and rave? Would that satisfy you?

I will shame her, I will expose her.

Oh, now that one shows remarkable sense. I can just see you handing her over to the hangman. Sir William did not even give a trial to that other fellow spy . . . what was his name? Howell . . . Hale, something like that.

Very well, Gabrielle Rhoads, I have married you. You are—with a little dramatic license—wholly in my power. Believe me, I will exercise that power.

Bravo, Darcy! A splendid plan. Marriage means, of course, that the twain—that's you and her—can never, ever be parted short of death. Your second great step forward was to agree never to take her unwillingly into your arms.

My boy, you are nothing short of a genius. You are planning to be married but not married, to be enemies always together, to hate where once you loved, to endure sleepless nights—lying still and in torment with passion and mutual desire, then bragging to her each morning of how well-rested you are.

Gradually, as Gaby had done, helped by the rhythmic motion of the coach, with the practicality of a soldier, he leaned back against the cushions. Gaby, awakening several hours later, found him soundly asleep.

Gingerly, she reached out to touch his hair, his own hair, powdered and tied at the back with a sober black ribbon. She had, many times, wished he would not wear a wig—knowing that he must. Proper attire for a British officer demanded it. *Perhaps, since he was not in the army . . . at home in England at Ashford Hall . . . the customs may be different!*

My, oh, my Gaby, you certainly are a reluctant bride. Home in England at Ashford Hall. How very cozy and comfortable you sound, my dear.

Never mind how I sound. Sooner or later, I shall have my revenge. He will not get the better of me, my word on it. He will be sorry he even tried to draw swords with me. Perhaps he already is.

You are one observant girl, Gaby Foote. He looks the picture of unhappiness, doesn't he, fast asleep and snoring.

"He is *not* snoring!" Gaby said aloud indignantly. Oh well, maybe just a little snort now and then. It's this chaise. She stroked Darcy's arm. *In bed, he slept—oh, hours in my arms and I never hear him so much as sniff.*

Oh, fiddle-de-dee! Your poor injured warrior, who never so much as sniffed. I have seldom in my life encountered such hate as yours. Lying in bed with him, sweating and sleepless. Wanting him. Yearning for him. Aching to hear some of the words spoken on your pillow so long ago. Praying for him to tumble into your arms so you can have his passion without hauling down your flag.

Go away. Go away. Go *far* away. I have enough on my mind without having to endure your pinpricks.

Gabrielle, use the little wit he claimed you have. Do you love him? Do you hate him? Do you even know how you feel? You had better discover the truth in the less than twenty-four hours there are before he forces you onto that ship. Or would it be by force? Now think, girl, think, and do him a bit of justice. Has he not reason for complaint? Did he not give you his whole heart only to have it trampled? Did you not use him? Did you not lie to him? One lie after another, if you are honest? Had you ever been uncovered as spy, would he not have suffered in his career and been ridiculed throughout the army as a susceptible fool?

It was cold in the chaise despite a woolen afghan and a carriage rug. In spite of which, when Gaby put her hands to her cheeks they were damp and burning.

Darcy, Darcy, I never meant—it was never my intent—to hurt you so. At first, it was just a game . . . I never thought the game would become so deadly earnest. I only wanted America to be free of Britain. After all, we have a right to our own country. I never meant for the two of us to wind up the way we did. It began that day in the hackney, when I felt so strange . . . I did not realize what it meant . . . I just thought of meeting you again on equal terms and . . .

And what?

Gaby bowed her head.

Falling in love, I guess.

Ah. The truth begins to rise from the murky depths. And what then?

Gaby sighed wearily. "Let me be," she whispered aloud, "I must think."

Never did a journey seem so long, though they made very good time in terms of hours. When they made a number of stops to refresh themselves, as well as to bait the horses, which in Amboy, Darcy had described in the early morning, as "sorry nags."

Over fish stew and ale, he acknowledged that they would never earn a prize for looks but they were steady and had proved themselves to be goers.

Gaby, who was weary as well as bedeviled, wanted only a small bowl of broth and then bread and tea.

"Are you sure?" Darcy asked. "This may be our last stop."

"I am sure," Gaby answered, smiling slightly. "All these days together you appeared to be fattening me up like a Christmas goose. Then, when I am stout and squat, you will not want me; which is most unfair. I would regret being tossed overboard as a meal for sharks."

Darcy chose to take this raillery seriously. "I could not cease to love any woman for such cause as that. You are lovely to look at, which is pleasant, but I was attracted to more than mere beauty when I met you . . . intelligence . . . charm . . . wit, and a speaking voice that does not grate on a man's ears. You may laugh at my naiveté, if you will, as *I* have done all too often. One of the more sterling qualities I thought you possessed was honesty. Honesty and a total lack of the affectations and coy pretenses of so many women in society."

"You were not naive, Darcy, neither then nor now. I was as honest as any spy may be. I could not foresee what would happen between us. When I did . . ." She made a helpless gesture and put her suddenly chilled hands around the teapot for warming. "Once I had started, there was no way to stop," she said softly. "I could not betray my country."

"Why not?" he told her bitterly. "I am in the process of betraying mine."

Gaby shook her head.

"I ceased being a spy before you found me in New Jersey, so you have not betrayed anyone or anything. Will it ease your conscience to know that *my* group has been dispersed? Several of them departed from New York."

"How do you know that?"

"I—I had word in Setauket."

"My," he told her mockingly, "your sources are a little behind the times. They ceased operations, then decamped from New York at *my* suggestion."

"Oh!" said Gaby in the guilty manner of a child making off with forbidden sweets. "Oh!" Her second was indignant. "You could have given them parole or some such thing . . . they would have kept to their word."

"I do not think your friend, the Quaker lady, was unwilling to leave New York. Knowing her usefulness to *your* cause had ceased, she has returned to Philadelphia, which I believe is her native city. She traveled in the carriage of an elderly coachman who seemed also quite glad to rid himself of the dirt and the smell of New York."

"M-my maid?"

"She traveled right along with them, which reminds me, I have a message she left you, subject, of course, to my reading it."

"Of course," said Gaby drearily.

What right had *she,* he asked himself irritably, to be resentful.

"It was not the least personal," he said aloud. "It was just a few words of farewell. If it turns out to be in code, it has no value. I—*we* will destroy it when we are on the ship. Perhaps the sharks will cease coveting you and take a fancy to the torn bits of paper."

He finally found the note in an inside pocket of his greatcoat and handed it across the table to Gaby, who seized her letter, taking note of the broken seal with an ironic lift of her brows. She read eagerly.

My Dear Gaby,

As you will know by now, our former employer no longer offers us work, so the lot of us must all take up new situations.

Do not fret abowt it, child. The Wheel of Progress sometimes grind exseeding slow . . . but in the end, it triumphs.

Your work is done in New York, child, so go home now, wherever home may be. You have done your duty and must now look to your own happyness wether it lies here or akross the ocean.

Helth and Happyness and allso prosperrity to you, my dear Gaby. My time with you has been Deliteful to me. You are as dear to me as any Dawter. The Lady of Mercy sends her great Afecjtion, also of my own Wishes for you and her grattitude for all past favirs.

Yours very truly.

P.

P.S. Our mutuel frend goes home to her own Kith and Kin, so says *thee* need not fret over her. As to my self, worry not, love. Our coachman reminds me grattely of my dear forth husband.

All through the reading of the letter, Gaby fought hard to resist weeping. The P.S., so typically Penelope, caused her to laugh out loud.

Darcy stared strongly at her as she folded her letter small. "Tears I can understand. The parting from friends—particularly friends such as these—is naturally painful. But I cannot recall a single word or even sentence that could provoke such laughter!"

"That," chortled Gaby, sopping up her tears with the serving cloth in her lap, "is because you do not know the person in question."

"Your oh-so-prim-and-proper Quaker lady?"

"No, not my dear Quaker lady, who is goodness itself, but probably the least prim and proper lady we have ever—either of us—met."

"Who then?"

"I am not telling tales out of school, since you obviously met with her, and they are now safe away."

"You refer, I believe to your plump, much-married friend. The lady's maid. The one who has gone through *four* husbands, has she not?" He paused as Gaby continued to laugh hysterically, then continued his summing up.

"If I were a man, I would sheer off from that particular woman. Her husbands of middle years do not seem to fare well. Four times widowed and not the last bit shy to admit she is looking about her for number five."

"No. I keep telling you, she has only three deceased husbands. She is looking about her for number four, not five."

"I am certain . . . here, let me look at that letter . . . let us both look . . . Ah, see here, I am right. Look at the last sentence. 'As to myself, do not worry,' " he read aloud triumphantly. " 'Our coachman reminds me greatly of my dear fourth husband.' Does this not clearly indicate that she has been married four times and is now willing to have the coachman fill that post?"

Gaby rolled her eyes heavenward. "Oh, what simple, guileless fools men are! The meaning of the sentence is subtle but quite certain. Any *woman* would fathom it in a minute . . . *I* know, for a fact, that Penelope has been married to only three husbands. She—"

"A mere three times," he interrupted. "Poor fellows. She undoubtedly wears them out."

Gaby's face grew a delicate pink, but she continued doggedly, as though his last dig had neither been said, heard, nor heeded. "This is her way of telling me that she has decided on the coachman for her fourth husband. I am willing to make a wager with you about it."

"How do we prove—"

Their coachman approached their table hesitantly, hat in hand. "Horses be ready and rarin' to go, sir."

"We will be with you in a moment."

"Right, sir."

With a waggle of his hand that was somewhere between a greeting and a salute, the coachman departed.

"Finish your tea," Darcy urged her. Gaby swallowed it quickly, which was much easier than starting an argument. Struck by the smell of the sweet rolls, she tasted one tentatively, then picked up the small basket of four.

"These will be fine for my hunger on the road," she announced cheerfully. "Don't forget to pay for the basket, too."

"It horrifies me to think of the many years I got on very well without you as the voice of my conscience."

Gaby's skirts were wedged between the chair leg and the table. She pulled them loose and spoke ever so sweetly.

"I wonder, too, sir. You British—of the officer class—who have got your rank by purchase, rather than merit, just cannot seem to accustom yourself to minor privation. That is why, no matter the odds, *we,* not *you,* will eventually win this war and the mighty empire go down in ignominious defeat."

"Nonsense!"

"Not nonsense at all. Ours, however shabby, however ignorant, however raw, is a volunteer army. We have purpose; we fight for a cause. You British, with your moneyed class, who buy their commissions, and all the poor devils in the ranks with no other way to live—or, rather, to exist—cannot begin to understand Americans. Even worse are your Hessian lackeys, literally sold by their rulers into semislavery at so many pence a head. America's desire for freedom is outside your comprehension... which is why, no matter how many battles you win, we will be the victors in this war."

He rose from the table and came behind her to pull out her chair.

"Do you never weary of dispute, Madam Wife?"

Gaby rose without the aid of his outstretched hand.

"Seldom," she said, with a guileless smile that he knew was as false as her past protestations of love.

Gaby saw the thundercloud that erased his own smile and reminded him of past grievances. She shrugged. There was no help for it. She could not *make* him believe her. If he would not, if he could not, nothing she could say or do would convince him.

"What a pity!" she said softly, more to herself than to him.

"What is a pity?"

"That you deliberately choose to be unhappy when you need not."

"I trusted you once; I loved you once. It is not an agony I care to repeat."

"Then why not leave me here when you depart tomorrow? Just think—you need never see me again. Once home, you could begin to live your life anew. You could thrust both America and me out of your mind and your heart. Don't you realize I will be more trouble than I am worth?"

"I know it damn well," he said, "and aboard ship, I will begin the process of molding you into the kind of woman who is acceptable in the social circles in which I live. If necessary, I will hire a distressed gentlewoman who, for a fee, will teach you how to go on."

Gaby looked at him in horror.

"You must be mad!" she declared ringingly. "I would hate it *and* you."

He shrugged. "That would be your problem."

"I would make your life a misery."

"And *I*," he promised with a smile brimful of teeth, "intend to make yours a hell on earth."

Forty-five

They both slept fitfully through the long, tiring journey, awakened when they reached New York by the uneven jostling of the chaise. The cobbled streets of the city were kind to feet of neither horses nor humans . . .

In no time at all, Fraunces Tavern was reached. Darcy descended first without bothering to let down the steps. He held out his arms to Gaby. "Jump."

Gaby lifted up skirts and petticoats and flung herself down into his arms, aware that every bone and muscle in her body protested its abuse. She was quite content not to let go of him.

"How trusting of you," said a low voice in her ear. "I might have let you fall."

Gaby rallied her spirits sufficiently to say, "That would be too easy a way out for you."

"True. Ah, there she is," as a motherly woman approached. "Go upstairs with Smithson. She will make you comfortable. I will see to a light supper in our rooms."

Too weary to require further explanation, Gaby stumbled upstairs in the wake of the unknown Smithson, who carried the smallest of the portmanteaus that Gaby had packed.

A fire was blazing inside the room whose door Smithson held open for her. Gaby sped across to the fire, getting as near as she safely could. Having toasted her backside, she turned around and lowered her hands, first warming the palms and then the backs.

When she had thawed sufficiently, she looked about her.

Smithson had just taken her warmest flannel gown out of the portmanteau. She smiled cheerfully at Gaby.

"I will hang your gown over the firescreen so as to warm it before I slip it over you . . ."

"Thank you," murmured Gaby.

She was so bone-weary, she would have uttered polite consent to any proposal put to her. She walked across to the enormous sleigh bed, and plumped herself down on the gay red and white checked counterpane.

Her eyes closed again. She did not have sufficient strength to protest even when she began to be undressed. Better Smithson than herself.

The flannel gown, as promised, was deliciously warm when Smithson pulled it over her head, then tugged it down over her body.

"Mmm, mmm," Gaby murmured ecstatically, enveloped in warmth all over.

"Now, if you will excuse me, mum, I will go down to get your tray."

"Never mind. I want to sleep, not eat."

"Just pop off for a minute while I fetch your tray, Mrs. Rhoads. You will sleep all the better for a little hot food inside you. But first, the bed needs warming. If there's one thing I can't abide it is getting betwixt icy sheets."

"Mmm," Gaby agreed, as Smithson trotted briskly back from the fire with a copper pan and thrust it under the sheets, assuring herself that every inch of linen that might encounter Gaby's flesh would not cause her any discomfort.

Gaby was helped into bed, as though incapable of performing such a difficult task by herself and Smithson put the warming pan back near the fire, then quietly left the room.

Gaby tried to stay awake, fighting the Gaby who wanted sleep. She would nibble only a little something from the tray. Only the least little bit. She closed her eyes just to ease them. Then she slept, reluctant to be awakened by the hand on her shoulder. Smithson appeared to share some of Gaby's doubts.

"There now," she clucked as Mrs. Rhoads tried to push herself up. "It seemed a great shame to wake you, and you so spent, but the major—Mr. Rhoads, I should say—was most urgent that you take just a bite or two, you not having eaten at your supper stop."

"Besides," when Gaby sat all the way up, moaning slightly as she rubbed her bottom, "the major reminded me to tell you that, believe it or not, you may soon be longing for a meal of lobster bisque and fresh shrimp."

"That will be the millennium," grumbled Gaby, nevertheless carefully balancing the tray set on her knees.

She drank her soup with increasing appetite. Lobster or not, it was tasty. And the shrimp ... broiled just right with small roast potatoes in their jackets. Tea, of course, and several delicious little cakes. She drank every last drop and consumed everything on the tray except the plates and silver.

Smithson stood across the room, refilling the warming pan with coals.

"There now," she said delightedly, when she came to remove the tray. "You made a good meal, after all. The major—Mr. Rhoads—he had the right of it."

Gaby made a face. "Don't tell him," she said glumly. "He thinks he knows everything as it is."

Smithson looked startled at first, then gave a great peal of laughter.

"You young things," she said tolerantly, "how you do like to cover up your feelings. But I know the major too well not to see he has tumbled deep into love, and I can see it's the same for you."

Gaby's eyes rolled up in disbelief. With the tray removed, she snuggled down in bed again.

"Good night, Mrs. Rhoads."

"Good night," Gaby murmured. "Is it Miss or Mrs. Smithson?"

"It's plain Smithson, just as it always is for anyone hired out to serve in to a gentleman's house."

Gaby opened her eyes only partially.

"How incredibly like the English. I think it is downright rude!"

"No, ma'am," said Smithson philosophically. "It's just one of the ways of the world."

"Have you ever been married?"

"I married Samuel Smithson when I was sixteen and he only a corporal. We had twenty-seven good years together, though neither a chick nor child. *That* was a grief. He fought in battle after battle, most of them in foreign climes and never once did he get wounded. Lord, Lord, no bullet was ever made could hurt my Sam. He got to be a sergeant; and the rank and file liked to be beside him in the fighting. It was said he had a charmed life. And so he did in war! It took a dread disease to fell my man."

Gaby opened her eyes wide.

"Oh, he is—he has—"

"Two years ago come Easter, of the measles."

"I am so sorry."

"Ah well, it's not many who can say, as I do, that I have had a good life. There now," quite briskly, "I shouldn't be talking with you this way about matters of no interest to you. Good night, Mrs. Rhoads."

"Good night, Mrs. Smithson," said Gaby politely and slid down again in bed before the lady's maid opened the door.

It seemed only minutes but was actually an hour before Darcy came into the room. His entrance did not wake her, nor his undressing, but she awoke the moment he entered the bed.

When he leaned across, meaning to press one kiss on her forehead, Gaby opened her eyes to find his face extremely close to hers.

"Still awake, my sleeping beauty?" he said teasingly.

Her eyes closed again. "Major Darcy Rhoads, I am so exhausted, I do not have the strength either to resist or to fight you. Do with me as you will."

"But, my dear Gabrielle, I do not and will not."

Darcy made himself comfortable and lay down on his side of the bed and chuckled aloud. "What a pity to have found you so meek and yielding, because I know only too well that you may never be either or both again."

Gaby lay rigidly beside him, mortified beyond words.

Darcy turned over on his back and stared up at the ceiling. "In view of your kind offer, I am particularly distressed that I must refuse. I know only too well I may never meet with such generosity again."

He sighed deeply. "The truth is that I am so exhausted myself, I am afraid I could not do justice to the occasion—or to you."

Gaby gasped, then blinked her eyes several times, wishing she had a gun, an ax, a sword, a knife . . . even a hammer or any instrument of destruction she could use on him.

"I expect," he said, "that your elderly husband and your too-young lover who came before me—that is, if you didn't lie about the others, too—did not educate you in a few niceties of the marriage bed. Oh . . . you wanted to say something?"

Since the only sound had been the grinding of her teeth, Gaby remained stonily silent.

"Now, let me see, where were we . . . ? Oh, yes, the matter of strength in love-making. Actually, my dear, though it is seldom spoken of, your sex has it all over mine in the matter of endurance. Having exerted ourselves greatly in the—shall we call it *prelude?*—I am sure you learned *that* at least from me—"

He sighed again. "Next comes the matter of performance. Once a man has shot his bolt, so to speak, he often desires only sleep. Oh, many may go on forever, but if there is to be *quality* . . . a decent rest period is required."

He turned over on one side, propped himself up on an elbow and said with an air of great candor. "Several years ago I came to the conclusion that you are—your sex—a great deal more fortunate than mine. We must recruit our strength, while *you* appear to be untiring. Considered honestly, it is obvious that it takes a very good man to satisfy one woman, provided, of course, that she is a warm-blooded, passionate creature."

"I wish," said Gaby viciously, "that you were as wearied in

tongue as you are in body. Then, I would not be forced to listen to another word from you tonight."

"Not one single word?"

"Not one!"

"But that would be too rude," he protested solemnly. "When sharing a bed with a woman—even your wife—it is only proper to wish her a good night and good dreams."

He bent swiftly and his lips were the merest brushing of her mouth.

"Sleep well, my wife."

Two minutes later, he was asleep.

Gaby lay awake, hating him, for another forty minutes.

Forty-six

My dearest of Aunts,

My journeys have been ever so much longer, taking me much farther than either of us could have foreseen that winter morning when I set out on my travels. I regret, dear Aunt Emily, that just when my return seemed a matter of days, not months or years, I am forced to give you news of more delay.

I have married—for reasons you surely understood—a man who loves me. He has penetrated my disguise . . . which you know to mean the artifices we all of us use to ensnare reluctant, bachelor-minded men to take the final step.

Feeling as we both do—you and I—about wedded bliss—it need not be explained to you why I became inclined to accept the married state. It is, after all, a woman's only way to secure her future, such fragile, helpless creatures as our pitiful education trains us to be.

Alas, that we do have the thinking power of man's superior brain. Even now, as I write to you, I am being unmercifully bounced along hard roads in the chaise my husband hired to take us back to British-occupied New York.

From the harbor of that city, my husband and I will take ship for England. He intends to take me to his home, unaware home is where you are and that I have a father living in his country and dear Lydia as well. The refuge they offer is important. The need to have an alternative plan is something I learned watching British officers when they play piquet. They all seem to spend prodigious amounts in gambling. My frugal New England soul abhors the enormous sums wagered daily on the turn of a card or the amount of a doxy's undergarments, which (for a shilling or two) she is only too willing to exhibit.

I once approached one such woman in New York—really, she was only a girl—and protested against her humiliation. Fancy my astonishment when she smiled rather pityingly at me and said: "Now, miss, think of this: I get better pay for showing off me petticoats than lying on me back for a gentleman's pleasure. And the work's much easier, too!"

Oh, Aunt, you instructed me so rightly. There is much in this world that needs amendment if women are ever to cease to be men's playthings (wed or not).

To return to the subject of my plans and schemes. I have not much faith that I will find happiness in this marriage, which was undertaken in a spirit of anger and resentment on his side and much trepidation on mine. I must try to see if there is even the slimmest probability that one or both of us can be happy together.

If my forebodings prove correct, Papa (however grieved he may be when I confess all) will be my rock, my strength, in England just as you, dear Aunt, are my refuge in America.

The major (who I sometimes forget is no longer a major, only a Mr.) knows nothing about either of you. He fancies that once I am on the ship, and ever after, I will be totally subject to his domination. You, my dear Aunt, know me too well to believe I will ever allow myself to be entrapped in any relationship . . . even marriage . . . that does not suit my own notions of peace, happiness and propriety. Especially with the example of your own courageous stand against wedded slavery and a cruel owner.

It is time I ended this communication, which I am loath to do. When I speak to you, even by letter, it seems to reinforce the bond between us. Still, the bumping of the chaise has reduced my writing to a scrawl, which I know you will find difficult to read. Between this and the crossed lines (paper is scarce and fearfully expensive, even in New York), I pity you the difficulty in making sense of it.

Moreover, my companion—I supposed I should say, my husband is consumed with curiosity. He thinks I am composing verse, and I have allowed him to believe so.

"Is not a husband allowed a private reading?" he has teased me more than just the one time, and I tease back.

Really, we both sound delightfully in rapport. "No, you must buy it with coin like every other reader." Any outsider who listened might conclude that ours is a heaven-made match. More like hell, I have murmured under my breath any number of times in this last several days. (Papa would grieve about such blasphemy as I just uttered. You and my unwicked stepmama would not.)

Whatever the outcome, dear, dear Aunt Emily, as soon as we reach England, I will write to inform you of my safe arrival. After my first letter, I will faithfully report to you my each and every move. I so very much long to receive news from you, but for the time being, much as I regret it, I think it better that you do not write to me . . . until anonymity is no longer needed.

Therefore, I will not send the address of my husband's relations in England to prevent their learning *you* exist; and for the same reason, I have no intention of furnishing Papa's direction, so if I leave, Darcy will not succeed in following his wayward wife. The *why* would not trouble him; the *where* would bring trouble to *me*.

In New York City, I will endeavor to find someone to whom I may entrust this letter. I want to feel secure of its being delivered.

Again, dear Aunt, and always with the same reluctance, I bid you—not good-bye, which sounds too final—but, *adieu,* in the French fashion, which presumes this to be only a temporary fare-thee-well.

> Your affectionate niece,
>
> G.

Gaby was quite surprised in the morning to find her boastful husband still beside her, sleeping so soundly that his eyelids did not even flutter when she slipped slowly and cautiously out of their shared bed and took her reticule from beneath her pillow.

This was the happenstance she had been longing for since they arrived at Fraunces Tavern.

The nearest dressing gown happened to be his, not her own. She slipped into the too-long sleeves and sashed it around her. The gown trailed ridiculously, but what did it matter? In fact, it might be for the best that she was wearing it. She might appear at the worst, slightly silly, but if he appeared in *her* gown, he would be made to look ridiculous and the butt of much mockery and snickers. And for the same reason, he would not venture forth in his bedgown.

She stumbled along the corridor, trying to keep the gown hitched up. At the farthest end, a chambermaid with her arms full of linens stood in front of a cupboard counting sheets.

"Young woman." Gaby tried hard to sound authoritative.

The girl whirled around, not flustered at all. "Good morning, ma'am," she said with a friendly smile. "You were that quiet, I didn't hear you coming up on me." A small smile tugged at the corners of her mouth. "Though, probably I would have heard the sound of your falling when your skirts tripped you up."

Now, here's a girl with spirit, thank God.

"I need," Gaby said, "someone to do a small service for me. Not difficult at all," she hastened to add, "just the delivery of a letter. But it must be done immediately, as well as secretly and speedily. My husband and I leave on the packet for England today. I want to be certain you have been successful."

The girl was staring at her, open-mouthed.

"I will pay handsomely," Gaby assured her. "Perhaps a bit more if you turn out to be a good hand at bargaining."

"I'm from the Hampshire Grants, ma'am, there's no better bargainers to be found than there."

"Indeed? In Massachusetts we say—"

Exclaiming at her foolishness, for entering such a discussion, when so little time was left, Gaby interrupted herself.

"Here is what I want done." She produced the creased letter from her reticule. "Do you know Mr. Rivington's print shop?"

"That I do."

"Then take this"—she produced her letter—"to Mr. Rivington himself and . . . he will be able to see—here is the direction—where it must be sent. Give him the letter, pay him his fee, and ask him for a receipt . . . a *written* receipt, mind, on his own billing paper . . . what are you laughing at?"

"I thought you were half-flash and half-foolish till you mentioned a receipt," the chambermaid confessed laughingly. "So, it's this way," said the girl. "I walk—"

"No, a hackney will be ever so much faster." Gaby produced a pile of coins from her purse and one folded bank note.

The girl accepted both the letter and money, then parroted, "I take a hackney to Mr. Rivington's shop, give him this letter to post, pay his fee, get a receipt signed by him on his business paper, then I return—by hackney again?"

"Certainly. My husband will want to board the packet early."

"There is only one problem I can think of, ma'am . . . and here she comes like a ship in full sail herself."

The housekeeper was indeed sailing majestically down the hallway toward them. "Jenny, why are you not about your work?" she scolded.

"Oh, ma'am. Please don't scold Jenny. It was my fault. There's a small errand I want her to perform for me, but she said she was sorry, she had too many chores. Won't you please let her out for an hour? I will gladly pay for her time. Just add it to our bill."

The housekeeper thawed visibly. "Well, if you put it that way..."

"Thank you so much, ma'am." Gaby put out her hands to grasp the housekeeper's. When the friendly shake of their hands ceased, a handsome tip had changed hands and was being thrust down into the housekeeper's bodice.

"Now mind, Jenny"—her face was wreathed in smiles—"you are not to dawdle on the way."

"No, ma'am." Jenny bobbed a brief curtsey, then reprehensibly made a far-from-respectful face at the departing back.

"Bless you, Jenny," said Gaby fervently. "When you come back..."

"With a signed receipt?"

"Yes, with a signed receipt... you may keep all the change if there is any after the hackney rides and the posting, and I will give you, as well, five pounds sterling."

"English?" gasped Jenny with popping eyes.

"English," Gaby confirmed.

"God be praised. He must be looking after me this day," said Jenny. "Why, I have known a girl come to her man on their wedding day with less hard money for their dowry than that."

She looked at Gaby, suddenly beseeching. "You wouldn't be after jesting a girl, would you, ma'am?"

"Jesting! And me, as I told you, from Massachusetts. No one jests about money Boston way, I assure you, and I have already invested a great deal of mine."

Jenny's face cleared magically. She whisked off her apron and flung it carelessly on top of the sheets in the linen cupboard.

"Fancy me forgetting," she apologized, "that you came from Massachusetts, where they contrive to make tuppence buy sixpence worth of goods! Good-bye, ma'am," she added. "I'm off to get me a hackney just like a grand lady. Oh—*how* shall I find you when I come back? Will you be in your chamber or having your breakfast?"

"One of those two, but whatever you do or don't, remember not to approach me unless I am alone. If I am accompanied, I will make some excuse and come looking for you. Now, go, please. I will feel uneasy until you actually return."

When Gaby returned to her room, Darcy was up and fully dressed. His brows lifted at the sight and sound of her, as she tried not to trip over the tangled skirt of her husband's dressing down, and her efforts, especially combined with a few words Gaby had never heard on Papa's lips, were not a notable success.

"My dear," Darcy drawled in the too-British voice he used when he wished to provoke her, "why did you not tell me you had a fondness for that garment? It is yours—everything I own is yours, my dear, if you will only mention your wants to me."

"Oh, stop acting so English!" Gaby told him crossly. "I just took the garment nearest to hand when I was going . . . when I needed . . ."

"You blush so charmingly, my love. Shall I save you further embarrassment by admitting that I am perfectly cognizant of the fact that women, too, need sometimes to retire to the necessary?"

"Oh, the devil take you!" she said impotently. "I prefer you to be disagreeable rather than so detestably patronizing."

"But, my dear wife," he protested mildly, "there is so much you have cause to complain of in both my speech and my manners, I do not know how we are going to go on together. Shall I not speak at all?"

"*That* would be ideal." She tried to equal him in nonchalance. "I know you too well, however, to believe you capable of such restraint."

"You never knew me at all, Mrs. Forsyth-Foote, if you thought you could use me and then fade away, happily, into anonymity."

"But you see," Gaby explained carefully, "until a week ago, I never had experienced your vindictive streak. If asked, I might have said you did not have one."

"Everything you *thought* you knew about me until a week ago was totally wrong. You never understood my character at all."

"I realize that now."

"Fret not, dear wife. If you will obey all my orders as the head of our household, and get it into your own scheming head that I am not a dolt nor your own personal dunderhead, we will live more or less amicably together. There is one more matter . . . a rather delicate matter . . . we need to discuss . . ."

Gaby fought free of the long sleeve and enveloping prison of his dressing gown. She allowed it to drop to the floor and stood before him in her nightdress.

"Discuss away, then," she said curtly, crossing over to the rocking chair, where someone—no doubt, Mrs. Smithson—had laid out a full set of clothing for her, including a rather plain, serviceable dress and stout leather boots.

"It is the matter of our chastity."

Gaby dropped a pair of woolen stockings. "Our *what?*"

"Chastity," he repeated helpfully. "Yours and mine."

While she stood there, quite bewildered, he picked up his dressing gown with one hand and her stockings with the other.

She accepted the stockings. "What on earth are you talking about?" she demanded caustically, sitting on the edge of the rocker and kicking off her slippers. "My chastity is my own affair."

"Exactly!" he cried out eagerly. "That is the substance of the subject. You propose to be a wife to me only on paper, inasmuch as I hold the certificate of our marriage. You do not intend to render me any of the services which usually are considered an obligation when married. Now, I—perhaps foolishly, but necessary to my own honor—will never thrust myself upon—"

Gaby had already made two snags in her stockings in her savage need to be through with them. These last four words restored her to good humor. She began to laugh hilariously and when there was no more laughter in her, she began to cry. She cried loudly, robustly, and with her whole heart. Darcy came over to the rocker to inform her in doubtful tones, "I think you may be hysterical."

This, just as she was returning to some semblance of sobriety, set her off again.

"I think," he ventured uneasily, "I may have to slap you."

Gaby, having no handkerchief at hand, reached down and around for her petticoat and wiped her eyes and face with it. Before she could blow her nose in it, too, Darcy hastily handed her one of his large handkerchiefs.

"Now what," he said, when she seemed utterly calm, "was that about?"

"You were promising . . ." She sputtered just a little . . . "not to thrust yourself upon me. I presume you meant that in the metaphorical sense; I could not help thinking of the literal."

He smiled, the smile of the Darcy of old, sharing another previous exchange with her. One of those meetings of their minds, over and above even the joining of their bodies, that had been such a source of delight in their past relationship.

He quickly reviewed his past remarks and said sheepishly, "Thrust upon you—trust you to immediately think of its bawdier meaning."

Gaby gave him an almost friendly grin, then reached for her shift.

"Well, sir," she asked mockingly, "do you stay to watch me attire myself? Or am I allowed a modicum of privacy while I do so and then pack my portmanteau?"

"Smithson will do your packing," he said, "as soon as you dress and come downstairs. If I may suggest, come as quickly as you can. Shipboard food, even at the captain's table, runs the gamut from plain monotonous and unvaried, to unappetizing. It is often ill-prepared and gamy. You will think longingly a few weeks from now of the meal I propose to order downstairs. Fresh eggs—at least half a dozen to be eaten with the finest steak to be had anywhere in New York, as well as potatoes fried with slices of onions. Also, lean, tasty slices of bacon, as much as we can eat."

Gaby had closed her eyes in silent ecstasy. "I can almost smell them."

"You probably do. Are you ready to go down?"

Gaby had proposed to take her time dressing so as to give

Jenny more time to accomplish her errand and return; but the lure of the food was too strong. She could do her lingering more happily over breakfast.

"You go down first," she urged. "I will finish dressing and be with you as soon as I may."

He lingered. "If you take too long, the griddlecakes may get cold."

Gaby's mouth watered. "I won't delay."

Darcy walked over to the door, then turned—he would have her believe—uncertainly.

"But we did not finish discussing our chastity."

"For the love of heaven, we can discuss it over breakfast."

"Very well." His hand was on the doorknob. "China tea or coffee?"

"Either. Both. Go away."

"Corn bread or biscuits, muffins—"

Gaby picked up the rocker cushion and aimed it at his head, but was satisfied when it struck his chest. "I want every dish on the menu. I want to eat until I explode. I want anything and everything."

Forty-seven

To Darcy's awed admiration, as well as the waiter's and the cook's, Gaby had demolished—in short order and without conversation—a small steak, three eggs, one large helping of potatoes with onions, and two cups of strong coffee.

"The edge is off my appetite"—she fluttered her eyes flirtatiously at Darcy. "I think I can eat quite slowly now, if you want to converse."

"I would not dream of it. How could I be so cruel as to come between you and your breakfast?"

"Thank you."

"What shall I ask the waiter to bring you now? Another steak, perhaps."

"No, indeed. If you must know, I feel extremely guilty about having eaten just the one."

"Why?"

"Any good piece of beef in New York could only have been brought here by cowboys who stole it from Dutch farmers along the Hudson River estates in upper New York."

"I promise I will keep your shameful secret forever. No word of it will ever pass my lips."

"Of course, I would not feel guilty about such local fare as flapjacks with maple syrup," Gaby ventured.

"How many?"

"Four or five . . . or so."

Darcy beckoned to the waiter. "Half a dozen griddlecakes for my wife and . . ."

"Coffee," Gaby broke in eagerly, "and perhaps just a few strips of bacon."

"And you, sir?"

"Eggs, bacon, coffee and toasted bread."

Gaby nibbled on a biscuit while they waited. "Do you want to talk about our chastity now?" she asked chattily without troubling to lower her voice.

An elderly couple were sitting at a nearby table. The woman flushed to her ears and the man broke into loud guffaws.

"I think we can save it for shipboard," he answered casually, apparently uncaring, determined not to yield her every hit in their prolonged fencing match.

"Do you know Gabrielle, you have always enjoyed a good meal, but it seems to me now that your appetite is considerably greater than it used to be. What a pity you wasted so much time running away from me. If I had known how much it would cost to feed you, I might have fled from you myself."

"Possibly. But on the other hand"—with a beatific smile—"knowing your resolute, not to say obstinate nature—I could not take the risk."

Just as the waiter was returning with their second breakfast, Gaby spied Jenny hovering in the doorway near the rear. When they caught each other's eye, Jenny smiled, nodding her head. Gaby smiled back, signaling with her own eyes. Both appeared to understand the other's unspoken message.

Done.
Good.
Payment?
Later. After breakfast.
When?
Any time before we leave.

No fear of a mishap. Each had what the other wanted. Money for Jenny. Certainty—by way of receipt—so Gaby felt assured her letter would be safely conveyed to Aunt Emily.

Giddy and gleeful, Gaby attacked her second breakfast, only

discovering halfway through the proceedings, that it was impossible for her to take another bite.

She announced this conclusion to her husband.

"Thank God," he said, throwing down knife and fork. "I could not manage another bite myself, though I tried as manfully as I could to keep up with you."

He consulted his pocket watch. "Time to go. If you have any last-minute chores, better do them now, while I settle the bill with our host."

Gaby smiled and nodded. He had given her the needed minutes to consult with Jenny.

The maid was upstairs and working at the linen closet again. She came when Gaby called her name, and the two entered her room together. It was empty of all the bags, too.

"Where are my things?"

"Oh, your husband arranged for the servants to take all the trunks and parcels over to the ship."

Gaby's face cleared. "I really made it just in time," she murmured.

"Here's your receipt." Jenny held out a folded piece of paper. "I hope it says what you wanted. I can't read nor write except my name," she said.

One quick glance told Gaby all.

"Just what I wanted," she said, wondering why Jenny looked so uneasy.

She started hunting in her reticule for the bank note she had put aside for the girl.

"Your man is so handsome and pleasant-like," she said a bit uneasily, and at once Gaby understood her problem.

Between the secrecy and such a lavish bribe, the young maid who (thankfully) could not read, felt her own guilt at having participated in what she imagined might be illicit goings-on between Gaby and another man.

Gaby looked cautiously around them, as though some unseen person might pop out from underneath the bed or perhaps from behind a piece of furniture.

"Just between you and me, Jenny, so he doesn't hear me, my man is handsome and pleasant plus a good many other things I could praise him for. He is also stubborn as a mule and can't forgive his young brother for joining the American Army. Until now, every generation in their family has had a son, always the second son, in the British Army. Such idiocy. So I—oh, good, here is your money."

Jenny lost track of everyone and everything else as she took the precious bank note into her hands, poring over the numbers (which apparently she had learned).

"So" concluded Gaby, not at all certain she was heard, "I decided to have none of this foolishness. I am keeping up a writing acquaintance with Daniel—my husband's brother—so that when the war is over, he may be sure of a welcome home at any time."

"Yes, mum," said Jenny gloatingly, her fingers caressing the money as she folded it small and tucked it way below her bodice, just as the housekeeper had done. Just as I might, Gaby realized, struck by what a safe hiding place the area just between one's breasts could be, so long, of course as one didn't expect a gentleman in the vicinity when one undressed.

It all happened so quickly. Their schedule allowed so little time for reflection or rest that, almost before Gaby realized it, they were bundled into the waiting carriage and leaving Fraunces Tavern.

The trip to the harbor was not very long, and Darcy kept her mind occupied with tales of the changes in the city since the great fire. His notions about the dread night the burning of Manhattan lit up the sky, and many, even innocent folk, who were seen with matches or a candle, had become a part of the blazing inferno.

Some of the facts her husband marshaled together and tossed into his account were as incendiary as the fire itself. Gaby was too busy refuting them to be aware of their coach's uneven pace along the streets and down to the harbor.

On deck, when they arrived, she was still feeling nostalgic about the past and temporarily unconcerned about her future. How she had loved to visit Boston and walk along the pier and sniff the wonderful aroma of ships and sails combined with the heavenly scent of the rum and molasses, tobacco, and tea from the orient. Or later, goods sent the longabout way to and from England so as to be doubly taxed for Americans. How the fish must have rejoiced when those 342 chests of tea were thrown into the sea! No matter the consequences in London, the British had learned then what Americans thought of the tax on tea.

With her husband's stubborn, wrongheaded opinions to refute and the wonderful memories, half-forgotten, of long ago, almost before she realized it, Gaby was on the ship, *Pandora*. She would have stood at the rail for a while, but Darcy suggested they check their trunk and belongings to make sure everything had been brought on board.

Yielding to this piece of commonsense, Gaby agreed. They had a pair of adjoining cabins.

"Yours," Darcy pointed out virtuously, "is by far the larger."

"Always the gentleman."

There were some flowers for her, too, and on top of the one small table in the room, a bowl of fruit. "In case," he mentioned solicitously, "you become hungry before lunch is served."

"How thoughtful of you, my dear," simpered Gaby.

"I may not succeed, but I always try."

She had begun to shake out her dresses and decide how they could be arranged in the cramped wardrobe when there was a quick knock followed almost at once by the entrance of Smithson.

They both spoke at the same time.

"Mrs. Smithson, what on earth are you doing here?"

"Don't you worry about that, Mrs. Rhoads. I'll see to your clothes."

Mrs. Smithson took the dress from Gaby's hands. "The major

is on the top deck now. Perhaps," she suggested gently, "you will want to see New York Harbor before it disappears from view."

The force, the meaning of these words, struck Gaby with stunning impact. She was on a British ship with Darcy Rhoads, who was more or less her husband and was exercising one right at least of that office. On what could only be interpreted as a command, no matter the honeyed accents in which it had been sheathed, she was on her way to England with him. England, the enemy country.

She dashed out of the room and up the nearest flight of stairs, then paused uncertainly. A passing sailor came by.

"Sir, can you please tell me how to reach the top deck?"

He grinned, showing huge empty spaces where teeth should have been. "Just around that corner there and up a small flight for the starboard side."

"Thank you."

"Missy, just a word of advice?"

"Certainly."

"On shipboard a lady passenger doesn't say *sir* to the likes of me."

"What is your name?"

" 'Enry."

"Is it permissible to call you Henry?"

"Don't know for sure. No passenger ever did."

"How then does one get your attention to ask a question or make a request?"

Henry took off his knit cap, scratched the top of his head and returned the cap to its proper place.

"Never gave much thought to it. No one ever did. Some say, sailor, and some say, you, boy. Others just snap their fingers like and some only nod their heads."

"Since *you* seem uncomfortable with sir, I shall call you Henry," Gaby informed him. "I do not like the other alternatives."

With a smile and a friendly flip of her hands, Gaby turned the corner, went up the stairs, and arrived on the top deck. Darcy was a few feet away, both hands on the rail, his body slightly inclined as he looked his last at New York.

Gaby said the moment she was within hearing distance, "What *is* the quality in the British that makes them so pretentious?"

Darcy continued his survey of New York. "What," he asked wearily, "has one of them done *now* to earn your contempt?"

"I just asked directions of a sailor old enough to be my grandfather and he said I must not call him *sir*. Evidently, he is not considered deserving of such courtesy."

"It is the prevailing custom."

"It's a horrible custom."

"Agreed. *Must* we discuss all the faults and failures of my county now? Would you not prefer to take in the last glimpse of *your* country? You may not see it again for a long, long time."

"Oh!"

Gaby whirled around and the wind whipped up her skirts. There, in the distance—with the scars of fire and battle and occupation—was New York. There she lay in all her splendor. Dirty, unhealthy, scarred, polyglot . . .

Gaby had not thought the sight would affect her so.

After all, it was not the place of her heart. She was a New Englander, and her home was now in New Jersey. Nevertheless, there was a huge constriction in her throat and the tears in her eyes threatened to roll down her cheeks any minute now. She could not help herself.

The very first day she arrived in New York, she had met her true love, literally wriggled about on his lap in their moment of meeting. She had been kissed as no one had ever kissed her before she met Darcy.

She had found a wife for Papa and sent the two of them happily on their way across the Atlantic, before establishing her own new role in life in New York.

She had turned into an agent, a spy for the new nation of thirteen states under British occupation.

She became the most well-known poet in the exciting city. She had found such joy in Darcy's arms, as she had never before believed mere mortals could achieve.

For a moment, her eyes were so drowned in tears, she could not see. She kept brushing them away with her hands, only to have others well up and roll down her cheeks anew.

Darcy responded as he had so many times to her tear-without-a-handkerchief emergency. He mopped her face up himself, then turned her around again, facing the shore. He stood behind her, with his arms clasped around her, for protection from the wind. His hands clasped her hands as they rested on the deck rail, keeping them warm.

They stayed in that position for what might have been an eternity or only another half hour.

When the city was only a speck in the distance, and then suddenly not there, Gaby gave a prolonged sigh as she looked around. "There is only ocean," she said unsteadily.

"Yes, dear," said Darcy with unwanted gentleness. "I think you should go down to your cabin. The last week has been hectic, to say the least. Perhaps you might be able to rest a while."

As he descended the stairs slightly ahead of her, his arm under hers, his hand holding hers in case she stumbled. Gaby said, "I just recalled what I wanted to say to you. Why on earth did you bring a lady's maid for me? I never heard of such nonsense. Is she to mind my clothes and dress my hair on this ship? It would take less than an hour in each of twenty-four."

"I must needs have purchased her passage home in any event, since she was widowed in America while her husband served as my batman. A good man. I miss him. And when I pressed a small salary on her, it was because I thought you would need her greatly when you succumb to seasickness."

"Seasickness. I?"

Now Gaby was truly affronted. "What on earth makes you suppose I will become seasick?" she asked haughtily.

"It is not unusual for a new sailor. I have suffered some bouts of it myself, I must admit."

"Then perhaps I should send her to *your* cabin," Gaby suggested sweetly. "My parents and I visited family members often during the summer. I have been out on lobster boats in Gloucester, fishing trawlers in the Hamptons, and one glorious time we were able—my cousin Elijah of Nantucket and I—to go out to the sea on a whaler for a day. It would not have been possible had not the captain of a small schooner agreed to rendezvous with important mail to take back to Nantucket. Therefore, I did not, I have never been, and I will never allow myself to be seasick."

"If you say so, my dear Gabrielle," with a burlesqued bow, "you will not be seasick. In which case, I may beg the services of Mrs. Smithson for myself."

"Granted," said Gaby with a slight giggle. With her hand on the door to her cabin, her face suddenly crumpled.

"What is it, Gaby?"

"I am leaving my country." Her voice trembled. "My own country, my land, all that is dear to me. Can you know—can you possibly feel what that means to me?"

"I left England a few years back, wondering if perhaps I would never see it again. I faced the possibility of having my bones lie in foreign soil."

"But you did it of your own free will. Your have said yourself that generations of your family elected to be in the British Army. The difference is *you* are forcing *me* to go to England."

"I have no intention of wandering down that path with you again, Gabrielle. You chose to be a spy, you chose me as your dupe, you pretended to be my loyal and enduring love. You made all the choices that led to my *persuasion,* shall we call it, to get you aboard this ship."

He opened the door to her cabin and stood aside courteously.

"Thank you," said Gaby frostily, and walked by him, her back stiff, her head high, and her face frozen.

Mrs. Smithson was no longer there, but the cabin was neat as a pin, with a lovelier arrangement of the flowers, the fruit divided into two bowls, one near to the bed and the other on a tray above the wardrobe.

The trunk was not visible, but all its contents were neatly hung or put away. The ship's skimpy pillow had been replaced by two of goose down, which were Gaby's own. The colorful afghan folded at the bottom of the bed had been knit by Abigail many a year ago.

Gaby sat down on the side of the bed, thinking hard, trying to be honest with herself. She thought of her mother and her lost home, her lost dreams, and she wept. She thought of dear Aunt Emily and the home that would be hers one day, and she wept a little more.

She thought of the women's league which punished brutal men; and her heart lifted. To have been, even briefly, a part of it, rejoiced her heart. Perhaps some day, she would be part of it again.

She thought of her years in New York, first the city, then Long Island; and she would not—she realized—have changed a single thing. She had served her country . . . the very highest service, the riskiest that one could give, and she had loved it. The challenge, the excitement, and—face it, Gaby, face the truth . . . Darcy.

It was an exciting game you played, and you loved it. You loved him. You love him still.

If she were in New York now and he was on this ship without her, she would feel even more bereft and forlorn.

He, going back to England, me staying behind in America. The two of them parting forever.

Unthinkable.

So?

So the unthinkable truth had to be faced.

In no real sense had he forced her. She was here where she wanted to be. On a six- or seven-week voyage where they would be alone and very, very married. Very, very thrown upon each other's companionship.

England may not work out for you . . . that is a stark possibility. This . . . *this* time aboard ship might be all they were ever to have together.

In which case, why so contrary and contentious? Why not enjoy this brief, idyllic period that will never come again?

Quarreling with him had always had a certain spice of its own, when it was political rather than personal, when it was his-county-against-mine in the sense of minor courtesies (why should a sailor be thought of as more than some lower form of life or a woman like Smithson not be granted the dignity of Mrs. before her name?).

It had always been invigorating to match wits with him, with neither minding who had the better arguments and who came out ahead.

It was the more bitter spats that made them so unpleasant to one another, the frequent accusations and denials of betrayal. She had given him every reason to believe her guilty of using his love to gather information. Yet she wanted him to believe in her against the force of intelligence and sound reason.

He had held her in his arms so often in the nights . . . sometimes in the day . . . He would not believe in the proof she had given with body, heart and soul—not the least of these her body. Did he despise her so much as to believe that just *any* man could have induced her to give herself to him with such profoundly exciting abandon?

Each seemed to want the other to be clairvoyant.

Each seemed to think the other should believe in love's intuition rather than the evidence.

Each wanted the other to throw prudence and perception out the window.

Darcy must ignore all her lies and pretenses, as though they had never happened.

Gaby must admit she had given him cause to feel betrayed and, therefore, he had every right in the world to doubt her protestations of love.

Worn out and wearied by the thoughts going round and round in her brain, Gaby kicked off her shoes and lay down on her bed, smothering sobs in her goose-down pillow.

After a while, she cried herself to sleep.

Mrs. Smithson entered her cabin once, threw a light blanket over her and retired.

Darcy came into her room later from his adjoining cabin. She was fast asleep, clutching the pillow to her, and the marks of tear stains were still there on her face.

He stood for several minutes looking down at her. Who would ever have suspected the treachery that lay behind the mask? She was not beautiful. Even at the height of his infatuation, he had never considered her a classic beauty, but something much more... Lovely always to look at with or without her clothes.... capable of intelligent conversation—nothing of the "Oh, Major Rhoads, how can you be so naughty?" or "Major Rhoads, you put me to the blush. No, *his* girl, *his* (long before she refused his offer) chosen bride was capable of good sense and good judgment. She was charming in exchanges of wit, intelligent in ordinary conversation over a dinner for two, equally so in a group of people. And, above all, she had always known when it was time for silence.

Her air of lively, playful sportiveness... how enchanting it was. How it had captivated him.

He had fought hard against believing what he finally was forced to believe of her. He would have given his present fortune and his future earldom to be able to deny that she was *not* the enemy and had *not* dealt with him so honorably.

So bewitching... and so false!

Forty-eight

They were less than a day out from New York, and Gaby was too busy, too exhausted to have much time for brooding.

She was playing nurse not only to Mrs. Smithson (who had been brought along on this voyage to take care of *her*), but also to her own lawfully wedded spouse.

Both had been attacked by seasickness in a particularly virulent form, while Gaby (smugly pleased that her boasts were fulfilled) did not experience the slightest queasiness, and certainly not any reduction in her appetite.

With Mrs. Smithson (mortified beyond words that the mistress should wait on the maid), Gaby was unfailingly gentle and soothing.

With Darcy, although she performed many of the same tasks, holding his head, mopping his brow, cleaning him up) she could not deny herself the pleasure—when he was not in the throes of nausea—of exercising a degree of sadism.

After all, she reminded herself righteously, it was the very first time since their meeting on a New Jersey highway, that she felt she was the one to have the upper hand.

Unfortunately, the upper hand did not entail any form of retaliation. With ocean, only ocean all about them, there was no ship magically appearing onto which she could be spirited away and taken back to New York. Aware of this, she had to settle for a little mild torture.

"Really, Darcy, I think you defamed this vessel and the cook, too. Why, this morning's breakfast was almost as satisfying as our last meal at Fraunces Tavern. In some respects, it was better. The biscuits were made with blueberries, bottled ones, I fancy, but baked, there was no difference at all in taste. And the bacon, la, it was cut so lean and just the right degree of crispness. I vow—"

Darcy struggled up, leaning on one elbow. "And I vow, too," he uttered in a strangled voice, "that if you do not cease to discuss food of any sort, I will strangle you. I still have enough strength left in me to do that."

"Very, well, sir," Gaby answered meekly. "I only thought that you would be happy to learn that I am not sick."

"Gabrielle!"

"Yes, sir?"

"I want—oh God!" His voice thickened and his eyes rolled around. With his pallor turned greenish, Gaby—not truly unsympathetic—knew what was about to happen.

"Chamber mug?"

"Yes."

She seized it from its pride of place on the washstand and shoved it under his nose.

He uttered guttural sounds. "Tng oo, go bay," she had become used to such tense speeches and translated, "Thank you. Go away."

"You *are* more than welcome," said Gaby. "At least *I* know a wife's obligations. Are you *sure* you don't need me?"

He shuddered. "Bositivb."

"Positive," Gaby's mind told her after three seconds of debate. "Very well, dear husband. Since you so wish, I shall leave you to your misery."

With a farewell flip of her hand, Gaby retired through the adjoining door and closed it firmly.

On a cloth which she had spread across her trunk to serve her as a shelf, she picked up the last of her stale muffins brought from Fraunces Tavern, and the second volume of *Robinson Crusoe*. With her own two pillows set behind her back to serve as a comfortable prop, she opened her book and set aside the silver bookmark that had marked her place.

Both mark and the book had been long-ago gifts from Darcy, who had marveled greatly at the extent of her reading. Novels and histories, poetry, the Bible—as well as present-day newspapers and periodicals so she would be in touch with what was going on at home and abroad. Gaby read them all.

Now, though, Gaby delayed looking down at her book. She leaned back against the pillows, a multitude of thoughts scrambling around in her brain, each one trying to gain ascendance.

Darcy. Darcy. Every road led back to him. And so did all her thoughts . . . all her longing . . . all her yearning . . .

She knew full well that one great stumbling block which could never be surmounted . . . soldier versus spy . . . patriot versus loyalist . . . independence versus monarchy . . . the rebellious thirteen states versus the taxable thirteen colonies, and—Gaby sighed deeply . . . what it all added up to was England, the unloving mother country, versus America, standing firm on her own feet.

Mrs. Smithson was the first to recover and within a day or two, she was able to express her undying gratitude to Mrs. Rhoads for her many acts of kindness. She could now, she added firmly, take care of herself and of her mistress, too.

Gaby agreed meekly to be served, which she realized was necessary to the older woman's pride. Then, she sped to her own suite, impetuously entering Darcy's room—without knocking—to see if he was improved, too.

The surprise was hers. Darcy was not only out of his bed, he was partly dressed. Boots, smalls and breeches, he stood, stooping to peer into a small mirror as he shaved. He was bare from the waist up.

"Oh!" said Gaby. "I mean . . . you are feeling better?"

"Obviously."

"Then you don't . . . you won't need . . ."

She was walking backwards through the door as she spoke.

"No, my wife," he said banteringly. "I appear to be coming to life again, so I have no further need of a ministering angel. Nor," he added smoothly, "of my tormentor either."

Gaby had the grace to blush.

"How could I resist," she asked defensively, "when you have had the upper hand so long?"

"I? The upper hand? Are you daft, girl? You have held me in the palm of your hand since the first time we met."

"The first time we met," Gaby repeated, blushing and stammering.

He looked at her in surprise.

"Yes, I suppose . . ." she murmured uncomfortably. Then, more composed, "I suppose it did seem that way to you."

For some reason or other, this mild acknowledgment made him angrier than the wildest disagreement. "*It* seemed so to you. Only *seemed*? Are you under the impression—has it never entered your mind—from the first you have held me in the palm of your hand for good or ill?"

"What shall I say, Darcy? What do you want me to say? That you are right? That you are always annoyingly right? Let me say it all for you, and then be completely done. I used you. I was on the lookout, not specifically for you, but for any British officers that night we met at Mrs. Loring's. If I had been able to annex an officer of higher rank than you, I would have tried for him. If you had not succumbed to my charms, I would have looked about me for a susceptible captain. Are you satisfied? Have you done with me? Is there any other disagreeable detail you would like me to give you?"

"I doubt it. What you have said is more than enough—too much, if the truth be told. The facts were known to me even before I came hunting you in New Jersey, but I could not still the wild hope I cherished that it had all been a gigantic mistake. When I finally found you, when I knew the truth, how could I not feel ashamed of having believed in your innocence?"

"You told me once," Gaby said quite steadily, "that you have never relished this war because it is one of brother against brother. And it is exactly that, brother against brother. Father against son. Women against husbands. My own father was, as I have told you, loyalist to the core. He knew full well I held vastly different views, but we ignored them rather than argue. Dear as he was, tolerant as he tried to be, Papa and I seldom discussed our differences... In one way he did not understand his women at all. He thought our political opinions of very little importance. Women do not vote. Married women do not own property nor have any say in law or government, so he could be patronizingly indulgent about our point of view. *You* are blind in a different way, Major Rhoads. You never cared a fig for my politics. You indulged me at times in the same game as Papa. Such notions as we women get in our pretty little heads!" she mimicked bitterly.

Darcy nicked himself and swore as he swiped at a spot of blood on his a chin.

"Are you quite through with your diatribe?" he asked freezingly.

"Not quite. There is one other thing I want to say, Darcy Rhoads. You are *not* angry for most of your stated reasons. What you cannot forgive me is that I tricked you, I made a fool of you. Your brain was addled by love and you fell under my spell. I played the pipe and you danced to my tune. I was the wiser of the two of us—I knew what I was doing and what I wanted, you played Simple Simon. For the love of heaven, what did you expect of me? That I wring my hands and say to my... to those who were above me, 'Oh dear, oh dearie me, I have fallen in love with the major. Shall I resign from the service and go away?' Or perhaps you would have preferred 'Dear Major Rhoads, this is difficult to say to you, but I must confess that I am an American spy. Since I am and I find myself unexpectedly in love with you, I can no longer be an agent. What shall I do? Where shall I go?' "

Darcy set his razor carefully on the washstand.

"You talk too much," he said quietly. "I have never known a woman who can talk so often and so much at the wrong time."

Before Gaby could anticipate his next move, he had come

close enough to scoop her up in his arms and sit down on the side of his unmade bed, lavishing kisses on the top of her head, then on her closed eyelids.

She lay perfectly still in her husband's arms while he took the combs and pins out of her hair and wrapped it around his hands. As he braided the silky mass through his fingers, he kissed vulnerable spots behind her ears and then his lips brushed lightly across her throat, to and fro, to and fro . . .

Gaby had closed her eyes.

"Open them." He tickled her under the chin.

"I would rather not."

He tickled her some more. "I would rather you did."

She curled up closer so his knees were taking her full weight and he could not get at her chin. Then, she jumped, as his hands took advantage of the opportunity to slip beneath her petticoats and move purposefully up her legs, pausing briefly at her knees, but a little longer at their thighs before moving upward to lusher territory.

"No," Gaby moaned, and the hand withdrew. Then, "Don't go. Please. Please, PLEASE!"

She was ready, she was eager. And on his terms, too. She would be no unwilling bride.

As soon as she made this clear to him—with a great many incoherent sounds and one clearly stated admission—she was rolled off his knees and onto the floor as he stood up.

"I will hold your consent in abeyance until I can be sure you will not change your mind again," he said casually. "Shall we go to breakfast now? It is the first time in a week that I have felt inclined to eat."

"You utter and complete beast!" yelped Gaby breathlessly from her half-sitting, half-lying position on the floor. You despicable barbarian! You—you—there are not words enough for me to tell you what you are, other than the lowest form of life on this continent or any other."

Laughing, he reached down to help her to her feet.

"Shall we go arm-in-arm together, the very picture of happy domesticity?"

"Why certainly, Major," simpered Gaby, allowing him to hoist her to her feet. *Everyone on the ship has been utterly beguiled by my touching loyalty to my poor, dear seasick husband. Of course*"—she smiled, casting her eyes down modestly—"*they could not help being slightly amused, too, to see* me, *graceful creature that I am*"—she placed one splayed hand against her breast—"*in such looks and health while my husband, strong and stalwart soldier that he is, should be prostrate with such a laughable ailment as seasickness.*"

"Gabrielle Rhoads," Darcy enunciated in words that might have petrified a far more daring young woman even than Gaby, "you are treading in dangerous waters, and I do not refer to the seas beneath this ship. Provoke me again at your peril."

One last tug, and she was pulled against the solid strength of his chest. She could feel his heart beating against her. It was more than likely that he was experiencing the tumultuous reaction of her own heart.

She was convinced of it when the beginning of a smile (quickly suppressed) played around his lips.

"Yes," said Gaby quickly stepping away from him. "I am hungry, too."

"When are you not?" he murmured.

Darcy opened the door and held out his arm. "No, don't draw away my wild one. To be carried into the dining room would embarrass even so independent-minded a young woman as you."

Forty-nine

Gaby came to the captain's table that night, leaning on her husband's arm. She managed somehow to exude the quiet assurance that seemed to be self-taught in lovely, not necessarily beautiful women. Eve must have looked just so, sitting under the apple tree while the wily serpent persuaded her to pluck and eat a single, juicy sample.

Darcy was directed to a seat well away from his wife. On his right was Lady Litton, and on his left Mrs. Horace Sunderby.

They were so short a time into their voyage that the fresh meats and vegetables were still plentiful. The meal was much better than he had expected.

It was the only satisfaction the next ninety minutes brought him. Mrs. Sunderby's hobby appeared to be genealogy—not her own but other people's. She had questioned Darcy (mercifully, most often when his mouth was full) and she had learned every scrap he knew concerning his own family and she was able to expound on accounts of his forebears that Darcy had never heard before (and hopefully, never would again). She had enlightened him as to why his Uncle Percival bore such a startling resemblance to King George II. The explanation was simple; they were closely related on the wrong side of the blanket. Entirely owing to his wife's excursions in the king's bed, a simple baronet had been elevated to an Earldom and appropriate estates bestowed on him to give both wealth and rank to the new earl's heir. In gracious acknowledgment (raising gales of laughter in succeeding generations), the child had been named George.

"So you see," Mrs. Sunderby finished her last monologue in a piercing voice, "you, yourself are indirectly related to our present monarch."

"Amazing." murmured Darcy, catching Gaby's eye. At the look on his face, she started to sputter and choke into her water glass.

Heaven help me, that little witch will never allow me to hear the end of this.

When Darcy turned to Lady Litton, he received no relief. Lady Litton was a sportswoman . . . hunting was her life and the breeding of beagles for the hunt came second.

Mrs. Sunderby had harangued him endlessly on the breeding of his family; Lady Litton was concerned only with the breeding of her dogs.

Gaby seemed to be faring a great deal better than he. The captain was on her right, young Sir Anthony Gray on her left. Whether talking to one companion or another, she seemed to be in the greatest spirits, and they laughed so often, and so immoderately as to make it appear they were all three well satisfied with their places and their company.

Into the sudden silence that occasionally falls on even the most congenial group, Lady Litton's deep bass voice was heard declaiming, ". . . so, and in no uncertain tone, I assure you, I said to him 'Clive Montgomery,' I said 'if you fancy I will accept that worthless mongrel of yours as having serviced my bitch, Briney, you had better consider your accusations before you look for help to the law!' And that," she finished triumphantly, "was the last I heard of Clive *or* his nasty little whelp."

It was Darcy's turn to choke, which he did in wine rather than in water.

Gaby continued to sparkle at the captain and Sir Anthony, but her heart was no longer in the witticisms or the gossip. She watched Darcy covertly when she could, her mind in chaos, her heart turned upside down.

Nothing has changed, Gaby . . . but then you always knew so, did you not? You tried to explain it to Mercy Enough that long-

ago day. For some women there is only one man. Compromise is not in their natures.

You could not tell him the truth. You were too proud to marry him, in your role of merry widow.

You still play games with his heart—and your own—but you can no longer shy away from one incontrovertible fact.

You love him still.

Nonsense.

You have loved him always.

Ridiculous.

You gave your strength, your wits, your devotion and your honor to the cause of American independence. To Darcy, you gave your heart.

I don't want to hear any more of this flummery.

But you must hear, Mrs. Gabrielle Forsyth-Foote and that additional name taken quite lately—Rhoads.

Why must I?

Listen, little Gaby Foote, and listen well.

You must decide what to do about Darcy Rhoads, who is, after all, your wedded husband.

Will you leave him? Will you stay? How will you make him believe in your love? He now knows most of the facts, almost all of the lies. He has learned of the double role you played . . . Mrs. Forsyth-Foote, the spy versus Mrs. Forsyth-Foote, his eager and ardent lover. Happily—not here on the ship but after we land in England, he will wonder if the unchaste Mrs. Forsyth-Foote exists, if the Lady of New York is a trumped-up identity.

It appears to me, Gaby, that you must contrive on this voyage to keep him far, far too busy to ask himself—or you—any questions.

And how is this to be accomplished?

Spell it out, madame. Say it as it is.

In your bed, Gaby. Do you remember that in your bed, he had heart and mind only for you? We have five or six or seven weeks more across the ocean to England. If you cannot keep him diverted for that small period of time . . .

Besides, Gaby . . . stop shrinking from the truth, known so well by the Lady of New York. You want him in your bed again.

Hell's bells! Put an end to this hypocrisy. Tell the truth, Gaby, and confound the devil! Your bad humor is frustration . . . you are shaking inside with the intensity of your desire.

Ah, so you admit it. Well then, what are you going to do about it?

Darcy had just solemnly agreed with Lady Litton's pronouncement that no man of decency would permit his beagle of dubious ancestry to have at her own dear pedigreed bitch, Juliet.

"But, perhaps, Lady Litton," he continued gravely, "Juliet is not so much to be pitied as yourself. You seem to have been the greatest sufferer. It appears, from your account that she—Juliet—enjoyed the—er—encounter. Occasionally, in dogs as well as people, infusion of new blood has been considered desirable. Why should your Juliet not have her own Romeo? Show compassion if the high-born lady now and then shows the need of a little romance in her life."

Lady Litton listened, a bit overwhelmed by this spate of eloquence. She sensed that there was something a bit convoluted in Mr. Rhoads's reasoning, but for the life of her, she could not think what it was.

She turned to her other table partner, resolving to mull over the problem at her leisure, while Darcy returned to his dinner, hoping for a small interlude of peace. He was unprepared for the sight of his wife, smiling at him across the table. Her smile was brilliant, her eyes full of warm laughter.

He sucked in his breath, remembering for the first time in a long time how that same smile, bespeaking both love and passion, was intended for him only.

God, how I loved her. How—to my sorrow—I believed in her. I would have pledged my own honor that she was true. Heaven help me, how I love her still, even though I know she is not to be trusted.

Even now, I do not know much about her except for her occupation. And that I was the lovesick fool who offered the lady my heart to trample upon and permitted her access to military information.

The ugly truth cannot be made more palatable. Face it, Darcy, you were the source from which her bits of intelligence, great or small were garnered.

On the other hand, there is this. My wife is a very tasty morsel, indeed. And we are far from land and civilization. The Lady of New York that I knew would have—in her own mind—two alternatives. She would endure me if I made my intention plain, because I am stronger, and she would be impotent against that strength. But I know two other things. One, she would lie under me, limp and passive to make sure I received no iota of pleasure in the encounter. Or, two, she would protest so loudly and violently, as to make fools of us both; and again, she would do it in a way that ensured we would neither of us derive the least enjoyment. It would be war, not peace and pleasure.

Even as he tried to analyze the meaning of Gaby's smile, he found himself responding to it.

God help me, I have been down that path before and I have no wish to travel it again.

When the meal was finally done, the ladies withdrew, leaving the gentlemen to their wine and to more intellectual conversation than womens' puny minds were able to comprehend. The price of a good stallion . . . Lord Mainwaring's curious infatuation for his wife's personal maid . . . the impossibility of finding a valet who could polish boots well and be equally as skillful dealing with his gentleman's hair and makeup.

Bursting with barely concealed impatience, as soon as he could do so without too great rudeness, Darcy excused himself.

When he got to his cabin, he crossed the room in darkness to light a candle. He would listen for sounds behind the door that separated them, symbolically as well as physically, one from the other.

Holding up the brass lamp in one hand, he turned around frozen with surprise for only seconds. He was aware of being shocked, startled, and then so overwhelmed by joy that he could not help the great glow of happiness lighting up his eyes, his face, his being.

Gaby could not help but see it, too, but he no longer cared.

He set the light down on the closest flat surface, his washstand, and said, "I am minded of an old folk tale. At this point in the story, I should be saying, 'Someone has been sleeping in *my* bed . . . and there she is.' Is that what you expect to hear, Madam Wife?"

"You would not be strictly accurate if you did so," Gaby answered. "For one"—she waved a bare arm about—"it is a bunk, not a bed. For another, I have not slept, only waited."

"Waited for what."

"Not what? Who? And the answer to who, is you."

"For what purpose."

"I promise you, I am not intelligence gathering."

"Promise? You promise more easily than you perform, Gabrielle. I have learned to be quite wary of your pledges."

"Darcy," she said in some exasperation, "how can you be so silly? What possible information is there to be given or gotten aboard this ship? The people we will most likely spend the greater part of our time with have not one completely whole brain between them. *You* may have had a good time—I admit I enjoyed the lady's discomfiture, too—in trying to prove to Lady Litton that little Juliet has a right to her Romeo, even though he is not of equal birth . . . but such amusement would pall . . . for both of us, I fear. Do you disagree?"

"No."

"Most eloquent."

"The eloquence must come from you, my dear wife. Why are you in my bed?"

"Dear me," Gaby answered, pouting the least bit. "I should have thought that was self-evident. Your bed was the one place on this ship that, sooner or later, you would be bound to come to."

"True, but what has that to do with you? I also said I wanted no unwilling woman, whether she be lover or wife."

"Do I look unwilling?"

She sat up, allowing the blankets to fall away. She was wearing a lacy garment that was completely ridiculous for a voyage across the Atlantic, but decidedly appropriate for seduction.

"What do you really want, Gaby?"

"For the love of God, what do you think? We have a long, tedious voyage ahead of us. Much as I love the water, I occasionally long for a change. As for the other people on this ship . . . *wearisome* is the kindest word that I can use for most of them."

"So?"

"So I would rather be making love with you—*to* you—than be flirting with the captain or the callow younger gentlemen. Certainly, I anticipate you would find more delight in sharing your bed with me than in hearing of the bastard who was foisted onto your family by your revered monarch's grandfather. As for Mrs. Sunderby and her precious bitch Juliet . . . I as well as you know you will hear her story again and again, becoming even more bored with each repetition."

"Ah, so I am intended to be solace for you and to keep boredom at bay?"

"A rather tactless way of putting it, but—on the whole—true."

"And do you think the offer is one that I should accept?"

Gaby shrugged. "Why not? It's a very pleasant way of passing time. As newlyweds, we would not occasion too much comment if we both seem to prefer each other's company to any other person's."

"And when the voyage is over, what then?"

"Our brief amnesty will be over. We can return to being enemies. As you so kindly pointed out, I am only a possession with the worthless title, wife."

He stared at her broodingly for a few minutes, and Gaby threw back the covers, prepared to leave his bed.

"Very well, my dear husband. I will importune you no longer." She shook her head regretfully. "So indecisive as you have become. Perhaps another time. And then again, perhaps not. It is an offer I have not ever made to any other man and, in view of this rebuff, I doubt that I will ever make it again."

Her feet were on the cabin floor, seeking her slippers when Darcy spoke.

"Get back into that bed."

Gaby hesitated.

"You heard me!"

"Yes, I heard you, but you took your time about agreeing, too much time to make me satisfied that this will be good. No, I will amend that. Not so much good as it would be wise. No more than you, do I want an unwilling bed partner. You must be able to give up your anger, your resentment, your sense of having been betrayed, and your wish to hurt me. I do not refer to physical hurt as much as to emotional wounding. Words, contrary to what poets say, can be extremely painful. They have a way of enduring quite a long time, sometimes forever."

"There is no need for *you* to tell me about emotional scars," Darcy said.

"Will you be able to refrain from talking about them for six weeks? Will you be able, for this short time, to suppress your grievances? Will you—"

"I will be able to do anything . . . say anything, or contrariwise, say or do nothing at all. When I have you in my arms, all is forgiven, all is forgotten. Does that satisfy you?"

Gaby gave him a friendly smile as she got back under the blankets. She smiled up at him—the brilliant, blinding, beguiling smile of the past—as she moved over to make room for him.

Fifty

After he joined her in his own bunk, Darcy admired the lacy garment, then proceeded to divest her of it. It lay, diaphanous and fragile, at the foot of the bed.

"Lovely," he had murmured as he rid her of it. He returned to her. "Ah," lifting up the covers so as to view her bare body. "Lovelier still."

"I would curtsey my thanks," Gaby said sedately, "but as you can see, I am not in the best position for doing so."

"On the contrary, you are in the position which of all others I prefer. It is *you* at your most delightful . . . and also trustworthy. While you are here with me, Delilah of the many thousand delights, I can be certain you are not conspiring with my enemies to bring me down."

He felt the stiffening of her body; he saw the sparkling joy leave her face and the enchantment all drain away.

"I beg your pardon," he said quietly.

She made a small gesture of helplessness.

"You need not," she said tonelessly, pulling the covers way up to her chin. "I accept it; I even understand that you cannot help yourself. In your situation, my reactions might well be the same. But it also shows how wide the gap is between us and how impossible to bridge. Even in just these few minutes since we made our agreement, you cannot put aside your bitterness. You cannot refrain from uttering your little pinpricks."

"I have tried," he said wearily.

"I know, it is what I find most heartbreaking about our situation. You try so hard, Darcy, and so fruitlessly. I cannot say that I am sorry for my spying, but I am appalled at what I have done to you. I never thought that my love would turn *you* into an angry, embittered man."

She came out from the covers and faced him briefly, sitting on her haunches. She extended one hand tentatively, to caress his cheek.

"I am sorry, Darcy, truly sorry I hurt you so. Forgive me."

Having made her little speech, she crawled down to the foot of the bunk to retrieve her two-ounce black lace shift, only to feel a pair of strong arms hugging the breath out of her from behind.

"I suppose," said a loud, as well as ironic voice in her ears, "you thought the view of your delicious little rump wriggling away from me would be a major inducement to let you go."

Her head swiveled round. He had thrown aside the covers, too, and there could be no denying that, despite what was going on in his head, every bit of the rest of him bespoke his need of her.

She allowed him to pull her back and over him.

"Oh! On top?"

"It is not," said Darcy in the half-satiric, half-loving tone of previous days, "a position that is unknown to you. And since you are already *there*, with me *here*, will you please put an end to this torture?"

"Since you asked me so prettily, I will" said Gaby, throwing herself forward to kiss his mouth with lusty abandon. Then, she slid down along the length of his body.

The last words she remembered saying—or, come to think of it, shouting—were "Go! Go! GO!" which appeared to be invitation enough. They joined with much sound and fury, arrived together at the desired destination, and fell deeply asleep tangled in each other's arms and legs in the bed that was a tight fit even for one.

Both revived from unconsciousness, more or less at the same time. The one candle still threw shadows on the cabin wall. Bed seemed the proper place to be, since there was only darkness through the porthole.

"Comfortable?"

"No."

"Shall I—"

"No. Are *you* comfortable?"

"Mmmm. I don't think so."

"Shall I—"

"Nooo . . . don't want to move . . ."

"Me either."

"So go back to sleep."

"You're wriggling."

"Am not."

"Are too."

"You're wiggling more."

"Not wiggle, wriggle."

"Stop shouting in my ear."

"For God's sake, go to sleep."

"If you will, too."

"Whatever you want."

They both yawned hugely and slept again, this time till the rising sun sent red streaks through the porthole to tell the lazy lovers that a new day had dawned.

In a sudden excess of modesty, Gaby gathered a blanket around her body, clutching at the neck where the two ends met.

Prudently, Darcy refrained from informing his wife that although extremely modest from the waist up, from the waist down, she was a sight to make a man return to his bed, not desert it.

Darcy continued to watch as Gaby, with the blanket half-tripping her up, executed small, mincing steps toward their connecting door.

"Is it time for breakfast?" she asked sleepily.

"Not much more than a quarter hour."

"I will never make it," she moaned.

"Why the despair? Are you hungry?"

"Ravenous!"

"Me, too.

"On the whole," he said judiciously, "a good sign. Vigorous lovers who expend so much energy need to be stoked up now and then."

"Yes," Gaby uttered an unregretful deep sigh. "I seem to recollect that many, many meetings between us centered around food."

"Food and love."

"Yes," said Gaby again, and braced herself. The night's romance over, was he about to deliver another one of his stinging gibes?

She was unaware that her posture grew suddenly tense, as though she was expecting some ill-natured remark, waiting for one of the little verbal pinpricks that he so adroitly threw into conversations.

He walked across to her and bent slightly to kiss her lips. It was a gentle, kindly *almost* friendly kiss. In the kiss there was nothing of passion or sexual yearning.

It was a most reassuring kiss.

She looked up at him with her eyes going wide and dark . . . and slightly confused.

"May I—we try again, Gabrielle? On the same terms as before?"

"Husband and wife for the length of our sea voyage?"

"Lovers for the length of our sea voyage," he corrected firmly.

"Why? Isn't it the same thing?" she asked hesitantly.

"If you go back to the beginning, as lovers, we were beyond compare. We have not done as well being husband and wife."

"Very well, sir. We will be lovers. After breakfast or before?"

"After," he said firmly. "Remember, I need stoking."

"Not a romantic decision," Gaby said thoughtfully, "but, on the whole, sensible."

They dressed with such speed, they entered the breakfast quarters just after the others had been seated. The two empty chairs were side by side, and two of the gentlemen started to rise, but Gaby forestalled them.

"No, indeed, you must not discommode yourselves," she insisted. "After all"—she ducked her head, now the shy bride—"my dear husband and I must needs practice this business of living together side by side."

Gaby and Darcy seated themselves amidst chuckles, smiles and sly allusions. She rolled her eyes at him, and he, under the pretext of inspecting her coffee spoon for cleanliness, whispered "Now, thank God, I may not be forced to listen to harangues about amorous bitches or my grandfather the king's bastard. I will be forever grateful."

"How grateful?"

"Whatever boon you desire."

"Is after breakfast too soon?"

"For *that,* it is never too soon."

"Very well."

"A firm assignation?"

"Certainly."

"Doors locked? Servants and sailors not admitted?"

"I would hardly want visitors *or* spectators."

"I am forced to admit that in some matters you have a logical mind."

"Thank you . . . I think."

"You are heartily welcome, and I will prove it after breakfast, my lady fair."

"I am afraid, sir, that Lady Litton is trying to attract your notice."

"Damn."

He smiled across the table. "I am afraid, Lady Litton, that I did not hear the whole of your remark."

Surprised that anyone should not be able to hear her booming voice, Lady Litton increased her volume enough to penetrate to the farthest corner of the ship. Everyone at the table was forced to listen to her comment.

"Mr. Rhoads, I have given much thought to the kind opinion you expressed at our supper last night, and it has vastly eased my mind. Even though Juliet did not produce the pure-bred I expected, what does it matter? She will whelp again."

She gave a good-natured neighing laugh and several at the table could not suppress the notion that a bark would have been more appropriate. "As you said to me, a sweet bitch like my Juliet should have her Romeo at least one time in her life. She will be breeding for many years after."

I will not look at him. I will not laugh.
I will not look at her, or I will succumb to wild hilarity.

Never had breakfast stretched out longer. Was it Gaby's imagination or did the food already seem to suffer from lack of freshness and too long a time at sea?

Never had an inferior meal gone on and on so endlessly—or had the seasickness affected his sense of taste?

For all that they were sitting side by side, they might have been at opposite ends of a huge table.

He dared not look at Gaby for fear of a fit of uncontrollable laughter.

She dared not look at him for fear of an outrageous allusion to their after-breakfast plans.

When breakfast was finally done, he pulled out Gaby's chair for her. "Your cabin or mine?" she murmured shamelessly.

"Yours. Definitely yours."

"I'm willing, but why so certain?"

"Yours is larger."

She stood up and they came face to face, body to body.

"Mine is larger!" she said incredulously, looking him up and down, then shamelessly down and down. She shrugged. "If you say so, Darcy."

"You shameless baggage! I will punish you for that."

"Oh. Is it now called punishment? Fancy that. And I always thought that pleasure was—"

"Be still, you little witch. Can't you see that Mrs. Sunderby is straining to hear our conversation?"

"Oh, poor dear. Perhaps I should help by giving her just the substance of it so—"

"Gabrielle Rhoads, if you utter one single other word until we reach our quarters, I will strangle you here before witnesses."

"Oh, very well; but I think marriage has made you very stuffy and pompous."

As she turned to move away, the captain came to bid her good morning with wishes for a pleasant day.

"I would like to wish *you* a good day and thank *you* for your kindness, Captain, but I cannot. Mr. Darcy," she added sadly, "has forbidden me to speak." She looked sadder still. "Captain, you listened to my conversation all those days my husband was so sorely seasick. Do *you* think I talk too much?"

"The captain has other things on his mind than your conversation, dear wife." said Darcy, darting such a poisonous look at the lady, that the captain was considerably startled. Just as he was wondering if, underneath his soft words and pleasant manner, Mr. Rhoads, might be brutal to the lady, husband and wife exchanged glances.

The shared look was laughing, tender, mirthful and above all lascivious.

Well, well, the captain conceded kindly as he moved away. If not on their honeymoon . . . when?

Fifty-one

It was a period of love and laughter. It was day after day of lust and passion. Week followed week and there seemed no end to awakened desire and then sleepy satisfaction.

There were interludes of new acquaintanceship . . . when neither could talk fast enough to learn all there was to know about the other.

There were intervals of silence when they were content to sit or to walk on deck or lie in one or the other of their bunks, holding hands, communing but without the need to speak.

Occasionally, Gaby would remind herself, fearfully, *Hold onto happiness. We will be in England all too soon. It may never be this way again.*

One day, they unexpectedly encountered the captain on a lower deck. They all exchanged greetings and were suddenly brought back to a world of unpleasant reality as he sniffed the air.

"Smell that, madam, sir; it's the smell of England not that long over the horizon."

Gaby's heart plummeted; Darcy's was a stone inside his body.

"Wh-when?" she asked fearfully.

"I would say, we are not more than two days out of London, ma'am."

The married pair walked on in silence . . . the first one of their many silences that was awkward and uncomfortable.

"Fancy that! Only two days out from England!" Gaby spoke in a high, artificial voice.

"The weeks have certainly gone by swiftly." It was an awkward remark and he felt his own clumsiness, even as he answered her.

That night, they entered their quarters at Gaby's door and Darcy opened the adjoining one and turned to her questioningly.

"I am very tired, Darcy," she said softly. "Perhaps, not tonight—"

He lifted her hand and kissed it gently; but he could not hide the momentary look of relief on his face.

The look broke her heart.

The kiss was salt upon the open, bleeding wound.

Their sole attempt at love-making in the last days on the ship was restrained and gave pleasure to neither.

If this is how it will become, I want none of it, Gaby told herself fiercely, even as Darcy pondered the way to achieve, not just a truce, but acceptable harmony.

Alternative plans began to take shape in Gabrielle's mind.

The day before they docked, she asked Darcy, "How far is your uncle's home from London? In what county is it located?"

Pleased at her show of interest—Darcy answered eagerly, "Not far at all. Near Salisbury Plain in the County of Wiltshire. It puts the pleasures of London just an easy journey away."

"How nice," Gaby murmured temperately. "From all I have heard, the theater and concerts in London are without peer, and the shops, too. Lady Litton heaped praise on them. They are infinitely superior, she says, to those of New York."

Oh, of great interest, thought Darcy gloomily, knowing what his wife thought of Lady Litton and how unlikely she was to fall in love with England for the theaters and shops.

Gaby was pursuing another line of thought.

"Will we be able to stay on in London for a few days?"

He hesitated. "I had not thought of. . . . my uncle will be impatient . . ."

Gaby looked at him beseechingly. "But he cannot even know of your arrival yet. Just a little shopping would be rather pleasant, especially since it will take me time to walk on even ground again. I want to see the bookstores, too. And, naturally, I wish to look and feel at my best when I meet your family . . . so, if you please, Darcy . . ."

If you please, Darcy.

Damnation, she felt sickened to hear the pleading words upon her tongue. Next, it will be *May I?* or *If I may beg your indulgence, sir,* or some such fawning phrases.

No, Darcy Rhoads. Love you, I may. Want you, I do. But not, sir, never, on such terms as these. We are equals or we are nothing.

She would prepare for several different futures, she decided resolutely, and then take the one that would serve her best. *If need be,* Gaby planned, *a life lived without him. I managed it for a year in Setaucket. I am capable of doing so again.*

In London, the passengers from the *Pandora* bade each other hasty good-byes and quickly went about their own business. The carriage that took Darcy and Gabrielle to their hotel rattled along the streets, making both of them a little queasy and amused that it should be so.

They exchanged laughing glances of commiseration, more in tune than they had been for several days.

When they arrived at the Selkirk, Gaby stuck her head out through the window, which she had insisted be left open so she could see all the sights along the way.

"Good God, Darcy!" she exclaimed, "It looks more like a castle than an inn or hotel."

"So, you are a country girl at heart?"

"I admit that up until today, Fraunces Tavern was my idea of the biggest and the best, but I am already willing to admit that my country cannot compete with yours on matters of show or elegance."

"Now, why do I feel," said Darcy, as the door was opened and the steps let down, "that the compliment you offered was no such thing?"

"I cannot imagine," said Gaby innocently, as she accepted his outstretched hand and proceeded down the steps like a lady.

Most of their baggage was put into storage at the hotel, to be taken out when they left for Darcy's home. The small trunk apiece that each had used on the would *Pandora* would suffice—"But I shall buy some fashionable gowns so I will feel more at my ease."

Even Darcy admitted that after so long a time of needing only fresh uniforms, his clothes could hardly be considered fashionable.

For two days, they accompanied each other on tedious shopping trips and went to the theater one night to see *Romeo and Juliet*.

At the first intermission, Gaby said thoughtfully to her husband, "On the whole, I think we would have been more entertained by Lady Litton's Juliet with *her* Romeo.

At the end of the play, he waited quizzically for her opinion.

"What incredibly silly people!" she said to her husband, who laughed and agreed.

By their third day in London, just as she had intended, Darcy was worn down.

"Have mercy," he implored when she mentioned long gloves and slippers.

"Poor darling!" Gaby cooed. "You may rest or order new boots or go to your uncle's club or whatever you wish. The carriage and coachman you hired will take me wherever I decide to go."

He hesitated, uncertain, but she urged him so much in the direction of his inclination, he finally agreed that she would go alone, though he assuaged a feeling of guilt by escorting her to the coach and ordering Jeremiah not to let her out of his sight.

Being back in England must have addled his brain, Gaby decided with unwifely lack of charity. True, London was far bigger, much dirtier, and a great deal noisier than New York. Still, how absurd of Darcy suddenly to cast her in the role of a witless child who must be protected by someone stronger, wiser and—of course—male.

Jeremiah was directed to a milliner's first. She strolled about in it for a quarter of an hour, then selected a handsome fringed silk shawl, with a design in a Chinese pattern. The shawl would make a fine gift for Darcy's Aunt Charlotte.

Her second stop was to a mantua-maker, where there were only two or three customers, but some of the loveliest gowns Gaby had ever seen. One or two were hanging casually from a wooden rack; others were draped over the backs and caned seats of chairs.

There was a dress of Spitalfields silk in a rich and dazzling floral pattern, to be worn over a quilted lavender petticoat. She longed to buy it for Lydia, but realized that for a clergyman's wife, living modestly in the country, it would not be considered appropriate.

Circling the room, she found a handsome striped poplin with a blue silk underdress in a pattern of a small butterflies and leaves.

When she left the shop, she carried a box with a fashionable name, containing Lydia's gown. Her own—the Spitalfields silk—needed minor alterations. It would be delivered to the Selkirk.

Jeremiah was waiting patiently, and Gaby felt sure now that she had given a good enough impression of a gentlewoman's shopping day. She asked if he knew the name of and could take her to the best bookshop in London. He eyed her with interest, as though he had picked up what seemed an ordinary frog and discovered it to be a rare museum specimen.

"You're a reading lady, then," he said. "I thought you was from the colonies."

"The colonies," said the lady tartly, "are no longer British colonies, but the United States of North America. And, you may find this hard to believe, but we are not total barbarians. Many of us actually write, as well as read, good sir."

"And are most of the women of a sort like you, ma'am?"

"What sort would that be?"

Jeremiah chuckled. "Plenty of spirit, enough to keep your man on tenterhooks the rest of his days."

"I am not like that at all," said Gaby loftily. "I am meek and mild and submissive."

"That's a good one. Ah, now, that's a good one indeed."

She could hear the slap of his hand on his leg. "That's me best laugh for the day."

When she entered the bookstore, Gaby drew in her breath; her eyes began to glisten like stars. Wherever she looked, books, books and more books.

Oh, this was truly wealth beyond compare!

Row after row, shelf after shelf; on stands, in special trays, even some heaps of them behind desks on the floor. In this one case, she must do England justice. Never before had she seen in one place such a vast amount and variety of books.

She moved about here and there, plucking one and another off a shelf. Even as she glanced through the pages of one book, she was eagerly reaching up for the next.

The shopkeeper in charge appeared to be a round little man, almost hidden by his desk. He pushed his framed spectacles back along his nose.

"If you need help, madam," he said in an avuncular way, "you have only to ask."

Having given her this modicum of attention, he retired behind a book of his own. Apparently, it was a matter of indifference to him whether she bought from him or not.

"I want to buy out your whole shop!" Gaby declared extravagantly. "I want to buy *everything*."

Apparently interested by this comment, he put his book aside. "You have a strange way of speech—or, rather accent."

"I am American."

"Ah, then, that accounts for it."

"Accounts for what?"

"You have a pleasant easy way about you. And though you may look like an English lady, very few would care to admit they have a fondness for books."

"Idiots!" Gaby snorted.

"Exactly." He smiled, duty done, and returned to his book.

Gaby flitted here and there, choosing volume after volume, returning to his desk now and then to add another book to the growing heap.

She had chosen a baker's dozen when she was struck by a sudden thought. She returned to the desk.

"Sir, I have a problem. I want to buy all these, but—"

"You don't have sufficient money?"

"No, money is not my problem, but the lack of a permanent residence. I do not yet know where they should be sent."

"Will you know soon?"

"I think . . . yes, of course."

"In that case, I will box the books and put them in the warehouse. A cash payment must be made if I am to take them out of circulation; but I will make a list of the books and give you a signed receipt. Then, when you are settled, you may send me word."

Gaby beamed at him. "What a splendid idea! You start the list and I will see if there are just . . . perhaps one or two more."

In the end, she came back with three that she decided to take along with her. Shakespeare's *Sonnets*, *A Woman's View of the History of England*, and a long (probably boring) *Essay on the Difficulties Leading to the Rebellion of His Majesty's Colonies in America*. Since she was to spend some time in England, she might as well try to see the American War for Independence from the British point of view.

By the time Gaby left the store, with her three books neatly tied up in a parcel tied with string, and the others all set aside, she had her list and the receipt neatly tucked away in her reticule, and the bookshop owner had become friendly enough for her to inquire about the publishing house of Egerton.

"A pretty good house," he said judiciously, and then slightly cocked one eyebrow. "Are you in hopes of becoming a lady writer?"

"I" said Gaby majestically, "am a poet and I have been published in newspapers for several years. My own book of poems, was sold a few years ago and published in New York. I am amazed and disappointed at what I sense is your attitude. You are obviously a man of learning, but there was a touch of disdain in the way you said 'lady writer.' What is the woman of knowledge and some talent at writing to do? Hide her capabilities so as not to alarm men who fear an educated woman? Speak silly nothings so she will never be suspected of having a brain? Tell the—"

"Enough. Enough. I concede you complete victory. I am guilty of all the snobberies you have mentioned. *Mea culpa.* Forgive me, my dear young woman. When your book is published, I shall order immense quantities and praise it to one and all."

"But suppose"—Gaby gave him her gamin grin—"it is not praiseworthy?"

"I shall stock it all the same."

"You need not fear." Gaby said wryly. "Good or bad, even indifferent, it will sell."

"Why?"

"Because my first book, *Amorous Verse* by a Lady of New York, has already won great favor with the British residing in occupied New York. They will look for—and get—something even racier in *More Amorous Verse."*

"And *you* are the Lady of New York?"

"Yes."

His eyes twinkled merrily behind his steel-framed spectacles. "Does the lady have any other name?"

"In New York, she is known as Gabrielle Forsyth-Foote. Here in England, she is reduced to plain ordinary Mrs. Rhoads. Let me write the names down for you."

"And today, both these ladies-in-one are in my shop, to indulge more than a passion for books, I think. It seems to be the opening gambit in a match that smacks strongly of high-stakes gambling."

Gaby smiled but did not speak.

"Will there be a gentleman some day who will ask for the information you have given so freely to me?"

Gaby's smile faded. "It is possible," she said, "but not at all certain."

"And if he comes to me full of questions?"

"Then it is up to you."

"To me alone? You have no instructions and trust my independent action then?"

"Certainly. I have no choice."

"May I tell you my plan?"

"If you wish."

"I will part with a little information the first time, a little more the second. If I can incite him to return a third time, he will have wrung me dry."

Gaby looked at him with great respect. "You did very well without instruction. I bow to your judgment."

"I would like to take full credit, but I fear Sophocles said it before I did . . . *they are not wise, then, who stand forth to buffet against Love; for Love rules the gods as he wills.*"

He could see only the blush on her face. Gaby felt it all over her body.

"His name is Darcy Rhoads, Major in the British Army until quite recently. He knows of the first book, but not that Egerton, the publisher wrote me to suggest an English edition. He—*we*—Mr. Rhoads and I—had so many difficulties . . . our politics, our outlook on life, our interests, our backgrounds. We really should not have loved or married. Prudence and good sense made it folly, but it is, as you have just said, *Love rules the gods as he wills.*"

"I look forward to the drama due to be enacted in my shop."

"Understand," Gaby said anxiously, "that you must not expect him to be walking in here any time soon. It may be a long time—if at all."

"He will come," said the bookshop owner quite confidently.

"What makes you so certain?"

"You love him?"

"Ye-es."

"He loves you?"

Gaby nodded. "Ye-es, but very much against his will," she added quickly.

He suppressed a smile.

"He will come."

"I would like to be as sure as you are," she said rather resentfully.

"If you love him, he cannot be a fool. If he is not a fool, then he will surely come."

He tapped his own copy of her receipt. "I will file this with any material concerning your purchases that might be of interest and concern."

"Thank you," said Gaby rather faintly, then held out her hand.

He took it in his own hand for a minute, then reminded her. "Among the gentry in England, dear Lady of New York, the well-born do not permit a lowly shopkeeper this gesture of respect."

"In America," said Gaby, "We show respect where respect has been earned."

She held out her hand again.

Fifty-two

There had been times during their halcyon days and weeks aboard the *Pandora* when Gabrielle was convinced that somehow, in some way unknown to her, she must have done a good deed. More, come to think of it, than just good.

It must have been a deed of incredible magnitude. How else could she explain the services of such a superior fairy godmother keeping constant watch on Darcy and on her all their weeks at sea.

The godmother (Gabrielle called her Mercy) seemed to be always at their elbows, making sure that there was no more bitter remarks, no hanging onto past grievances, no recalling the past except in the most joyous fashion.

Their truce was so honorably kept that they could talk together laughingly about matters that had seemed far from comical a month or two before.

One such matter was the means by which Darcy had tracked her down.

"My dear wife," Darcy said sanctimoniously when she first brought the subject up. "I never claimed to be anything except a simple soldier. *You* were the spy."

They were in bed at the time (as so often they were).

Gaby sat up and began pummeling him with her pillow. They struggled together for a while, with Darcy pretending he was getting the worst of it.

When he decided to stop the pretense, Gaby was soon lying

flat on her back and he was holding her down with both hands and a knee.

Gaby squirmed and struggled, then finally went limp.

"Pax?"

"Yes, *pax,* you brute." Gaby pretended to be wiping away tears.

"Do not cry, beautiful maiden." His eyes rolled in their sockets. "You have no idea what a lascivious brute I can be."

Gaby sighed soulfully and gazed at the ceiling. "Anyone can *talk,"* she said.

The next half hour was—to say the least—exceedingly breathless.

"But . . . you . . . never . . . told me . . ."

Darcy removed several strands of her hair from his mouth and returned them to their proper place on her head. "Later," he mumbled. "M-much later."

When he woke, he found the wife of his bosom sitting crossed-legged at the foot of the bed, wearing only a light lawn shift and a threatening expression.

"Tell me now."

"If you are not the complete scold," Darcy told her grumpily.

"It takes one," said Gaby graciously, "to know one. Talk sir."

"Very well," Darcy capitulated. "It was not that difficult, now that I think back. In fact, it makes me wonder—" He looked at her with a condescending air. "Were you a successful spy or merely adequate?"

"Extremely successful." Gaby pointed her nose to a spot way past him.

"It makes me wonder. I mean—after all, *I* had little trouble in pursuit."

"That is far different. You were—" She faltered a moment, then fell silent.

"You were about to say that love made a fool of me," said Darcy smoothly. But it was too late.

"After I returned from Philadelphia," Darcy said, "I paid a weekly call at our river house. My patience finally was rewarded. The army wife now residing there described you to a T . . . not the powdered, painted lady of fashion, not the brittle loyalist widow, but *my* Gabrielle, my harum-scarum Gaby, the passionate wench I had seen so often with her head upon my pillow, her natural beautiful hair, neither powdered nor covered by one of those hard, stylish wigs of monstrous proportions which ladies wear so as to seem à la mode."

Gaby murmured, "I am being diverted from the subject at hand."

He saluted her and continued his report.

"I now safely assumed that you were still in New York, although for several weeks I heard no word *of* you or *from* you. Then, I had a stroke of good fortune. Captain Sir Anthony Drexel and I had occasion to attend a card party at Mrs. Loring's. A comparatively dull evening until the very end."

"I kept sniffing the air," he said with a rueful smile, "wondering why Drexel seemed to smell so abominably of fish."

"For Heaven's sakes, Rhoads!" he snapped at last. "Stop sniffing about me like a hound after a fox. Yes, I smell of fish. Lord, the sacrifices one makes for one's country!"

The other three at the table stopped their play to look at him inquiringly.

"Some idiot from on high"—he looked around quickly to make sure his comments could not be heard—"some idiot gave a report implicating a certain lady in clandestine operations here in New York. The lady in question was elderly, past sixty at the least. She was also a midwife and of good repute; and her second occupation, consisted of preparing the dead for burial."

The three gentleman at his table, including Darcy, laughed immoderately.

Sir Anthony looked at them all with disfavor.

"Laugh all you please!" he said cantankerously. *"You* were not the ones who had to assume the role of fishmonger for several days. And to fulfill the role, it was necessary for me to spend time at a wretched place called the Fly Market. I had also to stink of fish."

His friends wipe away tears of merriment.

DARCY'S KISS

"I gather," said Darcy, "that your mission did not prosper? Else you would not be so gloomy now."

"It definitely did not prosper. It was, in my opinion, a complete waste of time. The Lady in question was a Quaker. A genuine, thee-and-thou practicing Quaker, just the sort to be a spy."

His friends, who had been laughing a little less became, once again, almost convulsed with mirth.

"Nothing like sympathy from one's friends!" said Sir Anthony ironically.

"Did you not fall upon even one little shred of evidence?"

"Not a single one. There was just one time when I thought— but no, I did not."

"Was there any basis for your one time of doubt?"

"Every week or ten days, the Quaker lady sold fish, mainly at the Fly Market, on behalf of a young cousin, a fisherman. I stationed myself at a little stand next to hers and peddled my fish bought elsewhere the same day."

He shrugged. "One day a girl came by . . . a colonial miss. Nothing the least bit fashionable in her manner of dress, but oh, her figure and her face! Her unpowdered hair was so thick and soft! How I would have loved to be a welcome guest in my lady's chamber, sinking my hands into the mass of it. After all, her lack of cosmetics, plain stuff gown, and rustic manner would not have mattered at all when the lady was lying naked in my bed."

Darcy managed to hold his tongue; Bartlett asked, "What color was her hair?"

"Black."

"And her eyes?"

"Black, too."

"And her other parts?"

"I told you," Sir Anthony said in great irritation of spirits, "she was not a spy, merely another colonial. In addition to a lovely face and a lissome body, she was—as most of these damned colonials appear to be—undaunted. There was a great congregation of half-starved brats trailing after her. She bought a great many of my fish and most of the Quaker's lobsters, then gave us both a tongue lashing for not showing the brats some compassion and giving them food. Once she gave the fish and lobsters to the children—she told them where to go and how to cook them. I tell you again, nothing daunts these colonials. What an acid tongue the wretched girl had."

"Have you never seen her since?" Darcy asked in what he hoped was a casual-sounding way.

"Not once," Air Anthony said regretfully. "Quite a shame. If she had taken a bath, brushed her hair, and kept her mouth shut, I would not have minded the least bit having her in my bed."

"But what a fate for the poor girl!" said Captain Pointdexter.

"Would you have been willing to share her?" Major Bartlett asked.

Fortunately, during this exchange, the jests flew back and forth so fast, no one observed that Darcy did not take part in the badinage.

When the game resumed, laughter lessened and then Darcy was able to say without much concern, "So you have retired from the business of being a fish peddler, Anthony?"

Sir Anthony shuddered. "Yes, thank God, though not immediately."

"And your good Quaker lady's reputation has been cleared?"

"So far as I am concerned, most assuredly, yes. I cannot even imagine how anyone came to suspect her. Do you know what I was forced to do for the two days more that I was assigned to watch over the Quaker lady?"

"We haven't a notion," Captain Pointdexter answered solemnly.

"Prepare yourself for suffering of no small a nature," said Sir Anthony. "I was forced, by the necessity of not letting her out of my sight, to attend—not just one, but *two* wakes while she laid out the corpses. One of the worst of my experiences in this uncivilized country . . . but not so awful as—"

He paused dramatically, and the other three, still laughing, urged him to finish his sentence.

Sir Anthony took a linen handkerchief from his sleeve and

wiped his brow. "I had to linger," he said in sepulchral tones, "while one of the wretched Mercy's patients was giving birth to a child."

"Did the child live?"

"An eight-pound boy with lungs like a baritone," Sir Anthony replied quite gloomily.

"The mother, then . . . was she the one to succumb?"

"Not at all. She was talking and laughing a quarter of an hour later. Why must your minds run on dying!" he exclaimed in great irritation.

"You were the one to give us the notion," said Major Bartlett.

"You most certainly did," Darcy chimed in.

"You gave us the impression it was your worst experience in America!" Captain Pointdexter reminded him.

"Well, by God, it was," Sir Anthony reiterated with great feeling. "Do you have any idea what it is like to be present at a birthing? I never heard such caterwauling in my life. Enough to drive a man to drink. Anyone hearing her would have been certain murder was being done. Not at all the way I pictured. Always before had the notion"—he shook his head dejectedly—"these American women were good peasant stock . . . a few hours in bed, then the foal is dropped—and—"

"Not foal, man, babe. A mare drops a foal, but a woman drops a baby," Major Bartlett instructed gravely, though his shoulders shook.

"Whatever," said Sir Anthony in the most melancholy way. "It was enough to put a man off marriage for life."

"Why?"

"Wouldn't want to go through that again." Sir Anthony paled at the thought. "Not for a thousand pounds."

"You could always go away until it was over."

Sir Anthony shook his head. "Wouldn't be a sporting thing to do. After all, if it's my wife, the only gentlemanly thing would be to stick around."

"Well, since you are not at the present time either married or betrothed, you have plenty of time to make up your mind," Darcy said, genuinely amused but still with his eye on the ball. "Did the Quaker lady—what did you say her name was? Did she—"

"That's another thing," Sir Anthony broke in, "Never heard such a rubbishing name in my life."

"The baby's?"

"No, they were sensible about *him,* named him George. Mother thought of it—rather clever. When we beat these damned colonials, they will be able to claim he was named after the King."

"And if they should by some odd chance win?" suggested Darcy.

"That's the beauty of it. They can then say he was named after their confounded general."

The other three did not even try to restrain their laughter.

"And the Quaker midwife," said Darcy cunningly, "Did she think the name was a good choice, too?"

"Never asked her," snorted Sir Anthony. "Not that she was in a position to throw stones. Never heard such an outlandish name as her own. Mercy Enough Godwin! Can you believe it?"

Darcy not only heard; he cherished the name. Mercy Enough Godwin. He had made great strides forward, he was convinced, in running down his quarry.

Fifty-three

For the brief time they stayed on at the hotel in London, as well as when they arrived at Ashford Hall, their blithe period on the *Pandora* might have been shared by two other people.

In London, they had often been engaged in separate activities with only their two selves, shut up in a carriage. Neither was at ease, they had little to say. There seemed to be an embargo on every subject.

When each of them occasionally made a remark, it appeared to be more in keeping with their own private thoughts than of anything they were discussing.

At one point, just as she had made a slight observation about the rows of magnificent poplar trees in an area they were passing through, Darcy said abruptly, "You will not speak of your—alliances in New York when we get to Ashford Hall."

"I certainly hope you have told them I am American."

"Naturally, since they would know by your speech and accent."

"My accent?"

"You do not sound English."

Gaby's hands balled into fists. "I thank God for even small favors," she said haughtily.

He gave her a sharp look, then shrugged and let both the speech and the moment pass.

About twenty minutes later, Gaby cried out eagerly, "Look, a lake. How wonderful! I can't imagine living far away from water."

"Did you think England was a wilderness? We have lakes and ponds, streams and rivers, and the English Channel, as well as the ocean. Our country, you must remember, is called the British Isles. There is water everywhere."

"Thank you for advancing my education," said Gaby politely as she again glanced out the window.

A quarter of an hour later, she asked, "You spent all your boyhood there. Can you describe your uncle's home?"

He thought for a minute, then said almost pleasantly, "It is always hard to describe one's home to a stranger."

A stranger, thought Gaby and shivered.

"It is, after all, mostly memories, and memories are difficult to describe. When we turn into the last fork that takes us to Ashford, there will be a deer park, a fishing stream, and an unusual formation of high rock, mostly covered with moss. As children, we called it the Hump; but several men of science have told my uncle that it dates back to the dawn of recorded history."

"How interesting," Gaby said tepidly, unwilling to be snubbed again.

"When we go through a huge pair of gates decorated with the lion and unicorn of England and inscribed with our family crest in Latin, then we are home."

He spoke the Latin words aloud and Gaby asked eagerly, "What is the English, please? In Latin, I know no more than *amo, amas, amat.*"

"In English," he told her slowly, "the translation is this: Men of Valor and Honor," he paused deliberately, then he repeated, "Men of Valor and Honor, Women of Virtue and Truth."

A slap across her face could not have made his meaning more blatant. "What a pity you did not recall the legend before you kidnapped me in New Jersey," Gaby said idly. "Surely you knew that your chosen bride could not lay claim to either of those traits."

He turned coldly away and did not trouble to answer her.

What am I doing in this far-off country, traveling with this stick of a man who has suddenly become a stranger, too?

Gaby felt the cold creeping over her body, seeping into her bones.

Oh, what folly to believe you could make this work, Gaby. You may as well have married the coachman, Jeremiah. Or the round, bespectacled bookshop owner. With him, Gaby, she told herself mournfully, *you would have had more in common.*

When their carriage turned at the fork Darcy had indicated, Gaby deliberately closed her eyes. It was silly . . . eventually she would have to see it . . . or face the fact that it was there . . . but she saw no need to disturb herself further by looking at the damned Latin legend.

By her husband's standards, she was not *a woman of virtue*. She had chosen to be his mistress long before she was his wife. By his standards, she was not *a woman of honor.* He believed she had lied to him again and again, with her tongue and endlessly with her body.

As though she were capable of such skillful deceit. But try to convince him of *that!* More easily might she have walked on water!

I was a virgin, dear sir, the first time you took me into your bed. You see, it was the only way I could remain a spy and yet have you make love to me.

I wanted you to make love to me. How could I not? I fell in love with you, not as Gaby Foote, the minister's daughter or Gabrielle Forsyth-Foote, the dashing loyalist widow . . . but as that innocent, ignorant simpleton, Emily Washington. She sat down on the lap of the very wrongest man she could have chosen and gave him her heart forever.

They came to a halt in the circular driveway of an imposing brick residence. Gaby could see that wings of a different stone and color had been added at later times.

Even as she pretended bored indifference, she had to admit that she had never seen a more handsome residence. No wonder Darcy had longed to return home. This was his background. It was a part of himself—oh, why could she not have realized it before?

Here was the house with lands all about it and—what had he said? A deer park, a pond, a stream for fishing . . .

Oh, God, this was his history!

And worst of all, it was his future!

But not hers. Never hers.

Even if their marriage was conducted on the most amiable and amorous turns, she would always be a misfit. She would never belong or be happy in his world.

Darcy was so focused on the reunion about to take place, he did not notice her shivering. She was glad. This was something she would have to deal with on her own.

As her husband gave his hand to assist her down the carriage steps, a growing number of servants were running toward him from the house.

They were calling out greetings. "This is a happy day, sir!"

"Good to have you home, Mr. Darcy."

"Oh, my stars, the master will be elated to see you safely arrived."

Darcy was the center of all their eyes until the first hullabaloo died down. Gradually, their eyes shifted to Gabrielle, who stood by, enjoying the scene. Thank God, for this small mercy . . . the Earl's home was not so formal as she had feared.

Darcy sprang to her side and brought her to the little knot of servants.

"May I introduce the very finest import from America to England, my wife Gabrielle."

There was a murmur of congratulations as he made each servant known to Gaby, who held out her hand, hoping she was doing the right thing.

Since Darcy did not frown nor object, she presumed she was not being too much of a green country girl.

The butler was giving instructions to the coachman as Darcy and Gaby, with the rest of their entourage, went up the broad stairway leading to the house.

"My uncle? My aunt?" Darcy asked eagerly. "Are they at home?"

"Not your uncle, sir. This is his day for the assizes, but we were just about to bring the tea tray to my lady in the blue parlor."

"Then by all means, do so, but triple the contents—if you please. We have been traveling all day and are both"—he smiled politely at his wife—"extremely hungry.

"Never mind announcing me, Hockley. I still remember where the blue parlor is located."

With Gaby's arm tucked into his, he hastened her so quickly across a great marble hallway, she was quite breathless when they arrived at the blue parlor.

A stout lady, with a matron's cap atop her head, looked up eagerly, expecting her tea.

Her momentary look of disappointment gave way to one of shock.

She had considerable trouble rising to her feet, and in seconds Darcy was beside her, making her struggle unnecessary. "My dear Aunt," he said, pressing her gently down, then kissing her on the cheek. "How very happy I am to see you."

He half-turned, indicating to Gabrielle that she should come forward.

"Why not a dog whistle?" she muttered under her breath, but not so low he could not hear her.

Even as he said, "My wife, Gabrielle, ma'am," he was administering a retaliatory pinch to her arm.

"I am happy to meet you, madam," Gaby said, grimacing at the pinch.

Darcy handed her to a chair.

"And I am most happy, dear Aunt," said Darcy, "to see you in such a fine glow of health and spirits."

His aunt gulped aloud even as she cast a beseeching look at her husband's nephew.

"Darcy dear," she quavered, "surely you know how fond I have always been of you? You know I would not for worlds have injured you in any way?"

"Of course, I know. Of course, you would not," said Darcy in some bewilderment.

He must not have been convincing because Aunt Charlotte burst into tears.

Amidst heavy sobs, she confessed the awful truth.

"I am . . . I am . . . it just happened . . . even your uncle could not believe that I am . . . I have . . ."

"You are pregnant?" suggested Gaby helpfully, having noticed this condition the moment she set eyes on the supposedly barren lady.

Aunt Charlotte paused to give her recently wed niece-by-marriage a look of shocked reproach.

"With child," she murmured.

"Ah, yes," said Gaby at her blandest. "With child."

Darcy shot her a murderous look as he tenderly helped Aunt Charlottte back in the armchair where she had been sitting.

Darcy sat on the sofa near to his aunt.

"You know . . . you have long known," quavered Lady Ashford, "that every surgeon I ever consulted said I could not conceive. It was a great grief during the early years, but then you and your father came to live here at the Hall and we were all so happy. Percy said you were as dear to him as a son, so were both well satisfied. We have been wed for twenty-five years. *Twenty-five,* dear Darcy. And for . . . *this* to happen now, I'm sure I don't know how."

As she gestured helplessly, Gaby leaned forward, "Oh, ma'am," she said earnestly, "I am sure if you put your mind to it, you will remember how . . ."

A footman entered with the tea tray, which probably, thought Gaby, smiling sweetly at her husband, saved her from immediate strangulation.

Aunt Charlotte groped for her handkerchief. "If you would be so kind as to pour," Aunt Charlotte said flutteringly to Gaby. "I feel so faint, I am sure I could not safely hold the pot."

Gaby moved at once to the seat in front of the tea tray, pleasurably surprised and happy to see such a great variety and such a large amount of food. Small sandwiches of cheese and paper-thin slices of beef. Boiled eggs and ham. Scones. Small cakes. Honey. Marmalade. Warm rolls.

"Tea, my dear. Both sugar and milk," said Aunt Charlotte in her die-away voice, which already grated on Gaby's nerves.

As Gaby lifted the silver teapot in one hand and a fine Wedgwood cup and saucer in the other, Aunt Charlotte continued. "Two of the sandwiches—since Mrs. Arnold has cut them so small today. And a boiled egg. Just one boiled egg will do. And some rolls . . . I cannot eat a boiled egg without a roll. And perhaps just . . . well, never mind now. I will perhaps have some scones later with my second cup. We shall see if my appetite is good."

For several seconds, the Wedgwood cup had been wobbling rather perilously in the Wedgwood saucer. Gaby was trying her best neither to shake nor to laugh, but she was having a hard time of it.

Fortunately, Darcy recognized her problem. He took the cup and saucer in his own hand and brought the tea and sandwiches to Aunt Charlotte.

"And you, Darcy?" Gaby asked, although she already knew.

"Coffee, please."

Gabrielle poured his coffee, adding no sugar and only a little milk. Then she heaped a plate with sandwiches and passed that to him, too.

"Thank you."

There was a slight pause in conversation while they all ate and drank.

When Aunt Charlotte had emptied her cup and plate, she looked toward the tray again.

"More tea, my lady?" asked Gabrielle with great concern. "These scones and the cakes are marvelous. You must have a wonderful cook."

"Oh, yes. Pierre came to us direct from Paris. His pastry is superb. And my dear doctor reminded me that I am now eating for two."

Gaby, who privately thought the lady was eating for five, carefully avoided her husband's eyes.

Watching Aunt Charlotte's intake of food with awe, he dared not look into his wife's face. She was most probably holding back gales of laughter.

When there was little left to eat, Aunt Charlotte got unsteadily to her feet. "Doctor Ingram says I must rest after any exertion," she told her nephew and his wife. "Mullins—my midwife, you know—will come down for me. We thought it was best for her to come live with us toward the end."

The words were no sooner said, than Mullins was with them and tenderly guiding her mistress's footsteps toward the stairway.

"You do forgive me, Darcy, do you not?"

Since Darcy looked ready to explode, Gaby answered for him.

"There is nothing he needs to forgive you for, dear Aunt Charlotte. Your son—even a daughter—as his new cousin is a lovely surprise for dear, *dear* Darcy."

A little later, Darcy and Gabrielle were shown to their apartment—separate bedrooms for each and a private dressing room and a small sitting room shared between.

Gaby gazed, entranced, out the long windows in her bedroom. Acres of lush green lawn and, in the distance, water. She could not tell if it was pond, lake or stream. Poor Darcy. How awful for him.

To be reared in this wonderful house knowing one day, someday, all of it would be his to cleave unto, cherish and sustain all of his life.

Really, in a way, one could say it was the propertied equivalent of marriage. Stewardship for one's lifetime. The land to love and cherish and pass down to the next generation.

It might seem odd to make the comparison, but had she not felt the same when Aunt Emily told her that she would inherit Hillpoint one day?

It had brought a thrill of pride amid many other jumbled emotions. It was impossible to sort them out all at once.

As Aunt Emily's heiress she would have years of happiness living free and independent.

When, eventually, ownership passed to her, she would have all and more than most women in the world today. She would control her own destiny.

It might be odd for her to be thinking about a life of her own. She had the trifling impediment of a husband.

Gaby wandered through to the sitting room. It was warmed by a heavenly fire; and the sheepskin rug in front of the screen beckoned invitingly.

She took off her shoes and lay on her back.

"Fire-watching?" asked an ironic voice behind her.

"I am toasting," Gaby said, turning onto her stomach and looking up at him. "Do sit down, Darcy. It gives me a crick in my neck to look up at you."

Darcy sat.

"Do you understand the situation here?" he asked tersely.

"I understand that for many years *you* have been tacitly acknowledged as the heir to all of this and—"

"Now?"

"You may not be the heir, after all."

"True. If the child to be born—in four months, by the way—is a boy, as the son of the older son rather than the son of his brother, that child would have precedence over me."

"And a girl would not?"

"Correct. My uncle's daughter would have a handsome portion, but the Ashford Hall earldom, and the other entailed estates would come to me."

"I see."

"I doubt if you do."

"Well, make it clear then."

"It is not just the question of boy versus girl. My uncle is now fifty-six, Aunt Charlotte, ten years younger. It is a very chancy time for Aunt Charlotte to have a child."

Gaby nibbled on one finger. "Yes," she said, "It had not occurred to me before. You are considering the third possibility," said Gaby. "It is always good to consider all alternatives." She added as disagreeably as she could, ". . . that the child may die, although that one . . . do you not feel it to be just the least bit ghoulish?"

She could see the pulse beating in his forehead, and the flare of his nostrils. Would smoke and fire come out of his mouth and nose next.

"This conversation," Darcy said in a clipped English voice, "is not over, but I do not trust myself alone with you now."

Gaby rose from the sheepskin and curtsied low.

"Oh, la, sir, I am most flattered, but with all the servants running about and coming at one from corners like a jack in the box, I fear it will be a long, long time before we will know one another again. I am thinking of the biblical sense, you understand? Did I ever mention that my father was a minister?"

"You may or you may not have, I can hardly remember. There were so very many things—most of them lies—that you told me. And you overrate your attractions if you fancied I came here to indulge myself with your so accommodating body. I wanted merely, as I thought was only right, to bring you up to date on my—I should say *our* situation. I see now it would be a waste of time. Besides which, since we cannot speak without wrangling, the less we see of one another, the better."

"I entirely agree."

"I am glad." He turned back at the door to his bedroom. "You, my girl, incite violence to your person. My honor forbids, though I feel it might do *you* a world of good."

He bowed briefly. Gaby curtsied.

She giggled. He swore.

"Oh, go to blazes."

"Only if you go with me."

Fifty-four

Even when she was living in such close contact with the British in New York, Gaby had never realized the extent to which they were bound by the influence of family name, title and inherited wealth.

The Earl, when he came home, was exactly that to her—the Earl. Aunt Charlotte was not cozy, comfy pregnant Aunt Charlotte. She was the Countess.

My lord, my lady did not come easily to Gaby's lips; she continued to find it odd that a man who earned a living by his own endeavors—whether he be a farmer, a lawyer, or apothecary—was the inferior of anyone fortunate enough to have no occupation at all.

Incredible that for a man (or woman) to be expensive and idle made him (or her) of more worth, given greater respect and entitled to obsequious deference by all others (except those of superior birth, more fortune and with greater titles).

One fact was very plain to Gabrielle. She had noted it again and again and could only wonder since their talk if Darcy perceived it, too.

His uncle was not quite comfortable with him no matter how many times "my dear nephew" was uttered in the course of the day.

The Earl was truly devoted to that "dear nephew," but the dizzying prospect of an heir so unexpectedly and at his time of life had thrown him into a state of shock and perturbation, which she did not believe—looking back on all the times Darcy had spoken of his uncle—to be Lord Ashford's usual condition.

She did not discuss it with Darcy because their physical intimacy—resumed since coming to Ashford Hall—had never again extended the intimacy of the emotional bond between them.

Au contraire. The more often he crossed through the sitting room to come to her bed, the wider the division between them seemed to grow.

When he returned to his own bed . . . he never stayed the night in hers . . . Gaby often cried herself to sleep or stayed awake, unhappily rolling about her bed and punching the pillows.

She would never forget—returning to her room shortly after she had left it to get a handkerchief—hearing one of the chambermaids snickering to another, "When he's been with her, I can always tell. It looks like one of those there elly-funts has been ram-pag-inn about the bed."

Blushing but amused, tiptoeing, Gaby retreated backwards.

Going downstairs again without her handkerchief, she felt anger rising. Even the servants were convinced of a closeness between Darcy and herself that no longer existed.

No elephant had rampaged around her bed, nor her husband either.

They had merely engaged in a sedate, formal, and unsatisfactory exchange of she-didn't-quite-know-what. At its conclusion, he had departed, and she had rampaged in a fury of frustration and resentment all by herself.

On reaching the first floor, Gaby's state had gone from red-hot anger to uncontrollable amusement. Really, if one looked far enough, the situation did have its humorous side.

Having looked far enough to be diverted, Gaby sat down on the third stair from the bottom and laughed until she cried. A servant passed her silently, uncertain what to do.

Apparently, his solution was to approach her husband, because in about two minutes Darcy came out of the dining room, where breakfast had already begun.

"What on earth . . . ?" he began, then stepped back as Gaby took one look up at his prepared-to-rebuke-her face. Then she dissolved again in gales of laughter.

She was also muttering fractured remarks, which he found difficult to make sense of.

"Ell-y-funts," gurgled Gaby. "Oh, dear. Ram-pag-inn. P-please D-Darcy, lend me a hand-hand—"

She could not complete the whole of the last word, but seeing her streaming eyes and hearing sniffles, he interpreted her need and passed over a neat square of linen from his own pocket.

Gaby wiped her eyes and blew her nose hard, and in the fleeting few seconds when she caught his eye, she saw a trace of the Darcy of old . . . Darcy in their house on the river . . . Darcy aboard the *Pandora*.

When she tucked the handkerchief in her sleeve, the latest, most disagreeable version of Darcy had returned.

"You know my uncle dislikes unpunctuality at mealtime."

"As it happens, I am not hungry. I will skip breakfast, so as not to ruffle your uncle's sensibilities."

"Nonsense. *You* skip a meal?"

Since, as a matter of fact, Gaby was extremely hungry, she accepted his outstretched hand.

Resolving suddenly that from this moment on, she would begin as she meant to go on, Gaby said cheerfully as Darcy pulled out her chair, "Sorry to be late, Aunt Charlotte."

Aunt Charlotte looked taken aback. (She did much care what time someone came to breakfast or if she came at all.)

Darcy frowned slightly while the Earl gave Gaby a look of haughty inquiry.

"Something appeared to amuse you greatly, *dear* Niece." (There he went again, the *dear* that did not really mean *dear*.)

"Yes, it did."

"Will you not share your jest with us?"

"I am afraid," Gaby said gentle, "it was an extremely private jest."

"I see," said the Earl, who obviously did *not* see at all. By way of showing his displeasure, he took up the newspaper lying near his plate and retired behind it with a great crackling of paper.

"Any news from America?" asked Gaby cheerfully.

"Good God!" The Earl exploded at the same moment.

The Earl's wife, nephew and Gaby—all three cried out, "What?"

"Major John André, Sir Henry Clinton's aide, has been captured by those damned rapscallions, and there is talk—my God, the dirty devils! Who could conceive of such infamy? They are actually threatening to have him hanged as a spy."

"André was in intelligence, was he not?" asked Gaby politely. "Does it say in your article whether or not he was a spy?"

"I had begun to suspect," said Darcy thoughtfully, "that André might be engaged in intelligence work."

"You know him, Darcy?"

"Not well, but it is almost impossible in New York not to become acquainted with anyone of officer rank."

"Hockley. Hockley!" roared the Earl. And upon the butler's appearing, "Send to town immediately! Immediately! I want all the latest papers."

Hockley bowed and withdrew.

The Earl threw down his paper. "Infamous! Infamous!"

"May I?" Gaby took up the discarded paper and quickly found the offending article. "It appears," she said after a quick reading, "that, in all likelihood, Major André *was* a spy. This dispatch is not quite clear on this point, but admits he was taken in enemy territory without uniform. He may well have been a spy."

"He is an English gentleman and an officer. What right has your rabble to threaten him?"

"Did you ever hear of an American officer, Captain Nathan Hale?"

"Certainly not!" the Earl said testily.

"It is unfortunate you did not, my Lord," said Gabrielle kindly. "He was a former schoolteacher who accepted the risk of spying on the British at Long Island in '76. He was captured, admitted the truth and was sentenced to hang by Sir William Howe without the formality of a trial."

"What has this to do with André's capture?"

"Their situations are the same, sir, except that André is being granted the courtesy of a trial to discover his guilt or innocence."

"You equate these situations as alike? An English officer and gentleman as compared to a scrubby American schoolteacher?"

"Yes," said Gaby gently, "I do. And it is because they do *not* understand this that the English gentry and your monarch himself are losing America forever. We will be our own nation, Lord Ashford, not an undervalued pawn in Great Britain's game of chess."

He was looking at her with genuine horror. He could not— Englishmen of his stamp would never understand . . .

"Hockley! Hockley!" the Earl roared again.

When the harried butler returned to the dining room, his master ordered hastily, "Have the carriage prepared; I am going to London. Never mind sending for the papers. Darcy, my boy," turning emotionally to his nephew, "I would be most obliged if you came with me. Having so recently returned from America, you may be able to discuss this matter at the War Office. It cannot be. English gentlemen do not spy. And how can the activities of the two men be compared?"

Lord Ashford left the table first, though only halfway through his breakfast. He was followed almost immediately by Darcy.

Gabrielle rose from the table next. "Do not let us hurry you, Aunt Charlotte," she said soothingly, "Darcy may need my help with his packing, having no man yet."

She beckoned to Hockley, who hastened over to Lady Ashford to offer to fill her plate for her. While the difficult task of what more she could eat was discussed, Gaby fled upstairs and through their sitting room to Darcy's chamber.

"My I help you, Darcy?"

"There is very little to take. I doubt we will stay above one night or two. It is my uncle's way," he explained apologetically. "He needs to be doing something when it is obvious there is nothing to be done."

"If André is found guilty, he will be hanged," said Gaby soberly. "Not because anyone in the military wishes him to be, but because our general has no other choice. How will *your* general, *your* people regard America's life-and-death struggle if we make a distinction between your spies and our own?"

Darcy turned from his wardrobe, holding the blue coat they had bought together in London.

"I know."

"Your general would have hung *me*, Darcy."

"Good God! Do you think I do not know it? Do you think I have not tortured myself about it night and day?"

He flung down the coat and set his hands upon her shoulders.

"We must talk, Gabrielle, when I return. First, I must talk seriously to my uncle, which is my main reason for going with him."

As he reluctantly freed her shoulders, Gaby stepped back. "Yes, Darcy," she said. "We must talk, but first—as your friend, not your wife—remember, Darcy, when we were friends a long time ago?—there is something I feel that I must say."

"Say it then."

"I do not know if you are aware of what, as an interested party, you may, perhaps, not have observed. Your uncle is devoted to you . . . more than that, he loves you dearly, but—"

"But?"

"He is in a state of excitement that transcends all affectionate bonds of the past. He longs *so* for a son. His own son. Yet, he knows that it may not be. There might be a son, *true*. There might just as likely be a daughter. Or at your aunt's present age and condition, she might lose the child, or die herself."

"I have considered all those possibilities, Gabrielle."

"Then, you have considered, too, that he dearly wants a son of his own but also—if his wish is not granted—a much-loved nephew in reserve if he does not obtain his heir."

Darcy put his hands on her shoulders again and gave her a small, gentle shake. He was laughing.

"I am not altogether an idiot, my dear wife. I look and I listen, too."

He kissed the tip of her nose and said again. "When I come back, we will talk."

Fifty-five

When Darcy got back, there was no wife at Ashford to talk with. She had taken off, a bewildered Aunt Charlotte explained, only a few hours after Darcy left with his uncle. She left any number of gowns and combs, and bits of jewelry behind in her haste to leave Ashford Hall.

Her farewell note was brief. It left him feeling no less murderous toward her on the fortieth reading than on the first.

My dear Darcy,

Forgive me, for bolting without explanation, but I find that I cannot live the life of an English lady, whether she is a ladyship or simply Mrs. Rhoads.

At Ashford Hall, I am *cabin'd, cribb'd, confin'd,* and I simply cannot contemplate so tedious a life. Just think how often in the next twenty years or so I would be a sore embarrassment to you.

Based on this letter alone, I feel quite certain you would have no difficulty at all in obtaining an annulment of our marriage or a divorce. You need not worry about *my* reputation. No one at home in America is likely to learn of it. We would both be able to marry again.

In case you are worried about my safety . . . you need not be. I must confess, this is another matter I lied about to you. My father is alive and well, married to a dear friend of mine, and living in England. He is a minister, and since he is a loyalist as well, he knows nothing about my activities of these . . . last years. I plan a short visit with Papa and Lydia before I go.

Home is New Jersey and I was on my way there when you played highwayman. You see, Darcy, in a much more modest way, I am an heiress, too. I will inherit my Aunt Emily's home and land (ten thousand acres) and all the farms.

So, you need not worry about my being comfortably settled.

Good-bye, my dear. There was much joy along with all the grief.

Gabrielle

The contents of every drawer, every wardrobe, every trunk or piece of baggage was ordered dumped on Gaby's bed. When this was done, Darcy shouted all the maids out of the room. One item at a time, he went through everything she had left behind. He emptied pockets, pored over every scrap of paper, questioned each servant and generally had the Hall in such turmoil as it had not known since the time the Earl of that day was executed by Cromwell's men.

When a maid came to him with the box of thirteen fans he had given her long ago, he swore so dreadfully that the maid, who had hoped to please him, fled from his sight.

This made another maid hesitate a full day before giving him a letter found on the desk in the lady's parlor.

"Sir," she quavered apologetically, standing a few feet from him and holding out the letter, "this was on the desk."

Darcy snatched it from her hand, and she stole away while he was reading it.

It was headed "Egerton, Publishers of Fine Works" with a London address below.

My dear Mrs. Forsyth-Foote,

We were much gratified to receive your signed confirmation of our agreement. The English version of *Amorous*

Verse by a Lady of New York will be in print three months hence. We expect to puff it up and feel very confident, it will cause as much a stir here as it did in America.

If it sells as well as we anticipate, we will follow up as speedily as possible with your second work, *Beloved Enemy and More Amorous Verse.*

Yours, etc. . . .

He looked hopefully among some of the books left behind for something—anything—that would help his search. In a leather-bound Bible, he found it.

There was an inscription inside the cover: "For my dear daughter Gabrielle on her twelfth birthday, from her loving father," and just below, "the Reverend Timothy Foote."

"That witch! That . . . I will catch up with her if only to kill her."

"Believe me, my dear Mr. Rhoads," said the elderly head of Egerton, Publishers, in an agitated voice, "I would be most happy to oblige you. But Mrs. Foote—"

"Mrs. Rhoads!"

"Yes. Yes. Mrs. Rhoads. Whatever you wish. You see, she instructed me most straightly not to give her present direction to anyone. Not anyone at all. If you will forgive me, my dear, sir, she must have anticipated your request because she said, I was most particularly *not* to give it to you."

"Then will you do this? Write to my wife. Say I came here and was denied, as she instructed. Then ask if you may now tell me where she is to be found."

"Yes, indeed. I would be most happy to oblige you if I may do so without violating a confidence. A very determined woman, if I may say so . . . and so talented, too. It is an American trait?"

"Very much so," Darcy snarled. "They are a most obstinate, independent, presumptuous sort of people.

"I am returning to Ashford Hall today," he continued with a trifle less heat. He scribbled a few lines on one of his uncle's cards. "As soon as you receive an answer, will you be so kind as to contact me?"

"Certainly." Mr. Egerton became agitated again. "That is, if she consents . . . if she has no objection . . ."

"I am, of course, in hopes of a favorable reply," Darcy said smoothly. "In any event, I would prefer to receive it direct from *you*, sir. I will return to London immediately if I receive any communication from this office."

"Certainly, sir, certainly. I only hope . . . oh dear."

"Your servant, sir," said Darcy brusquely and set the room rocking by the vehemence he used to vent his feelings when he slammed the outside door.

Ten days later, Darcy returned to London.

As soon as he was admitted to the inside office and strode across to Mr. Egerton's desk, the old gentleman held out a piece of paper.

The single page consisted of one sentence. "If Mr. Rhoads still wishes to know it, you may give him the direction of my father's residence."

In a small bit of crabbed writing below, someone had written in the Reverend Timothy Foote's address.

"I am obliged to you," Darcy said abruptly. "Forgive me if I have been lacking in courtesy, but that—my wife," he began over, "has led me a merry dance."

The older man twinkled up at him. " 'Tis a way they have, Mr. Rhoads, and yours, if I may say so, is more of a handful than most, but—"

"Do I not know it?"

"But she will give a spice to your life, it would never have without her, sir."

"I know that, too."
The pair shook hands solemnly.
"Nevertheless . . ." said Darcy.
"Ah," observed Mr. Egerton.
"Ah, indeed!" Darcy answered.

Fifty-six

Lydia was having a solitary tea with a book for company when Darcy's card was brought to her.

"Please ask Mr. Rhoads to join me," she said with a slight qualm of unease, "and bring another cup and perhaps the lemon cake."

"Yes, mum."

"Sit down, Mr. Rhoads," his hostess greeted Darcy moments later. "Will you have tea?"

"Gladly," he said briefly, just as the second cup and saucer and the lemon cake were brought in.

"I presume," said Lydia a bit nervously, cutting into the cake, "that you are here to see dear Gabrielle."

"I would like to see 'dear Gabrielle' very much, indeed, or is it *presuming* too much for a man to be interested in tracking down an errant wife?"

"It depends. If I may ask . . . why do you *want* to see Gaby?"

"Why, I wish to murder her," he said with a charming smile, "though I have not yet settled on the means I shall employ. There are so many delightful methods by which it could be done. Strangulation. Shooting. Drowning. I have not quite decided." He accepted his tea and a slice of cake. "Perhaps you might lend me your silver knife?"

Lydia leaned back, smiling. "Good," she said. "Encouraging."

"Madam!" he said heatedly, then, "I assume Mrs. Foote?"

"Yes, I am Mrs. Foote. Gaby's stepmother."

"Tell me, Mrs. Foote, are all American women mad? I sit here in your drawing room with murder in my heart and you observe that you find this encouraging."

"Of course," Lydia returned quietly. "You could never be as enraged about her as you are without feeling other very powerful emotions."

"Believe me, ma'am, my emotions are more than powerful. They are overwhelming."

"In what way are they overwhelming, Mr. Rhoads?" asked Lydia, less collectedly. "I love Gaby dearly. If you think you can enlist my aid to contribute to her discomfiture, then you are much mistaken."

"Would you consider it as adding 'discomfiture' for the two of us—to resume a normal relationship as husband and wife?"

"It depends. How do you define the word 'normal'?" asked Lydia with unexpected shrewdness. "Her descriptions of your 'relationship' at Ashford Hall sounded very far from normal to me!"

"A women's point of view *is*, of course, a great deal unlike a man's, but if you will consider what had gone before . . . How much do you know"—he interrupted himself—"of what went before?"

"I know that Gaby stayed on in New York for a long time after her father and I sailed for England under the happy conviction that she had returned to my husband's sister in New Jersey. Emily, having no child of her own, intended to leave a vast property and her money to Gabrielle.

"Letters from her came regularly and appeared to be posted from New Jersey. She received our letters, too, I know not for certain by what means.

"Her father does not know she became your mistress. She was planning to confess all to him, but I convinced her not to do so. She would only be giving him pain for no cause. So, he thinks she stayed on in New York as a rebel spy—that pained him, too, but not as much. Men," she murmured, half to herself, "have such a strange notion of morality.

"I think," she addressed the man who sat opposite her, holding a cupful of tea that was now cold, *"I* think there was nobility in what Gaby did."

"Making a fool of me—because I loved her—in order to learn military secrets?"

"What a fool your are!" He was startled to hear this soft-spoken, serene matron—who was obviously in the same interesting condition as Aunt Charlotte, suddenly turn into a spitting cat.

"What fools men are!" she repeated contemptuously. "As though Gaby would have allowed you to make love to her if she had not fallen so instantly, so violently into love with you. Why, I hardly knew her that afternoon she saw you at Fraunces Tavern, and I could tell how much in love with you she was when I helped her to get past your table without being recognized."

"What the hell," asked Darcy Rhoads, without apology, "are you talking about?"

"If you do not remember, it is not for me to tell you."

"Then will you please send a servant for my wife, and perhaps I may make some sense—though at this point, I doubt it—out of her."

"Gaby is not here, Mr. Rhoads. My husband escorted her back to London. I could not go"—she gestured—"because of the baby. My husband will oversee Gaby's publishing interests in England after she goes home. She wanted to see to his having a power of attorney."

"My God! Do you mean she has left for America already?"

"No. I doubt she could be gone so soon . . . what with publishers . . . lawyers . . . shopping for books and other English goods, which are more plentiful here, as well as untaxed.

"I also thought"—a slightly more astringent note crept into her voice—"they both needed to be alone as father and daughter before *you* caught up with them."

Tears filled Lydia's eyes suddenly. "For so long, it was just the two of them together . . . and now it may be many years—if ever—before we meet again."

"Your distress," said Darcy calmly, "is not necessary. If Gaby makes up her mind that it is time for all of us to unite, she will achieve it. So I will not say good-bye, Mrs. Foote, but only *au revoir.*"

Darcy rose from his chair.

"The thought of the *two* of you there together is enough to make a mere man tremble. I suppose you cannot tell me the ship on which she will sail?"

"I believe her publisher and my husband made the arrangements."

"I see. Do you mind if I take some of these little cakes with me?"

Lydia blinked in surprise. "Nooo."

"Good." He spread out his handkerchief and piled as many of the cakes as would fit on it, then tied up the corners and explained.

"I believe I will be there in plenty of time. On the other hand, Gaby's whim of iron may overcome her common sense, so I will drive through the night and this may be my only supper."

He was amused to see Lydia nod her head sagely.

Americans! He kept himself from saying aloud. *Was there ever before such a mad, mad breed?*

As Darcy came striding through the door, he was approached by a sober young clerk.

"Mr. Rhoads?"

"Yes."

"Follow me, please, sir. Mr. Egerton has been expecting you."

"Has he indeed?"

Mr. Egerton rose from behind his desk and nodded to the clerk to close the door behind him.

Darcy took the chair which his host indicated and accepted a glass of wine.

"I gather," said Darcy affably, "that my arrival is not unexpected?"

"Your wife mentioned that you might be making inquiries."

"Did she now?"

"I believe her exact words were 'He will be pounding on your door any time after today.'"

"And *today* was which day, if I may ask."

"Wednesday."

"Only two days," Darcy said sardonically. "She did not leave much leeway for delays on the journey."

Mr. Egerton coughed. "She seemed convinced—that is, she just happened to mention that the devil took care of his own."

"Such touching faith. Well, Mr. Egerton, you see me here again just as I am supposed to be. Do *you* provide the instructions?"

"Tomorrow on the morning tide. The ship is *Happy Sailor* of the Queens Own Line. A cabin has been reserved for you."

Darcy rose from his chair. "An excellent arrangement. She will have an extra day with her father, and I will have the pleasure of a hearty supper tonight and an equally hearty breakfast in the morning. My thanks, Mr. Egerton. I am sure you will not be unhappy to rid yourself of a troublesome pair."

"You mistake, sir. The affairs of the Lady of New York and her husband have greatly enlivened Egerton Publishers these last few weeks."

"Thank you for your kindness and your patience then, sir."

"Mr. Rhoads," as Darcy got up from his chair, "have you read your wife's last book?"

"Amorous Verse?"

"No, the latest *Beloved Enemy and More Amorous Verse.*"

"She has not shown it to me."

"It is not set up in type, but I have a hand-written copy of the lead poem."

"Which you have been instructed to give to me?"

"If you wished."

"I do."

Mr. Egerton pretended to ruffle through a good many papers on his desk before the copy he had spoken of was found. Darcy accepted it and leaned across the desk to shake the publisher's hand.

"Thank you."

In the hackney on his way to a hotel—*not* the Selkirk, Gaby might be staying there with her father—he held the paper toward the window the better to read.

> I will cherish my whole life long
> The memory of our encounter at an evening party
> Given by the mistress of your general,
> Sir William Howe.

Darcy's hands shook slightly. This was her story . . . her explanation . . . her apology . . . this was the why of Gabrielle Forsyth-Foote.

He read quickly, knowing he would do so many times; but this first time, he wanted only to understand. He wanted only for his love to be returned to him, untarnished.

> I somehow knew
> There existed no antidote
> For such love as I felt on the instant—
> Only you!

Some moisture welled up in his eyes—admit it, Darcy, tears of joy and relief.

> How poor Papa's blood would run cold if he ever knew
> That his dear virgin daughter
> . . . sought to seduce a man

How utterly completely Gaby-like!

"Oh, my love, my love," he said aloud, resisting with every fiber of his being the thought of changing his orders to the hackney driver and going to the hotel where he felt sure Gaby was to be found.

No, better not. She had directed every step of this chase so far. He could exert the strength to follow through to the very end.

He resumed his reading.

> Think back to a freezing day in New York
> Long before our marriage
> Remember a cold colonial girl
> Who commandeered your carriage.
> I told you my name was Emily
> (Emily *Washington* to rile you)
> When I said her name I lied . . .

Emily Washington! By God, he remembered her.

She had haunted his days, haunted his dreams! The little tart had made a fool of him. He had gone to Fraunces Tavern time after time, hoping to meet her . . . and then . . . Gabrielle entered his life and he thought no more of Emily, but *she* . . . she had not forgotten . . . she in her ridiculous, roundabout mad American way had gone looking for him.

He dropped the precious page and bent over to retrieve it.

> On our short hackney ride
> Poor Emily was so beguiled
> This sheltered Massachusetts miss
> Fell in love at just first kiss.

No wonder, after the night he found Gaby, he had no longer been haunted by Emily.

Deep down, in a part of him he did not know existed, the two had become one, and each had given her heart wholly to him.

Fifty-seven

Agonizing
Apologizing
Not only for what I did
But what I would do again

"Beloved Enemy"
More Amorous Verse

A group of passengers stood on the deck of the *Happy Sailor,* determined to look at England until there was no longer an England to see.

Gaby stood alone on the top deck, leaning against the rail, looking out across the ocean to America.

That would always be her way, he thought ruefully. Make peace with the past, but fix your sights on what will be.

She did not so much as turn her head when he came to stand beside her.

"I brought your thirteen fans."

After several minutes of silence, he spoke again. "The apologies are due to you, but the agony was mine."

"Why? Did my love seem such a puny thing to you, so insignificant an emotion that any man would have done in your stead?"

"Gaby, dear, beloved mule-headed Gabrielle, I did not think at all. You had rejected my offer of marriage—which *mea culpa*—I admit, I considered to be a great honor. After you declined, much to my astonishment, you appeared to tumble so immediately and so easily into bed, how in the hell was I to know it was your first time? True, you played the role of shy maiden, but that's what I thought it was, the play-acting of a mistress. I had never bedded a virgin before. It always seemed too much of a responsibility. That was a very merry chase you led me."

She smiled faintly and he noticed that her hands were gripping the deck rail so tightly her knuckles were completely white. So she had not been as absolutely certain as she pretended.

"You realized?"

"Not immediately . . . but fairly soon. There were too many clues, too many hints, too many players giving too much information . . . that is, unless you intended to be found. Why, Gaby?"

"It was not enough for me to know . . . *you* had to be sure. You could follow the chase and find me . . . or you could ignore the clues and relinquish me."

"And you would have been content to let our fate rest on such a flimsy happenstance."

"No happenstance at all, Darcy," she told him fiercely. "When I fell in love with you in a hackney, the fates were lined up against us a great deal more than they were in these last weeks. I planned what would happen, I pursued you shamelessly—however unaware you were of it—I made it happen. If you were willing to do less, then I did not want you. *You* had to know how much you wanted me. You had to make the choice based on what *you* were giving up."

She turned and looked at him for a moment. "Was it a hard thing to decide, Darcy?"

"Strangely, it was something of a relief to tell my uncle that I wished as strongly as he did for a fine, healthy son. He accepted almost gladly the idea that even if his wish was not granted, there are close cousins galore all over England for him to train as he had proposed to train me.

"He had made over one of his estates to me, so between the sale of it and my own inheritance from my mother, which is considerable, I am a wealthy man. There is no reason why we

DARCY'S KISS

cannot extend your aunt's acreage and build a fine home of our own right near to her."

She did not answer. He saw that she could not without breaking down in tears.

"I brought your thirteen fans," he said again.

"Th-thank you."

"Tell me the rest, dear one."

"I came to love you so truly, so overwhelmingly," she confessed, blinking, "I could not believe any aspect of that love could be wrong . . . or evil . . . or wicked in the eyes of God. I also believed we had no future together. What future *could* there be for an English earl and a minister's daughter, who was also an American agent?"

Slowly, he unpeeled her hands from the rail and brought them both together under her chin.

"Emily Washington," he said wonderingly, "and my own Gabrielle. I have thought of nothing else since last night when I read 'Beloved Enemy.' But I still find it hard to believe."

Her eyes sparkled brightly, the tears all gone.

"The times I have wanted to kill you!"

"And I you."

"There are so many things yet unsaid."

"No matter. We have seven weeks on this ship and all the rest of our lives."

"One thing I would like to know, Gaby mine. Why were you sitting on the stairs and laughing fit to bust, our last morning together at Ashford Hall?"

Gaby withdrew one hand from his and put one hand against her mouth. Even then, she could not control her laughter.

"I overheard two of the upstairs maids talking about us. Betty said to Gloria that she always knew when you had visited in the night. It looked like a herd of elly-funts had been ram-pagin' across my bed."

Darcy threw back his head and laughed aloud, then took her hands back, warming them in his own.

Despite all they had to say, neither seemed to feel the need for speech.

It was much later when England had faded away and there was only ocean about them that he came from his cabin (which was larger than hers) to petition gravely, "May a ram-pag-in' elly-funt come into your bed, love?"

Excerpts from
Beloved Enemy and More Amorous Verse

by a Lady of New York

Beloved Enemy:

I will cherish my whole life long
(As I do now)
The memory of our encounter at an evening party
Given by the mistress of your general,
Sir William Howe.
In the entrance way
While a servant took my hooded cloak from me,
I heard the muted voice of ribaldry,
Then immediately after,
Warm-hearted laughter.
Do you recollect, my love,
How I stepped into the drawing room
And looked around
To seek out the sound?
It was because my heart had told me
That I would see you.
I was not mistaken.
There you stood, glass in hand, wig ever so slightly askew,
Dressed—which was no surprise—
(However much the heart denies)

In that which I most despised
The uniform of a British officer.

During the first moment of painful awareness,
You seemed not the man I remembered.
Nevertheless, I felt the jolt of my heart . . .
Its convulsions of joy
Leaped all the way up to my throat.
I was stricken with a sudden strange ailment . . .
Although it had never come on me before
I somehow knew
There existed no antidote
For such sickness of love as I felt on the instant—
Only you!

I looked across the space between us
And softly, silently
As a butterfly folds its wings,
I sent my love across to you.
You must have heard the singing of my heart
Because, while I was willing you to look directly at me,
Suddenly you became still.
You put down your glass
You talked and gestured with your companions no longer.
I exerted my will even more strongly
And at once—O sweet victory!
You turned all the way to face me.
Our eyes met and clung,
You moistened your lips with the darting tip of your tongue.
O love, I became a woman
In that instant acknowledgement of our mutual yearning.
O love, I watched you become the man among men for me
And recognized in dismay
The moment when you remembered that
Not merely provincial loyalists ladies
Attended such gatherings as this one,

DARCY'S KISS 441

But those who were not considered ladies at all
(Like our hostess, Mrs. Loring,
The charming adulteress
Of whom the Commander-in-Chief of your own army
Was at that time so very adoring).
In my over-elaborate gown
And my powder and patches,
It seemed perfectly plain
That I sought for the gain
Of un-wedded matches
At once our eyes locked
And yours showed the shock
Of awareness
That I might belong to an even older profession
Then that of soldiering,
One which denied me the claim
To ever expect a gentleman-born
Might give me his name.

My heart leaped
With passionate love
That I knew was forbid.
The chasm betwixt us
Yawned so wide and deep,
This first love
This sweet love
This pure love of mine must be hid.
I might give you my heart
But never bestow
Either truth—or my hand—
My betrothed was a cause
More important than any one man.
For I played a game
With a deadlier aim
Than choosing a lover,
And it meant I might choose

To use
Any man for my cover.
Thus, the blossoming of passion
Before ever it could flower
Seemed at an end.
One day far in the future
Each of us might marry
And dutifully build a tree of life
To nurture the passing of our blood lines,
But my husband
And your wife
Would be strangers to us forever.
We would never hold them in our hearts
With the aching, loving longing we felt now,
As though both our hearts had been fiercely bound together
Then set on fire
With the same piercing arrow of desire.

I walked towards you, my dear love,
Observing with gladness
That your eyes were glazed over with yearning . . .
It was obvious you were deep in my spell.
Then I recollected . . .
I took three steps back from you,
My eyes sent a message of farewell.

You appeared to accept my decision
And retreated, too,
Looking back over your shoulder only once,
Your face overcast by sadness
Your eyes somber with regret
You were wretched in your relinquishment
And yet, having resisted temptation,
You mourned what could never be.
Suddenly, my own blood ran swift with the elation of love . . .

Relinquish you?
Not *me!*

Men may be bold in battle,
In affairs of business
And in the political arena
Where they most frequently conspire,
Also in the boudoir of a courtesan
Who has been highly paid for her services
And wants only to please her patron
In any way he desires.
But *I* was no man
On the field of honor
Easily yielding what I most wanted.
A woman is not so nice in her notions,
She would make a bid
Just as I did
For a brief time of happiness.
I maneuvered calculatingly
So as to be once more in your view.
How poor Papa's blood would run cold if he ever knew
That his dear virgin daughter,
In the throes of first lust,
Sought to seduce a man
At the same time she also planned
To abuse his trust.
If to take my love,
I had to slake my love
And become a fallen woman . . . then—
Fall I must!

As my heart beat with rapid, anxious strokes
Magically, you were beside me
I knew a day of reckoning
Was bound to be,
But with your eyes beckoning,

I chose my disguise—
Carefree
Impetuous
Rather than wise.

How exquisite our early rapture!
How impossible that it could last!
One day you uncovered my present
(Though without discovering my past).
Your anger was fearful
And did not abate
You could not forgive
You seemed almost to hate.
I endured your resentment
As long as I deemed fair
But . . . I am American . . .
We breathe freedom in with air.
To my own land, my own beliefs,
I tried to be true . . .
Dearest, did not you?
Understandably, a rebel love
Might cause you great distress.
Yet *you* gave your heart to me
Without loving England less.

Think back to a freezing day in New York
Much before our marriage,
Recall a cold colonial girl
Who commandeered your carriage.
She said her name was Emily
(Emily Washington to rile you).
When I spoke both names I lied,
You see, however hard I tried
I failed to resist you.
On our short hackney ride
Poor Emily was so beguiled,

This sheltered Massachusetts miss
Fell in love at just first kiss.

Unashamed, I must confess
When next we met, I loved no less
I love you still
And doubtless will
Until I die,
In spite of which, this is good-bye.
I cannot remain your wife
Existing for all my life
On a diet of humble pie
Agonizing—
Apologizing—
Not only for what I did
But what I would do again
So, farewell, beloved foe,
Farewell, most dear of men!

Dear Reader,

The American Revolution was the background of the first historical novel I ever read. I fell in love with the late 18th century and my love affair with that era of history continues until this day.

The historic eras in my books have a thousand-year span (from 1066, Norman Conquest to 1996, U.S.A.); but every four books or so, I start getting withdrawal symptoms and I know it is time to return to the American War for Independence from Britain, 1776-1781, and to some of my favorite characters, the amateur spies (both real and my fictional ones) who, without any special training, with no particular know-how, few guidelines, but rather intuition, innocence and guts, risked their lives for what was still a country-in-waiting, a more-or-less virgin nation to-be.

Darcy's Kiss is my latest return trip to the seventeen hundreds, and a thoroughly enjoyable one it was for me. The conversion of Gaby Foote, daughter of a New England minister, into Gabrielle Forsyth-Foote, writer of erotic poetry as a cover for her spying, was a joy to write about. (Creating the necessary poems was great fun, too!)

From their first kiss (at their first encounter) throughout their tumultuous relationship, Gaby and her dashing Darcy enchanted me completely. As characters tend to do, they wrote way ahead of me. I hope that you enjoy the journey, too.

I love to hear from my readers. You can write me at:

> Jacqueline Marten
> c/o Ethan Marten
> P.O. Box 665
> Virginia Beach, VA 23451

Please send a SASE if you'd like an answer.
All my best,

Jacqueline Marten

If you liked this book, be sure to look for others in the *Denise Little Presents* line:

MOONSHINE AND GLORY by Jacqueline Marten	(0079-1, $4.99)
COMING HOME by Ginna Gray	(0058-9, $4.99)
THE SILENT ROSE by Kasey Mars	(0081-3, $4.99)
DRAGON OF THE ISLAND by Mary Gillgannon	(0067-8, $4.99)
BOUNDLESS by Alexandra Thorne	(0059-7, $4.99)
MASQUERADE by Alexa Smart	(0080-5, $4.99)
THE PROMISE by Mandalyn Kaye	(0087-2, $4.99)
FIELDS OF FIRE by Carol Caldwell	(0088-0, $4.99)
HIGHLAND FLING by Amanda Scott	(0098-8, $4.99)
TRADEWINDS by Annee Cartier	(0099-6, $4.99)
A MARGIN IN TIME by Laura Hayden	(0109-7, $4.99)
REBEL WIND by Stobie Piel	(0110-0, $4.99)
SOMEDAY by Anna Hudson	(0119-4, $4.99)
THE IRISHMAN by Wynema McGowan	(0120-8, $4.99)
DREAM OF ME by Jan Hudson	(0130-5, $4.99)
ROAD TO THE ISLE by Megan Davidson	(0131-3, $4.99)

Available wherever paperbacks are sold, or order direct from the Publisher. Send cover price plus 50¢ per copy for mailing and handling to Penguin USA, P.O. Box 999, c/o Dept. 17109, Bergenfield, NJ 07621. Residents of New York and Tennessee must include sales tax. DO NOT SEND CASH.